"A charming love story rich with nineties nostalgia, *The Rewind* is Allison Winn Scotch's best book yet."

—#1 *New York Times* bestselling author Emily Giffin

"*The Rewind* is as much an endearing love story about the one that got away as it is a love letter to all things nineties, including Doc Martens, Y2K, and dial-up internet. Fresh, original, and compelling, this book is Allison Winn Scotch at her absolute best."

—*USA Today* bestselling author Colleen Oakley

"Sassy, engaging, and warm, *The Rewind* is a sharp and witty rom-com about the road not taken—and the people who find their way back to us anyway. Ezra and Frankie are magic together. You won't be able to put this down until happily ever after."

—#1 *New York Times* bestselling author Laura Dave

"A dazzling second-chance romance. . . . This is the Y2K new-millennium story I didn't know I needed."

—Washington Independent Review of Books

"Nineties nostalgia is alive and well in this moving story of a lost first love and second chances. Readers will enjoy piecing together both the story of the forgotten night and the reasons behind the relationship's disastrous first ending." —*Library Journal*

"An engaging . . . story of a couple that come to accept their faults and in the process find their future." —*Kirkus Reviews*

THE REWIND

ALSO BY ALLISON WINN SCOTCH

Take Two, BIRDIE MAXWELL

ALLISON WINN SCOTCH

BERKLEY ROMANCE
New York

BERKLEY ROMANCE
Published by Berkley
An imprint of Penguin Random House LLC
penguinrandomhouse.com

Library of Congress Cataloging-in-Publication Data

Names: Scotch, Allison Winn, author.
Title: Take two, Birdie Maxwell / Allison Winn Scotch.
Description: First edition. | New York: Berkley Romance, 2024.
Identifiers: LCCN 2023022023 (print) | LCCN 2023022024 (ebook) |
ISBN 9780593546550 (trade paperback) | ISBN 9780593546567 (ebook)
Subjects: LCGFT: Romance fiction. | Novels.
Classification: LCC PS3619.C64 T35 2024 (print) |
LCC PS3619.C64 (ebook) | DDC 813/.6—dc23/eng/20230512
LC record available at https://lccn.loc.gov/2023022023
LC ebook record available at https://lccn.loc.gov/2023022024

First Edition: March 2024

Printed in the United States of America
1st Printing

Book design by Daniel Brount

For my grandmothers, Birdie Dash and Dorothy Miller.
Legends both.

I am just a small girl in a big world
trying to find someone to love.

—MARILYN MONROE

Take Two,
BIRDIE
MAXWELL

BREAKING: AMERICA'S SWEETHEART GOES SOUR

Think America's favorite actress, who is all sugar, no spice on-screen, isn't pulling off an Oscar-worthy performance on the daily? Think again. Your favorite dimpled firework, Birdie Robinson, who has been Hollywood's go-to rom-com queen for the past half decade, has gone into hiding following her on-set meltdown and subsequent halt in production.

By now we've all seen the video of her fight with beloved director Sebastian Carol, of the acclaimed Carol family, who was brought on board to direct *Love Grenade*, the sequel to her smash *Love Bomb*. We've seen her throw her script at his head, we've seen her knock over all the water bottles on set on her way to her trailer. We've seen her slam her trailer door so hard that the hinges broke. We've seen the chilly press release from the studio, chastising the industry's highest-paid actress, who is as sunny to the public as the roles she plays, for her unprofessional behavior. Hollywood rushed to Mr. Carol's defense, and at last count, at least nine A-list actors have confirmed that he is an absolute joy to work with. Additionally, his brother, megastar Kai Carol, issued a statement saying he always stood by family. So if those long-standing rumors of a Kai-Birdie, aka Kaidie, entanglement have any truth to them, consider it officially *over*.

We have, of course, also seen her filmed apology, in which several perfectly timed tears slid down her perfectly blushed cheeks. An apology that, if the public's reaction online is any indication, has only made Ms. Robinson's current PR quagmire even worse. That she had to carefully script her contrition did not sit well with Carol stans everywhere.

More to come as we have it . . .

1

BIRDIE

BIRDIE ROBINSON ARRIVED on her childhood street much like she had left: unceremoniously, with little fanfare, and certainly with no red carpet. She dropped her leather duffel, stuffed only with clothes designed for a wellness retreat (she had in fact packed for a wellness retreat), and spun toward the stop sign on the corner. But her driver and his Escalade were long out of view, and she suspected sending him away was the first of many regrets she'd have about coming home. She dipped her head back and stared up toward the cloud-covered night sky. The air smelled just as she remembered her hometown's night air smelling: like threatening snow, like chopped firewood, but also like the neighbors had left out rotting garbage. Barton was complicated in that way, and certainly, it was complicated for Birdie.

She squeezed her eyes shut and groaned aloud. She hadn't meant to end up here, both in this moment and, well, ever again. She had fled New York earlier that morning, having booked a last-minute trip to the private, exclusive spa outside Los Angeles, the privacy being the most critical criterion for her choice. But as she ran from the paparazzi who greeted her at LAX and threw herself into the waiting car, she found herself directing the driver here. To Barton. A speck in the middle of California. She hadn't been home in four years, hadn't thought to call her father and stepmother, hadn't thought to text her younger sister, Andie, or DM her best friend, Mona, whose house Birdie could see from her spot on the sidewalk if she were to open her eyes.

So now she was moored to the sidewalk in front of her parents' bilevel home as the temperature dipped into the thirties, dressed in a caftan meant for a day spa, and talking herself into ringing the doorbell.

She heard her phone vibrate in her bag. Sydney, her agent, or Imani, her publicist. She should tell them she bolted, that she would miss their lunch tomorrow at the spa to "remaneuver" their next steps. That was Imani's word. "Well, the apology video didn't go *exactly* as planned, so let's meet up and discuss a re-maneuver." Birdie was relieved Imani had found a new word for it. She'd heard her publicist say *pivot* at least several hundred times in the past few weeks, and it was all Birdie could do to stop herself from proposing a drinking game. Every time Imani says *pivot*, we take a shot.

Needless to say, she'd be hospitalized for alcohol poisoning.

Birdie was tired of the news alerts on her phone blaring about the downfall of America's Sweetheart. She was tired of being a piñata for gossip sites, tired of getting dragged over hot coals because she couldn't take Sebastian Carol's on-set bad behavior for even one more second, which was the only reason she threw a fit in the first place. Sebastian Carol, of the famed Carol brothers duo, spawn of the famous director Milo Carol, was known to be handsy. He was known to leer at breasts and to entice actresses back to his trailer, all under the guise of bolstered parts, better lighting, future roles in blockbusters. Birdie knew this when she signed on. She also knew that Sebastian was complicated for her for plenty of other reasons: namely, the long-secret and very doomed relationship she'd had for five years with his brother. But the studio insisted on Sebastian for the sequel to Birdie's biggest box office hit. Frankly, the industry's biggest rom-com box office hit of the decade. The only thing that trumped Birdie's star power was the Carol brothers' star power, so she said yes. And then, when she watched him massaging one more day player's shoulders, she lost it.

How was she to know that someone was filming? How was she to know that while she was defending the honor of women everywhere, the public would choose to side with Sebastian? (This she really should have known.) How was she to know that the day player might give an interview to TMZ saying it was a perfectly innocuous massage? Or that Sebastian would threaten to quit if Birdie wasn't fired. Since *Love Grenade* couldn't work without Birdie or without Sebastian (according to the studio), they shuttered the film entirely. Rumors grew into legend and legends became truths, and soon, so, so quickly, Birdie Robinson, star extraordinaire, was hurtling toward her downfall. A dickhead director and a misogynistic media and a publicist who couldn't stop saying *pivot*: a toxic unexpected combination that led Birdie to the rash decision to flee to Barton after so many years away.

Birdie steeled herself again to ring the doorbell. She could probably swipe the key that was always under the doormat, because Barton was not the type of place where you worried about your neighbors stealing keys and then stealing your television, but she didn't want to startle her parents. Walking in unannounced after four years. Her father and Susana were professors at the state university about twenty miles south. Two brainy peas in a pod, Susana used to say, and Birdie, too young to understand that she didn't mean this literally, always envisioned them as green and round and pressing up against each other, which at the time she found disgusting. Birdie didn't want to stride in the door after so much time away and find them naked, which had happened when she was thirteen after she told them she was sleeping over at Mona and Elliot's—Mona's twin brother—three houses down, but forgot her toothbrush and returned home to retrieve it.

So the doorbell it was.

She bounced her head and talked herself up the stoop. Birdie the actor could talk herself into anything, become just about anyone. It was the only thing she was truly excellent at in life: assuming a role and inhabiting it until the director yelled cut. Sometimes long after that too. So now, how difficult could it be? It had to be better than being chased by photographers whenever she left her loft in Tribeca for the past three weeks. It had to be better than reading about the rumors that Page Six was inventing that were more fictional than half the scripts she read. *Birdie Robinson hates her neighbor's pugs! Birdie Robinson doesn't tip her barista! Birdie Robinson is America's Sweetheart no longer!* For the record, Birdie loved pugs, tipped well, and, if Sydney and Imani had anything to do with it, would be America's Sweetheart until she hit menopause, possibly longer, because then they'd issue a press release about ageism and shame the audience until they relented. *Pivot.* Birdie truly loathed the word, but it was hard not to admit that her team was good at it, right up until they were fucking awful at it. She knew the apology video was a mistake. She knew she didn't sound sincere, couldn't bring herself to sound sincere, but Imani snapped her fingers and told her it was handled. She trusted them that it was. It was not.

Birdie's hand was shaking as she pressed her finger to the

doorbell. She heard it chime in the house and waited for the thunder of footsteps, imagining her father, probably in some professorial tweed blazer, swinging it open and bear-hugging her in delight. She tilted her ear toward the door. She heard no thundering footsteps.

Birdie would explain that she just needed a place to hide out for a week, until everyone realized that they'd gotten the whole situation wrong.

She pressed the doorbell again.

Finally, there were footsteps behind the door, and then Birdie heard the bolt unlock, then the latch. She calmed and told herself that of course she could return home after so long. Of course everyone would be more or less mostly happy to see her.

The door swung open, and it took Birdie at least two solid seconds to see that it was not her father and not Susana in front of her. It was her sister, Andie, who had a pageboy haircut that rendered her unrecognizable from the last time Birdie had seen her, but still made her no less beautiful. The type of beauty that Birdie had to work for, had to be lasered over, toned down, shaved to the quick and tortured with daily personal training sessions for.

Andie's jaw dropped, and then her eyes narrowed.

Birdie started to speak but Andie was faster.

"Oh my god," she said. "Oh. My. Fucking. God."

And then she slammed the door right in Birdie's face.

2

BIRDIE

IRDIE KNEW THIS was a minor setback. She and Andie were not on the best of terms, it was true, but she didn't think that she deserved to have the door slammed right in her face and then dead-bolted.

She crouched down and lifted the welcome mat. She patted around on the cold stoop, but the key, the reliably ever-present key, was gone. Birdie wondered if Andie could have planned this, but then she knew that was impossible. Even though it felt very much like Andie had planned this.

Fine, she huffed. No matter.

In high school, Birdie had become an expert at scaling the side wall of her house, which led directly into her bedroom window, which had a broken lock and could easily be shimmied open. Birdie wasn't getting into the sort of trouble that true delinquents stirred up—more like losing track of time listening to show tunes with her drama friends while drinking wine coolers or breaking into the wardrobe room at school and holding a photo shoot while drinking wine coolers. But it was the sort of trouble that was endlessly frustrating to her parents, who spent loads of time blathering about her wasted potential, her untapped intelligence. Still, neither one of them had the stamina to stay up until Birdie's curfew, much less later, so she became an expert at scaling the wall under her bedroom and slipping in undetected. She imagined it as practice for when she was cast as the lead in a *Mission: Impossible* film.

Birdie unlatched the side gate and reached for the trellis, which wobbled and groaned under her weight but held. She was in better shape now than she was back in high school, though her caftan was not prepared for her scramble, nor were her open-toed shoes, but she quickly ascended to the second floor. For a brief moment, she was concerned that a paparazzi camera might catch her, but then just as quickly she remembered that almost no one knew she was from Barton. Which was precisely why it was the only place she could return to in her moment of calamity.

She had lied about her childhood in all her early interviews, and thus her Wikipedia page and IMDb profile and even her two *People* magazine cover stories cited Medford, Oregon, as her hometown, not Barton, California. It had started out with a simple untruth: she'd been young and hungry and auditioning for the part of a lonely lighthouse owner on the coast and had told Sydney, who was only working with her on a trial basis, that she knew Oregon like a second skin. The fog and the clouds and the way the mist rolled in from the ocean every day by sunset. The flannel and the fleece and the hybrid cars, which, fifteen years ago, almost no one was doing like they did now. Her mom had lived in Portland for a year, so was it even a lie? Regardless, Birdie inhabited a Pacific Northwesterner like a pro. Sydney told casting, and casting told the producers, and the producers told the director, and then, once she landed the role, she found it easier not to correct anyone. As work became more steady and her fame snowballed, she realized she liked that part of her make-believe biography: a crunchy granola who was homeschooled near the salty beach of the Pacific Ocean. And so Medford stuck.

Her hand made its way to the window latch, and she heard it pop, exactly as she remembered it would, then she shimmied it open and tilted forward, knowing the love seat below would break her fall. She somersaulted inside and instead of being greeted by a cushion, she landed flat on her back, with an ache radiating up from both hips, and staring at the ceiling. She looked to her left. The love seat was no longer there. She looked to her right. A stack of moving boxes greeted her, and her bed had been stripped bare. She wondered if she'd gotten the room wrong—it had been more than fifteen years since she'd scaled that wall—but the door flung open, and Andie stormed in like a paratrooper. No, she'd gotten it right.

"Oh no, you don't," Andie said, a little out of breath, like she'd been racing to beat Birdie here. "You don't get to backdoor your way into this either."

"Technically, not the back door," Birdie said from the floor. "Technically, a window." She winced. "Where is my couch? Did you do this on purpose?"

"Where is your couch? Seriously?"

Birdie rolled to her side and pressed herself toward sitting like she would do at the end of one of her yoga classes. She was pretty sure she had bruised her pelvis. They always had mats on set if she was going to do a stunt like this herself.

"Why is my room packed up?" she asked.

"Why is your *room* packed up?" Andie parroted.

"Are you just going to repeat everything I say back to me or are you going to explain?"

"Do you *ever* check your email?" Andie snapped.

No. Birdie really did not check her email. She had an assistant, Miranda, for that. If anyone truly needed to reach her urgently, they had her cell. Also, once the shit hit the fan with Sebastian and the studio and the public, Birdie certainly never checked her email.

"Yes," Birdie said. "Of course I check my email."

"Then you would know that I have sent you several messages asking what you wanted to keep and what you wanted to trash."

"Are they finally turning my room into that library they always threatened to?" Birdie asked. She thought her parents found this ironic and/or hilarious, that they'd stuff the room from floor to ceiling with books and first editions. "Possibly the first time a book made it across the threshold," her dad had joked, but it pricked Birdie all the same. She wanted to point out that she'd read *The Lord of the Rings* for pleasure when she was twelve, but that she could so clearly cite one book, one time, probably proved his thesis.

"Because they just left on sabbatical," Andie said. "Seriously? Do you *never* read your email?"

Now that she mentioned it, it did sound familiar. Birdie had glanced at something about her dad and Susana spending a year in Spain, but it was shortly before the dustup with Sebastian and then she was watching her entire career unravel, so she didn't think she should be blamed for forgetting.

"Spain," Birdie said, like she was an authority. "Madrid, yes?"

"Barcelona." Andie sighed. "And I packed up your room because they want to sublet the house. I emailed you to ask if you could come help. Then I emailed you to ask if—"

"I got it," Birdie said. "You sent me a lot of emails. Many, many emails. So many emails I'm the worst sister in the world, in the solar system. In case you didn't realize, my life has come un-tethered."

Andie made a face. "I did see that apology. Looked closer to a hostage video, if I'm being honest."

"No one asked you to be honest," Birdie said.

"Welcome home." Andie shrugged. "Sorry your fan club isn't waiting." She turned to leave. "I was taking all of these boxes to the dump tomorrow. Anything you want, I suggest you salvage it now."

3

BIRDIE

BIRDIE WOULD HAVE happily tossed every box, every last thing, but there were at least a couple of childhood mementos that she wanted to keep. The yearbook in which she was named Most Likely to Win an Oscar, the folder she'd stuffed with notes that she and Mona passed back and forth in middle school, all full of withering insults about their fellow classmates. The CD compilation she'd made for Mona's twin brother, Elliot, but had never screwed up the nerve to give to him; the dried-up corsage he'd bought for her at prom, even though it had been a pity date. Elliot, unlike Mona and Birdie, was ridiculously beloved, exceptionally handsome, and never without a girlfriend or at least someone to make out with, a habit that had stuck—at least the last Birdie had heard—well into his thirties. Elliot O'Brien was now a hotshot reporter whose byline landed on page one of the *New York Times* and whose face popped up on television more times than Birdie wished. Still, he'd been momentarily single for their senior prom, and when Mona prodded him, he did Birdie a kindness and took her as his date. When she first saw him in a tux, she honestly thought she would drop dead from shock. Chestnut hair, blue eyes, cheekbones to sharpen a knife on, a swimmer's body. No one should be that attractive.

She plunged her hands into the second box, the first filled with folders and mail from colleges that she never applied to and junk that had accumulated over the years. A hat from when she worked at Sbarro to earn money for a move to New York after her senior year, a Girl Scout sash that was patchless because she refused to join in for reasons she couldn't remember now and made Susana sign up Andie instead. (Andie, of course, had made an exceptional Girl Scout.)

Birdie was half glancing at the papers and trash that she had dumped on the floor when an envelope addressed to *Birdie Maxwell Robinson* landed at her feet. Almost no one ever called her by both her real name and her assumed one because almost no one ever *knew* about both her real name and her assumed one, and so she couldn't help but startle. She honestly nearly jumped out of her skin.

Her pulse was flying as she reached down, swiped the letter, and ran her finger under the lip of the plain white envelope.

She read the letter once, twice, then a third time to be certain because her brain had never been particularly good at math, and now she was trying to add it all up. She checked the postmark but it had faded so much it was barely detectable.

Once she reread it for a fourth time, she was sure: someone had sent her an anonymous love letter. Here. To Barton. Using her real name. Which meant—Birdie's blood was really racing now, her breath a little shallow, her cheeks a little flushed—that it wasn't a crazy fan, it wasn't her old stalker against whom she had filed a restraining order. Someone who had once loved her—

and whom she had evidently once loved—had concocted a romantic chess move straight out of one of her movies.

Bird—

Beautiful, complicated Birdie. This may come as a shock to you, as it did to me, or perhaps you understood this all along, but well, I'll cut to it, as I know you'd prefer dramatic plot points, big effects, maximum impact. So I'll just say: I regret everything.

All of it.

And I would have done it all differently.

I heard you were in Barton for a bit, so I thought I'd let you know—put it down on paper, let you decide. I guess I thought I'd put this out into the universe, see if it comes back to me.

If you have had the same regrets, the same what-ifs about where we went wrong when everything could have gone right, come find me. Consider it? Consider me again.

X

Birdie clutched the typed letter against her chest and spun through the list of hearts she had rejected, men who knew both her birth name *and* her true roots (her childhood roots, not her natural hair-color roots because that was a bridge too far). There were men she wished never to think of again and a few she thought back on with something akin to wistfulness, but who among them knew her secrets? That the letter writer noted that she was back in Barton again meant that the note must be several years old, which also meant she could eliminate any of her recent romantic failures, which was for the best. She couldn't remember the details she'd shared with her earlier boyfriends, but then, she realized with a start, perhaps that didn't matter.

Her heart lurched with electricity, as if the letter came armed with defibrillators.

What she needed, Birdie realized, was indeed a *pivot*. Exactly what Imani had suggested. But this time, Birdie could spearhead it herself, without the coddling and the strategizing with her in the room but with everyone pretending that she wasn't. Birdie had gotten too comfortable with all that, and look where it had gotten her. A punch line on gossip sites; a survey on People.com asking if you would rather be stranded on a desert island with Birdie Robinson or a coconut; a one-way ticket to Los Angeles and a three-hour drive to Barton. Which was to say, her team's pivots had gotten her nowhere other than careening straight into a brick wall.

But an honest-to-god anonymous love letter? That was an irresistible plot twist that even Imani couldn't dream up, a zig to her previous zags that would surely get her right back into the public's good graces. Indeed, up until three weeks ago, there was very little that America could agree upon, but they firmly agreed that Birdie Robinson was their anointed sweetheart. You couldn't turn on a streamer or a cable channel or sit through the trailers at the AMC and not see her wide, dimpled smile lighting up the screen. Birdie Robinson was the antidote to their woes, even if just for two hours in a darkened movie theater or sprawled on their sectional in front of their sixty-five-inch TVs.

And so, it dawned on her like the glorious radiant sunshine of a picture-perfect day, what America needed was simply to be reminded of how marvelous she was at the art of a rom-com, and what better way to remind them than to cast herself in her very own?

Birdie turned on her sandaled heels, flung open her door, and raced down the stairs. The living room was half–packed up, with boxes upon boxes of books and books and books. Her dad and Susana had more books in their living room than the Barton Public Library, a point Susana, her stepmom, made clear whenever they drove by the library, saying, "I actually think we have more books in our living room than they do in the library!"

Birdie flew around the corner into the room, where Andie was parked on a taped-up box in front of the flat-screen, which was a new addition to the household. Similar to Susana's book fetish was her anti-TV stance. Birdie and Andie were part of that insidious set of households that loudly proclaimed, "We don't believe in television," which meant that Birdie spent nearly every free minute possible at Mona and Elliot's, because their dad was a doctor who believed in moderation in all things and their mom was normal and paid for cable, giving the three of them access to R-rated movies and endless films that Birdie would envision herself starring in when she got older. Also, because Birdie had been in love with Elliot since the twins moved in when they were twelve. And of course, because Mona was her best friend.

"When did this happen?" Birdie asked, nudging her chin toward the flat-screen.

Andie was lost in a *60 Minutes* segment and didn't hear her at first. Birdie was about to prod her again—a TV under this roof was no small feat—when a face she recognized came on-screen. Elliot. *Elliot!* Elliot O'Brien was in front of her, holding a microphone to his mouth, reporting from some war-ravaged part of the world, yet looking just as delicious as the last time she had seen him in person, seven years back. Birdie reminded herself that the last time she'd seen him, they'd parted on unpleasant terms, extremely uncomfortable, unpleasant terms, in fact. So she recalibrated and pretended that he didn't look nearly as handsome as was plain to see. His dark wavy hair flopped in the wind of that war-ravaged country, his blue oxford unbuttoned just enough to turn Birdie's insides to lava, his intense stare penetrating the lens with both empathy and gravitas.

Goddammit. Birdie was already losing the thread.

"Andie," she said again.

"Elliot is so incredible at this," Andie said in reply. "If I didn't have a girlfriend, I would seriously consider giving it a go."

Birdie felt the muscles in her face point downward, as if Andie were her competition or as if Elliot were still even an option. He never had been but for one fleeting night, and then it was all the more clear that she'd been wrong about him too.

"I got this letter," she said, trying to *pivot*. "I found it in a box."

"Congrats," Andie replied without even turning from the screen.

"No, not congrats," Birdie said. "Did you put it in my room? Or in the box? Or . . . like, do you know when it showed up? Or who sent it?"

Her sister craned her neck toward her. "How would I know who sent you a letter? Isn't it signed?"

Birdie's adrenaline surged. This was indeed just the hook she needed, she could sense it, the way that she could sense exactly how to deliver a line reading to garner applause from the crew, the way that she could cry on cue, the way that she could take hold of a room once the cameras were rolling. Yes, this was the *remaneuver* she needed, and if she could sell it to her sister of all people, she could sell it to America.

"No, it's not signed, which is why I asked."

"Don't you get a million fan letters? Why is this of any interest to me? Ooh, unless—is it like a ransom note? Then you have my full attention."

Elliot was wrapping up his segment, and the sisters were momentarily distracted, watching him throw it back to the *60 Minutes* anchor. Anderson Cooper appeared on-screen, dapper and with twinkling eyes that made you want to listen to anything he told you.

"Hilarious but no, not a ransom note, at least not yet. I care because this is a *love letter,*" Birdie snipped. "And I think it could be my ticket back to normalcy."

Andie turned to face her now, and though she was not related to Susana by blood, she shared a remarkably similar expression to the one Birdie had grown so used to in her teenage years. Her lips were pressed into a flat line, her nostrils flaring as if she'd smelled something foul.

"You got an unsigned love letter and you think it's *your ticket back to normalcy?*"

"You really need to stop repeating everything I say," Birdie piped. "Aren't you supposed to be the one with the master's degree or whatever?"

"PhD." Andie tutted.

"Right, so then surely you can see how me tracking down this old boyfriend and throwing myself at his feet is the love story that America didn't know it needed? But I need to know where to start."

"How exactly would I know where you should start?" Andie said. "I haven't known anything about your life since I quit."

"Since I fired you."

"Since I *quit.*"

Birdie stared at Andie. Andie stared at Birdie.

And then Anderson Cooper broke their standoff by introducing the next segment.

"It's not often that we cover behind-the-scenes Hollywood drama here at the news magazine, but this is the story that won't go away: Did Birdie Robinson, who until several weeks ago was the rom-com queen of Hollywood, permanently destroy her career when she went toe-to-toe with Sebastian Carol? We're back after the break to put this story through its paces. Don't go anywhere. Trust me, this is a good one."

"Oh my god," Andie said, her palm moving to her mouth to conceal her grin.

"Oh my god!" Birdie shouted, both at Anderson and at her sister, because there was nothing else to say.

4

BIRDIE

BIRDIE HAD NOT driven a car since she left Los Angeles four years back and permanently moved to New York. Andie's 4Runner was a stick shift, which meant that Birdie unintentionally peeled out of their parents' driveway, the tires squealing on the cement, her body lurching forward then back as she remembered how to ease off the clutch.

She and Andie had gotten into what Mona referred to as "classic Bird and Andie shit" over *60 Minutes*, nearly coming to blows over the remote. Andie was the more physically fit between them, despite Birdie's mandated boot-camp and training sessions, and alas, Birdie could not wrestle the remote from her sister's palm. So she grabbed her sister's keys from the kitchen counter, threw her arms into a puffy parka she suspected had been bought at Costco, and ran out before Andie could follow her.

Mona. Mona would know what to do about this letter.

Birdie stopped and started and reminded herself to release the clutch as she lurched through Barton, past their old high school, past the turnoff for the strip mall with the Sbarro. Mona had opened Monads, a semi-shitty dive bar, shortly after their parents' inheritance had come down just over a decade ago, which made the payout sound grander than it was. But it was enough for her to buy out the floundering watering hole that mostly catered to underage high schoolers and tired nine-to-fivers in Barton. At the time, her best friend had intended to be an astrophysicist or head up NASA, but she'd dropped out of Caltech to come home and then stayed home, and Birdie didn't judge her for it. Now she got her galactical fix in on the weekends on alien-hunting excursions in various southwestern deserts, and for this, Birdie *almost* judged her, but Birdie didn't have so many friends that she could risk losing Mona, and besides, she didn't think she could handle it if she did lose Mona. They'd been inseparable since the O'Briens moved to her block from San Francisco, and even as Birdie's star ascended higher and higher, she knew she'd never find anyone to replace Mona.

Birdie remembered the route to the bar by heart and flipped her blinker on, turning into Monad's parking lot, then blessedly easing into a spot next to Mona's RV, which she had also inherited from her parents and used as an excuse to never buy a car. The 4Runner's gas gauge flared red, as if it were angry with Birdie for the three-mile trek, and she reminded herself to fill it up on her way home. One less thing Andie could be mad about.

The bar seemed quiet as she stepped down from the truck, which came as a relief. She hadn't thought her plan through—didn't really have a plan, in fact, other than she didn't want to watch *60 Minutes* and she didn't want to be in Andie's company for a moment longer than she had been. Fleeing to Monads made sense. But now she was standing in the parking lot in a Costco jacket and a flowy caftan, and it occurred to her that she would be completely exposed once inside. Camera phones would be raised, record buttons would be pressed. Her location would be shot across the internet in no time flat.

But Birdie was not in a position to barter with the universe, so she curled her toes in her misguided strappy sandals to keep them warm and strode across the lot as if a director had told her to march forward with all the confidence she could project. Birdie always found difficult moments easier to digest if she simply pretended she was acting out a scene; this meant she could be vulnerable on the surface but not so vulnerable that she risked emotional decimation. She thought of Elliot again—perhaps the last time she'd been completely vulnerable—just before she pushed the door to Monads open. Elliot had emotionally decimated her, but then that was her own fault—thinking she'd be something different to him, thinking that he'd spent years craving her the way that she'd spent so long craving him.

Monads hadn't changed much since the last time Birdie had been home, four years back. The first thing that hit you about the place was the scent. Birdie didn't know why Mona couldn't hire a deep cleaner to blast whatever the whiff was that assaulted your nose upon entry, but when she'd asked the last time she was here, Mona had flung a hand and said, "The smell is part of the charm. People would kill me if it smelled like Pine-Sol." So instead, Birdie was sledgehammered with an odor that fell somewhere between old shoes and spilled beer and Glade PlugIns. The walls were adorned with Barton High memorabilia—a banner from the year the basketball team won regional playoffs, another from the single season they'd come in first at football but quickly lost in the playoffs. (Elliot had invited Mona and Birdie to tailgate, and Birdie leapt at the chance but Mona waved him off, so Birdie acted cool like she wouldn't have thrown herself into his trunk for an opportunity to keg stand with him.) There were photos of beloved coaches over the years, and more than a few black-and-whites of Elliot on the podium at swim meets.

Birdie had lost track of today's exact date, but there were half-strung white doilies on the wall behind the bar and several dollar-store cupids hanging from the ceiling—Mona's attempt to draw out Valentine's Day into early March, no doubt. When she was first getting her start, Imani made a big push about how America's Future Sweetheart was obsessed with Valentine's Day. Her publicist secured the February *InStyle* cover, which blared, **BIRDIE ROBINSON LOVES LOVE!**, and an entire narrative was constructed around how much Birdie, well, loved love. No one stopped to ask Birdie if she'd really been in love by then, when she was twenty-five, and if anyone had asked such a thing, she couldn't have answered honestly, so it was just as well. *Yes, with my best friend's brother? Possibly with a chef who I ghosted once I got semifamous?* Regardless, Birdie eyed Mona's decorations and felt flush with relief that February was behind her, and March lay straight ahead.

From the front door at Monads, Birdie watched her best friend behind the bar for a beat. Dressed in overalls and a flannel shirt, her hair in two pigtailed braids, Mona still looked sixteen, but then that was part of her mystique: how she could be so disarmingly adorable while her brain ran circles around your own. Birdie knew that what she personally lacked in book smarts she made up for in emotional intelligence, but Mona was lucky to have both. Which was precisely why she was the one to ask about the letter, not Andie. Andie with the enormous chip on her shoulder. Andie with an ax to grind.

Mona organized the glassware while the overhead speakers started in with ABBA's "Dancing Queen," which reminded Birdie so acutely of driving to school in Elliot's car that she wondered if she were being set up, on *Candid Camera*, if that was a thing anymore. She glanced around but the bar was still quiet, mostly empty but for a few dart throwers in the back room, so the song, the memories, the way both washed over her, was simply chance.

Birdie had always been well aware that Elliot would never think of her as anything other than Mona's best friend. He was a star swimmer, editor of the newspaper his junior year even though that had always been reserved for a senior. He went through girls as quickly as he tore through a fifty free, which was to say extremely quickly, and even if Birdie had wanted him to go through her (she did, she very much wanted him to go *right* through her), she was not the type of girl he set his sights on. But there was a moment, a very brief hiccup, back when she'd entertained the notion of Elliot as more than just Mona's twin brother.

It became real, concrete for her, in the middle of high school. When her butterflies grew into something more adult, more electric. In the doorway to Monads, with ABBA blaring and her best friend shimmying her shoulders while wiping down the bar, Birdie remembered now that Elliot had just gotten his license— he and Mona were four months older than she was—and Elliot started driving to school. Mona, afraid of failure, refused to take the test initially. Their parents gifted them their old Honda Accord, and one week their junior year, Mona was out sick with mono so it was just the two of them every morning. Elliot, because he was gracious, had offered Andie a ride too, but Andie got to school early because she was already in advanced math classes and liked to meet with her teachers for extra work. (Birdie didn't think she could be blamed for hating her younger sister.)

Birdie had assumed that carpooling with Elliot alone would be exactly like carpooling with all three of them, but it wasn't. It wasn't at all. Though they'd been alone a zillion other times before, something charged passed between them those mornings. Or at least something charged passed through Birdie. Her mouth would run dry and her palms would grow clammy and she'd stay up all night the evening before trying to think of clever things to talk about. Elliot, so much more at ease at sixteen than she was, brought her his mom's banana bread every day (back when she still ate carbs) and let her choose the radio station, and Birdie always opted for songs that showed off her range. There were a couple of moments when their hands brushed each other's, reaching for the volume to turn it up to full blast, and Birdie felt something reverberate deep in her gut. But she didn't allow herself to consider anything more about it. For a variety of and plentiful reasons: (1) Elliot O'Brien, varsity swim star and editor of the paper, was so far out of her drama-dork league that she didn't even think she qualified for the minors, while he was the anointed MVP, (2) Mona would kill her (not that there was anything to kill her over—see point number one), and (3) Birdie hadn't yet even kissed a boy, and she honestly didn't know what could happen next, what *would* happen next. She knew in theory of course: Susana had academically explained sex to her and Andie when they were nine and seven, so it wasn't that she didn't *know*; it was that her imagination either went too far—popping the buttons off his shirt and pants on the side of the road before they made it to school—or not far enough—that she was a fool to even think that Elliot would enjoy kissing her.

Years later, he proved her suspicion correct.

Still, though. During that heady week of carpooling, there was something about the way he looked at her when she turned up the dial and belted ABBA, like he was discovering something new about her, or the way he asked her opinion on a story he was crafting for the paper because he said she always considered things differently than everyone else, that made her wonder: *Maybe?*

But then Mona recovered quickly—it probably was never mono, her pediatrician decided—and was back in the carpool, and Elliot was more measured, more brotherly, and Birdie convinced herself that, like many things about boys, she'd gotten him wrong. Maybe he did understand her, but that didn't mean he wanted to careen the car over to the side of the road and drop the passenger seat back and climb atop her. Birdie's imagination always worked too hard. There was a reason she was still a virgin.

Tonight, ABBA finished the final harmony and the stereo switched over to some new pop song that Birdie didn't recognize. She saw Mona's face furrow as if she didn't know who had come up with this playlist either, and then her friend's eyes glanced up and her mouth dropped open in joy.

"Birdie!" she shrieked and threw herself over the bar in a single bound, like Tom Cruise in *Cocktail*, if *Cocktail* had been set in a dingy dive in the middle of nowhere California. Mona barreled into her best friend, and Birdie was surprised at how much she needed it. She reached her arms around Mona's neck and hung on tight until Mona pulled back and stared at her. "What? How? I don't— Wait, come sit. Let me pour you a drink. Actually, I don't even care what or how! I'm so damn happy you're home!" She linked her elbow into Birdie's and marched her to a stool, squeezing her shoulders as Birdie sat, as if Mona needed to ensure that her friend was solid, real, and wasn't going anywhere. Mona then slipped behind the bar and reached for the gin, pouring a heavy glass doused with tonic. Then she slid it across the bar and plopped her elbows down and leaned over with wide eyes.

"So tell me everything. If you're home, it must be a real shitstorm."

Birdie dug into the enormous side pocket of Andie's Costco jacket for the letter, which she'd folded up and tucked away for safekeeping.

"It's a five-alarm shitstorm," Birdie conceded.

"So an extremely gross shitstorm. You can't take a step without landing in it. "

"An accurate summation of my past few weeks. As you probably know. And . . . I'm sorry for not being in better touch. My team . . ." Birdie drifted as if she wasn't sure what she wanted to say. Her team hadn't kept her from texting Mona. She'd simply been too swept up in the whirlwind of everything to seek advice from the one person who probably would have looked out for her. She'd gotten used to self-reliance, and when she'd gotten tired of self-reliance, she'd gotten used to listening to Imani and Sydney. She could see the mistake of that now. "Anyway, yes, it's been an absolute massacre of a shitstorm." She nodded. "And also, I needed to show you this."

She thrust the folded envelope toward Mona, who frowned and opened it like she used to back in middle school when she'd find a note in her locker from a girl who inevitably wanted an introduction to Elliot or a boy who wanted to mock her over her undying belief in UFOs.

"What am I looking at?" Mona asked.

"An unsigned love letter," Birdie said.

"An unsigned love letter?" Mona's eyes grew wide, and Birdie saw her friend's cheeks flush with excitement. This was exactly the sort of thing a romantic like Mona, a grown woman who still got swept up in Valentine's Day, would adore. "When did *this* happen? Tell me *everything*!"

"This is . . . as much as I know. Also, are we still doing this?"

Birdie flapped a hand at the Valentine's decorations behind her best friend. "Love is dead, Mona. Didn't you know?"

"Birdie Maxwell," Mona chastised, and Birdie knew she was in for an earful about her cynicism, but then the door swung open behind them and a blast of cold air jetted in, and Mona lost focus. She raised her palm to wave to a group of locals, then to a second group right behind them. Birdie swiveled on her stool, keeping her head down while trying to scope out a few of the faces as they milled past and plunked down in the side booths. No one took note of her just yet. Still, she sneered at Nelson Pratt, who had ruined her prom with Elliot. And she scowled at AnnaMarie Baker, who she was pretty sure had taken Elliot's virginity and now, last Birdie heard, had four kids yet was still at Monad's on a Sunday night. Birdie, even to this day, loathed AnnaMarie Baker for no other reason than she got to sleep with Elliot first.

"So an anonymous letter!" Mona sang, returning her attention to the paper in her hand, her eyes coasting over the paragraphs, then resting back on Birdie. "This is exciting? Or terrifying? Which do you want me to feel? I will feel whatever you want but I have to say that I'm leaning toward thrilled. Titillated? Already too far out over my own skis with possibilities?"

Birdie grabbed her gin and tonic and tipped a long sip down her throat. "I'm thinking I want to find the man who sent it."

"Yes!" Mona cheered.

"I'm thinking that maybe that will help remind people that I'm likable, that I'm just a girl, standing in front of a boy, asking him to love her."

"And I'm thinking that's . . . brilliant," Mona said. "Though I never took you for a romantic, even though I tried my hardest, god knows." She had. It had been Mona's idea that Elliot take

Birdie to prom, after all, even though she'd suggested it platonically, completely platonically, ridiculously platonically, as a kindness since Mona already had a date in Nelson Pratt, who was her lab partner in AP Bio but also not-so-secretly loved her, and Elliot could have had his pick of anyone, the cheerleading squad, the math club, the orchestra kids.

"Which is why I came to you," Birdie said. "Because *you're* the one with the good heart."

"No, your heart is goodness too, Bird," Mona said, then held up a finger toward one of the back booths as if their beer order was urgent but not as urgent as an anonymous love letter that could save her best friend's life. "You just sometimes forget that."

"My heart is half-goodness, half-bullshit, let's be real," Birdie said.

"The perfect combination for Hollywood," Mona replied. "Me? I'm still holding out hope that you'll base a movie on a small-town girl who runs the local watering hole until a brilliant scientist wanders in one day and makes all of her dreams come true."

"Your dreams involve waiting in Monads for, like, a biologist to sweep you off your feet?"

"Well, it's that or Nelson," Mona said, nudging her chin toward her prom date. "He asks me to marry him at least every four months, but I think he mostly likes that I give him free beer sometimes."

"People have married for less."

"People have. But not this gal," Mona said, then shouted to the booth, who were now hollering in her direction, "One goddamn second, you will not wither from dehydration without a pitcher in your hands at this exact moment!" Her eyes slid back to Birdie. "So, this letter. Who are your suspects?"

"None of them? All of them?" Birdie honestly didn't have a

clue. She wasn't sure she'd truly even loved many men, other than Elliot—who was the one secret she had kept from Mona, and, she hoped, the one secret Elliot had kept from her as well—they'd agreed upon as much before he bolted from her place seven years ago after their regrettable night together. There was Kai, of course, but given all that had unraveled with his brother, how he hadn't reached out these past few weeks to even tell her privately that he was sorry for Sebastian's unhinged behavior, she couldn't stomach even entertaining that he'd made a play to win her back. Cutting Kai Carol out of her life was, other than watching Elliot walk away, the single hardest test of willpower she'd endured. Likely harder than Elliot because with Kai, she had a choice. His door was always open. But with Elliot, he closed it firmly behind him, so there wasn't even a road back to him if Birdie wanted it.

"The chef!" Mona snapped her fingers. "He's a possibility."

"Ian." Birdie said and thought about how Ian used to bring her leftovers from the restaurant because he didn't want her getting too skinny.

"Or the tennis guy—from Santa Barbara," Mona noted. She and Mona had spent a week in Santa Barbara celebrating her thirtieth birthday, and Carter had been the tennis pro at the resort. Carter, who was genuinely lovely and, last Birdie had heard, lived in Los Angeles. Theirs hadn't been a great love affair, but she wouldn't mind seeing him again, sleeping with him again either. They'd had absolutely spectacular sex.

"Oh, what about Simon?" Mona asked.

"You are remarkably adept at remembering all the men I've dated," Birdie replied.

"I liked Simon," her friend said. "But possibly because his British accent made me weak in the knees. I think Elliot keeps up with him, I can ask."

"Oh, you don't have to ask Elliot," Birdie said, suddenly unable to meet her friend's eyes. "Please don't bother him with this."

Mona shrugged. "Okay, well, that's a start. Anyone else I'm forgetting?"

Yes, Birdie thought. "No," she said.

"Well, three is not exactly a lengthy list, but three is better than zero. So now what?"

Birdie raised an eyebrow and chewed the side of her lip, repressing a smile. Only Mona would know that this was her conspiratorial look, the face she'd made when they were kids and Birdie was out of cash so pocketed a KitKat from the 7-Eleven because they absolutely would *die* without a KitKat, then would whip it from her pocket with sly triumph. (Her petty-theft phase was limited to a three-month period in eighth grade, no need to alert the tabloids.) Or the face she'd make when she decided that she and Mona should pull a Ferris Bueller and bail on school for the day. There wasn't nearly as much to do in their neighboring towns of Fresno or, if they really pushed it, Bakersfield, as there was in Chicago like in the movie, but they took the Honda Accord for a joyride as soon as Birdie called the school to sign Mona out under the guise of her grandmother dying. (Her grandmother had already died, so Birdie didn't feel too guilty.)

"Are you . . . No, you're not . . . You are!" Mona cheered because their brains were so synced, even now, that her friend could almost read her mind. "You're gonna make this into a thing, and you think it's going to save your ass with the public, don't you?" Her eyes grew to globes and a grin spread across her face. Birdie didn't even need to explain the rest. Her best friend loved a great rom-com, and so she knew a brilliant plot device when she saw one. "And maybe you'll even find love along the way!"

The front door opened again before Birdie could reply and tell her that finding love was honestly the least important criterion in her plan. A breeze strong enough to kick up the hem on her caftan swooped in, and if she'd been thinking straight, she would have seen it as an omen, a sign, a warning. Like when the chilly winds blew in from the north in some medieval HBO series, and with them, death and crows and bloodshed and all of those harbingers soon followed. As it was, she was completely shell-shocked and ill prepared when in following Mona's gaze and subsequent smile toward the door, she spun on her stool and found herself staring at Elliot O'Brien, star reporter in a war-ravaged land no longer.

Birdie's insides torpedoed and her sweat glands kicked into immediate overdrive. She worried she was going to vomit, right there on top of her seasonally inappropriate sandals, or possibly dissolve into a puddle of nervous perspiration that would require patting down her forehead and armpits and definitely the waistband of her underwear with those little cocktail napkins piled on the bar.

She hadn't spoken to him in seven years, since he'd walked out of her Tribeca apartment. She'd tried not to even *think* of him in seven years. And now Elliot O'Brien had come home, just in time for her own return.

The stars, Birdie thought, had aligned against her.

5

BIRDIE

B IRDIE'S FIRST INSTINCT, obviously, was to run. She jumped from the barstool just as Elliot's eyes met hers, and then she plopped back down just as quickly. If she ran now, he'd know it was because of him, and that would start a whole thing that Birdie didn't have the emotional fortitude to withstand. Besides, it felt critically important—for reasons she didn't understand—that Elliot think she was calm, totally collected. That seeing him for the first time since they'd slept together was no different from seeing, say, Nelson Pratt. Who, it was true, Birdie would have been happy to put in a headlock, but that wasn't the point, and she needed to focus.

"Elliot!" Mona shrieked from behind the bar. "Look who surprised us with a visit!"

Birdie felt herself wince as heads swiveled and stares lingered. A hush fell over the room as everyone registered that Birdie Robinson* (*Maxwell) was among them, and then slowly, an electric buzz pulsed through the bar. Or that could have been the rate of her pulse, which had taken flight and was only gaining speed.

Calm. Stay calm, she thought, though it was already a losing battle.

Elliot's hand floated up in an awkward wave as blood flooded her cheeks. And then he walked across the bar and was right in front of her. If she could have crawled underneath her stool without giving herself away, she would have.

"Birdie," he said, and she thought she heard his voice catch. "To what do we owe this honor?"

"Elliot," she replied, and he tipped forward to kiss her cheek. She was so surprised that she was late on reciprocating, so she semi-kissed the air as he pulled back, and she was certain she'd never been more mortified. He could kiss *anyone*, he could make *anyone* go weak in the knees, and here she was screwing up a hello.

"What's wrong with you? Why do you look like you've swallowed a toad?" Mona belted at her brother. Birdie was too busy trying not to come completely unraveled to realize that Elliot himself looked a little peaked. "Please don't tell me that you, of all people, are intimidated by our friend Birdie?"

Elliot wasn't intimidated by her fame, and Birdie knew it, and Elliot knew that Birdie knew it. Still, the question bought Birdie a few seconds to compose herself, to stitch herself back together and, ideally, white-knuckle her way back from a nervous breakdown.

"You know that fame is just a construct," Birdie managed sweetly, which was entirely for Mona's benefit. "It's just me, Elliot. Just the same old me."

Elliot narrowed his eyes, and Birdie batted hers at him over-dramatically, and there were a million things to say to each other that couldn't be said because Mona had no clue they'd spent a night together seven years ago, and it had to stay that way forever.

"It's good to see you, Bird," Elliot said, then pulled back the stool beside her. "Do you mind?"

"You're already sitting, so is it too late to say that I do?" she replied. She reached for whatever she was drinking and drained it. She minded, very much.

"So, Birdie Maxwell, what brings you back to Barton?" Elliot asked, and Birdie tried to assess if he genuinely had no idea that she had spiraled into an internet punching bag or if he simply didn't care. She knew that Elliot spent his days jet-setting across the globe, reporting on "real things" (as Andie had once explained it to her), and so perhaps was the only person on the planet who had not seen her ill-advised apology video. She hated that she wished that he had, and then she hated that she wished for that wish too.

"I thought you were in, like . . ." Birdie decided to dodge his question, meet indifference with indifference. Yes, that was the way to play this. "I just saw you on TV in some far-flung country. What brings *you* back to Barton?"

"We pretape things, you know. That's the magic of television," Elliot said. "I've been back for three days. And back in Barton for two."

"So then I can only assume that you have borne witness to my public downfall," she said before she could reorient herself and remember that she was supposed to be playing indifferent. "Did you take the time to vote in the *People* magazine poll? 'Should We Banish BiRo to a Desert Island?'"

"I . . . did not vote in the *People* poll," he said. Which of course he hadn't. He reported on "real things," and Birdie now truly wanted to crawl under her stool and possibly die there.

"Fuck the *People* magazine poll!" Mona chimed in. "I got Nelson's nephew to write an algorithm to spam bot it."

"Even *you* saw the *People* magazine poll?" Birdie groaned. "Mona, no offense, but you don't need to be wasting your time defending my honor by screwing with the algorithms."

"That's what I'm always telling her," Elliot said.

"That she shouldn't be defending my honor?" Birdie narrowed her eyes.

"No, that she's too brilliant for any of this ridiculousness."

"I'm not doing this with you right now, Elliot. We have more important things to discuss," Mona replied.

"More important than you graduating from college?" Elliot asked.

"Yes, Birdie got a love letter!"

Birdie slapped her hand over her eyes.

"It's nothing," Birdie said, because the last thing she needed was further humiliation in front of Elliot.

"You got a love letter . . . and . . . that's news?" he asked. "I'd think you'd get a lot of those."

"It was sent *to her house*. With *both* of her names. Which means it's a real person. But anonymous, unsigned, a complete mystery!" Mona sang. "Isn't that amazing?" Mona, for once, was not reading Birdie's cues.

"It's not amazing, Mon," Birdie mumbled and dodged Elliot's eyes. "But it could be helpful, that's all."

"Mona, I need tequila," Elliot said. "Just give me the whole bottle." He reached over the bar and helped himself before she could protest. "And, Birdie, how exactly is an anonymous love letter helpful? I don't follow."

"She's going to find out who sent it!" Mona was practically levitating now. For someone who was such a scientific genius, Birdie thought, she really could let her imagination get the better of her. "She's going to track him down and remind America that she was their sweetheart all along. And also, maybe, probably, potentially find the man of her dreams."

"I don't have a man of my dreams, Mona. Really. Please," Birdie muttered. Was it too late to run straight out into the night and pretend none of this had happened?

Elliot took a deep glug from the tequila bottle, as if he had his own things to forget. Probably including sleeping with Birdie, but then, she remembered, he *had* forgotten. Quite easily. "Explain," he said. "What exactly does that look like? You email various exes and ask them if they sent you an anonymous letter, and if someone admits to it, you issue a press release?"

Birdie felt herself scowl. "I don't issue a press release."

"You call the paparazzi to catch you guys covertly hand in hand?"

"I don't call the paparazzi *ever*," she seethed. Forget running out into the night. She wanted to strangle him. That would work too.

"Okay, so, then, what? How exactly does this work?"

Birdie glared at him, then darted her eyes to the floor.

"I haven't thought through all the details," she said with a huff. "I just knew that this was the opening scene of sorts. 'Publicly reviled former America's Sweetheart gets a chance at love again.' Who wouldn't green-light that?"

"I would, that's for sure," Mona said, just as Nelson Pratt shouted, "Mona O'Brien, if you don't get us pitchers of Bud Light in the next thirty seconds, I'm going to get down on one knee and beg you to marry me in front of everyone here!" Mona reddened and said, "Excuse me, I'll be back. Hold that thought."

Birdie and Elliot stared at their knees until she was across the room.

"Did you tell her?" Birdie hissed. "Please tell me that you didn't tell her."

"Did *I* tell her?" Elliot whispered back. "Would I still be alive if I had?"

"So she knows nothing?" Birdie said. She firmed her jaw and flared her nostrils just like she would in a close-up. She had the scowl down perfectly.

"I mean, Mona knows a lot of things, but does she know that we slept together and you kicked me out the next morning? No, she does not."

"That is *not* what—" Birdie snapped, but then Mona was ambling back to the bar, and Birdie said, "So how long are you in town for, Elliot?" She grabbed the tequila from him and tipped her own sip back, as if the two of them were accustomed to sharing bottles all the time, as if everything were perfectly normal between them. She really was an exceptional actress, she thought.

"Unclear," Elliot replied. "Just wanted to catch up with my twin sister, lie low, get some rest."

"I had the most brilliant idea," Mona said. "While talking to Nelson."

"Talking to Nelson about me?" Birdie asked.

"He's so much more normal now, Bird, I promise."

Elliot rolled his eyes, and Birdie wondered if they were both thinking of the time at prom when Nelson narc'd them out to Mona. How they had slipped away into the faculty lounge because Birdie had always wanted to break in (their principal literally hung an "Off Limits" sign on the door), and Elliot was already accepted to Berkeley, so neither of them cared if they got caught. And so Birdie picked the lock (she honed various skills on her free afternoons because she took her talent résumé seriously), and they raided the fridge, which mostly had yogurts, but someone had left three boxes of Girl Scout cookies there too, so the two of them curled up on a tweed love seat and ate sleeve after sleeve of Samoas. Birdie licked the chocolate residue off her fingers and wondered if she was misreading that Elliot very much looked like he wanted to kiss her when Mona flew through the door of the lounge, and they each jumped to opposite corners of the couch.

"What's the brilliant idea?" Birdie asked Mona now, ignoring the idea that Nelson Pratt could be any less annoying at thirty-four than he'd been at seventeen, even if Mona vouched for him.

"You can't just issue a press release," she said. "No one would buy that. That *reeks* of self-aggrandizing."

"Are you my publicist now? Because I already have one who I'm pretty pissed off at. The apology video was her idea, well, my agent's too. Which is to say that I was outvoted, and now I would like to fire them both, but for obvious reasons, because my reputation is in the shitter, I cannot."

"It's not *that* bad," Mona tried.

"The only current offer I have, with all the others having been pulled, is an independent horror film that I'm pretty sure they want me for because they could claim they got to kill off America's Sweetheart."

"Yikes," Elliot said.

"Nice," Birdie replied. "Extremely helpful."

"I'm just saying, the video was not your best—" he started.

"So you *have* seen it," Birdie said before she remembered that she was supposed to be pretending not to care.

"But why doesn't Elliot write it for you?" Mona was talking right over them, a million words per minute like her mouth couldn't keep up with her brain. Which, given the speed at which her synapses fired, was probably true.

"Write . . . the letter? Elliot didn't write the letter," Birdie said. She heard her voice teeter into an octave too high. If Mona suspected that Elliot wrote the letter, then Mona knew much more than they realized. Which meant that her best friend and his twin sister was well aware that they'd been lying to her for seven years, which meant that they were about to drown at the bottom of shit's creek. Birdie thought of ways that she could save herself, pin it all on him. He was known to have slept with women across the globe, so Birdie thought she could build a case around that.

"I didn't write the letter!" Elliot said, tutting, also too strident to be normal. "Why would I have written the letter? I don't even know what this letter *is*!" he bleated.

"Jesus, calm your tits," Mona said, passing him the open page, and Elliot, Birdie noticed, was the color of an overripe tomato. "Seriously, will you two just relax?" Mona was still going. "No, Elliot, I was proposing that *you* write *the story* of how Birdie is trying to *find* the person who wrote it. Then, Bird, it looks objective, and, Elliot, maybe you need to stop covering, like, the bleakest news on the planet, literally the entire planet, so you'll get some sleep at night."

He and Birdie both yelped *No!* so loudly, so in sync, that anyone who didn't know better would think they had something to hide.

"Yes!" Mona responded. "Absolutely yes. Give me one reason why this isn't perfect."

Birdie waited for Elliot. Elliot waited for Birdie. And when neither of them could come up with a plausible explanation, Mona clapped her hands together, poured them a round of shots, and said, "Perfect, we're doing this. I don't want to hear another word of protest."

6

BIRDIE

BIRDIE WAS TOO drunk to drive Andie's 4Runner home, and besides, she was pretty sure it was out of gas. Elliot, because he was always such a goddamn Boy Scout (he wasn't, he really wasn't, though), had the foresight to lay off the tequila two hours prior, and thus, at midnight, when Mona told Elliot to take Birdie home, once again neither of them could offer a compelling explanation why he shouldn't.

Birdie well knew that Nelson Pratt had been snapping pictures of her all night, and god only knew how soon they'd be racing around the internet, chum for the bottom-feeders. That Birdie Robinson's prospects were so bleak that she'd cozied up to a shitty bar and drowned her sorrows in cheap booze while swathed in a parka that resembled an REI sleeping bag. Until now, Imani and Sydney had managed to bury any leaks about her fictitious background, doubling down with a *Vogue* shoot on the Oregon coast five years back. She knew that promises had been made for juicier scoops to outlets who threatened to run the truth, and she further suspected that Imani had an assistant dedicated to weekly internet deep dives: Reddit, Twitter, various gossip forums where catty women named something like mom2soccer4some eviscerated everything from her posture to the way she tucked her hair behind her ear when a costar was about to kiss her. But since Birdie so rarely came home, she'd never placed herself in the crosshairs of people who actually knew her back when she was Birdie Maxwell. And anyway, for a long time, Birdie coasted by on goodwill and general adoration, and if there was dirt to be scooped, few reporters were interested in doing the necessary digging.

Now she was a gazelle out on an open plain. Fresh meat.

If Nelson Pratt wanted to expose her past the way that Sebastian Carol had manipulated her present, there wasn't much that Birdie could do to stop him. It didn't help matters that on the way out of Monads, she marched up to his booth, rooted herself to the floor with her hands on her hips, and said,

"You, Nelson Pratt, are a fuckwad who ruins everything. So I would like to say, seventeen years postmortem, that you should fuck all the way off."

Elliot yanked her by the elbow, and she stumbled forward into his chest, and she nearly rested her head there, right on his heart, until she realized what she was doing and recoiled.

"Birdie," he said low, quiet, right in her ear. "Let's not do this now, make it messier. Come on. Nelson isn't worth it." Still, she turned and hissed at Nelson like a pissed-off feline on the way out, just so he was a little scared, a tad intimidated. In high school, Birdie Maxwell couldn't scare a cricket off their front porch. Now at least she could make someone flinch.

A few minutes later, they were each sitting in his car rigidly, as if any sort of movement might cause them to touch, as if any sort of touching might make them combustible. Birdie tried not to think about that night they'd spent together seven years ago. How was it seven years when she could still remember the crackle of sparks that ran through her when his fingers snaked over her thighs and up the hem of her dress? How she pressed him against the wall in her apartment foyer, how they couldn't even wait to make it to the bedroom. How his lips had felt like salvation, how his touch had felt like coming home.

Elliot, Birdie noticed, gripped the steering wheel until his knuckles were nearly dead white and didn't dare look in her direction. Was he thinking about it too? How they braided their legs together in her king-sized bed, how he flipped her on her stomach and straddled her to dig his elbows into her sore spots just below her shoulder blades, then how his palms wound their way to her breasts?

His phone started buzzing as soon as they pulled out of the parking lot. Birdie glanced down at it, then at him, then down at it, then back to him. Elliot was still staring straight ahead as if he couldn't hear it, which Birdie found suspicious. Ludicrous.

"A girl from one of your ports?" she said.

"No," he replied. She watched a muscle in his neck twitch. Why were even the muscles in his neck so goddamn alluring?

His phone blared again. This time, Birdie reached for it and flipped it over.

"Francesca," she said. "So certainly a girl. Possibly not in a port."

Elliot's hand shot off the wheel and grabbed the phone. "Do not answer that."

"Okay, wow," Birdie said. "It's cute that you think I'm interested in speaking with one of your girlfriends."

"She's not my—" Elliot started, then stopped himself. "It

doesn't matter. Also, you don't seriously think that I can write this article, do you?"

"Because it's beneath you?"

"What? No, because . . ." He trailed off, which was just as well. What was he going to say to Birdie, that, yes, covering her love life was beneath him when there were wars being fought, diseases to cure, politicians to expose?

"Is it because *you* were the one who wrote it, the letter?" Birdie felt her eyes go wide as soon as the question was out of her mouth. That was the gin and tequila talking, and if she had been in any sort of coherent state, she would never have asked such a thing. This was Elliot O'Brien, childhood crush, one-night stand, and the man who hadn't reached out to her since. Then, because she really had no self-control evidently, she added, "I mean, let's be honest, that would actually make a whole lot of sense. You know where I live. Lived. You know my real name. Who's to say that you, Elliot, don't regret everything?"

Stop talking stop talking stop talking.

But she couldn't. Seven years was a long time to stay quiet.

"Because," she continued, "I'm pretty famous, as you may know; I'm pretty much queen of the mountain, a pretty massive deal. Maybe you realized that I'm the one who got away. I wasn't just another notch in your very well-notched bedpost. Would you estimate that you have *ever* managed a sustained relationship, other than that with your own ego, or is a revolving door of perpetual women going to be your thing forever?"

Elliot pursed his lips together and didn't reply, so Birdie let the booze sink in and closed her eyes and eased her head against the window. She was half-asleep when his phone bleated again, and so, too, did hers.

She flipped her cell over in her lap and saw that Imani was calling, though it was well past midnight. Imani calling well past midnight was almost never a good sign. She swiped her screen and jabbed at the speakerphone.

"Are you in some shitty bar telling people to fuck off?" her publicist asked by way of greeting.

Birdie jolted up straighter, and Elliot immediately silenced his own ringer.

"In fact, I am not," Birdie said, and it wasn't even a lie. "I am in a car, being escorted home by a very esteemed journalist."

"Okay." Imani sighed. "*Were* you in a shitty bar telling people to fuck off?"

"Not people," Birdie said. "One person. His name is Nelson Pratt, and if I explain what a loser he is, you'll be glad I didn't get more graphic."

"Biiiiirdiiiiieeeee," her publicist howled.

"Chirp-chirp," she replied. Goddamn, she was drunk.

"Your little spout-off is all over the internet now. We barely had a chance to dig out of your apology vid—"

"The apology video is on *you*!" Birdie interrupted. "I told you it was a terrible idea! You *know* I can't act when I don't believe in it!"

"Respectfully, Birdie, you've signed on to scripts that shouldn't have made it out of someone's 1990s trash files, scripts that my cat could have vomited up, so I don't buy that for a second," Imani said.

"Well, look who's being honest with me *now*," Birdie said.

Imani sighed, and Birdie could picture her at her home in Santa Monica, in her kitty-cat pajamas that Birdie had gifted her last Christmas, nursing a hefty glass of wine to manage her stress.

"Birdie, things are going to get worse before they even have any hope of getting better. I thought we could do some splashy profiles, some redemption-arc pieces, and this would all go away. But, look, can you just . . . lie low, draw absolutely no attention to yourself, and let Sydney and me and your team put our heads together to figure out how to move forward?"

"I *am* lying low. That was the whole point of the dive bar, of coming ho—"

But Imani had hung up on her before she could finish her sentence. Which was what Imani did when she was issuing a decree, not making a request.

Elliot let out a whistle, and for a second, Birdie had forgotten he was there, driving her home like a gallant escort, a noble hero of sorts, even though he certainly was *not* a gallant escort, despite feigning the fact that he was that exactly when they were teenagers. Would a gallant escort have left her in bed seven years ago? Would a gallant escort not have even bothered to send an email, a text, a goddamn Facebook message after walking out?

"So. You're obviously scrapping your plan to hunt down this anonymous long-lost pathetic sad sack of a lover, correct?"

"Ah, he finally speaks," Birdie said. "And I'm sure that you would be delighted if he were a pathetic sad sack of a man. Like that's the only type I could have pining over me?"

Elliot's face folded into confusion. "What? No. I was joking, Birdie. Trying to lighten the mood."

"Well, you should stick to nonfiction, then. Comedy isn't your forte. Do not recommend. Zero stars."

"I wasn't—" He shook his head and fell silent. "You're right. I've never been funny. That was always Mona. And you." This wasn't true at all, but Birdie didn't feel like boosting the man when he was down.

"I'm going to ask again," she managed, ignoring his compliment, because Elliot was so adept at telling women what they didn't even know they wanted to hear that she couldn't let herself get hoodwinked. "Just so that we're clear. Was it you? Because if I find out that it—"

"No," he said, and Birdie thought she heard his voice wobble, but then, she was also very drunk, so she couldn't be sure. Wouldn't swear on it in court. "You know I don't do regret."

"'Elliot O'Brien. I don't do regret.'" Birdie managed a laugh and hoped it was one that conveyed disgust. "That should be the name of your memoir."

"Put it on my grave."

"Or at least in your Twitter bio. Give all those fangirls fair warning when they slide into your DMs."

"They don't slide into—" His phone buzzed again in the cup holder, and he fell silent, just as he turned into the darkened street where they used to play kick the can in the summer after dark. Birdie would lie on the couch all day thinking of quippy things to say to Elliot, who spent the summer at swim training and then, when they were older, lifeguarding at the YMCA pool, and there was nothing more satisfying than when she nailed the pithy one-liner. Making him double over in hyena howls, pressing his fingers into the sides of his waist to ward off a cramp. If Mona noticed that her best friend had long-simmering feelings for her twin, she never said a word. At least not at the time. There was nothing threatening about Birdie's feelings because it was so one-sided, and neither of them—Mona nor Birdie—ever dared to imagine that anything would come of it. Besides, half the school had crushes on Elliot. Mona was so used to his public adoration, the low-level, ever-present flirting by just about everyone that she seemed to be immune to it. Also, there was the fact that even when Birdie was dreaming up those devastatingly acerbic, hilarious one-liners (Elliot was perhaps her first audience), she was always steadfastly in Mona's corner: when boys tried to tell her that she wasn't smart enough to join their honors science study group, when girls asked her if she and Elliot were really twins because he had gotten all the looks in the family. (Not all the looks, of course. Mona was adorable and plucky and had the same annoying facial symmetry of her brother. It was just that Elliot's features all fell together much like Michelangelo's *David*: perfectly, all at once, in total harmony.) Birdie was always there, Mona's ride or die, shit-talking those boys, eye-rolling at those girls. It wasn't hard to love Elliot from a distance and cherish Mona much more closely.

Tonight, by the time they pulled up to Mona's house, Elliot's old childhood house, Birdie's eyelids were being tugged lower with every inhale, lower still with every exhale. It was easier to get drunk, chew out Nelson Pratt, imagine that this anonymous letter could be her professional salvation, than to face the consequences of getting drunk and chewing out Nelson Pratt, the video of which (though Birdie did not yet know this) already had two million views on YouTube.

When Elliot said, "Well, we're home," she was halfway asleep and, for a very brief moment, forgot the entire mess before her and believed him.

7

ELLIOT

BY 2 A.M., Elliot was still wide awake but could feel the throb of his eyeballs imploring him to get some rest. But he was right on the cusp of a professional breakthrough—he was actually somewhat desperate for a professional breakthrough—and as was always the case when a thread was tugging at his brain, he practically levitated with energy, and short of a tranquilizer gun, sleep was never going to find him. Birdie evidently had no such problems and had passed out down the hall in the guest room, stumbling inside and rebuffing his efforts to lend her a shoulder on which to lean as she wobbled up the steps. Neither of them ever considered that he drop her at her old house; it was muscle memory that she'd crash here, down the hallway lined with framed photos of their trio at birthday parties, at Disneyland, at high school graduation, from his own boyhood room.

His phone blared again, and this time, when Francesca's name popped up, he had a plan and answered it.

"Francesca," he said to his editor in his best honeyed voice. "Just who I wanted to speak with."

This was, of course, a lie, and they both knew it. Elliot had been back in the States for three days, home in Barton for two, and Francesca had been up his ass ever since. She wasn't out of line—he knew he deserved it—but still, all he wanted was a few days off to not think about work, to not live and breathe his work. The issue at hand, however, was that Francesca was primed to give him plenty of days off from work. Too many days.

"Why didn't you tell me that you knew Birdie Robinson?" Francesca hadn't smoked since her thirtieth birthday, but she still sounded like a barking seal when she was running hot. "How have I made your career without knowing that you were friends with the biggest movie star on the planet?"

"Is she?" Elliot asked, though he knew she was. He hadn't thought that this was where the conversation would start—he figured he'd have to beg a bit and lie a bit and convince her a bit—but he wasn't disappointed that she was already playing into his hand.

"Seriously, how do you know Birdie Robinson?" she pestered.

Something occurred to Elliot: "How do you know that I know Birdie Robinson? Which, between us, that's not even her real name. She's Birdie Maxwell here in Barton."

"The video, from tonight," his editor replied. "You two muttering into each other's ears, and I couldn't tell if you were in love with her or *had* been in love with her, but then I realized: What? Elliot doesn't have a shot with the world's most beautiful movie star."

"Your hyperbole is a little out of hand, Francesca," he said.

"That you wouldn't have a shot or that she's the most beautiful?"

"Anyway," he said. "You were calling me at two in the morning just to ask me that?"

Francesca sighed. "Well, I've called you at every other hour, and you've dodged me. I thought that Birdie Robinson might be a good entry point, a soft landing."

"I have an idea," Elliot interjected.

"I'm sure you do. Your problem is never ideas, O'Brien; it's the ethical execution of them."

He wasn't surprised that his editor cut right to the heart of the issue; it's what he loved about her if he wasn't so terrified of her right now. He'd been working for Francesca since his start at the *Times* in New York, and when she jumped to San Francisco to run the newsroom, she took him with her. But presumably, in her next breath tonight, she was going to can him, and so Elliot spun his brain like a kaleidoscope: he'd do anything, promise her anything, to keep his job. He knew that she'd let him off with warnings before. But now—*now?*—Francesca had been on a rampage (so he'd been told, as he'd been declining her calls) when she heard from a competitor that Elliot paid for intel required to break his story on the Senate bribery scandal last month. Even though he'd gotten his facts right. Even though the Senate was now opening an inquiry into the seven colleagues who'd laundered money from a corrupt overseas government. *Sue me*, he wanted to say to Francesca, but actually, she could. If the *Times* booted him, there, too, would go the *60 Minutes* gig, and then he'd be left with, like, a shitty newsletter that barely covered his monthly Wi-Fi bill.

"Let me pitch you," he said, trying to keep his tone professional, not panicky. "If you hate it, then you can fire me. If you love it—or if I'm even in the ballpark of lukewarm—let me at least stick around and prove my worth."

"Again, your problem has never been your *worth*. Your problem is your ego."

"I thought it was my ethics," he said.

"O'Brien!" she snapped. "Cut the banter. Give me your pitch. You have one minute before my Ambien kicks in. Go."

"Birdie got a love letter," he said.

"I'm sure she did. I'm practically willing to send one to her myself. Can you ask what serum she uses for her skin?"

"Sure, if that will help my case, no problem."

"It might, but it probably won't," she acknowledged.

"Anyway, let me clarify: *Birdie got an anonymous love letter.* And she wants to track down the guy—or girl, I suppose—who sent it. And I would like to pitch, or, I should say, my pitch is that you let me cover it for the *Times.* Hit the road with her, kick the tires, rattle some ghosts."

Elliot was working this all out in real time, flying by the seat of his pants. He didn't stop to think, couldn't stop to think, that revisiting Birdie's exes—and, god forbid, reuniting her with some dude who might have gotten away—would gut him, puncture his otherwise steely armor that served him well professionally and honestly served him pretty well romantically, since he had no desire to linger in a relationship.

"I'm intrigued," Francesca murmured. "What, exactly, is the plan? How would you craft the feature?"

"Features," he said, because he figured that the more pages she gave him, the more chances he had to prove he was invaluable. "Still working on that with Birdie. I'm thinking we road trip it? Maybe take a quickie flight if we need to?"

"And I'm budgeting for that? I don't see Ms. Robinson staying at the roadside hotels you're used to."

Elliot thought of the Birdie he knew as a kid. Rough-and-tumble, with scrapes on her knees from capture the flag, with sharp elbows during kick the can as her ponytail flew behind her and her Converse laces unraveled as she ran.

"Also still working on that. Let me talk to her."

"Who else knows about this letter?" Francesca asked.

"No one? I mean, my sister."

"So we won't be scooped."

"Not if you green-light me right now. But *right now*, because I have to get to work."

Elliot held his breath. He knew he was pushing his luck, but he also knew that a story had fallen into his lap that he, solely, could report. If he could land this plane, the headlines would be everywhere. His byline would be everywhere. Ironically, it would be the most widely read story of his career, and sure, it wasn't the hard-hitting pieces that garnered him Pulitzer nominations (he had two), and it wasn't even all that interesting to him other than the fact that it involved the unrequited love of his childhood (so it was actually extremely interesting to him), but Elliot had built an entire life around his work, and if he had to cover Birdie's ex-lovers to salvage that, then so be it. Without his career, Elliot couldn't even fathom what he'd do with himself. He was thirty-five, single, child-free, he had more airline and hotel points than any human should ever hope to accrue, and the only thing tangible he had for himself was his byline under headlines and a once-a-month-or-so *60 Minutes* gig.

"I'm not saying yes," Francesca said. "But I'm not saying no. My Ambien kicked in, and I'm not dumb enough to commit to anything while inebriated. Call me by nine tomorrow with your plan."

"Okay," he said. *Okay.*

"And I want the name of her serum regimen too. That's mandatory." She hung up. Elliot exhaled a bubble of stress that was pressing against his breastbone.

He groaned and stood to stretch, his lower back cracking as

he did, and glanced around his old bedroom. He assumed his parents had plans for it one day—his mom always joked that she'd turn it into a home gym—but then they died, and that was that. His old trophies still cluttered the bookshelves; his old 49ers posters still adorned the walls. He scooted to his closet and pulled an old Barton High Swim Team hoodie off a hanger, slipping it on like he used to all those early mornings when he'd head out the door in the darkness for practice, like this was arming him now with the bravado he had back at sixteen. Then he gingerly eased the door open and tiptoed down the hall. Birdie had left the guest room door ajar, and he didn't want to be a creep, but he just wanted to be sure that she was okay.

He padded next to her bed. Her arm was flung over her face, and her hair fanned like a wild mane across the pillow. He remembered how he woke up in the middle of the night when they were finally together, that night, just to stare at her, at the way she had a flurry of freckles across her nose, at the way her lashes flitted while she was dreaming, at the way she looked so peaceful. Tonight, she had asked him if he voted in the *People* poll, and he'd lied because of course he had. Would he rather be banished to a desert island with Birdie Robinson or a coconut? If Birdie were banished to a desert island, he'd have wanted to be banished too. He would have marooned himself on the island, spearing fish and cracking said coconuts if that's what she asked for. He would have endured sunburns and shark bites and jellyfish stings. He would have searched for driftwood and built them shelters and hunted for dry wood and started fires. He would have swum to the end of the ocean for her, which his high school self nearly could have done. He pictured it: papayas and fish meat and them naked and salty and sunburnt. It honestly sounded wonderful.

Tonight, she was snoring, not particularly quietly either, and he watched her for a second, then a few seconds more, amazed that she was so exactly the same as she had been at twelve or sixteen or twenty-seven but also so transformed. Not just by age or maturity. Maybe by fame. Maybe by cynicism or the exhaustion that came along with that fame—sharper cheekbones, skin that had been lasered to within an inch of an open pore, like even the slightest imperfection could be held against her. (He really couldn't blame Francesca for demanding details about her skin care.)

He should have reached out when the on-set video went viral, when the unkind leaks and unflattering hot takes starting zooming around the internet at supersonic speed. He should have texted and said, *Hey, sometimes I also get raked across the coals, called a traitor, called a shitbag, called a motherfucking idiotic enemy of the people on Twitter.* He could have helped her craft a more honest apology; he could have, he thought, simply helped her. But they really hadn't spoken in so long that it felt stilted, maybe even selfish, to make such a gesture.

In the guest room, Birdie let out a snort, and Elliot jumped, then he quietly retreated and eased the door shut, the latch clicking into place. He darted back to his room and opened his laptop, ready to plug some names into Google, ready to do whatever he needed to convince Francesca that he was invaluable. He knew Birdie had dated that chef, Ian, before she was famous. And he knew that she'd spent about a year with his friend Simon, the hotelier, when she was twenty-nine or so. Add in the tennis pro, Carter, for that thirtieth birthday in Santa Barbara that led to a whole thing, and Elliot at least had a place to start. He had stopped asking Mona questions about Birdie after their own fling, but he was lucky to have a sister who liked to talk. And he was lucky that he had a brain that always, always paid attention when Birdie's name came up. There were also very questionable rumors about Kai Carol over the years—every once in a while, Elliot did a deep, deep, deep internet dive into Birdie when he was lonely in a run-down hotel somewhere—but given the fallout with Sebastian, he couldn't quite make the logic work: that a world-famous movie star wouldn't publicly defend the woman he loved if their romance had been legitimate in any way. Besides, he couldn't envision a scenario in which he tracked down Kai Carol and got him on record about Birdie in the next few days. Elliot was good, but even he knew his limits.

He typed in *Chef Ian Sands*, and Google led him immediately to Chez Nous, a restaurant in San Francisco that was actually one of Elliot's favorites. He hadn't realized that Chef Ian was *her* Chef Ian, or maybe he wouldn't have raved about the mussels when Ian came out to greet him. (Ian knew Elliot by reputation so made a point to say hello.)

From downstairs, Elliot heard the front door slam, and then Mona's footsteps thumped up the stairs, and she burst through his door like they were still kids.

"Is she okay?" she asked.

"I don't think she needs you looking out for her, Mon."

"I never said that she *needs* me to. It's just something that normal people do for each other, Elliot. Normal people who don't have an allergy to attachment."

"I'm attached to you," he said.

"We shared a womb. That's a bare minimum, that's basically a requirement."

"She's asleep down the hall," Elliot conceded.

"Did you guys consider my idea? You and the story. Her and her letter?"

"Yes." Elliot nodded. "It's on my radar."

He needed to proceed carefully here. Mona didn't know anything about his professional complications, the gig he was holding on to by an extremely tenuous thread—he'd always played the part of the much more together sibling and wasn't ready to abandon that now. And even though the story had been her suggestion in the first place, Elliot suspected she wouldn't take kindly to him barreling ahead with Francesca in a bid to save his job. *Birdie shouldn't be bartered like that*, she'd chastise. And she wasn't wrong. But Elliot liked to think that he and Birdie both stood to gain with this plan—he was only using her as much as she was using him.

Also, he didn't like to think that he was *using* her at all. Birdie's fame didn't impress him. Birdie did that all on her own. She had since the very first time they met.

Since he was twelve.

Since he was twenty-seven.

Since he was thirty-five.

Then. Still. Now.

8

BIRDIE

BIRDIE WAS CERTAIN that she was dreaming. She heard a loud pounding on a door somewhere in the distance, then the doorbell clanging again and again, and when it blessedly stopped and she was drifting back into her hangover-induced slumber, she couldn't shake the sense that someone was standing at the foot of her bed, hissing her name. But her eyes didn't fly open until she felt hands clamped around her ankles, and her entire body being tugged off the footboard.

Then she was up with a start. She'd had a stalker before and, in her bleary-eyed confusion, assumed that he'd found her again. She kicked her feet as forcefully as she could, straight up in the air, and it was only when she heard her sister yelp, "Ow, you mother-fucker!" that she fully came to consciousness. As it was, her head was throbbing and her stomach was making medically worrying noises, still sloshing with the gin and the tequila and, oh, she remembered now, the microwaved fried cheese sticks that Mona had warmed up at the bar because Birdie needed something to absorb some of the booze and that was the best option on the menu.

When she opened her eyes, her sister was tilting her head back with a trickle of blood creeping down her left nostril.

"You gave me a bloody nose," she cried.

"Well, how was I supposed to know that it was you? I took self-defense classes a few years ago; you can't blame my reflexes." Indeed, the studio had enrolled her in jujitsu for the part of a single mom who agreed to try twelve new hobbies in an attempt to find her soulmate. (It wasn't Birdie's favorite script but they were paying her too much to say no.)

Andie stomped out of the room, then returned with toilet paper stuck up her nose and scowled.

"I don't know why I'm being blamed for this," Birdie said. "Also, why are you here? Also, I need some Tylenol. Also—"

"I'm no longer your assistant," Andie interrupted. "Get your own goddamn Tylenol. But I'm here because you have slept through the stampede that has barreled through Barton."

Birdie swallowed down something awful that had risen from her gut and tried to make sense of what Andie was saying. She couldn't.

"What? What stampede? And what does that have to do with me?"

Andie pulled out the wad of toilet paper before answering. She examined it, saw she was still gushing, and pushed it back in.

"The stampede of reporters," she snapped as if this should have been obvious. "I opened the door this morning to go for a run, and it was like a zombie horde out there. I do not like zombie hordes, Birdie. As you may remember."

Indeed, Birdie had been offered an eye-popping figure to *pivot* to the horror genre back when Andie was living with her in

Los Angeles, and Andie talked her out of it. The film flopped terribly, but by then Andie had returned to Barton, having quit (or having been fired—it depended on whose account you believed), and Birdie never had the chance to thank her.

"Seriously, you need to get out of Barton ASAP or else you need to go tell them, not to be too literal, to *get off my damn lawn*," her sister said. "I had to slip out the back alley to get here, and, Birdie, I do not *like* slipping out like I'm the one who has something to be ashamed of."

Now Birdie was awake. Wide-awake. Electrifyingly wide-awake. She flung the comforter to the floor and was on her feet before she realized her body wasn't ready for such rapid movements. The floor tilted and the room spun, and she staggered forward toward the windowsill, where she steadied herself. She angled her head so she could peer down the street, and sure enough, she saw at least five vans, some with satellite dishes on their roofs, parked in front of her house, along with crews milling about and reporters pacing with cell phones to their ears.

"Holy mother of hell." She spun around and caught a glimpse of herself in the mirror on the closet door. She'd fallen asleep in her ridiculous caftan, which, against the dated backdrop of Mona's guest room, looked even more absurd than it had last night, like she was a boozy housewife stuck in the late nineties. She had sheet marks embedded on the left side of her face; her mascara had flaked and run under her eyes, making her look even more exhausted than she already was. Her hair, which she'd been letting grow out for *Love Grenade*—focus groups liked Birdie better with soft, flowing waves—was matted in the back and snarled in the front, like she'd had a wrestling match with her pillow.

The guest room door flung open, and Elliot and Mona flanked the doorway. Elliot had that serious look on his face that was immediately so familiar. In high school, Birdie used to sit high in the stands at his swim meets—she was too mortified to let him know that she was always there when he already had a very vocal cheering section of significantly more popular girls sitting in the lower tiers, sometimes even carrying signs. Every time he stepped up on a block, she'd see that look, even from her bird's-eye perch. Elliot putting himself through the paces of the race; Elliot blocking out any distractions because distractions meant that he might slip up, and slipping up meant that he might lose, and losing was not something that Elliot O'Brien did.

"We need to get you out of here," he said.

"I can't leave," Birdie said. "Not . . . like this." She gestured frantically to the outfit meant for her wellness retreat. "They'll use this photo in my obituary and a hundred times before then."

Andie held up a bag. "Yes, I brought you this." She glared at her sister like she couldn't believe she was doing her this favor. "They're mine, so sorry that they're, like, from Target, but you'll survive."

"I love Target," Birdie said, like that was at all relevant.

"Elliot has my keys," Mona said. "I'll just use his car in the meantime."

"Wait, why does *Elliot* have your keys?"

"San Francisco," Elliot said. "Ian's there."

San Francisco? Ian? Birdie felt like she had gone to bed drunk and woken up in the twilight zone. Andie unzipped the overnight bag and handed her a neon tie-dye hoodie that was definitely intended for tweens.

"I can't wear—" Birdie started to protest. "Also, how did they find your address, our address, Andie?" Everything was starting to spin and absolutely nothing was making sense.

"That . . . might have been Nelson's fault." Mona cringed.

"Bird, we have about four minutes before they google Monads and find Mona's name and connect her to the house three doors down. So if you want to hold a press conference on our front stoop, then by all means, take your time," Elliot said, using his TV reporter voice and taking charge, which Birdie found both incredibly frustratingly sexy and also extremely annoying. "But I'm pretty sure your publicist told you to lie low, so I'm trying to do you a favor here."

Birdie threw the hoodie over her caftan and flopped her arms against her sides as if to say, *See, I told you I would look like an absolute ding-dong*, but no one paid her any mind.

"Can I at least brush my teeth?" she said.

"There's a sink in the RV," Elliot said. "Come on, we have to move."

There's. A. Sink. In. The. RV.

Birdie replayed the sentence over in her head again, as if she were expected to be up to speed.

"Wait . . ." The three of them had already hustled out the door, but she found her feet were firmly planted to the shag carpet that Mona's mom had installed when they moved in twenty-three years back. "Wait!" she cried again. "I didn't agree to an RV!"

The doorbell rang, and she jumped, her feet suddenly no longer stuck. She considered the enormity of her fictitious backstory about her childhood in Medford, Oregon; she'd spoken about it in at least a dozen interviews, she'd done that stupid *Vogue* shoot against the bluffs by the Pacific Ocean, which hadn't felt stupid at the time, but now, with the press literally pounding on her door, she could see that it was, indeed, ill-advised. The last thing that Birdie Robinson needed right now was even a whiff of another scandal. Imani had already warned her, and though she hadn't even glanced at her phone since Andie's rude awakening, she well knew that her confrontation with Nelson had likely gained speed like a cannonball shot out of the barrel overnight.

"Goddammit," she said to her reflection in the mirror. The violent yellow and orange sweatshirt turned her skin green, and she felt certain that Andie had chosen only the most putrid of her clothes to pack. The doorbell rang again.

And Birdie, ever the actress, met her eyes in the mirror and decided that she would improvise. And so she grabbed the duffel and ran.

9

ELLIOT

ELLIOT HAD PEELED the RV off the curb of the alley behind their house before anyone could take notice of the oddly dressed woman by his side who sprinted into the Winnebago ahead of him. He hated this thing, resented this thing, and now he couldn't believe he was piloting this thing. His parents had taken it to the Grand Canyon the summer before his mom's diagnosis. She'd blown off her mammogram—she was only in her fifties, what difference did a few months make? His dad had taken a two-month leave from running the local ER; he was burned out and needed the reprieve, so what harm did delaying a doctor's appointment do? What they would find in June, they'd find in August when they were done with their bucket-list road trip. But she couldn't get an appointment in August. And by October, when she finally did, the cancer that could have been caught in June had spread like wildfire. Elliot found it easier to blame the RV than his father. Or his mother. And then, when his father died a year later of a stress-related cardiac arrest, Elliot couldn't blame him at all. So the RV it was. That Mona tootled around in it every weekend when she should have been working for NASA only compounded his loathing.

Birdie had come up for both funerals. He glanced over at her in the passenger seat, with her oversized black sunglasses, and her feet, now in Andie's beat-up Vans, up on the dash. Though she had bolted to New York shortly after graduation, she was in LA when their mom died; she'd moved there for pilot season and had landed a part on a soap—*Power and Passion*—back when soaps still aired, and a few were shot in LA. He was in his junior year for his mom's funeral, then his senior year for his dad's, so he had plenty of time to watch *P and P* (as the diehards referred to it) in his dorm. Then she was sitting beside him at the funeral, her leg pressed against his, her palm squeezing his, her other palm holding Mona's. And it was so surreal, he recalled thinking, how he was swollen with grief but also so joyful to see her, to admire her success, to have her clutching his hand. When he saw her again in New York at that premiere party, the one where they slipped into the bathroom of that chichi lounge and locked the door before either one of them even had a chance to think it through, he really did think that he could stay forever.

Elliot put on the RV's blinker and checked his mirrors. So far, no one had tailed them, which meant they were exceptionally lucky. Which also made Elliot nervous. Because he dealt in facts, not good fortune, and on the road, he always believed that luck ran out.

He cleared his throat, trying to figure out where to start with her. He wanted to tell her that he'd already pitched Francesca, that this wasn't as spontaneous as it appeared, though he hadn't counted on the paparazzi and fleeing. It was the ethical thing, to let her know that he had some skin in the game. But he also wanted her to trust him, to rely on him as a confidant, not just a

journalist, and he worried if he mentioned that he'd already mon-
etized the story, already promised its delivery to his editor, she'd
recoil and add him to the list of people who capitalized on her
fame. Francesca had woken him up this morning and agreed to
give him one week. If he couldn't find the suitor, couldn't nail the
landing, that would be it, she conveyed.

"Let's go over the ground rules one more time," she had said.
It was only 7 a.m., and she was already in the office. She slurped
on what Elliot knew was pitch-black coffee, and Elliot thought
that he'd do just about anything to be back in the newsroom sip-
ping that pitch-black coffee beside her.

"Okay," Elliot said. "But you don't need to."

"Can you do this within the journalistic guidelines that I
know you are aware of but too often ignore? No bribery, no
blackmail, no twisting of elbows to the point where someone may
snap a tendon?" she quipped.

"Yes."

"And you can write objectively, without bias, through clear
eyes, despite the fact that you evidently have a long-term friend-
ship and never once mentioned that to me?"

"For sure," Elliot lied. "One hundred percent."

"*Love Bomb* is one of my favorite movies," she said, sounding
genuinely hurt for someone who Elliot occasionally doubted had
any feelings at all. "You could have at least told me that you
knew her."

"Sorry," he said. "She's protective of her privacy." Also, he
hadn't spoken to her in seven years. How well could he even
know her now? Elliot didn't like this notion, that he'd let the time
get away between them—but it had all the same.

Francesca went silent. Then: "O'Brien, you are absolutely sure
about this? Because you are already on thin ice, and by that I

mean the number one spot on my shit list of whom I cannot defend if they fuck up again. There's nothing else I need to know? Nothing that might prevent you from reporting objectively?"

"I promise. This is a clean, uncomplicated situation that I can dig into," Elliot lied for a second time. "She's my sister's best friend. That's it."

In the RV, he saw a sign for the freeway and lurched over a lane to the right.

Finally, he broke their silence. He wanted to make her feel like she was in charge. He suspected that Birdie preferred to control the narrative, and so the best shot he had at framing this story properly was to pretend that all of this was her idea.

"I'm sorry if this feels like a kidnapping," he said. "I think Andie panicked."

"Andie isn't really prone to panicking," she replied. "I think she probably just wanted me out of her hair. Which is fine. Just as well. I would have proposed starting with Ian anyway. He's safe, neutral territory. We were young, and it faded, and I can't imagine he wouldn't be happy to see me."

"Happy enough that he'd have written the letter?"

He watched Birdie consider this, her eyes out the window at the dull, flat, lifeless acres that were rushing by.

"He was my first love, you know? And he knew me straight off the bus from Barton. Literally. We met a week after I moved to New York, so he knew my real backstory." She flopped her shoulders and adjusted the seat belt. "I think young love has a way of sticking with you."

"I have a theory about first loves," Elliot said, and this time, she turned to look at him.

"I'm sure you do."

"No, but really. I think that whoever that first love is, I think you spend the rest of your life chasing that sensation of the thrill of falling. Because it's before you've been hurt, you know? Before your heart has been obliterated and you've spiraled into barely functioning and you don't want to eat and you can't sleep either, and you call them a million times and hang up."

"I can't imagine that you've ever had your heart obliterated, but I suppose in concept, the theory isn't a bad one." She returned her stare to the window.

Elliot wanted to ask her if she considered Ian her first love or if there had been someone earlier, but there was no way to ask this gracefully, and also, he would have already blown any semblance of objectivity if he did. She was right: he'd never fallen so headily in love that he lost his equilibrium, his sense of space and time. But then, he had been infatuated with Birdie since the day they met.

He remembered now how grouchy he was about the move down from San Francisco at twelve, how he'd given his mom a hard time because he was a preteen and had the hubris to do such a thing, like moving to Barton was some sort of conspiracy against him personally. It was a sweltering summer, like the rays of the sun were changing you on a cellular level, like you were a few degrees away from becoming a wildfire. The day after they moved in, Elliot's dad had gone to the hospital to get up to speed, and his mom was busy with the movers and the contractor who was renovating the kitchen that still stood today. So he and Mona were left on their own. They kicked around the neighborhood, glum and mopey, discontented to have been uprooted from the familiar beats of their old life: their middle school, their house on the top of a hill with bones that groaned but in a comforting way, their friends they'd known since birth. Here, everything was flat. Everything was dry. Everything was so completely scorching.

Mona's cheeks were sunburnt within the hour, her shoulders fried by the time they wound their way home. There was a girl sitting on her front steps at the end of the block, frantically racing to eat a Popsicle before it melted, licking her fingers as often as she was licking the stick. She had Band-Aids on both knees, and her hair fell along both shoulders in two tight braids. She had on a spaghetti-strapped tank top and denim shorts that needed a wash, and beside her, fanned out facedown, was a book. Elliot stopped two paces behind Mona, who was complaining about the agony of her sunburn already, and stared. This girl, he knew, was going to mean something to him. He'd kissed two girls back home in San Francisco, one on a dare during spin the bottle, and one because he had worked up the confidence after that first kiss. He watched Birdie from the sidewalk, where eventually she noticed his stare and returned it, and he couldn't explain it, but he was thunderstruck.

Finally, she finished her Popsicle and picked up her book, turning it right side over in her lap, and said, "Well, you can just stand there or you can introduce yourself."

Mona turned back to look at Elliot then, and whatever she saw made her howl. She nearly doubled over with laughter, like she had a cramp in her side from the hilarity of his expression. Blood rose to his cheeks, and then Mona righted herself and stepped forward and said, "Hey, I'm Mona, this is my dumb twin brother, Elliot."

And Birdie squinted and sized him up, screwing up her lips like she was really assessing him.

"You guys are twins? You don't look anything alike."

Elliot had cringed. Even at twelve, he got attention for his looks. He'd been stopped in Macy's with his mom and Mona and asked if he wanted to do commercials; he had girls who left him notes (*had* left him notes, back in San Francisco) in his locker all year; he got invited to things when he really didn't even know the kid who was hosting. Mona, their mom assured them, was beautiful, ethereal, but she was pale, where he was naturally tan; she lacked any semblance of muscle tone, where he was a born athlete.

That day, on their new street, Mona didn't bristle.

"Oh yeah, fraternal twins." She shrugged. "Too bad for him I'm the smarter one."

Birdie giggled at that, at the casualness of the insult, and said, "Well, hi. I'm Birdie. If you're into kick the can after dark, I'll rope in my little sister too. She's annoying but, well, you need at least four people to make it good."

"What are you reading?" Mona asked because Elliot still couldn't speak.

"Oh." Birdie held up the cover. "*Lord of the Rings*. It's not on the summer reading list but everything on there is stupid or boring, so I'm reading this instead because my stepmom is paying me twenty bucks to read a book this summer, so whatever. Have you read it?"

Elliot had, of course, read *The Lord of the Rings*. He'd snuck a flashlight into his room and pulled an all-nighter finishing it. None of the rest of his friends in San Francisco were nearly as excited about it as he was.

Elliot sensed something in his stomach that felt like butterflies taking flight, and he had to remind himself not to stare.

About a month later, he almost screwed up the nerve to tell her that he sometimes fell asleep thinking of her. Then again at fourteen. Then again at sixteen when they were alone in his car, with Mona out with pseudo-mono. Then again that night in New York. He had meant to that night. Until he remembered prom. And Mona's request. Not request, demand, how she'd yanked him out of the faculty lounge and said, "Elliot, you have everything you ever want. You *get* everything you ever want. So maybe don't screw up Birdie for me. Maybe just leave my best friend out of it." Elliot remembered, even now, how she shook her head and said, "No, definitely leave her out of it. Leave her alone." And then Nelson Pratt called her name down the hall, and she gave Elliot one last glare and went back into the auditorium.

And he had, he had left her alone! For years! She'd just looked so insanely delectable at that premiere party, and it wasn't just that she was delicious enough to eat, it was that she was *Birdie*, and he couldn't stop himself. She was all he'd wanted for what felt like as long as he'd existed, even as he slept with dozens of women who were beautiful and enjoyable and smart as hell. None of them were Birdie. And that night in New York was perfect, and it was heaven, and it was exactly like—no, better—it was better than he'd ever imagined. And he'd imagined it *a lot*. How he would touch her, how she would touch him, how her skin would feel under his fingertips, how she'd sigh when he'd kiss that delicate spot on her collarbone that he sometimes stared at for no reason other than he couldn't not stare.

And then he walked away before explaining himself. But in his defense, Birdie basically pushed him out the door and honestly seemed relieved when it was all over, when he walked out her door and he heard the bolt click behind him. Maybe theirs was an itch and, once scratched, the need would be alleviated. Except that now, sitting beside her in his sister's RV, he knew that the itch was just getting started.

"Tell me about Ian," he said, aiming for objective, as promised to Francesca. He and Birdie hadn't even gotten into any of the nitty-gritty, and he already was losing his reserve.

"You're using your television voice," Birdie replied.

"I don't have a television voice."

"This is your television voice," she said, dropping her tone lower, enunciating cleanly. She really was an excellent mimic. "And since you're using your television voice, I assume that you have decided to write about me. About this."

"Oh," he said, "I mean, only if you want me to. It's totally up to you. I'm happy to pitch my editor, though." He wondered if she could hear the lie as soon as it was out of his mouth.

"Can you make me look good? No, let me rephrase that: *Will* you make me look good? Because I am not here for any sort of dissection piece that I've seen you do about others."

"Understood." He nodded, too caught up in the hint that she read his byline to focus on the ethical squishiness he'd just agreed to. One hour in, and he was already making promises that no proper journalist would or should make to his subjects.

"I know that you're, like, a Pulitzer Prize winner, but I need to take the lead here. This is *my* life, my narrative. I never should have let Imani and Sydney force me into that stupid apology."

Elliot didn't correct her, that he'd only been nominated. He liked that she thought he'd won. The corners of his mouth shifted upward, and he repressed a grin: Birdie had tracked his career as much as he'd tracked hers. He didn't tell her that he'd always made a point to see her movies by himself in the theater in the middle of the afternoon, that her dubbed voice had kept him company late at night on televisions in at least a dozen countries. Birdie Robinson speaking French. Turkish. Chinese. She was perfection in any language. So it pleased him that she followed him too, and already, his imagination was taking flight with possibilities of what he could do to her if they swerved off the road into a rest stop and they found themselves in the twin bunk beds in the back.

"I'm merely here at your disposal," he offered in what he hoped was a neutral tone. "I'll do anything you ask."

She turned toward him and raised an eyebrow from behind her enormous insect-like sunglasses, and his cheeks blazed. So, less neutral than he'd aimed for. He suddenly remembered that night of the premiere, how he'd straddled her in her king-sized bed, her on her stomach, her face against a pillow that was likely custom-made with Turkish linens and more expensive than a week of his salary. She wasn't quite A-list yet, but she was ascending, the sort of fame where you're still excited for the recognition, where you don't mind the paparazzi, the autograph seekers, the way eyes lingered on you at a restaurant, where you're nearly at the top of the mountain but the climb is still a thrill.

She was already naked by then, when he straddled her in her king-sized bed, complaining about how the heels at the premiere pinched her feet, then cramped her legs, which twisted into an ache in her back. So he dug his thumbs into a sore spot on her left side by her shoulder as she groaned. Then he used an elbow in the small of her back and over toward her hip bones as she held her breath, and then he ran his fingers up and down her spine until she flipped over and pulled his lips toward hers. It wasn't often for Elliot that the foreplay was as good as the act itself, but with Birdie, every moment of his skin against hers, his breath in time with her own, was a revelation.

"I'll let you take the lead on this, of course," he said now, hoping she didn't notice the flush of his cheeks, the way that his reporter voice had tilted to a higher octave.

"Then we agree. We make me look as wonderful as possible,

we rehabilitate my image, and if I happen to find true love with an anonymous ex, that's just the cherry on top."

Elliot swallowed. Birdie reached for the radio and turned it up louder.

"Okay," he said above the noise, even though he didn't really want to hear the details. "Well then, tell me about Ian."

10

BIRDIE

BIRDIE TRIED TO pretend that Elliot was just another journalist, that this was just another profile. She'd spoken to hundreds of writers over the past decade and knew where to draw the line between revealing too little and revealing just enough, knew how to drop enticing morsels that made for incredible pull quotes but didn't give too much away about any sort of personal particulars. She knew which reporters she could trust with near honesty and which ones would do anything for a headline.

With Elliot, though, all of Birdie's normal instincts were muddled. How could she see him clearly when she'd spent her teenage years viewing him through a lust-tinted haze, and she'd spent the back half of her twenties mortified that she'd been yet another one-night stand to add to his ledger? So while he wanted to know everything about Ian, Birdie reminded herself to proceed with caution. Elliot O'Brien could extract bone marrow from her if she wasn't careful. As it was, Imani was already going to have a nuclear breakdown when she caught wind of Birdie's plan, so she needed to manage Elliot cautiously, needed to give him only enough to capture her brilliantly.

"I met Ian pretty much as soon as I got to New York," she said now. The radio in the RV was playing "Bohemian Rhapsody," and she wondered if Elliot remembered the time in the carpool when she and Mona would trade off verses. How Mona sang off-key but Birdie could hit all the high notes in nearly a full belt, and Elliot would dissolve into literal tears at how discordant the two of them sounded together. Birdie almost took it as a challenge: to see how hard she could make Elliot laugh, to see if he'd have to pull over on the side of the road to get a grip so they didn't careen into a telephone pole. Mona was better at the lyrics than she was, so Mona sang the wrong notes and Birdie sang the wrong words, and honestly, the whole thing was a messy delight.

Elliot reached over to the radio and turned the volume down. If he remembered anything, he didn't betray it, and maybe that was just as well, Birdie thought, since she had just vowed to keep this entirely professional.

"So you were eighteen. I remember when you left. In that maroon Volvo wagon without a functional tailpipe," he said.

Birdie was surprised that he remembered. That she'd agreed to drive one of her dad's friend's cars across the country for four hundred bucks, which got her to New York and helped with rent. Elliot and Mona had stood on the corner waving and cheering as she pulled away, like they were certain that she was going to be a wild success even before Birdie was.

"He was the sous chef at my first job," she said. "Waitressing. I wasn't particularly good at it, as you may imagine."

Elliot looked over from the driver's side, lingering too long, and the RV wandered into the middle lane before he pulled it back. "I'd think you could be good at anything you really wanted to do," he said, and Birdie felt her insides lurch. At his sincerity, at his flattery. Goddammit, she was such a sucker for a handsome man who paid her compliments. She unwillingly thought of Kai, and how she took him back so many times, too many times, because he knew exactly how to woo her.

But Ian; Ian had always been exactly who she thought him to be, exactly who he told her he was. She watched the farmlands whoosh past and wondered why she'd lost track of that, how she lost track of it. Maybe Ian sending her a plea for a second chance was just what she needed: a final cleanse to cast off the residue of Kai, whom she hadn't spoken to in several years but spent too much time thinking about now that his brother was looming large over both her mental health and the headlines. Maybe if she hadn't been so cavalier with Ian's devotion, she never would have entangled herself with Kai when they met on set when she was twenty-five: he already a superstar, she the hot new up-and-comer. Maybe she wouldn't have bumped into Elliot at that premiere party at twenty-seven and taken him home with her, a secret she'd keep from Mona until she died and a mistake that shattered her enough to send her running right back to Kai. Birdie had never thought of herself as a woman who needed a man; that's who she played on-screen, not who she was in actuality. But the more she filtered through the patterns of her poor choices—how often she'd let Kai back into her life because he pressed her weak spots, how many years she'd pined for Elliot thinking somehow she'd be different for him, not just another warm, naked body added to his well-documented history—the more she considered that she was closer to those parts she played than she realized.

Ian had been a beast in the kitchen when she met him. She'd wandered into Lucky's, a midtown hot spot catering to executive types and with a menu full of ingredients Birdie had never heard of, six days after she landed in New York. She needed a job and had made the mistake of being honest on all her other waitressing applications: *no*, she had no experience, but *yes*, she was a hard and eager worker. But in New York City, where customers demanded speed and accuracy in their orders, experience was required. Birdie hadn't imagined that she couldn't find gainful employment. She had about a thousand dollars in her bank account, money accrued from graduation, an occasional check from her mother, who now lived north outside Seattle, her Sbarro gig, and the four hundred dollars from driving the Volvo. When she saw the "Help Wanted" sign in the window of Lucky's, she started with her first lie. It was easier after that, to figure out what people wanted to hear and tell them. She knew she wasn't all that book smart compared to Andie or Mona or Elliot. But street smart? Birdie liked to think that there was no one wiser.

So she told the manager she'd worked at a pizza place in Central California. Was that even a lie? Not really, she didn't think.

Ian was working the lunch shift. He interrupted her job interview without an apology, cutting her off mid-sentence to tell the manager that if he didn't fire the other sous chef, he was quitting. He said it exactly like that, matter-of-fact, no melodrama, just a take-it-or-leave-it option. He wasn't prototypically handsome: his eyes were about a millimeter too close together; his nose looked like it had been broken in a fistfight. His top teeth were mostly straight but his bottom ones were a mess. His blond hair winged in places it probably wasn't meant to, and his arms looked like they got a better workout than the rest of him. But his skin was luminous, and those eyes were kind, and Birdie, who had spent her formative years swirling in her own imaginary melodrama— for Elliot, for actual drama class, for high school auditions—found this exact combination irresistible. After she'd been hired, she heard that the other sous chef kept making leering comments at the waitresses, and Ian had taken it upon himself to champion their cause, and she was all in. Later, when she finally had it out with Sebastian Carol over his own wandering eyes and hands, she would think of Ian briefly and assume that everyone would laud her like they had him. Yet another thing she'd get wrong.

She lingered by his station for two straight weeks, having clocked out of her shift but finding every excuse to stay. He talked to her as he worked, explaining why he held the knife the way he did, why he blended instead of whisked, why certain spices were too much and certain others were too little. Birdie didn't have much interest in the food—she'd already been told by one casting director that she could stand to lose some baby fat even though she was presently subsisting on ramen and air—but she had plenty of interest in Ian.

She'd been a virgin when they met. Birdie had forgotten a lot of details over the years about her life before she blew up on a global level, but she hadn't forgotten that. She lived in that shitty fifth-floor walk-up, and it was a sweltering late-August night, the type where the heat rises and threatens to suffocate you. She brought Ian back to her apartment, and he opened all the windows like that would help, and it did a little. He seemed like he knew things about the world that Birdie didn't, couldn't, because the only sort of worldly experience she'd had was in her own imagination. She'd never really traveled; this was the first time she'd been anywhere alone, on her own. She wanted to drink Ian in, eat him whole.

He took her clothes off slowly, keeping the lights on, and she watched his eyes move over every inch of her exposed skin, then ran her own fingers over the tattoo of three stars in the crook of his arm, then up his back, which was sinewy from long hours in the kitchen. But his stomach wasn't defined with a six-pack, and she fell a little bit more in love with him because of that. She remembered now that she thought of Elliot fleetingly when she was completely naked in bed. She'd always envisioned, based on absolutely nothing other than those few lost moments in carpool, one night spent raiding the vending machine with him their senior year, and a brief interrupted moment in the faculty lounge at prom, that she'd be doing this with Elliot. But then Ian asked her if she was okay, and if she wanted to keep going, and her whole body throbbed at how much she wanted him, so she forgot about Elliot and reminded herself that part of acting was living in the moment. So she did. And it was spectacular. And then she found that she rarely thought of Elliot again much at all. At least for a while.

They had pulled over to the side of the highway after Birdie relayed the important parts of the story, omitting the Elliot-specific asides. Elliot wanted to jot some of this down, he said, and while he was focused on his laptop, Birdie scampered to the little bathroom in the back. In their haste to flee Barton, she hadn't considered the lack of privacy that came with a home on wheels, and she couldn't exactly just lumber into a rest stop bathroom and not be noticed. The RV it was. She wrestled with the accordion door and found that it didn't quite close. She tugged harder and the handle made an alarming whine, as if to say, *Lady, you get what you get and you don't get upset*, and Birdie was sweating by then. She peered one eye out the not-insignificant crack and saw Elliot's back toward her, so she sat and peed as quickly as possible, which meant that it felt interminable. Birdie wasn't shy; she'd gotten used to stripping down in front of wardrobe crews, in front of camera crews, in front of audiences if the script required it. But that was always for make-believe. With Elliot twenty feet away, she felt significantly more vulnerable than when a script required a side-boob shot and millions of teen boys downloaded a freeze-frame to figuratively tuck under their mattress.

"You're sure you don't want me to give Ian a heads-up that we're coming?" Elliot called, just as she was finishing up. Birdie shoved the door farther ajar and slid through the open space. When she tried to tug the door closed, it refused. She shook it and pulled it and tried to shimmy it, but it was no use. If she wanted even a morsel of privacy in this vehicle, it wasn't going to come while she was in the bathroom. *Wonderful.*

"I prefer the element of surprise," she said, only now taking in the rest of the RV. There were bunk beds in the back that looked like they were better suited for summer camp—thin mattresses, sheets with alien decorations that Mona surely found whimsical, a sad deflated pillow at each head. She hoped that Elliot wasn't planning to actually *sleep* here. Birdie was not some prima donna, okay? But she needed at least three pillows and preferred percale cotton sheets, and almost always required a white-noise machine or at least a fan to lull her into dreamland. She hadn't even packed her other necessities: her eyeshade, her earplugs, her three-step serum. And second of all (third of all?), was she honestly expected to sleep directly under or directly over Elliot O'Brien? They'd rushed out of the house so quickly that they hadn't discussed logistics, how this would work, whether (ideally) they could park this thing in a Four Seasons valet lot and retire to housekeeping and room service.

Elliot noticed her assessing, recalibrating.

"Do you like to be on top or bottom?" he called, and when she turned an unnatural hue reserved for the deepest of sunburns, he jumped to his feet and took a few long steps toward her. "Sorry, *sorry.* Jesus. I meant . . ." He swallowed. "I meant the beds."

Birdie thought that she must be losing her mind. Was she the only one of them who thought that they wouldn't make it one night under such circumstances?

She chastised herself. Sex for Elliot wasn't any grand revelation. She'd known this before she brought him back to her Tribeca loft. She'd just assumed that she'd be the exception to the dozens of women who came before her. And for the hours between when she left the premiere and the ones when he walked out, she'd never felt more like herself.

"You can't be serious that we're sleeping in this thing," Birdie said. "San Francisco is full of nice hotels, you know." She thought of her favorite one in Union Square. They'd bring her egg whites and a fruit smoothie in the morning, and maybe she could book a massage, and certainly, the suite on the top floor with those jacuzzi jets sounded like her idea of nirvana right now. Or a different type of nirvana than she'd just been imagining with Elliot.

He shrugged. "You told me you're in charge. So you're in charge. I just worry that—"

Birdie pushed past him. "You don't worry, you write. And no, to answer your question, I don't want to tell Ian that I'm coming. The surprise makes it feel more romantic."

"Bird, you realize this isn't an actual rom-com, correct?" He slipped into the bathroom, which gave her a blessed moment to compose herself. Of course she knew this wasn't an actual rom-com! Elliot was business, *all* business, and it was good to be reminded all the same.

Birdie clutched the driver's seat of the RV, plopped down, and felt calmer about the sleeping arrangements, what with her doubling

down on her own professionalism and Elliot out of her eyesight in
the bathroom. He'd left the key in the ignition, so she turned the
engine over. "I don't need you telling me how to dictate my come-
back," she called over her shoulder. "I've taken advice from everyone
for the past decade, and it's been a disaster."

"Not quite a disaster," he shouted back, and then she heard
his footsteps heading toward her, her heart thumping louder in
time with each one. "You're not exactly hurting, if we're being
honest—highest salary in the industry, schedule booked for the
next year."

"What I meant," she growled, "was the past few weeks. Are
you now keeping tabs on me, checking my press hits in your
Google search?"

Elliot sank into the passenger seat and shook his head *no*, and
Birdie wondered if it was possible to actually die of humiliation.
Of course he wasn't checking up on her. He was off breaking, like,
Middle East peace talk news, certainly not following the dire
downfall of a girl he once knew and a woman he once slept with.

"Just do this on my terms," she said with a huff. "Once we find
the guy who wrote this, I'll be redeemed, you'll probably get loads
of, like, women sliding into your DMs, and you'll never have to
think of me again."

"You're the boss," he said, and she waited for him to refute the
DM insinuation, but he did not.

Birdie replied by pressing her foot to the gas and lurching
back onto the highway. Ian Sands was due north. She couldn't
wait to surprise him.

11

ELLIOT

BIRDIE IS A *terrible driver*. Elliot was simultaneously attempting to type notes about Ian and keep from vomiting, and this was all he could think. *Birdie drives like she lives: like she has something to prove, like she's up for the fight, even though no one else is throwing punches.* She was honking and lane changing and not above giving someone the finger, which Elliot thought was not the best way to stay inconspicuous, but then she also made it clear she wasn't interested in his opinion. But focusing on her driving was more palatable than focusing on Ian—on the breezy way she spoke about him, on the upturn in her voice when it became evident that she'd be happy to reunite with the esteemed chef if he were indeed the ex who hoped for his second chance.

Elliot tried to remember all the details about her time with Ian, what Mona would have filled him in on. Those first few years at Berkeley were a blur, though: he was no longer the big fish in a small pond, and he found that he had to work harder than he ever had before to maintain the air that everything came naturally to him. He walked onto the swim team but almost never got to compete. He applied for the college paper and was given a position copyediting, not nearly what he'd hoped for. He'd figured that the coaches would fall all over themselves, that the editors would fling open their doors. So maybe he didn't know many details about Ian because he hadn't asked Mona or maybe he was just so busy keeping his head above water that he knew if he lingered on Birdie, how she was brave in chasing her dreams and courageous in doing it in New York and falling in love with someone who wasn't him, he might fall apart.

"We lost track of each other for those years, I guess." His voice was low, husky, and he almost didn't sound like himself. "I don't remember any of this. This is all news to me."

"I guess I sort of disappeared," Birdie said. "It felt important to try to make it on my own. Leave Barton behind."

He started to say that he wished she hadn't disappeared from him, but then that was rewriting history. Wishing for something like that now when he'd been busy losing himself to the beautiful women he met on campus were two wildly divergent realities. The easy attention from classmates who wanted to spend the night with him felt familiar, safe. Birdie was anything but.

"The beginning of Birdie Robinson," Elliot said instead.

"In my defense, there was already a Birdie Maxwell in SAG."

"And the 'Robinson'?"

"It just sounded like a movie star's name."

Elliot stuttered out a sharp laugh. His fingers flew over his keyboard.

"Please don't write that," she said, quickly glancing toward him. "That makes me sound ridiculous."

"Nothing about you is ever ridiculous," he said before he could think otherwise. He felt Birdie's gaze lingering on him, and he found that he couldn't return her stare.

They were close to San Francisco now, the early-March sky nearly dark by 5:45 p.m. He stood, stretched, and took three strides to the fridge, which he opened, seeing only a six-pack from one of Mona's weekend adventures, and closed again. He had a rule that he never drank on the job, and even though he knew that was unlikely to stick for the duration of this reporting gig—because Birdie, if anyone, could drive him to inebriation— he still thought he should at least make the effort. Birdie changed lanes unexpectedly, and the RV swayed, and Elliot reached above to grab on to anything available before he went toppling. He steadied himself on a cabinet door, which swung open, and weathered road maps spilled out. Relics of a bygone era. Relics of his parents.

Elliot wasn't prone to sentimentality, but he lost himself for a beat. That they could be so long gone and yet still so present. He squatted down, and when the motor home heaved yet again, he simply plopped on the floor, running his hands over the unex- pected poignancy of the memory of his parents, side by side, poring over the paper maps, exploring wherever their whims took them.

"Sorry," Birdie called over her shoulder. "I did warn you."

She had. She had warned him that she rarely drove herself anywhere anymore, so perhaps she should remain in the passen- ger seat for the journey, but then she'd gone and plunked down behind the wheel anyway. Classic Birdie Maxwell. He gingerly eased himself to his feet, slowly, nervous that she would lurch forward or brake hard or peel into another lane. That was the thing about her: Birdie was infuriatingly stubborn, extremely self- reliant, honest when she wanted to be, vague when she needed to be. But she at least leveled with you while doing so.

She even had after their night together in New York.

"Don't go just yet," she'd said the next morning. They were

both naked in her bed, and in reply, he raised the top sheet and peered at her body underneath and replied, "Well, I certainly don't have to for a while," and then slid lower and disappeared beneath her bedding, and she didn't bring it up again until they'd finally dragged themselves out of bed for some sustenance. He remembered how she had only some wilted unidentifiable greens in the veggie drawer and some moldy cheese that looked like cheddar, but that was really just a wild guess. She was never really home anymore, she said. And when she was, she didn't cook. Cooking reminded her of an ex, she'd said. Because Elliot was the one naked beside her, that hadn't even resonated, hadn't bothered him one bit. Instead, he suggested running out for bagels, and she moaned and said, "Ooh, carbs, yes." And he dressed himself and took a long glance at her still in bed, and he wanted to press himself close to her heart, tell her that he'd take care of her, assure her that she didn't have to use sharp elbows to stride through life anymore because he could be there beside her. So he said, "I'll be back, and don't go anywhere." And he meant every word. Until plans changed.

Elliot's phone buzzed, breaking him free from the memory.

FRANCESCA

update?

ELLIOT

Sending you a teaser asap. Can go live tonight.

FRANCESCA

then what

ELLIOT

first entry will be filed by morning

that's a lock?

Elliot didn't know what he was promising, but committing to a deadline was at least one thing he was good at.

Birdie noticed his phone's constant vibrations.

"Someone at this port of call?"

Elliot wondered if it was possible for ears to blush, and if they could, whether she noticed that his felt like they were on fire.

"You know that I don't just bounce from city to city looking to fall into bed with someone, right?"

Birdie raised and lowered her eyebrows like she'd heard differently, and Elliot wanted to argue with her, prove to her that she didn't know him as well as she thought she did, but he did often fall into bed with women in different cities, so he lost his will to debate the finer points of the argument before it even started.

"It's my editor," he said instead.

"Tell her we'll get her the most amazing happily-ever-after," Birdie replied. "I genuinely think this is brilliant. Absolutely brilliant. I didn't expect to be this excited to see Ian, but, honestly, I am."

Elliot tried not to let it get to him, the way that her demeanor had shifted, the way that she seemed lighter at the idea of a reunion with her first love.

"So you and Ian. How did it end? It can't be because of his cooking. Because, wow, I do love his mussels."

"You love his muscles?" Birdie replied. "That's a little weird, but I don't tell you how to do your job. Is he, like, super in shape now or something?"

Elliot laughed and thought again of how she got the lyrics

wrong all those years ago in the back of his Honda. "No, mussels. The seafood. I love his mussels."

"Oh, he used to make me those too," she said, then something passed over her face, unreadable. Another pause. "Though they were never my thing. I pretended for him, though. I didn't want to let him down."

"Can I ask you something?" Elliot posited.

"You can ask me anything you want." Her eyes were dead ahead, her posture ramrod straight.

"Okay, let me rephrase. If I ask you something, will you answer honestly?" Birdie chewed her lip and didn't answer him. "Fine," he continued. "I'll ask, and you decide."

She offered a curt nod and adjusted both hands on the wheel. He could see that she wasn't comfortable, that she'd give him a pat answer or some clipped little sound bite. One of Elliot's better qualities as a journalist was being able to read his subjects, and he knew that this was not the time to press her, rather the time to ease off and let her come to trust him. He'd just thought that she would already—that trust between them would be innate. Though he knew he'd given her reasons to be wary.

"It's okay, actually," he said. "We have time to get into everything else." There was a shift, small but still detectable, in her body language. Like this was exactly what she needed from him. He took note. "Do you think that Ian was intimidated by your fame?"

Birdie shook her head. "I wasn't famous when we were together. Also, fame is . . . I mean, I don't want to sound too woo-woo Hollywood, but it's what I said to you yesterday, and I mean it: fame is just, like, it's window dressing, it's an extra complication to having a normal life. It's, not to sound too much like a ridiculous movie star, but it really is a construct. And Ian would be the first one to point that out."

"It's way more than a construct, Birdie," Elliot pushed back. "It's changed everything about you."

She froze, and he realized that he hadn't meant to say it like that. Goddammit. He should have said: *I would like you if no one on the planet knew your name. I would like you if you were so famous that they planted a flag on the moon with your photo. I would like you under any circumstance.* But why would she believe that from him? They'd had their chance, and they hadn't spoken to each other in seven years.

Words were words were words. Elliot was very good at words. Actions were a totally different beast entirely.

Dear Readers:

I am excited to introduce you to the first in a multipart spotlight series set over the course of a whirlwind week, give or take a day, contingent on just how deep we get into this. I know some of you through your emails and through social media, but I'm taking a different beat here, one that I am no less exhilarated by. I don't have to be embedded in a war in a far-flung country to tell thrilling, blood-pounding stories. This time out, we're uncovering a mystery in real time, and I'll be reporting developments as we go.

Nearly everyone on the planet knows Birdie Robinson, which also means, let's be honest, that nearly everyone has devoured the on-set tantrum and subsequent leaked emails and attacks on her character. As it turns out, I know Birdie too, albeit a little bit differently. Birdie is my twin sister's best friend, so I have viewed this public backlash through a slightly different lens. I viewed it as an attempt to undermine a woman I knew as ridiculously talented and equally enjoyable to be around. She and my sister, and thus yours truly, spent unquantifiable hours together as children, and yes, people can change, but still, I maintain that the Birdie of my childhood is not altogether different from the Birdie of now. She is kind. She is good. She is brilliant.

As the internet has determined, I was at a bar with Birdie two nights ago, when she showed me an anony-

mous love letter that she'd received. Through various behind-the-scenes vetting processes, we determined, blessedly, that the letter was not from a stalker or an obsessive fan. In fact, the letter appears to be genuine, an attempt of an ex to stake his claim, to put his feelings out into the world and see, as he said in the note, if they come back to him.

And so, we are going to do that, readers. You and I and Birdie. She and I are visiting a few of the potential old loves of her life. I'll be writing about them and revealing the facts—unbiased, I promise you—as we go. To maintain her safety and privacy, the location of each ex will not be disclosed until the story is filed.

Stay tuned! This is just a teaser for all the excitement to come. Let's try to give our Sweetheart the happily-ever-after we all root for when she's on the screen in front of us.

⇒ **12** ⇐

BIDIE

IAN RAN A fast-paced, *en vogue* restaurant on a mostly unre-markable block where the air smelled slightly of the sea and sidewalks were adorned with elegant, barren trees. By no small turn of fate, they found a half-empty street, and Birdie eased the RV to the inclined curb, then mistakenly went atop it, then eased back to the pavement. The RV clunked and clattered but it was parked, and Birdie figured they should both be relieved. She'd warned Elliot that she was out of practice driving, and full disclo-sure, she'd been flying on adrenaline on the highway and felt more than a little lucky that she didn't drive straight on top of at least three Priuses (they were so small compared to the RV). But she hadn't wanted to show him that she was nervous or faltering or in any way vulnerable, so she kept her grip on the wheel and her eyes on the road, and she pretended. Because she was always very good at pretending. Now she flipped the key in the ignition and flopped back in her seat, unsure if the churn in her gut was from the prospect of seeing Ian again or possibly taking their lives into her hands on the streets of San Francisco, which were wholly not designed for a vehicle the size of a small yacht.

"Right," Elliot said. "I made a six thirty reservation, so we should hustle."

Elliot had called ahead to at least secure a table. Birdie hadn't really thought through exactly how it was going to go or what she was going to say. Only that she imagined something like him seeing her face from across the room, and her matching his penetrating eyes. And then she would rise from her chair, and they would meet in the middle of the restaurant, and yes, people would be staring and some others would be filming, but then that would make their feel-good reunion blaze around the internet at a world-record pace. Maybe Ian would clasp her face in his palms or maybe he would leak happy tears. Maybe he would sweep her off her feet and spin her in a circle while the diners cheered. Birdie hadn't quite narrowed it down, but any of those sounded great to her.

She would ask him about the letter, and either he would have written it or he wouldn't have, but maybe it didn't matter because the start of her heralded reputational rehabilitation would have begun.

Birdie had changed out of the caftan into a pair of Andie's oversized cargo pants and still wore the garish neon tie-dyed hoodie. She wished that she had something more presentable, something that wardrobe would approve of—a cashmere sweater and faded black jeans like she wasn't trying too hard—but Andie had packed the dregs of her closet, likely intentionally, so Birdie had to do with whatever she had on hand. She thought she looked like a seventeen-year-old skate rat, but then there wasn't much to do about it, so she pushed her shoulders back and held her head high, like this was all part of the plan.

Chez Nous had a gilded door with three five-pronged stars across the middle. Ian had three five-pronged stars tattooed in the crux of his left arm, and Birdie's stomach unexpectedly cramped at the memory, of running her fingers over them absent-mindedly while he explained the notes of a Syrah or kissing it in the morning to wake him up for morning sex. An understated sign hung over the restaurant's corner entrance, which was abutted by two large olive trees, like Ian was beckoning you into the South of France by way of San Francisco. There was a huddle of patrons outside, and Elliot, who was a pace ahead of her, reached behind and grabbed her hand, as if she needed guidance to find her way through. Her body charged when his fingers laced with hers, but she reminded herself: Ian and his cooking and his kindness and his sexy tattooed arm and how he loved her before any of the rest of this. *Ian*, she said to her brain, *not Elliot*.

"Come on, we're late," he said.

But Birdie stopped, needing one more second before it all became real. Elliot spun around and placed his free palm on her elbow.

"Hey, it's okay. Whatever happens, I have your back."

Her eyes met his, and he held her gaze, and another charge coursed through her. *Goddammit*.

"Okay," she said.

"Okay," he said, then walked side by side with her through the door. When she took a step in front of him, she felt his hand on the small of her back, and something about it felt safe, felt like armor, even though she was used to arming herself: with the wardrobe of a skater kid who wasn't anything like her, with a script that was fiction, not her own, with lighting that illuminated her from every angle, with a costar who never stole her thunder.

Birdie wasn't one to linger retrospectively on her choices,

because in her business, there would be too many what-ifs to get caught up on. What if she'd better prepared for that audition? What if she'd agreed to sleep with that director? What if she had been more gracious to Sebastian Carol and pretended she hadn't minded his wandering hands, the way that he leered at the extras? What if she'd never let his brother, Kai, into her life? But now, standing in the hub of Chez Nous, with wineglasses clinking and peels of contented laughter loitering in the garlic-scented air, and patrons who just seemed *happy*, Birdie, for the first time since she walked away from Ian to head back west to LA for pilot season, considered that she could have gotten it all wrong.

The hostess, Birdie could tell, recognized her immediately. To be fair, everyone recognized Birdie immediately everywhere she went and had for the past decade, since her breakout film opposite Kai. But seeing the flare behind the hostess's eyes and the way that her jaw opened quickly then closed as the woman composed herself somehow calmed Birdie, even though she sometimes complained that what she wanted most was privacy, anonymity. But the hostess's momentary flummox reminded her that she was in charge here, she had the *influence* here, and she could march in and construct whatever narrative she wanted to. Even if Imani told her to lie low, even if Elliot thought that *he* could craft the narrative. (Birdie suspected that Elliot thought he could *still* craft the narrative.)

"I'm here to see Ian," she said to the hostess and put on her very best movie-star smile. *Entertainment Weekly* once said that "Birdie Robinson has a smile that could power the sun." She felt very much like she could currently power the sun.

"Do you have a reservation?" the hostess murmured.

"We do," Elliot said, but Birdie already had a hand in the air, shushing him. "Under O'Brien."

"But I am here to *see Ian*," she reiterated.

The hostess made a show of pretending to look up the reservation, as if she didn't know exactly who was standing in front of her, but Birdie didn't want to wait. And besides, she wasn't here to eat. She strode through the room as diners dropped their forks, hands stilled in midair. The kitchen was in the back but open, facing the diners, so whether Ian saw her or she saw him, it didn't really matter.

In less than a beat, he was in front of her: Chef Ian Sands, whom she hadn't seen in fourteen years, whom she hadn't spoken to in fourteen years. And Birdie felt calm. Birdie felt *great*.

Did he write the letter? Did it matter? She could already envision them as a new power couple; she could see the headlines, she could taste the homecooked meals that he would serve her while she was naked in bed or after a long day on set.

Ian looked significantly more rumpled and simultaneously more beautiful than he had when she last saw him when she was twenty and he was twenty-three. His blond hair was longer and shiny, which made him look more like a surfer who got lost in a kitchen. His baby fat had been shed and now the cut of his cheekbones matched the cut of his knife. Fine lines had crept in around his eyes, which Birdie found endearing and, well, lovely. He looked wise now, and though she had loved him before when he was just Ian the sous chef, he'd grown into real adult handsomeness, a beauty that caught her off guard. And though she'd had her reasons for walking away, an altogether new feeling clanged in Birdie—not just that she wanted this for the headlines, which she knew were likely already writing themselves. Rather she wished that Ian *had* been the one to regret their split. In their entire two years together, Ian had never been unkind, had never been anything less than devoted, had supported her peripatetic audition cycle by insisting on sending her out into the world with a hearty breakfast, by pinging her cell all day to see if she landed a part. He would massage her feet at night when she was still waitressing, and once she quit, slightly prematurely because money was still tight, he brought her home all the extras from the restaurant. He was protective and sweet, and her heart expanded when he kissed her. Birdie remembered all of this, suddenly, in a long rush right there in the dining room of Chez Nous, and dialed up her movie-star smile.

"Ian," she murmured and leaned over to kiss his cheek. "Surprise." She grinned so widely she felt like her dimples might crater.

When she would rewatch the video of this moment online tomorrow morning, she would see Ian's stony face, she would witness that not only did he not reciprocate her kiss, but rather he appeared to recoil from it. But Birdie was so swept up in the moment—in genuine nostalgia and belated appreciation for her first ex, her second love—that she overlooked his body language, missed his chilly vibe completely.

"Surprise?" he asked.

"Yes! Surprise!" she repeated. "I got an anonymous love letter, and, well, I'm here to see if it came from you."

13

ELLIOT

ELLIOT CHECKED THE side mirror to see if they'd been followed, but blessedly, miraculously, the not-exactly-inconspicuous RV had not been tailed by the paparazzi. If they'd lingered at Chez Nous for even another minute, he suspected he'd be driving like he was a costar in a Kai Carol action film, peeling around corners, possibly driving straight on top of slow-moving electric coupes. As it was, he was breaking all sorts of local speed limits as he navigated to his apartment on the opposite side of town.

He checked the rearview mirror and saw the soles of Birdie's Vans, Andie's Vans really, facing him; Birdie was still kneeling at the base of the toilet. He thought he heard her retch and reached for the radio to turn the dial down. Or up. He wasn't sure which was worse: listening to her puke to be sure that she was all right or listening to her puke, period.

"Bird?" he called over his shoulder. "Come on, it'll be okay."

It probably wouldn't be okay, but it sounded like something that he should say in this moment regardless. Professionally, Elliot tried to never say something he couldn't verify or back up with concrete facts. Personally, he was significantly more squishy. *He'd call her; he'd text her; hey, maybe we should get another drink sometime; hey, that was fun, we'll do it again sometime.*

He replayed the last few minutes in his brain, trying to get a handle on how he could frame it for his article to possibly make it any less humiliating for Birdie. But the video would be out there by now, photos and probably some live streams and hot takes were no doubt all over TikTok with some savvy Gen Zers offering up scathing commentary at her hubris.

It had taken a beat back at Chez Nous for Ian to comprehend what was happening. He blinked at Birdie several times, then slid his gaze over to Elliot, whom he'd met over the years. (As previously noted, Elliot did indeed love his mussels.)

"So you're with her now?" Ian asked, ignoring Birdie's question about the letter and whether he'd sent it, ignoring her entire presence, actually. "Please tell me that you are not with her now."

"No, no," Elliot said. "I'm just here as . . ." He intuited immediately, clearly, what Birdie had not. That they should have called ahead, that they should have warned Ian. That not only did he have no rosy feelings toward her, but he was entirely fine turning her surprise visit into a public dressing-down. Elliot wasn't sure why Birdie was oblivious, but it was likely because she was already playing the part, had already committed to her role. Elliot thought then of how he'd lingered outside the school auditorium their senior year. She was rehearsing for *Little Shop*, and he was done with swim practice but waiting around in case she needed a ride. He peeked his head through the door, just slightly, very quietly, so no one would notice he was even there, and he didn't even recognize Birdie at first. She was belting out "Suddenly Seymour" and wearing a short blond wig and a wide high-waisted skirt, and Elliot knew with complete clarity that she was going to be a star. She was unrecognizable, this girl whom he'd known since he was twelve. She could morph herself into anyone, she could will herself into believing she was *anyone*. And right then, at Chez Nous, Elliot realized, she was a rom-com heroine in need of a hero.

"He's here to document it," Birdie said to Ian, unaware of the storm that was brewing. "He's here to see if you wrote me the letter. I asked him to come. Also, did you know that he loves your mussels? The seafood, not your biceps. But, Ian, you are looking extremely fit."

"You think," he hissed at her, "that I would have sent you an anonymous love letter?"

"No, I didn't—" she started, then stopped, then shook her head as if she were rebooting, and tried again. "I guess I didn't know? And I thought, you know, maybe? It's been such a long time, so I wanted to see you and . . . check."

"It's been a long time so you thought you should *check*?" Ian's cheeks were pink now, his chest rising and falling. "It has been fourteen fucking years, Birdie. And now, *and now*, you think you can show up here—at my work—to *check*?" He pushed up the sleeves on his chef's jacket, and his forearms were covered in tattoos, and Elliot saw Birdie stare at them as if she were looking at a map she no longer understood.

"I guess I thought—" she started.

"I don't think you ever even *spoke* to me after you just dumped me with no, less than zero, explanation. I mean, I should say, you dumped me for '*Los Angeles*.'" He held up air quotes, like "Los Angeles" was some bullshit excuse when she was really sleeping with someone else.

"It *was* for that," Birdie protested, as if that made it any better.

"Bird," Elliot murmured, but she didn't seem to hear him. He wanted to intervene, but he also knew he shouldn't become part of the story. He'd promised Francesca he could be objective, unemotional.

"I went out there for pilot season," she cried. "And . . . I don't know. I don't know, Ian! Maybe I'm here because *I'm* the one who regrets it! Maybe all this time made me nostalgic, made me miss you."

Elliot's eyes narrowed. He knew, ostensibly, that he was here for a happily-ever-after reunion, but now that Birdie seemed genuinely up for it, he soured on the entire idea.

"You think," Ian yelled, "that I give one shit—no, four shits— if *you* regret how you dumped *me*? That you suddenly were struck by some sort of lightning bolt fourteen years later?"

The restaurant had fallen so silent that Elliot knew there was no hope for Birdie. They were witnessing a celebrity reputational execution, and there was nothing the public loved more. He glanced to his left, then his right, and cell phones were aloft and surrounding them like the fleet of an alien army.

"I'm not a supporting actor in one of your movies," Ian rasped. "I'm not here for your amusement."

"I didn't say—" Birdie hiccuped, and Elliot watched the veneer slip away, as if she had realized—slowly but then also quite immediately—that this wasn't another one of her roles she could try on for size.

"And I certainly have no intention of being the object of some ridiculous puff piece that Elliot O'Brien is writing for reasons that I don't even begin to understand." Ian lurched. Elliot reared a half step back and clicked his tongue as if there was no need to drag his own name into it, but then, well, he *had* agreed to do this. Not only agreed, he'd pitched it! And as far as content went, Francesca would sell more ad hits for this piece than she sold in a month. But. But, but, but, but, but.

But Birdie.

Elliot saw her eyes well, and he hoped that it wasn't performative, but then he hated that he hoped that, and hoped that it was genuine, but then he hated that he hoped for that too.

"Hey, Ian, come on, dude," he said. "Maybe just . . . you know, dial it back a bit? Go easy on her?"

"Go fucking easy on her?" Ian was absolutely apoplectic. "Are you kidding me? Do you have any idea what it's like to sit around waiting and waiting and waiting for your phone to ring, waiting and waiting and waiting for the girl you loved and devoted yourself to for two goddamn years to call you or at least not to fucking *ghost* you, all because she moved to 'Los Angeles'?" He did the quotes thing again, and Birdie let out a cry.

"It was for *Los Angeles*, okay? It was only for *Los Angeles*," she wailed.

"So you traded me in for a vapid city full of plastic people with plastic parts and plastic brains. Great. Absolutely wonderful. Thank you for stopping by. This has been a real joy." He crossed his tattooed arms, like he was a bouncer ready for their departure. The hostess was suddenly by his side and rested her hand on his arm.

"Ian," she murmured, "should I call someone?"

"Should you *call* someone?" Birdie yelped. "You think you should call *security* on me? I know that you know who—"

And that was when Elliot finally snapped to. He stepped between Birdie and Ian and turned toward the girl he used to love and said, "Bird, come on. Let's not do this. It wasn't Ian. We got what we came for, which was an answer."

Birdie blinked back a few tears, then met his eyes. Her own were hazy and confused, as if she had been in a fugue state for this whole incident, and maybe, honestly, she had been. Birdie had always handled difficult things by putting herself elsewhere, literally and mentally. And obviously, this was more than a difficult situation. None of this was ideal—certainly, the live streams were wholly *not* ideal—but all the rest of it felt irrelevant now. Now they just had to exit, and they had to exit quickly.

"What—no, really—*what* about me ever gave you the impression that I would . . ." Ian was still going. Elliot spun around, with Birdie now at his back, and saw Ian's red cheeks, the spittle that was about to land on the front of his shirt. "That I would 'regret' losing you? What would I possibly regret? You dumped me even when I offered to move to LA. You realize that I had made calls, been offered an executive chef position? You never even heard me out, never spoke with me again. Poof. You were just . . . gone. Do you know . . ." He trailed off, then gathered himself. "Do you know how that felt? Do you possibly have any idea how shitty that was?"

"Look, dude, I'm sorry about this," Elliot said.

But then Ian's face fell and went blank. He looked over Elliot's shoulder and then back to his sometimes patron who surely would never be welcome back into his restaurant for his delicious mussels again.

"Well, will you look at that," he said. "Be careful with her, friend. She's already left you."

Elliot turned, and Birdie was halfway out the door of the restaurant.

When he found her, she was cradling the toilet in the RV. So Elliot sprang into action, jumping into the driver's seat and heaving the RV away from Chez Nous, away from the gawkers and the filmers and the fans. For a very brief beat of a moment, he envisioned himself as Birdie's hero, just like in one of her movies.

But then Francesca began blowing up his phone, and he reminded himself that both he and Birdie were in this for professional salvation, and those paths to salvation might diverge. And it dawned on him that only one of them might end up coming out of it on top.

14

BIRDIE

BIRDIE RAISED HER head from the disgusting toilet bowl in the miniature bathroom of the RV and tried to stop her gagging. But the reflux was beyond her control, probably a lot more than just the reflux too. Her stomach lurched again. Elliot was driving like a banshee, and she wanted to be appreciative, that he was rescuing her, but she was prone to motion sickness, and the way he was careening around corners was not helping the situation one bit. Also, Birdie was entirely disinterested in being rescued, even by Elliot O'Brien.

Her plan had been a hotel for the night after a pleasant rendezvous with Ian. A little pampering, certainly some room service. Now, for obvious reasons, that was totally outside the realm of manageable. The press knew she was in San Francisco. The press knew she was vulnerable and in the middle of a nuclear meltdown in San Francisco. They'd swoop in and attack like vultures if they had a location.

"I'll sleep in the RV," Elliot called back to her after slamming on the brakes at a traffic light. "You take my bed." Birdie raised her head from the toilet and caught his eye in the rearview mirror even twenty feet away. He was looking at her with something that Birdie thought he meant to be sympathy but honestly felt a lot more like pity. And she hated it, that Elliot *pitied* her. He'd already spurned her seven years ago. This, his pity, was even worse.

She didn't want his bed. What she wanted was a safe space to anchor herself, a room with a locked door where no one could find her. But no one knew Elliot's address, or at least they didn't yet, so it was either his apartment or this landboat, and so, with no reasonably decent options, she agreed to the better of two terrible choices.

She tried not to replay the events at Chez Nous over and over again as she hovered over the toilet, but how did one simply ignore public humiliation? Her team had already called her four times; Imani had texted three. And the worst part about this— no, actually, not the worst, one of many god-awful things—was that she couldn't even shift the blame. This was entirely on her! Her idea, her tactics, her words! She'd only glanced at Imani's first text but already knew that she'd turned a medium-sized shit-storm into a full tornado of turds.

Birdie pushed herself away from the toilet and crawled down the aisle of the RV toward the passenger seat, trying not to consider how much about the conversation Ian had gotten right. She *had* ditched him for Los Angeles; she *had* ghosted him after two years together. Birdie had always thought of herself as lucky whenever she landed a boyfriend, as the ugly duckling, the girl whose parents and sister were the brightest bulbs while she burned dimmer, the square peg in Barton's paved streets of round holes. It never dawned on her that she wasn't the victim here, that she'd actually been the awful one, the one who was completely reckless with Ian's heart. She thought about Kai as she threw herself into the front seat—she hated thinking about Kai, but there he was in her brain all the same—and how it felt to have her own heart yanked around. Ian had it exactly right back there, which didn't make it better and didn't make it worse. It only made Birdie want to rewind time. Perhaps then she would have given Ian a more truthful explanation.

It *had* been Los Angeles; she'd been honest with him about that—she loved her bubble out there, filled with long days and actors who took themselves too seriously and *Soap Opera Digest* interviews and double takes at the grocery store when shoppers tried to figure out where they knew her from. But, well, it had also been Elliot.

Just as she was getting her sea legs in LA, Mona and Elliot's mom died. She went up for the funeral and sat between her best friend and her first love, and though it was obviously not the time for any sort of romantic entanglements, she couldn't slow her heart, couldn't stop her brain from racing with her own sort of fantastical fictions. By then it had been weeks since she left New York, left Ian. To be fair to her, she took a few of his calls in those early days, made a vague promise or two to find a date when he could come visit, but their hours were no longer synced—he was leaving for work when she was just crashing for bed.

Elliot had always lingered in the background of her mind, and then there he was at the funeral, in the foreground. Even when he returned to Berkeley and she drove back to her one-bedroom apartment in Burbank, she couldn't shake it. So rather than tell Ian the truth, she simply told him nothing. After the funeral, he kept calling, and she stopped answering. Fourteen years later, she could see how selfish and cruel she had been. But fourteen years ago, Birdie genuinely didn't think she was breaking his heart. Ian was so wholly wonderful, how on earth could a girl like her break his heart? She squeezed her eyes closed in the passenger seat as Elliot made one final turn toward his apartment, and tried to recalibrate everything she'd told herself about their breakup.

"Do you think that I'm generally full of shit?" she asked Elliot, who was digging into a backpack and pulled out a garage remote triumphantly. He clicked a button, and his condo's garage groaned, then opened. Birdie gazed at the clearance and unconsciously ducked her head.

"We'll make it," he said. "Trust me." He winced as he eased the RV forward, but naturally, like everything Elliot did, he turned out to be right. "I figured we hide it here for the night; maybe by morning everyone will have forgotten."

Birdie turned toward him as both of their phones bleated. He offered a little shrug like they both knew this was preposterous but wouldn't it be nice if he turned out to be correct.

"You didn't answer my question," Birdie said, aware that her mouth tasted like a rotten avocado, and hoped that Elliot couldn't smell her breath. She patted down Andie's cargo pants, thinking maybe she'd find a wayward breath mint. No luck. She suspected her mascara had flaked completely down her cheeks, that those cheeks were red and tear streaked, and that something mucusy was threatening to run out of her nose at any moment. She could not believe that she was in the middle of a near psychotic break in front of Elliot. She hiccuped and repeated herself: "Seriously, Elliot, do you think that I'm full of shit?"

Elliot turned the key in the ignition and the engine silenced itself. He sat staring at the Honda Accord parked opposite them, the newer version of his own car back in high school. God, Birdie thought, how she'd lived for those mornings when he would pull up and honk. How she'd tell herself today would be the day when she'd nail the lyrics to whatever they were listening to, how Elliot would glance into the back seat and marvel at her talent, how even though no one appreciated her in her own home, Elliot sometimes looked at her and made her feel like the road could open up with possibility.

She wiped her nose with the back of her hand and hoped he didn't notice.

"I think," Elliot said after another long beat, "that I don't really know you anymore, Bird. So how can I even begin to answer?"

15

ELLIOT

ELLIOT WISHED THAT he had answered Birdie differently. All it would have taken was a quick "of course you're not full of shit, Bird, you're the girl I've always loved" to placate her, to dial down the temperature, but, of course, he'd been a bumbling idiot and been honest. They were in his entryway, and Birdie was still sniffling, her posture in a slouch, her chin quaking as if tears were both imminent and unpredictable. Elliot had no problem with small white lies nearly all the time. What about Birdie made it impossible for him?

He took a step inside, glanced around his apartment, and tried to view the place from Birdie's perspective. He was rarely home, and when he was, décor was not a priority. He sometimes brought women back here, true, but the lights were always low, and they spent most of the time in the bedroom, so he didn't have to apologize for the couch whose foot had broken so it sat lopsided, for the rug that he had spilled coffee on two years back and never bothered to replace.

Birdie plopped at his kitchen counter, with her face in her

hands, moaning. Both their phones had buzzed with a new article: **IS BIRDIE ROBINSON BAD FOR WOMEN AND WHY IS THE ANSWER YES?** Elliot knew the reporter vaguely—they'd had drinks at some press event years back—and honestly, she was smart and pithy and didn't take shots below the belt, so he couldn't blame Birdie for moaning.

"Am I bad for women, *am I bad for women*?" She raised her face, which was ruddy and also simultaneously waxy and pale, and cried, "Can't you do something about this? How quickly can you write your article saying that they have it all wrong? That you were there too?"

He plunked down next to her on a wobbly stool and rested his hand on her back. He felt her flinch, then soften, so he left his palm there, wondering if she felt the same buzz of electricity that he did. *No, no, no. What was wrong with him?* Of course she didn't, and this wasn't the time. Birdie was in trouble, so why did it feel like there was a fire brewing in him that was going to run wild, too hot to put out when it eventually sparked. Besides, this wasn't one of her romantic comedies where the good guy who made poor decisions was granted a second chance.

Birdie pulled up the hood of that god-awful neon sweatshirt and tugged the cord, as if she wanted to disappear.

"Hey," he said. "Don't do that."

"Don't do what?"

"Try to make yourself invisible."

"In this thing, that's impossible," she replied. Then she turned toward him with her red-rimmed eyes. "I really think Andie was trying to make sure that I was visible from space. This sweatshirt is like a tracking device."

"Maybe that's where we went wrong tonight. The Target hoody."

"Let's blame Andie," Birdie sniffed.

"Absolutely," Elliot said. "This is all her fault."

Birdie emitted a bark of a sad laugh, then sighed. "I really can't believe that in trying to do the right thing in telling Sebastian Carol to fuck right off, I've been branded the worst person alive."

"Well, surely you're not *the worst* person alive," Elliot said. "There are dictators out there, you know?"

"So one step below a dictator," Birdie said.

"Well, also there are serial murderers," he offered.

"So not as bad as a *Dateline* episode," she said. "Well, thank god. That's a relief."

"I never said that," he replied. "Some *Dateline* episodes have killers you root for anyway."

She curled her hand into a fist and punched his left shoulder.

"Ow," he said. "That hurt!"

"I meant it to," she said. "Why else would someone punch you if not to make it hurt?"

Elliot made a show of massaging his shoulder, which wasn't all that painful, but he liked the way they were bantering, like maybe he was distracting her from her phone, which hadn't stopped vibrating, like maybe he was distracting himself from writing an article about the Chez Nous massacre.

"Can I ask you something?" he said.

"I already told you, you can ask me anything you like."

"Right." Elliot nodded. She had said that. "I guess, well, this isn't so much a question but something that I don't quite understand. If Sebastian was so awful, why did you agree to work with him? He didn't . . ." Elliot felt his anger rise as he worked up the nerve to ask her the next part. "He didn't do anything to you, right? Put his hands on you?" His blood was at a low simmer, just envisioning it.

"He didn't have to do anything to me to make it feel personal," she answered. "It doesn't work like that for women." Elliot waited for her to elaborate, and when she didn't, he flattened his palms against the counter and pushed himself to his feet.

"Okay, how about a grand tour of my apartment. It's quite the lap of luxury. I'm surprised that *Architectural Digest* hasn't asked for a photo shoot." Elliot hoped he was masking his mortification: he glanced around, and honestly, the apartment looked like a college student's move-out day. Her own apartment in Tribeca had been finely appointed, clearly decorated by a designer, and though Elliot was not one for insecurity, now, with Birdie Maxwell standing in front of his IKEA-lite furnishings, he wouldn't blame her for bolting. "I know it's not the Four Seasons," he said.

"It doesn't have to be the Four Seasons," she said, though Elliot thought she could have sold the line a bit more.

The tour of his apartment took about forty-five seconds, but he showed her the coffee maker for the morning and assured her that the sheets were clean and told her how to jigger the shower knob so the hot water worked.

"You don't have to sleep in the RV," Birdie reiterated as her eyes coasted over the framed family photographs, one of the few personal touches in the place. Elliot had forgotten that he had one of the three of them, Mona, Birdie, Elliot, that his mom had taken on their fourteenth birthday on their front lawn. He and Mona always had joint birthday parties, but that was the first year that it was obvious that Elliot's RSVP list was significantly longer than hers. Elliot proposed that they just invite Birdie over—she could even bring Andie, who still liked to tag along back then— for a water balloon fight, then for a cake that they could split into quarters and they'd each devour a quadrant. Andie hadn't come, which pleased Elliot because he just wanted Birdie alone. So it was just the three of them and water balloons and an enormous sheet cake that gave them all a stomachache when they finally put their forks down. Elliot's mom had insisted on a photo—all their shirts were damp from the balloons and Elliot knew, without looking at it now, that Birdie had blue icing around her lips.

She picked up the frame, peered at it, set it back down, her face unreadable.

"Elliot, really, we're adults. Just sleep here. Who even knows when Mona changed those RV sheets last."

Elliot hesitated. He wanted to sleep here, god did he want to sleep here. He watched Birdie sink into his lopsided couch and press the heels of her hands underneath her eyes. What he wanted to say was that he didn't trust himself to sleep in his queen-sized bed with her. Didn't trust that he wouldn't lie awake all night willing himself not to touch her, not to run his hands over her spine or along her dewy skin or simply ask her if she wanted to place her head atop his chest. What he wouldn't do to run his hands along her dewy skin. All over it. Every last spot, every last inch.

"Well," he stammered, "it's probably more professional if we sleep separately anyway."

She dropped her hands and screwed her face up. "We weren't going to sleep together. Did something about this evening give you the impression that I was looking to get laid?"

"No, no, that's not what I meant at—" he bleated. But then she raised her eyes and met his, and he could see she was only joking. "Ah," he said. "Gallows humor."

"First comes gallows humor, then comes the death of my career."

"No," he said. "That's what I'm here for."

She parted her lips to say something, then stopped. Then reconsidered. "Elliot, you know that I'm not looking for you to save me, right? I mean, whatever happens with this letter and, you know, like, my public image. Yes, I need your help, but no, I don't expect you to, like, be my white knight."

Elliot felt the blood pool in his cheeks, then his ears.

"Right, no, I never thought—" He turned away from her and opened the fridge in an attempt at normalcy, to reset the equilibrium. Of course that's what he'd thought if he really drilled down on it. Save her, rescue her, prove that he'd completely fucked up and regretted it seven years ago by doing so. Also, save his own career in the meantime. It was a real happily-ever-after, just like her movies. Elliot had never thought of himself as subscribing to fiction, much less fantasy, and yet, just twenty-four hours in with Birdie, and he was doing it all the same.

"Okay, well, can I get you anything before I head out to the RV?" he asked.

Birdie sighed. "A time machine?"

"Where would you go back to?" Elliot asked before he could stop himself.

Their night together? Before she invited him back to her apartment? After he walked away? After she didn't try to stop him?

"The dawn of time," she said. "I think I'd go back to the dawn of time."

"Fairly boring," Elliot said, shutting the fridge. "No internet."

"Oh right, for sure. That's exactly why it's appealing." She managed a grin, and he nearly tipped over with joy in getting her to smile.

They each fell silent. Elliot knew there was plenty to say, but he didn't quite know what needed to be said yet.

Instead, he tried to talk himself into leaving. Putting space between them. If he didn't now, he knew he was going to cross all sorts of ethical journalistic lines, not to mention all sorts of lines period.

"Okay," he finally said. "I'll head out. Make yourself at home. Just, uh, I don't know, don't look under the mattress?" It was meant to be a joke about the time that she and Mona had been snooping in his room and found a weathered copy of *Playboy* that his swim team friends gifted him for his sixteenth birthday. When he got home from practice the afternoon they found it, Birdie and Mona had torn out all the pages and taped them to the wall in an arch around his bed. He took them down before his parents got home, but not before the two of them howled until Birdie shrieked, "I'm going to pee in my pants," and she and Mona both raced toward the hall bathroom before one of their bladders exploded.

"Look," Birdie said, finding his stare, then faltering. "I wouldn't mind if you slept here. I guess that's what I'm trying to say. I'd like the company."

It was easier to convince him than he'd planned on. He simply heard her ask and caved.

"Okay," he said.

"Okay?" she replied.

"Okay," he said again. "Yes."

BIRDIE ROBINSON HUMILATED IN COLD-DISH REUNION WITH HOT EX

Birdie Robinson has more to worry about than just her scuttled reputation from the fallout of her on-set fight with beloved director Sebastian Carol, brother of Kai Carol, the rumored secret ex of Ms. Robinson. It seems that she is making a fool of herself all over the country, this time in San Francisco, where she arrived, hat in hand, at Chez Nous, the award-winning restaurant of acclaimed chef Ian Sands. Multiple diners confirm to *ET* that Ms. Robinson tried to blindside Mr. Sands into a lovey-dovey reconciliation. Indeed, Isabel Marie, the hostess at Chez Nous (and aspiring model—she is represented by More Models in the Bay Area), had to forcibly remove Ms. Robinson from the premises, even when she demanded a dish of Mr. Sands' much-heralded mussels.

"Ms. Robinson showed up here unannounced and unwelcome, and distracted Mr. Sands from his patrons and his award-winning meals and presentation," Ms. Marie said. "What a sad affair for a woman who had convinced the public that she was a dream girl, a perfect embodiment of romance. More like a nightmare if you were to ask me, and I'm sure if you were to ask Ian as well."

Calls to Ms. Robinson's representatives have not been returned at press time.

16

BIRDIE

IRDIE LISTENED TO Elliot's breath rise and fall and rise and fall. She was astonished that he fell asleep so easily. She didn't know what she'd thought, that they'd lie awake whispering secrets and adoring words to each other or something like that, because they'd tried that once and look how that had gone.

"Elliot," she whispered to his shoulder blades. "*Elliot.*"

But he didn't budge. She was almost insulted at how heavily he slept, but then having a woman in his bed was not particularly revelatory for him, Birdie knew. She adjusted her pillow, rolled to her other side, and tried not to replay this evening's entire disaster in slow motion.

Imani had texted her seven times and called her twice. Birdie ignored them all and eventually turned off her phone. The video from Chez Nous was circulating all over socials like wildfire, offering the public more fodder that Birdie Robinson was a better actor than anyone had given her credit for, since she'd convinced the public for nearly a decade that she was harmless and kind and soft and cuddly. Like a teddy bear, one gossip account said. Birdie Robinson used to be a teddy bear, when it turned out that she was a grizzly.

She pulled the pillow over her head and groaned into it. Then she placed it against the headboard and punched it straight in the middle and set her head down on it and inhaled because *oh god, it smelled just like Elliot*. She shouldn't delight in this so much, but she couldn't help herself, like his scent was a dopamine hit. She rolled over toward him again and allowed her fingertips to brush up against his back, over his neck, up through his hair.

The night that he'd stayed over seven years ago, there had been very little sleeping. But for the hour or two that they did, Birdie mostly pretended to sleep while occasionally flitting open her eyes and marveling at him. Dusting his cheeks with her fingers, laying his arm over her stomach so no space came between them. Now his back was toward her as if he didn't even remember that night, as if she were just another warm body on the right side of the mattress.

She shifted again, stared at the ceiling, then reached for her phone on his nightstand, which was actually just a tower of books stacked on top of a U-Haul box. She almost wanted to text Mona to tell her that her brother was more of a disaster than he let on, but she wasn't in a position to judge, and also, she didn't want Mona to start asking questions about why Birdie knew what her brother used as a nightstand.

Birdie hadn't meant to ever keep secrets from Mona. Her best friend had never explicitly warned Birdie off of Elliot, but she hadn't had to be explicit. Her expression at prom, when she yanked Elliot from the faculty lounge, was readable from the moon, and even without prom, it was always clear that she and

Mona were the partnership and that Elliot was the third wheel. So no, Birdie was not about to text Mona about his nightstand full of hardcovers and a moving box.

Instead, she powered on her phone and then googled Ian, spiraling further into what-ifs and should-have-beens. She clicked through pictures of Ian at charity meals, photos of him with beautiful women on his arm, and write-ups on how he was democratizing the dining scene in San Francisco—bringing reasonably priced haute cuisine to nonfoodies and turning them into believers. She lingered over his Levi's campaign, where he looked like a goddamn movie star (she would know), and then read about how he donated his fee to public school lunch programs. As Birdie scrolled through write-up after write-up, a small part of her lamented that she had let him go so easily. That she'd overlooked what a diamond he was. Or perhaps, with hindsight, that she knew he was a diamond at the time and rejected him all the same. She'd been twenty years old and on the cusp of a whole new life. She wasn't equipped for long-term love then.

No, that was a simple lie she could tell herself.

She was equipped for long-term love but not with Ian. Rather, with the man she sat next to at his mother's funeral, whose breath rose and fell beside her now, the man who had made clear to her half a decade after Ian that her heart was on a fool's errand in holding out hope for him.

Elliot sighed loudly in his sleep, and Birdie startled and threw her phone to the foot of the bed, like she didn't want him to catch her reading up on Ian. She inched a little closer to him and closed her eyes, trying to time her own breath with his. Eventually, her eyelids grew heavy. She was surprised to feel the tug of sleep. There was something comforting, something tender, about lying next to Elliot O'Brien, even if she'd done it before, and ostensibly, she knew not to expect that this meant anything. It meant less than nothing. Whatever that number was, she thought just before she slipped into dreaming, that's what this was. A negative of less than nothing.

The next thing she knew, dawn was breaking through his window, and she pushed up to her elbows, and Elliot was gone.

Déjà vu. Just like seven years ago.

17

ELLIOT

ELLIOT HAD WILDLY miscalculated. He'd been dumb enough to think that by parking the RV underground and whisking Birdie away to his apartment, he'd be able to outwit the press. Even though he was a *member* of the press. This was at least part of Francesca's problem with him: his tendency to presume that he was the smartest person in the figurative room. He didn't even want to consider what Francesca would say if she knew that he'd shared a bed with Birdie last night.

He hadn't been able to sleep, of course. He heard her whisper his name, and it took every ounce of cellular willpower in his entire limbic system not to roll over and face her. But if he faced her, then he'd kiss her, and if he kissed her, then he'd sleep with her, and if he slept with her, then he'd never be able to *not* sleep with her again, and, well, okay, now he was spiraling. He'd felt her run her fingers over his back and neck and up through his hair, and he'd stilled himself to near paralysis so that he didn't do the one thing his body was aching to do. And when she finally fell asleep, he did roll over so he could memorize her perfect long lashes, the spread of her hair on his pillow, her spray of freckles. And then because there was no point in pretending that he wasn't wide awake, he pushed himself up to start his day. Because he owed Francesca an article before morning, and if he lingered even another minute longer in bed with Birdie, certainly, nothing was going to be written. And nothing good would come of it.

Once the sun had cracked the San Francisco skyline and after an hour or so hunched over his laptop, he felt reasonably decent about saving Birdie's dignity in the piece, hit send, and then slipped out to get coffee. On his route home, that's when he noticed a van parked across the street. He loitered behind a tree to be sure and saw a reporter he knew from around, Jaren Anders, asleep in the driver's seat. Elliot had never liked Jaren, and now he fucking hated Jaren, who had probably texted a few mutuals and gotten his intentionally unlisted address and lurched over in his stupid TV truck. Elliot wanted to march right up to the passenger seat and pop Jaren squarely on the nose, but then Francesca would certainly have grounds for firing him—and also, he had to get to Birdie.

He ran into the back entrance of his condo, flew through the door of the apartment, and raced into his bedroom. He'd envisioned that he'd wake her, she'd be grateful, and together they'd triumphantly outsmart Jaren and cruise out of San Francisco undetected. Also, if Jaren had figured out where he lived, he suspected that the rest of the local press—and probably the national press, for that matter—couldn't be far behind.

Birdie, however, was awake. He burst through the door, and before he could say a word, she scowled at him with what he felt like was her whole body. Could you scowl with your whole body? If anyone could, it was Birdie Robinson.

"I thought you left me," she snapped.

"I didn't—"

"I thought you left me *again*," she snapped even more sharply.

"I didn't—" Elliot remembered the coffee in his hand and thrust it forward like a peace offering. "I went to get coffee. But we need to move. Now." She didn't reach for the to-go cup, so Elliot's arm remained extended between them until he gave up. "There's a guy out there." He added, "Jaren. And he's a real douche."

"And this is my problem because?"

"He's out there because of *you*. So I'm going to say again, we need to hustle. Unless you want them chasing us all the way to Los Angeles."

"Los Angeles?" Birdie's voice tipped into a higher octave. "Why are we going to Los Angeles?"

"Carter."

"Carter?"

"Yes, Carter," Elliot repeated. "He's next on my list."

"You mean to tell me that after last night, you still expect me to go through with this?"

"I think after last night, it's even more important that you do go through with this," Elliot said.

"That's your TV reporter voice again," she griped.

"It's not my TV—" He stopped. It was. It was his goddamn TV voice. It was easier to handle her this way, not to think about the blurred lines of sharing a bed, of all the things he wanted to do to her while next to her in bed. He wanted to ask her: Why did you run your fingers up my back? Why did you trace them over my neck and up through my hair when you thought I was asleep? But he worried he couldn't stay reasonably composed when he heard her answer, and then he worried about what would happen if he misread her answer. What if Birdie, who was out here chasing true love, just wanted him for mindless sex? To scratch an itch? To enjoy him because of proximity?

They'd already done that. Elliot couldn't bear it again, and besides, this had to be kept professional. His career was hanging in the balance.

Also, there was Mona.

"Fine," he said. "It was my TV voice. But really, we have to go. It's six hours to LA, and if we slip out now, Jaren's asleep. He'll be waiting here all day while we're halfway to SoCal."

Birdie groaned. "I'm not going. I'm not doing this again."

"You're going," he said, and he wasn't sure if he was being strident because of Francesca or because it meant spending more time with Birdie or because he really did think he could help her. His brain ran through the options without him even realizing, and it dawned on him: yes, all three. But it would be so much more convenient if this was solely about saving his job.

"I'm not." She crossed her arms and jutted her chin. "You can't, like, kidnap me and take me to LA."

"It's not kidnapping, Bird," Elliot said. "We agreed to do this. Together."

"Nobody agreed to anything! Did I agree? I don't remember agreeing."

"Well, you got in the RV, and you spoke with Ian," Elliot said. "I took that to be agreement."

"You are an extremely unethical reporter if that's all you need for consent," she said.

You don't know the half of it, Elliot thought, but said, "I always get consent. *Always.*" And now he wondered if they weren't talking about something else entirely. Birdie scowled. Yes, they were talking about something else entirely.

"I don't want to see Carter," she said. "I don't want to see *anyone.*" She swiped Andie's neon hoody from the floor and started to throw it over her head.

"No, not that." Elliot sighed. "I really do think the paparazzi could see you from Mars." He stepped to his closet, grabbed a blue cotton oxford, and offered it.

"The paparazzi don't have to see me at all. That's what I'm telling you."

"Bird, they're either going to see you here, in my place, or they're going to see you somewhere else. And may I suggest that you'd rather do this on your terms than on theirs?"

Birdie scowled even deeper, her eyes narrowing to slits, her chin turning upward toward her pursed lips. But she swiped his oxford from his hand and shoved her arms into the sleeves. A concession. Also, a relief because Elliot couldn't begin to imagine how he was going to explain to Francesca that he'd blown the assignment one day into the job. Birdie had slept in a camisole, but Elliot averted his eyes all the same, as if watching her button up one of his shirts was too intimate for him to handle.

When she was dressed, she slipped into the bathroom and splashed water on her face, then used his toothbrush without asking. He didn't know why he was surprised that she still did that; back when she was sleeping at their house every weekend, she always had a spare toothbrush in Mona's bathroom. But occasionally it went missing, so she'd steal Elliot's because he was almost always still out with his friends while she and Mona were already crashing for the night. He'd get home at some point in the early hours and find a wet toothbrush, and for a while, he accused Mona of being super disgusting, but Birdie shrugged and said it was her, and then he found that he didn't mind so much.

"Okay," she said from the bathroom.

"You're ready?" he asked.

"Not at all," she replied. "Please note that I am doing all of this against my will."

"Birdie, I can't think of a single thing you've ever done against your will." He flipped off the lights and took a long look around like he could be forgetting something.

"Hostage video, Exhibit A."

"Apology video," he corrected. "And point taken." Elliot thought of the article he'd filed with Francesca just an hour ago. How he'd tried to report objectively while still making Birdie shine. He couldn't do all that much to salvage her humiliation in today's story, and he knew it, so he mostly stuck to factual reporting. Still, it was something.

He closed his apartment door behind him and dead-bolted the lock, just in case Jaren got any ideas about breaking in under the guise of investigative reporting, and Birdie jabbed the elevator button down to the garage.

The elevator doors opened quickly, she stepped in, and Elliot followed, acutely aware of how closely they were standing, as if he could feel her body heat. Maybe he *could* feel her body heat. Maybe the only thing he wanted in the world was to feel her body heat.

"Look." Birdie sighed. "All I'm saying is that I'm a sinking ship. I suggest you jump while you still can."

He said nothing because she wasn't wrong, and she said nothing because she knew that she wasn't wrong. That's how it had always been between them. One hundred percent honest until it became too difficult to speak the truth.

But he wasn't jumping, he knew. If she wanted him gone, she was going to have to march him down a plank and push.

18

BIRDIE

I F BIRDIE HAD been reading about anyone other than herself, she would have thought that Elliot was an outstanding writer. As it was, he was indeed an outstanding writer, but since the article outlined her humiliations from the past evening, she could not bring herself to compliment him. They were cruising through the South Bay now, having managed to eke out a narrow escape from Jaren—Birdie wondered, what sort of name was Jaren?—and she was poring back over every sentence, every nuance.

Elliot kept glancing over at her from the driver's seat. He'd tried to soften the blows, she could tell. He didn't mention how Ian had screeched at her to never set foot in Chez Nous again, how he didn't care if she made ten million a movie (she held her tongue on her actual fee), how he would have been entirely *wonderful* if he never had to see her face on another billboard again. How he'd thought her last movie with "one of the Chrises" was a pile of dog shit (that was a direct quote), how it was beyond him that anyone thought she could be the lovable girl from across the street with the heart of gold.

So that was nice of Elliot. To strike all that.

He cleared his throat. "Francesca is super happy. Evidently, it's getting record traffic, and it's only been up for an hour."

"Oh, well, if Francesca is happy," Birdie said.

"Have you checked your notifications?" he asked, ignoring her tone. "Facebook? Instagram? Email? Text? Twitter?" She flopped her shoulders. "Birdie, I promise I'm on your side here. This might take a few bites of the apple. Give me a chance to build my case."

Birdie didn't reply. Her hand found its way to the buttons on Elliot's oxford shirt, and she closed it up to her neck. She liked how it felt, to be enveloped in his things, but also, she was too raw, too vulnerable, to feel protected by it.

"You don't believe me?" he asked.

"I'm not in a position these days to trust anyone," she said.

"Anyone . . . or me?" he asked.

Birdie's heart accelerated. She knew it would probably be prudent to discuss their one night together, to dig in and pull it up from the roots, but she also firmly, surely, certainly did *not* want to discuss anything about it. It would be so much less mortifying if they just let it all go unspoken, that she had been pie-in-the-sky in love with him, and still, she hadn't been anything more than another woman in another bed on another night for him. That still, he left.

"Not just you," she said finally, and hoped he didn't notice the burn in her cheeks, though Elliot noticed everything. "I mean, obviously, everyone. The studio that told me to work with Sebastian, then didn't have my back. Imani and Sydney, who told me to do the apology video, then, well, look at how that went. Jesus, one night home, and even Nelson Pratt is now my mortal enemy."

"I think we can agree that Nelson Pratt is a dweebish knob."

"A knob?"

"Simon taught me that," he said, as if bringing up Simon was a way to remind her of their mission here. That Elliot was literally steering her toward a reunion with someone else. Birdie's gut churned with something like emotional acid at her naivete, that she'd run her hands up his spine last night, that part of her probably hoped he'd roll over and kiss her. Not probably. Definitely. Birdie didn't know what she wanted from Elliot any more than she knew what she wanted out of this whole mission. She'd told herself it was simply for professional redemption, but seeing Ian changed something about that. Maybe it was too simplistic, that it could rebuild her in the public's eyes. Maybe she could hope for something more profound. It wasn't that she needed a man or a husband or a boyfriend. But a partner, that sounded nice. Someone to call after bruising days, someone to come home to instead of her empty king-sized bed and a phone full of work emails. Someone who understood her in the moments between action and cut. Someone who looked at her the way Elliot used to in carpool when they were alone.

"But me," Elliot asked again. "You still don't trust me? I promise you, you'll never have a reason not to, not with work, not with this."

Not with work. Not with this.

Message received. Elliot wasn't daydreaming about someone to share a king-sized bed with, much less daydreaming about her.

Birdie exhaled and ran her hands over her face. "Seeing Ian . . ." She drifted and tried to reframe their focus. "He was always so kind to me. I think I really messed that up."

Elliot nodded, like he got it. Like he'd messed up his own set of circumstances along the way, though clearly not with her. With Birdie, he'd been certain, and good god, it was all so mortifying.

But he didn't elaborate, so she reread the article again, letting the silence balloon between them and repressing the growing urge to say, despite everything: *I think I really messed up a lot of things. Like with you. I should have begged you to stay.*

Even if it wouldn't have made one difference in the end.

19

ELLIOT

ELLIOT GRIPPED THE wheel of the RV and trained his eyes on the traffic ahead, trying to distract himself from the fact that Birdie was still reading, rereading, the article beside him in the passenger seat. He promised her that he'd look out for her, and that was the easiest promise to make. Of course, he well knew that she didn't have to hand over her trust just because he wanted her to, and he also knew that she had ample reason to tell him to fuck right off. But she hadn't. She didn't. Elliot felt something flutter in him at this recognition: that he missed her inherent goodness so very much, that he'd lost track of the way she grounded him, that he'd lied to himself and pretended Birdie wasn't valuable, wasn't worth clutching onto. His heart lurched at how acutely he had missed her, like it was making up for the years away by pummeling him with nostalgia and regret and wistfulness all at once.

He blew out his breath, waiting for her assessment of the story that was currently trending on Twitter. The car in front of him had a MY KID IS AN HONORS STUDENT AT FRESNO JUNIOR HIGH bumper sticker, and he recalled that time in tenth grade when he forbade his mom from advertising his own success on the back of her minivan. Elliot and Mona had gone head to head for top of the class. He thought Mona won that year, but it could have been the next. His mom always brought home a cake that had both of their names on it, as if their class ranking didn't mean a thing, and really, it didn't.

He was old enough to live a life without his parents now, but sometimes he still missed her, missed them, acutely, painfully. He suspected his mother would have none of this, this pussyfooting around his complications with Birdie, with Mona now, but then, she wasn't here to ask. So he kept running on instinct. Which served him professionally. Personally, he was beginning to understand that he was a disaster. He knew his short-lived relationships with women were a crutch so that he never had to do any heavy lifting: his barren apartment, his round-the-clock job, the distance he kept between him and just about everyone else so he could do that job well. It was one thing to know this; however, it was another to change. He stole a sidelong glance at Birdie again and wondered if she were the cure he needed. Even though he was also wise enough to know that no one could cure anyone else; that would be too easy.

"I do appreciate this part," Birdie said, reading aloud.

Privately, after the confrontation that is now racing around the internet, Ms. Robinson appeared genuinely remorseful that she had caused Chef Sands such pain, even though it was over a decade ago, and most of us don't harbor grudges for the better part of our adulthood. She offered insightful reflections in the quiet moments afterward: what she could have done differently,

how she was an inexperienced kid who was careless
with his heart, how she hoped that one day they could
be friends because he was the first man to cook for her.
Lasagna.

"I didn't say any of that," Birdie said, cocking an eyebrow toward him.

Elliot laughed. "I told you I had your back. And what's he going to do—issue a press release that he never made you lasagna?
You mentioned that he used to cook for you; I felt like this was in
the ballpark of accurate."

"Journalistically squishy."

"I've been way more squished."

Birdie considered it, then: "I suppose a reporter reads between the lines. Not all that different from being an actress,
really."

"Incredibly different," Elliot batted back. "Not even in the
same ballpark. I deal with facts. You deal with fiction."

"And yet, here you are, playing fast and loose with my own
story."

Elliot checked his mirrors, tried to distract himself. Something about sitting with Birdie while she read his words made
him anxious, and he wondered if she'd feel the same. If he were
to confess that he'd gone to every one of her films on opening
weekend if he was in the country or sometimes in a foreign one.
It was almost spiritual for him, seeing the girl he'd loved since he
was sixteen projected on the screen in front of him. Seeing that
girl end up with a happily-ever-after every time, a heated kiss in
the snow with her family cheering from the living room window,
a race to the airport to chase down the one who had gotten away.

They were flying down the highway on the way to Los Angeles now. Birdie had set down her phone when the cell service got spotty and seemed to relax once it was out of reach. Elliot watched the furrow in her brow soften, her posture slide into a soft C, her head start to bop along with the music. The radio came in and out, but outside Merced, Birdie landed on an eighties station that stuck. She was singing low, under her breath, to Annie Lennox, the Eurythmics, just like she used to in carpool. *I'd travel the world and the seven seas . . .* Once Mona would join in, Birdie would ramp up, get going. By the time they reached school, the two of them would be hanging out the windows.

Birdie amped the radio up louder and raised her voice to match, uninhibited, perfect. Elliot launched himself right back to his sixteen-year-old self and clamped down on his lip to keep from laughing. But it was no use.

"What?" she said, turning to glance at him. "I'm a good singer. You can't make fun of my singing. Not when I'm already at rock bottom."

He shook his head, tears threatening to spill. His giggles were morphing into full-blown howls, a cramp building in his side, and he had to blink quickly to keep focus on the road.

"What did you just sing? What exactly do you think the lyrics are?" he managed, his voice breaking halfway through the question.

"*Sweet dreams are made of cheese,*" she sang. It was pitch-perfect, that was true.

And Elliot just lost it. He accidently swerved toward the divider, and Birdie reached over with a shriek to grab the wheel.

"What?" she asked once they were steady. "*What?*"

"Why would sweet dreams be made of *cheese*?" He couldn't stop himself. He broke into cackles again. His face felt like it was going to be permanently stuck in some sort of hyena smile, but it was out of his control now, like his brain was willing his face to calm down but it was no use.

"Because cheese is delicious!"

"Birdie, why would it be *cheese*? It's *these*. 'Sweet dreams are made of *these*,'" Elliot cried.

"That's ridiculous. What are 'these'? That could be anything."

She had a point, but Elliot knew for certain that it was not *cheese*.

"Who dreams of *cheese*?" he asked, then felt his face contort again. If he didn't get it together soon, he was going to drive the RV right off the freeway. He tried to think of serious things. His parents dying. Getting fired. Mona finding out that he and Birdie had slept together.

"I mean, have you never met a starving actress? I bet I dream of cheese at least fifty percent of the time," she said, but she was grinning now too. "Okay, yeah. I can see that I may not have gotten it right." Annie Lennox was hitting the chorus again, so Birdie belted out *cheese* with extra emphasis, and they both shrieked when she did, Elliot wiping away literal tears, Birdie pressing into her side as if that helped her breathe.

The radio faded as they drove on, and Birdie sighed, then started to speak, then sighed again. Elliot felt his pulse accelerate. He knew that at some point, they were going to have to discuss that night in New York, but he was panicked about what to confess, how to say it, if he should lay all his truths bare. He glanced over at her, but she was focused out the front window at that bumper sticker they still trailed. He decided if she brought it up, he'd tell her the truth.

"What happens if we find him—whoever this is—and he's changed his mind?" she asked finally, just as the stretch of silence was growing unbearable.

So she was not at all thinking about what he had been thinking about. Not even close. Not even in the same universe.

"Birdie, how could someone change his mind? With you?" he asked, and he saw her still beside him.

Fuck.

What an idiotic thing to say when she thought that was precisely what had happened. That he'd changed his mind. As if he could ever change his mind about something as foundational as his feelings for her. That would be like scientists declaring that they'd gotten gravity all wrong or that the sky was actually magenta, not blue. Some things were simply true forever.

But maybe *he'd* gotten it wrong. Maybe he was the only one who still felt his blood throb, literally throb, whenever he thought of that night. When he remembered how he felt split in two when he realized he was going to have to walk away. Maybe she never even revisited that night, the sex, the whispers, the way she called in sick for a rehearsal for some show she was doing so he didn't have to leave just yet. So she didn't have to leave just yet either.

"When I leave and head into work," she'd said from her king-sized bed. "Then maybe this perfect bubble will burst. Like Cinderella's slipper expiring at midnight."

"I don't think it was her slipper that expired," he said, though he knew what she meant, and adored that like the lyrics in their carpool, she'd get it slightly wrong. They were tangled up together. He was running his hand over her naked back, her hair pushed to the side, her eyes closed like this was all a mirage. To him, it was much closer to a dream.

"What if I don't want it to expire?" she had asked, rolling over and meeting his eyes. Vulnerable, honest, Birdie Maxwell even when she was already Birdie Robinson to everyone else.

"Then maybe I won't want it to expire either," he'd said, and kissed the tip of her nose, then moved on top of her. Of course, a few hours later, that all changed. He couldn't blame her if she'd held a grudge, refused to entertain any memory of just the two of them.

He'd explain everything if she asked, he vowed now. But he couldn't bear to bring it up and confess and be met with disbelief that he still regretted it, still questioned it, which he did all the time. He said, "Tell me what happened with Carter."

She pushed up her sunglasses and hesitated.

Finally, she said, "It was amicable. But then, I thought Ian was amicable. And, well, after last night, I think I'm no longer welcome in the entire San Francisco vicinity. Napa and Sonoma might even be out. Certainly Oakland and Marin."

"It wasn't that bad," Elliot said, though it was.

She looked over at him, her eyebrows raised. "I think there was a point where he threatened to sue you."

"True, but that happens on, like, a daily basis. If I *don't* get threatened with litigation, I consider the story a failure." He laughed but she did not.

Instead, she went quiet for a moment, and he worried that he'd offended her in some way, reducing her to just another story, just another file to live on the hard drive of his laptop.

"Maybe I could walk away from everything," she said. "No, maybe I *should* walk away from everything. I definitely could. It's much easier to exit this industry than it is to enter it. I doubt there would be any fanfare. Maybe an article or two about what a loser I am while still being bad for women. But at least then it'd be over. One last pitiful humiliation. I could handle that."

"Birdie Maxwell is not a quitter. Never has been. Never will be."

"But maybe I am. Maybe that's exactly why I ran back to Barton. Maybe all I had was Plan A, and now that I need to pivot to Plan B, I . . . just can't pivot." She cringed when she said *pivot*, and Elliot wondered if she'd been told before to be someone else, to be someone different. He wanted to say that she was exquisite exactly as she was, but then, well, that wasn't his compliment to share anymore.

Still, he wanted to show her that even if he'd been reckless, careless with her heart, he wouldn't be now, if given the chance. He said, "I remember that my mom used to tell me that you should never make a major decision when something hasn't gone your way." He thought of his mother again, a pang reverberating. "I think maybe we don't make any decisions about your career just because something hasn't gone your way."

She squinted out the window and didn't respond for a very long time.

Then she said, "I'm glad you're doing this with me, El. Glad you're keeping me from making major decisions when I shouldn't be."

She reached over and squeezed his bicep, and he moved his left hand atop hers. She lingered in his grip for a minute, maybe two, and Elliot stayed warm to the touch, even long after she pulled away.

Heeeeeey, bitches! Did you see the latest BiRo scuttlebutt? Well, if you haven't, put on your detective hats and pull up a chair! For those of you who have been in a coma for the past few days, America's favorite sweetheart who we now love to hate is on the hunt for an anonymous ex who still holds a torch for her.

Sound like something she scripted?

Yeah, we think so too. A little too on the nose for our taste, and as a few recent emails have revealed, BiRo is chillier than a Chicago winter, not the warm fuzzy who would be out there looking for love. More devious than sweet, that's for SURE. We are totes #teamsebastian on this one.

But in the interest of playing along (and also, let's be real, bitches, we wanna see who this dude IS), we're taking a survey. Enter the poll below to who your best bet is for that sad sack ex who wants to come to BiRo's rescue. (Let's be clear here, if this is legit, we are all in, and are rooting for her happy ending. We're not monsters.)

VOTE HERE:

- 1. Chef Ian Sands
- 2. Simon someone? (Wasn't she bumping uglies up with a hotelier?)

- 3. Kai Carol (never confirmed but we're going with it—what a twist that would be)
- 4. Random dude no one ever saw coming
- 5. She wrote this to herself, don't be played

20

BIRDIE

BIRDIE STILL HADN'T told Elliot about Kai, that he should probably be added to the list of possibilities of who wrote the letter. Kai, Sebastian's brother. Kai, whom she hadn't heard from in several years, since she permanently fled the city they were now barreling toward in this rickety RV. At the time, she told everyone that she couldn't stay sane under the relentless sunshine, but really, she couldn't stay sane when Kai lurked around every studio lot, every West Hollywood coffee spot, every street, every wine bar, every memory.

They were still a ways out from Los Angeles due to traffic, not mileage, and she could have sat on the freeway for hours rather than nose forward to the City of Angels. Her dread had very little to do with Carter. Rather, Los Angeles was complicated for Birdie, who had lived there off and on since her career took off. She only permanently settled in New York once she and Carter split three and a half years ago. So, since she'd been single. Stayed single.

Her phone buzzed again while the RV lurched a few feet forward in traffic every minute or so. Birdie was no mechanic, but she didn't think the engine was exactly purring. Elliot, who was scowling at the dashboard and occasionally smacked the front gauges with the butt of his hand, seemed to agree.

"Please just answer that," Elliot said, pointing at her phone. "I honestly think your team is going to put out a warrant for my arrest if you don't at least give them proof of life."

In the five hours that they'd been on the road, one of Elliot's neighbors had messaged a few times with updates: that one TV van had turned into two; that two had turned into four; that more than he could count on one hand now clogged the street, and their super was out there screaming at them about how this over-stepped freedom of the press. Elliot had laughed at that because his super was, he said, an aging hippie who loved to stick it to the man, but mostly Elliot seemed relieved that no one had realized that they were a hundred and fifty miles down the highway by then. Or maybe Birdie was the one who was relieved. She had to deal with the hassle of photographers from time to time in New York, but mostly, people there, even when they noticed her—and they always did—left her alone. This recent frenzy made her feel a little hunted, made her feel a little out of control, and also, worst of all, made her think of Kai, since he was the one who had taught her how to dodge the cameras, how to manipulate them, how to bait and switch them.

Her phone buzzed again, and this time she answered.

"What was the one thing I asked you to do?" Imani shouted. "I told you to *lie low*. Do you consider lying low showing up at a James Beard winner's restaurant and getting into a spat in front of dozens of diners?"

"Not dozens," Birdie said. She pinched the bridge of her nose and wished she had the ability to unwind time so that she didn't answer the call. Or so that she didn't confront Ian. Or so that she hadn't gotten into it with Sebastian. Why couldn't she have just kept her mouth shut and not gotten into it with Sebastian? They'd be halfway through filming by now, and sure, he'd be leering at the extras and possibly groping a day player or two, but *Jesus fucking Christ*, Imani was right, why couldn't she just *shut up*? What was wrong with her that she simply couldn't get out of her own way? She'd trained herself since leaving Barton: do better than everyone else, be better than everyone else. Somehow, she'd slipped backward into her childhood self who constantly caused Susana to press her lips into that thin, displeased line.

"Birdie," Imani continued, "I am now watching a live shot of TMZ outside an apartment in San Francisco. Please tell me that you are not making plans to emerge and give a statement."

"I am not making plans to emerge and give a statement."

Birdie heard Imani sigh.

"Okay, well, that is at least *good*. Now, is it too much to ask for you to just stay quiet and let me clean this up?"

"It is not too much to ask, no," Birdie said, as Elliot looked toward her with his mouth open. "What did you think of the article, though?"

Imani sighed again. Louder. "I think you can polish shit into a diamond, but it's still just a pile of turds at the end of the day."

Elliot made a sound like he'd never been so insulted, and Birdie held out a finger that matched her glare, which indicated that he should *zip it*. She heard him blow air out of his nose.

"Stay *low*, Birdie," Imani reiterated.

"Chirp-chirp," Birdie whispered and hung up.

"So," Elliot started.

"Well," Birdie said.

"Are you going to tell me about Carter or am I left to assume that he's another turd that I'll polish into a diamond?"

"Oh, just to clarify, she wasn't talking about Ian," Birdie said. "She was talking about your story."

"Birdie!" Elliot thumped the wheel, which accidentally triggered the horn, and the guy in front of them shot his hand out his window with a middle finger.

"Fine," Birdie exhaled. "But to be clear, I *am* lying low. If you want to go talk to Carter, you're on your own."

Birdie had met Carter on her thirtieth birthday. She'd been back in LA full-time by then for several years and had invited Mona to Santa Barbara to celebrate the milestone birthday. Mona had asked if Elliot could join, and Birdie demurred because they hadn't spoken since *that night*. She lied to Mona and said that she really just wanted it to be a girls' trip, and Mona accepted this at face value. Also, Birdie really *did* just want it to be a girls' trip. She and Kai had ended things yet again—and this time permanently, after a fight in his hotel room at the Wynn—when Kai panicked because the tabloids started sniffing around the rumors of the two of them. By then, Kai was on year three of a quasi-engagement: his team had thought he needed a stable, household-friendly woman by his side, and so Kai publicly proposed to his high school sweetheart. *People* magazine put them on their cover. He promised Birdie it was just for show, just to bolster his reputation, that Haley, his fiancée, was in on it, signed a lucrative contract. Stupidly, Birdie decided to believe him. Still, she cut off contact but sometimes caved and took his calls, so didn't quite cut off contact. And she'd gone to his room that night at the Wynn, and once again left single. It had ended mostly on her terms, but was it really her terms when she would have stayed if he'd offered something more than he had?

Kai Carol was the biggest action star on the planet, the yang to Birdie's romantic comedy yin. They'd met on set right as Birdie's celebrity was exploding in her mid-twenties and had danced in and out of each other's lives ever since. Kai mostly did the dancing, to be honest. Birdie mostly did the standing around and waiting. But the breakup at the Wynn, just before Birdie's thirtieth, felt permanent. Birdie needed a weekend with Mona to unwind, to pretend that she hadn't made a catastrophic mistake by getting entangled with Kai Carol in the first place at twenty-five, and then off and on ever since.

Carter was the tennis instructor at the resort. He'd gone pro after college but peaked in the rankings at forty-first in the world and retired when his lower vertebrae refused to forgive him for a punishing match at Indian Wells. He spent weekends in Santa Barbara and ran a private clinic for fancy people in LA. At the resort, Birdie had signed herself and Mona up for a semiprivate lesson—she thought the *thwack* of the racket against the ball would be cathartic—but Mona wanted to sleep in. So Birdie pulled on her tennis whites (she could always dress the part, even if she knew next to nothing about tennis) and made her way in the blinding sunshine to the courts, where Carter welcomed her with a dazzling smile, luminescent dark brown skin that glowed from within, and an unwillingness to go easy on her, despite the fact that he complimented her last film when they met. But he was seemingly completely unimpressed with her fame, nor was he put off by her ambition. By then, Birdie had leaned into this ambition. She no longer apologized for asking for what she wanted on set, she no longer cowered when she was given an executive producer credit and then actually wanted to have input. The girl who had grown up feeling like an outcast in her family discovered that she was actually pretty brilliant, just at something entirely different than what she'd been told mattered. So she relished this curiosity, and she relished the power that came with this curiosity, and she relished her professional contributions, which were unique and unmatched and celebrated. So yes, she leaned *way* into this, even her tantrums, which she thought came as part of the package deal. She'd seen famous men excused as difficult but genius in her industry, and no one held their difficulty against them because the latter canceled out the former. And when she threw her racket and cracked the frame because she hit thirteen backhands in a row into the net while envisioning Kai's face on that stupid yellow ball, Carter barely raised an eyebrow, though he made a passing comment about reining in her temper to improve her mental game.

All of this she found sexy. Extremely, incredibly sexy. So she paid for a three-hour block of lessons the next day before finally giving him her number and asking him to call her back in LA. He did that Monday. She was impressed with his no BS games even more than with his backhand or the way his quad muscle popped when he ran to the net.

Carter now lived in a small bungalow in Silver Lake, which, much like San Francisco, was hilly and winding and dizzying. Elliot had to consult the map on his phone four times before they finally turned down the right street and tottered by the well-appointed house with a lacquered navy door and well-maintained topiaries, and Birdie felt something like an ache for Carter. Still not a strong enough ache to convince her to confront him. If anything, the ache convinced her to leave it alone—why ruin something beautiful with reality?

Birdie and Elliot swapped places in the RV because he had to take a bathroom break—Birdie tried *extremely hard* not to look in the rearview mirror toward the bathroom door that didn't quite close, but she did catch a quick glimpse of his naked waistline before snapping her eyes forward. There was no parking because there was never any parking in Los Angeles, so she circled the area for a solid thirty minutes while Elliot, back in the passenger seat, groaned and griped and moaned about his deadline. As far as Birdie was concerned, they could have circled the block all day. The sun would set in a couple of hours, and then they could just slip into the darkness as if they were never here. Her pulse was beating loudly in her neck, and her mouth was as dry as her palms were sweaty, but still, she wasn't going to see Carter; she wasn't going to step into this any deeper than she already had. She sighed, and Elliot sighed louder.

"I hate Los Angeles," Elliot said, as if complaining made finding a parking spot on the street any easier. "Just breathing in its air makes me crazy."

"Too much sunshine for you?" she said. "Too many beautiful women?"

"Ha," he said just once, though he didn't deny the latter. Birdie knew she shouldn't be envious of all the other women he'd slept with, but she was envious all the same.

"You know Hollywood," he said. "Fun for about three days, then you wake up in the Valley and realize you're crashing in a house where they shot a porno."

"Well, you'd have to have watched the porno to know such things."

Elliot half grinned. "Fair point," he said. "If you ever need a recommendation—"

"You should know more important people," Birdie cut him off because getting porn recommendations from Elliot was honestly just a bridge too far right now. "If you're crashing at a porno house in Van Nuys, you don't know the important people."

Elliot cocked an eyebrow and let it go. Birdie wasn't quite sure what she was insinuating. That if he'd called her up, back when she'd lived here, he could have crashed with her? They'd tried that once. He left.

"It's not the porno houses I mind," he said, and Birdie thought, *Well, that figures*. "But it's just an endless string of highways connecting people whose ambition outsizes their talent. It's just a complete land of make-believe."

"Ouch," she said. "Brutal."

"Not you," he said.

"I live in New York now. So I don't take it personally."

Elliot nodded and said nothing else because they both knew exactly where she lived now.

They circled the block two more times until Birdie took a sharp left down a side street and blessedly found a stretch of about a hundred feet of free sidewalk.

"Okay, well, good luck in there," Birdie said.

"You're seriously not coming in?"

"I am seriously not coming in. I don't know why you thought I'd have changed my mind." She reached for her phone in the cup holder and held it aloft toward him. Dozens of notifications littered the screen. "I told Imani I was staying low, so I am."

"You also told Imani that you were huddled up in my apartment in San Francisco, so I'm not quite ready to award you with a medal for nobility."

Birdie shrugged. Elliot made a show of unclicking his seat belt while shaking his head in frustration.

"Well, you can't blame me if you don't like what I write, then," he said.

Birdie thought that she could blame him for whatever she wanted to and started to say as much, but then that was probably an entirely different conversation. And sitting in front of Carter's house while wearing Elliot's oxford button-down with memories of Kai swimming around her cerebral cortex was not the time to say any of it. For someone who had never set out to tie herself to a man, Birdie thought, she certainly had stitched herself into plenty of knots.

"Okay," he tried again. "Can you at least tell me why it didn't work out? Or why you thought maybe he would have sent the letter?"

Birdie didn't really think that Carter *had* sent the letter. But Elliot had mentioned him when pitching her the idea, and, well, it was easier not to correct him. She wouldn't mind hiding out in his bungalow with its navy blue door and rosebushes. It wouldn't be the love-swept ending that one of her writers would dream up, but Birdie was ready to settle for a little less. What had she told Mona back in the bar about Nelson? People settled for a little less every day, all the time. If Carter had written the letter, Birdie resolved, she'd embrace it, not just for the good press (because there would be good press) but because he was also a good man.

The truth was, though, Birdie couldn't think of anything that Carter would regret. Theirs had been a diplomatic, grown-up ending. The best type you could hope for, really. Yes, he'd been the one to end things with her, though it was more of an understanding. He'd wanted kids and a family, and Birdie hadn't, probably still didn't. There wasn't much middle ground once that was established. But they had an ease between them that she hadn't felt in a long time. Carter was funny and smart and obviously athletic, and they had fabulous sex. In hindsight, maybe Birdie was looking for an off-ramp from the mess of Kai and the lingering residue of Elliot, the thought of whom still bruised her, and so she and Carter fell into each other, and it worked until falling into each other wasn't enough for him.

"Last chance," Elliot said. He hesitated in the passenger seat and met her eyes, and Birdie saw his chest rise and fall, and she knew hers was beating in time too.

"I'm not budging." She shrugged.

"A woman who knows what she wants," he replied, like that was some sort of answer.

Then he opened the RV door, jumped out like he was parachuting into a war zone, and was gone.

21

ELLIOT

ELLIOT HAD ABSOLUTELY no idea what he was doing when he marched up to Carter's lacquered blue door and knocked three times, then popped back down the steps to wait. It was rare that he felt discombobulated at work or really, actually, at anything, but he had expected Birdie to cave, and now he was just some sort of lecherous gossip reporter beating down the door of one of her exes. This wasn't what he had pitched Francesca, and though he knew he could zig when he thought he'd be zagging, mostly he was thinking of Birdie in that striped blue oxford of his and how the only thing he wanted to do was pop each button one by one and certainly not give an ex of hers the fourth degree to see if he wanted to get back together.

The truth was that Birdie Maxwell made Elliot crazy. She had since forever. She continued to do so. He didn't know why he thought that this assignment would be any different. He'd been a fool to believe that she could just be *work*, just another story. Birdie had never been just another anything.

The front door to Carter's home swung open, and Elliot

sincerely began to regret his choice, much like he began to sweat around his neck as panic crept in over this entire calamity. He could be back in the RV, giving Birdie a pep talk, giving Birdie a massage, giving Birdie . . . He told himself to focus, to take this as seriously as an embedded piece in the Middle East. Then he glanced up the three steps of the stoop and found himself staring at a ridiculously gorgeous Black man who had at least five inches on Elliot and a wingspan that anyone on Elliot's swim team would envy. He was in a white T-shirt and tapered gray sweat-pants and barefoot and grinning, as if he was delighted that someone had rung his doorbell, and as if he was delighted that the someone was Elliot O'Brien.

"I thought you might show up," he said, his velvet voice filled with nothing but joy. "But where's my girl? No offense, she's much easier on the eyes than you."

"Elliot O'Brien," Elliot stammered, scooting up the stairs, ex-tending a hand, which Carter shook; then he wrapped his other palm around their grasp because he was that welcoming. Elliot decided he hated him, this beautiful man who got to sleep with Birdie for the better part of a year. This beautiful man who had been ranked forty-first in the world on the ATP.

"I came without her," Elliot lied because he needed to prove to Birdie that he was an intrepid reporter all on his own. He was. He had Pulitzers! Or nominations anyway. Why was he out here trying to prove himself to a girl he'd slept with seven years ago? Why was he swimming in envy at this beautiful specimen in front of him, who was whisking him into his house with nothing but graciousness?

Birdie Maxwell was dangerous, Elliot thought. Birdie Max-well scrambled his fucking brain.

Carter led him through the house, which was tastefully

decorated and not at all like Elliot's embarrassing crashpad, and out to the backyard, where a dog, a midsized mutt of some sort, yapped and hurled itself toward him. Elliot tried to pat its head to calm it down, but it wasn't the type of dog that seemed interested in being calmed, so it spun in circles and then launched itself into the pool.

"Oh, ignore Lucy," Carter said. "She's working through some things."

Elliot liked how he said that: that she was working through some things. Weren't they all? But then he caught himself liking Carter and felt like he was walking into a trap. Carter stepped back into the kitchen and returned with two Amstels. He gestured to the teak chairs and table.

"I suppose you're here because I'm on Birdie's list," he said, getting straight to the point.

"You've seen the news?" Elliot also sat up straighter, put on his reporter voice. *Damn you, Birdie*, he did have a TV reporter voice.

"I think you'd have to be a mole person not to have seen the news," Carter said. "And actually, they've probably seen it too. Poor Bird."

"Well, this was her idea," Elliot replied. "So she knew what she was getting into."

Carter chewed on this for a beat. "I suppose that's true, but the Birdie I knew tended to think that she could always rewrite her story, and maybe she thinks—or thought—she could do the same here. With that prick."

"Ian?"

"Oh god, no, not him. Have you ever eaten at his restaurant? He is a magician. Best mussels on the planet."

Elliot laughed despite himself. Muscles. Mussels. Hearing it objectively, he could see how Birdie had gotten it wrong. *Sweet dreams are made of cheese.* He wished very much that she were here doing this beside him, and not just because he thought he might fall in love with Carter if he lingered too long. The man was that amiable.

"Ah. You mean Sebastian Carol," Elliot said. "He is indeed a prick."

Carter started to say something but stopped himself. He raised two fingers to his lips as if caught in a thought. Elliot took it as an opportunity.

"So was it you?"

That smile again. Dammit. A slight shake of his head. "I've gotten a few texts asking the same thing today."

"That is not an answer to the question," Elliot said, irked that he was dodging, irked that it annoyed him that Carter's friends were raising the same suspicions. Birdie was meant to be *his*. The clarity of that idea alarmed him, so he corrected himself: no, that was just a narrative he'd spent his childhood buying into. They'd had their shot. One of them, maybe him, maybe her, had blown it.

"People have long memories when you date the most famous woman on the planet," Carter said.

"She's not the most famous woman on the planet. Think of Michelle Obama. Oprah. Taylor Swift."

"Well, no one thinks I've dated Michelle Obama." Carter grinned again, and his whole face danced with joy. "But that would be a dream."

Elliot laughed again in spite of himself. If he weren't still stuck on Birdie in the RV in his button-down, he'd probably be rooting for Carter too.

"But you still haven't answered the question. Did you send her an unsigned love letter?"

It was at this exact moment that Lucy launched out of the pool and careened right toward Elliot, as if she could sense that her owner needed a moment to gather himself. Carter jumped to his feet and grabbed a towel from the other side of the patio, but not before Lucy could shake herself off violently, coating Elliot in damp doggy pool water.

"Sorry." Carter laughed, handing him the towel. "Indoctrination by Lucy."

"And a perfect excuse to keep me in suspense," Elliot said, dancing his voice between official reporter and nice guy who wasn't trying to prod. (He was, but he tried to modulate his tone accordingly.)

"I've never been interested in that fame stuff," Carter said, like he was offering an explanation. "In my experience, fame is like food left out on the counter a day too long."

"Rotting? Attractive to fruit flies?"

There it was again, the deep bellow of a laugh. Elliot thought he might crater from envy. This man who was so comfortable in himself, so content with his damp feral dog and a beer. "Something like that," he said. "More like: gets old fast, then it starts to stink."

"I feel like I'm missing something here, like there are parts of the story we're skipping right over," Elliot said. He'd patted himself off by now, but Lucy was plunked by his feet and her wet dog smell was curdling his stomach. Or it could have been his jealousy.

Carter hummed under his breath, taking his time, mulling his answer. "I didn't write her a letter," he said finally. "I'm engaged."

"Oh," Elliot said, and was surprised at the relief that flooded over him. "Congratulations."

"But even before then," Carter said. "I love Birdie, she's the greatest, but . . ." He drifted and stared over Elliot's shoulder, then stood to get an errant tennis ball in the corner of the yard. "Lucy!" he called, and the dog was up with a start, then threw herself back into the pool to retrieve the ball. Elliot's phone buzzed in his pocket at the same time she landed with a tidal-wave splash, which served as an excuse to step inside and slide the glass door closed. As it was, he likely reeked from Lucy's first dousing; he wasn't going to sit around and wait for an encore.

"Yeah?" he asked. This was how he and Mona often greeted each other. A term of both endearment and sibling annoyance. He glanced around Carter's kitchen. High-end appliances, a fancy espresso machine, a KitchenAid mixer that looked new and was probably an engagement present. Elliot had flitted through enough registries to know one when he saw one.

"How's it going?" Mona asked. He could hear the edge in her voice.

"It's going fine," he said. "But I'm sort of in the middle of—"

"I read the Ian piece," she interrupted. "I wouldn't say it's going *fine.*

"'When Mr. Sands realized that Ms. Robinson was there to see him, his posture went rigid, the tone of his voice—and the entire restaurant—turned chilly,'" Mona read. "'The patrons of Chez Nous fell deathly quiet as the revered chef berated Ms. Robinson for having the gall to show up to his establishment, but more so, to reopen wounds that he clearly had barely managed to stitch closed. Once he was in front of Birdie—or she in front of him—blood was about to be spilled.'"

"Hey, if her exes are mad, I can't exactly control that," Elliot said. The excuse felt flimsy as soon as it was out of his mouth. This was why he preferred the page. He could be deliberate and think things all the way through on the page.

"Well, that doesn't mean you have to leave her out there to

dry," Mona batted back. "She was blindsided. What good does this do if she's blindsided?"

"Whose side are you on?" he asked. "And didn't you read the second half or did you make up your mind in the first paragraph? I made it quite clear that she was contrite, falling all over herself with apologies."

"We both know that Birdie didn't do any of that," she said.

"That's because we know her. But the world does not." Elliot stepped toward the stainless-steel refrigerator, which had pictures tacked up on its door, just like his mom used to have when he was in high school. Carter with a stunning Black woman on the beach, with Lucy posing between them. Carter and his fiancée at what looked like Wimbledon. The two of them at the Colosseum in Rome. He'd built an entire life without Birdie, had seemingly moved on totally unscathed. Elliot found that he had a whole world of questions for him entirely unrelated to the letter. Questions like: *How? How on earth did you do that?*

"It's your assignment to ensure that the world *does*," she said.

"Why are you so goddamn invested in this?" Elliot spun back toward the glass door. Carter was toweling Lucy off, which made it slightly safer for him to step back outside.

"Why aren't you *more* invested in this?" Mona snapped. "She's out there publicly drowning, and you, you've never failed at a thing in your life. The least you could do is have her back when she is."

Elliot blew out his breath and told himself that this, right now, was the time to tell her about the tenuous job situation. That he had his own set of troubles. That, oh, also, this whole deal with Birdie was complicated and messy and he was doing the best he could to lean into every ounce of his willpower but maybe that wouldn't work this time.

"Hello?" Mona bleated. "Are you just ignoring me, ignoring my constructive criticism?"

"I'm in the middle of something, Mona, you can't just call me and order me around."

Mona sighed like she absolutely could but would humor him for now. "Fine. Where are you guys?"

"LA. Carter. I'm actually in his—"

"Oh," Mona interrupted, her voice both lighter and still all business. "Yeah, he's not your guy. You're wasting your time there."

"How would you know *that*?" Elliot was irritated all over again: if she knew how to report this story, maybe she should be out here doing it alongside him and Birdie.

"I know a lot of things that you're not privy to," Mona said. "I know that seems impossible to believe—"

"I'm not doing this with you right now," Elliot said. "I don't need your diatribe. When I have a few things to lecture you about myself."

"Fine."

"Fine," he said.

"*Fine,*" she hissed.

They hung up on each other simultaneously.

Elliot took a deep breath and focused. He opened up the back door to the patio, where Carter was now seated, nursing his beer and scrolling through his phone.

"So it wasn't you," Elliot said.

"Birdie and I had a great thing," he replied like it was simple math. "But she was always more interested in losing herself to the story on the page, not the one she and I were writing."

"Sounds like something you could regret."

Carter bellowed that infectious laugh. "You really don't like to take no for an answer. My fiancée's a lawyer; you two would get along."

"I sense that there's a *but* coming."

Carter sighed, seemed to chew it over, then said, "But there was always someone else."

"Someone else?" Elliot felt his breath catch in his chest.

"She wasn't cheating. I don't mean that. There was someone else, *emotionally*." He paused. "I never had the full her. For a while, I thought it was, you know, that thing she does when she's half-present—losing herself to her characters, that whole other made-up life. But it was someone real. And, you know what, that was fine. Not everything is meant to be *everything*."

Elliot nodded, trying to keep his cool.

"I can see that she didn't mention this to you," Carter said, rising from his chair as if maybe he'd just realized it was time to escort Elliot out.

"No," he said, keeping his professional voice steady. "She did not."

"Ah, well, I'm not in the business of divulging my friend's secrets," Carter said.

"Come on," Elliot said. "You can't just shoot me a blind item like that."

Carter grinned, which turned into another bellow. "Welcome to the conundrum of Birdie Robinson. She tells you only what she wants, which only makes you want it more." They were at his front door now, Lucy by Carter's side, as if she, too, understood that Elliot was a wolf in sheep's clothing.

Carter swung open the beautiful blue lacquered door and offered Elliot a firm shake of his hand.

"Give Birdie my love," he said, and Elliot knew that he meant it. "I'm here for her in any way I can be supportive. I miss that girl in a way you miss your annoying little sister once you move out. Which is to say, my door is always open."

Then he closed the actual door behind him, and Elliot heard the bolt latch. In other circumstances, with anyone else, Elliot would have bounded back up the steps and pounded on the door for more, but his mind was spinning, his heart close to exploding from the adrenaline rush. He'd barely heard Carter's good tidings because all he could think was: *me me me me me.*

He stood there frozen. What if . . . Birdie had been out here pining for him all these years? Just like he had been for her. What did he do next, then, if it was him all along?

22

BIRDIE

BIRDIE WAS BLASTING the radio to Gloria Gaynor and sing-ing along when she thought she saw a woman walking a golden retriever do a double take. No, she definitely saw a woman walking a golden retriever do a double take. She didn't know what was taking Elliot so long—how long did it take to ask Carter a simple question?—but she wasn't about to wait around for the paparazzi in Los Angeles, who could find a vulnerable celebrity just about anywhere they didn't want to be found, to hunt her down. She shoved the key into the ignition and spun it with righteous dramatic flair while Gloria belted, "I will survive!"

In high school, it was not hyperbole to say that Birdie and Mona *lived* for this song. And so she turned it up louder and thought of her best friend, and how, of the two of them, everyone probably (and reasonably) thought that Mona would be the grand success. She wondered now if Mona was happy with Nelson Pratt, if she was happy living in her old house, if she was happy running Monads. Birdie had always aspired for *more more more*, which was what she probably found so seductive about dating

Kai Carol, and which was probably what tricked her into believing that once she was on top of the world, she'd never stumble downward. How easy it had been, though. To somersault to the bottom.

"You think I'd tumble, you think I'd lay down and cry?" she shouted, then remembered Mona correcting her. *Crumble*, Birdie. *Die, not cry*. Well, she wouldn't do those things either.

The dog owner who had gaped was definitely filming her now while her golden ate a neighbor's grass, so she peeled the RV away from the curb and figured Elliot would call her when he was done. She careened around a corner, narrowly missing a Mercedes SUV, then overcorrecting and nearly shaving the mirror off a minivan. A man out powerwalking shouted, "Slow down, kids live here!" and Birdie ducked lower in her seat, which was not conducive to better driving. She turned another corner and hit a dead end. She tried not to think that this was some sort of metaphor, some sort of sign. She backed up, moved forward, backed up, moved forward, like a painfully slow snail who was trying to U-turn its way out of a jam. The RV's engine made an alarming clattering sound, as if it wanted to alert the entire neighborhood that Birdie Robinson was out here attempting a road maneuver that she should leave to her stuntwoman, but Birdie was undeterred. *Nobody puts Birdie Robinson in a corner*, she thought, as she often did when she needed to lose herself to someone else's narrative.

Finally, she righted the camper, which was definitely unhappy with her—the clattering was more of a rumble, and if anyone nearby had been napping, they were surely awake now and wondering if a plane might land on their lawn—but she pressed her foot on the gas and tried to pretend that she was Thelma or Louise. Getting the hell out of Dodge either way. She lumbered the RV up to Carter's house, where Elliot was on the sidewalk holding his phone aloft, likely trying to get a signal, then waving her down like she couldn't see him plainly in front of her.

He flung open the door and huffed up the steps, looking frazzled, sighing with an exasperated flair. He reached for the volume just as Gloria was wrapping up her anthem and dialed it down to silent.

"Hey," Birdie snapped. "That is the perfect song."

Elliot rolled his eyes like he didn't remember how cute she and Mona were in carpool. *Well, la-di-da*, Birdie thought, then said, "Sorry if you're pissy because I kept your ass waiting." Her tone implied she wasn't at all sorry. He wasn't the one out here being filmed; he wasn't the one out here being judged.

"It's fine," Elliot said, like it wasn't. Birdie was now well aware that something had shifted in the half hour that he'd been gone, and honestly, she didn't think she had the energy to ask him what it was. If he wanted to tell her, then fine. But she wasn't going to drag it out of him like she thought he wanted her to. She was the one with problems here. She was the one who needed counsel and open ears and shoulders on which to lean.

"It was like two minutes," Birdie replied and turned the volume back up, but the station was now playing some croony seventies song that she didn't recognize, so her entire rock diva vibe was now ruined. "Sorry that you had to wait, like, two minutes."

"I thought you had ditched me," he said, but it sounded like an accusation, not an explanation, which rankled Birdie even more.

"Why are you being such a jerk?" she asked. "Like *I apologize* that some lady was filming me, so I went around the block."

"I'm not being a jerk."

"Right there. That tone. That's jerkish."

"Do you want to hear if Carter regrets it or do you want to argue with me over if my tone offends you?" he asked.

"Do I want to argue with you . . . over if your tone *offends* me?" Birdie raised her voice. "Is that supposed to be an olive branch over your slightly less offensive tone?"

She was racing down the winding Silver Lake roads, knowing they had a limited window before her anonymity ran out, and ran straight through a stop sign. In her defense, she didn't see the mini Cooper that slammed on its brakes just before it nearly T-boned into the side of the RV, and Elliot clutched his armrests and shouted, "Holy shit! I've had safer drives in Afghanistan!" which Birdie took as a reminder that he was doing her a favor here. Which she hadn't asked for. Or maybe she had. But she didn't want it to feel like she owed him at all.

She finally hit Sunset Boulevard and crossed two lanes at once aiming for the freeway exit.

"Where are you even going?" Elliot bleated. "Why are you driving like we've robbed a bank? What exactly did you do in the thirty minutes that I was gone?"

Birdie didn't know herself, so she certainly didn't want to explain herself to Elliot. She only knew that if Carter's neighbor posted a photo of her behind the wheel of Mona's Winnebago, then she really wouldn't have any peace, and yes, she knew that ostensibly she had embarked on this endeavor to drum up the very publicity she was now fleeing—but, as she would have said to Mona when she forced her into playing hooky for a day, *Life comes at you fast.*

"I'm going home," she said, which she hadn't even meant to say, but there it was.

"To New York? You're driving us back to New York in this thing?"

As if on cue, the motor let out a belch, and Birdie held her breath wondering if the RV was going to blow. Maybe that was just something that happened in movies, but she couldn't be sure, having never driven such a monstrosity, much less having never driven a monstrosity with an engine that sounded like it last had a tune-up when she was still in diapers.

"Not to New York," Birdie said. "Barton."

"So Barton is now home? Interesting," he replied.

"What's that supposed to—" Birdie hissed, then stopped herself. She knew exactly what it was supposed to mean. That she only fled to Barton when it was convenient. That she only considered it home when it was on her terms. She didn't know why Elliot was judging. He wasn't all that different. She thwacked her blinker and lunged over one more lane, just narrowly missing a Tesla, toward the ramp to the freeway. She knew that Elliot was swallowing whatever he wanted to say about her driving, which— and she knew this wasn't great, okay?—made her drive even more erratically. He was grunting and hemming and hawing and blowing air out of his nose until, finally, they were through the slug of traffic on the ramp and into the slug of traffic on the four-lane highway.

They sat there, unmoving, and occasionally inching forward, in silence. Birdie could feel his irritation radiating off him, and she hoped that he could intuit her own. She didn't even know what she was angry with, but it was like an acting exercise from her early days: you mirrored the emotion of the partner in front of you, and eventually "hello" became "*hello*," which became "*HELLO*," and suddenly you were screaming *HELLO* in a stew of rage that hadn't been there at the start.

The sun was starting to dip in the sky when Elliot sighed, fidgeted, and sighed again.

Finally, he asked, "Who was the other guy who was around when you were with Carter?"

"What?" She felt her breath quicken. She didn't know what Carter had said, but she wasn't expecting this. "I never cheated on Carter." Was this why Elliot was angry? "And besides, who are you to point fingers about juggling?"

"I didn't say anything about cheating." He was using his stupid reporter voice again. "And I didn't ask anything about juggling. So you don't get to make this about me."

"I have no idea what you're talking about," she said. She did, though.

"What is it that you're not telling me?"

"Elliot, I have been an open book!" She was overcorrecting, going too dramatic. She knew this would be the director's note— *We need you to pare it back about ten degrees, Birdie, let's go again on one*—but she couldn't help herself.

"Then why is Carter dropping blind items, why is Carter telling me that you were never his because there was always someone else?" His voice was no longer level. Birdie would have been turned on if she weren't genuinely irritated about what he'd intimated previously, that he was the one with the clean track record, that he was the one who was wholly honest, completely forthcoming.

The windows were down, and Birdie knew that their voices were carrying in the clog of traffic. She needed to be more prudent; it was only a matter of time before someone heard her, spotted her, called the media. It was so exhausting, never having anything for herself. She reached for his baseball hat on the dashboard and slapped it on her head.

"You don't get to do that," he said. "Hide."

"I'm not hiding from you," she said. Though that could have been it too.

"Then *who*?" he shouted. "How am I expected to write this story if you're not being honest with me?"

Birdie didn't want to say it. She wanted him to ask it. She wanted him to say: *Was it me? Who you were pining over?* Just so she could have the satisfaction of saying *no*. Even if that wasn't entirely true. Deep down, she had been pining for him nearly her whole life. But she found that in the heat of the moment, she wanted to cut him, bruise him, hurt him so that he knew what it felt like.

Because seven years later, he still had the power to take her breath away.

23

ELLIOT

ELLIOT WANTED TO tell Birdie to slow down, that the last thing they needed was to have some overzealous cop pull over a rickety motor home and discover that the most famous actress in the world was flying up the 405, but it had been an hour, and they still weren't speaking. And he wasn't going to be the first one to break, even though it wasn't a tough ask for him to apologize. But if he apologized, he'd have to explain that he was behaving like a jealous twit, and if he admitted that he was behaving like a jealous twit, then she'd be well within her rights to ask why, and then all his emotions would spill wide open onto the RV floor.

Also, he couldn't discount the fact that maybe he was acting a little melodramatic because, well, Birdie Maxwell made him crazy. So he wasn't in a generous enough mood to forge a peace anyway. And he certainly wasn't in a mood to pass along Carter's hellos, to tell her about the fiancée, to say that he thought Carter could be a good friend to her if she ever wanted to open herself up to him again.

Instead, they simply did not speak. Not when an eighties station played Queen and reminded them both of their carpool days in high school. Not when Birdie was desperate to pee and rather than pull to the side of the road and ask Elliot to drive so she could run to the back of the RV, she veered to the off-ramp too quickly and nearly leveled a car in each lane as she did. She careened into a pitstop parking spot, hopped out, donning extra-large sunglasses and his Cal hat tilted at an angle, and returned fifteen minutes later with Diet Coke and Mentos and an over-sized bag of Cheetos, which she was already eating when she sunk back into the driver's seat.

She caught him staring and said, "I guess you don't remember. This is my surprised face."

He didn't remember whatever it was that he was supposed to remember, so he stared at her wonderfully beautiful face, though he knew that wasn't the point, and she stared at him, and naturally, because Birdie had never lost a staring contest even when they were kids, he wilted first and flopped into the passenger seat.

She flipped the key in the ignition and turned up the radio, and they lumbered toward their hometown. After another thirty minutes of silence, he made a show of moving to the well-worn dinette table behind her seat and banged his keyboard loudly enough to let her know that even the infuriating Birdie Robinson couldn't stymie his discipline. If she didn't want to talk, then they wouldn't talk. Who said he needed her for the story? Who said that he needed her *at all*?

Elliot ran his hands over his cheeks, cracked his knuckles, and redoubled his efforts until he had a semi-decent workable draft, but he was mostly distracted by the fact that he was still circling Carter's hint about another man, and that his heart lurched constantly with the desperate hope that it was him. He glanced forward and watched her lick the Cheeto dust off her fingertips, and it was so human, so real, so normal, that he knew damn well he wasn't going to abandon that hope anytime soon, even if it was for the best for his career, even if it was for the best with Mona. Even if, even if, even if. He watched her blow out her breath, then straighten her spine, then hunch over and sigh all over again.

Finally, she turned and said, "Look, don't take this as a truce because we are still fighting, but I think there's something wrong with this stupid truck."

"We're not *fighting*," he started, then stopped, because actually, that was exactly what they were doing. "I just don't like—"

The engine made an alarming popping sound, and the RV sputtered and lurched.

"Shit." Elliot felt his eyebrows skew. "What was *that*?"

"Do I look like a mechanic?" Birdie bleated. "It's not my fault that Mona hasn't taken it for a tune-up in a decade."

The engine belched again, followed by an endless fwop fwop fwop, and something smelling like an erupted volcano filtered through the air-conditioning vents. And Elliot, who had been in plenty of dubious vehicles all over the world, began to worry the thing was poised to explode.

"Pull over! The next exit is right there," he shouted over the increasingly loud fwops. He jumped into her eyeline and pointed. "I'm not going to die in the middle of nowhere California."

"You think that I'm trying to kill you?" she shouted. "I didn't even want to drive! I don't even know *how* to drive. I never agreed to this RV in the first place!"

"Your driving is only part of the problem!"

"What are the rest of my problems?" she yelled, peeling over, then barely making the exit ramp.

"How much time do you have before we end up in a ditch?"

Elliot started compiling a mental list of all the ways she'd aggrieved him, all the ways she pushed his buttons, all the things she did that were just so goddamn infuriating. But then he considered that the brakes on his sister's hunk of junk could go along with the engine, and because he was a reporter through and through, he grabbed his laptop and uploaded the draft of tomorrow's story to the *Times* server in case the entire vehicle blew or they landed upside down and unconscious on the side of the road and his words were lost forever. He'd make his deadline if it literally killed him.

Birdie wrestled the RV into a deserted lot off the highway, the wheels or the engine or some sort of exhaust pipe now braying out its dissatisfaction. The smell of sulfur filled the cabin, and Birdie raised the collar of Elliot's button-down over her nose, then Elliot did the same with his own sweatshirt. She unlatched her seat belt and threw herself down the steps to assess the damage outside. Elliot gave it a beat because he was still feeling testy, then followed.

The front of the camper was smoking. Actually smoking. Birdie stood out in front with her hands curled into fists and pressed into her hips, like she was about to scold the engine.

"Now what?" she said, as a low but audible hiss emerged from somewhere that neither of them could identify.

"I guess we pop the hood?" Elliot said.

Birdie swiveled her head toward him and scrunched every muscle in her face.

"Am I supposed to know how to do that?" she asked. "I barely knew how to drive up until like a day ago when it was foisted upon me."

He wanted to remind her that he was pretty certain she had

played a down-on-her-luck mechanic in a film half a decade ago, but it didn't seem like the time. Also, he very much wanted to point out that this entire situation was her suggestion—the way to redeem herself in the eyes of America—but she wasn't totally off base that she hadn't actually suggested the road trip, and she certainly hadn't suggested the ancient Winnebago that he probably couldn't even sell for parts. Not that Mona would let him.

Elliot gingerly stepped forward toward the engine. He thought he'd feel around to see if there was some sort of latch, some sort of button to push. But when he was a few inches away, he could feel the heat emanating from the hood. He wasn't exactly sure what that foretold, but he tried to sound like he was an expert, like he wasn't rattled the way that Birdie appeared to be.

"I think maybe a belt snapped," he said with gravitas.

"You think maybe a belt snapped?"

"Or it could be the oil."

"It could be the oil?" she repeated.

"Possibly needs some fluid? Water?" Elliot tried again.

"So." Birdie flapped her arms around. "It could be anything? That's what you meant to say. It could be anything, and for once in your life, you have no actual idea?"

"I have an idea!"

"Admit that you have *no* idea."

"I have plenty of ideas!" Elliot echoed. "I just listed three of them!"

Birdie shook her head and stomped back into the RV, then stomped back out with her phone in her hand. She punched at the screen, then held it up to her ear. Then she lowered it again and said, "Great, no signal. Do you have a signal?"

"Why, are you calling your mystery man to save us?" Elliot snipped, then felt his eyes go wide because he couldn't believe that came out of his mouth. *Mortification.* Elliot O'Brien was known for being grace under literal pressure, and Birdie had reduced him to *this.*

She narrowed her eyes at him. "Are you, like, twelve?"

Twelve! If Elliot were twelve, he'd be running around his front yard with her, gawky and unselfconscious. They'd be playing capture the flag until dusk, when his mom would call them into the house, and Birdie would trail them because she never wanted to head home, where she felt like an outcast. She'd pile into Mona's bed at night, and Elliot would sit on the floor, and they'd try to tell each other creepy stories until one got too scary, and Birdie would tell him to shut up and stop, and Elliot would because he wanted to prove to her that he was her match but also never wanted to upset her. So now, yes, Elliot could only wish he were twelve and things were that simple. At least things were pure and easy in the way that they can be in late adolescence before you grew up and the world got so much messier.

"Also," Birdie added, "*you* left *me.* Has your brain completely blocked that out? Do we need to fact-check this with someone at your paper? Because if you're jealous or childish or whatever the hell this is, *you* left *me.*" She marched off to look for a signal in one of the far corners of the parking lot.

No. Elliot hadn't blocked it out. Not one bit. Not for even one day. But she had pushed him out, nearly *kicked* him out, and he wasn't about to spill his guts that morning when she was holding the door wide open. Now he should tell her the truth of his feelings after all this time, of how far he'd go if he was given the chance to act on them again. Maybe he'd write her a love letter. Maybe he'd put it down on paper and tell her that she was both his biggest mistake and his best chance for happiness. Maybe he could do something to fix all this. But also, Birdie was rewriting history again, like she had decided to give notes on their story arc.

"Hey," he shouted across the parking lot before he could over-think it. "*You* kicked *me* out that morning!"

Birdie made a face at him from a hundred feet away like either she couldn't hear him or he was completely pathological, and El-liot wasn't interested in asking which.

He sighed and checked his phone, which also had no service. He turned around with his hand aloft, waiting desperately for bars to appear on his screen. The sun had nearly set by now, and unless another traveler rolled in with a working cell phone, Elliot realized they were going to be marooned here until morning, when it would be safe to walk toward the highway and flag some-one down.

"Well," he said, calling toward her, trying to hold his voice steady. "I guess this is when an RV comes in handy."

"When's *that*?" she yelled back, like she preferred the expanse of concrete between them.

"When you have to sleep over by the side of the road for the night."

Now Elliot could see her face clearly, and she was looking at him like he had lost his fucking mind, but then she tilted her head back and screamed, her voice reverberating over the pavement and out into the void of the surrounding dead air.

"The only time in my life that I've wanted to be noticed, we're absolutely screwed."

"That's not true," he said, walking toward her.

"We're not screwed?"

"No, we may be," he conceded. "But the noticing part. There was a long time when that's what you wanted." He had to stop himself from saying *and I was the only one who did*. But he was being snide, not sentimental, and she knew it. "It's one night, Birdie," Elliot chided, his TV voice making another appearance. "We've spent plenty of nights together in smaller quarters." He meant, of course, in Mona's room when they were kids, but as soon as he said it, he realized that they could finally, really, fully and completely, be talking about their one-night stand.

Birdie went statue still, and he knew that she was thinking about it too. She turned and stormed back into the RV, closing the door behind her, as if Elliot were going to have to work harder to join her.

He titled his head back and fought back his own urge to scream. He didn't want to let Birdie know how much she still got to him, how easily she still rattled him, how she was the only person who ever made him feel vulnerable, exposed. He gritted his teeth and doubled down: focus on the work, focus on being the best goddamn reporter in Francesca's arsenal, focus on his salary, which would be down to zero if he blew this. All he needed to do was keep this aboveboard for a few more days, keep his distance for a few more days.

How difficult could that be?

24

BIRDIE

BIRDIE WOKE AT sunrise in the middle of a dream, her phone vibrating like it was looking for a fight. Cell service had come back up last night once darkness had set in, but by then, any nearby repair shop was closed, and Elliot left three messages on different auto shop voicemails before giving up. Now she patted down the sheets until she found her phone and cracked a crusty eye to check the screen: 6:53 a.m. Too early.

Five missed calls from Imani.

It was never good news when there were five missed calls from Imani.

In the bunk bed above her, Elliot shifted in his sleep, and the springs in the twenty-year-old mattress groaned. She'd fallen asleep before him last night, if you could call what she did sleep. Elliot had tried to forge a truce by making dinner. Mona had stocked the cabinets with some basics for her weekend trips, so he pulled out an ancient-looking stockpot, croaked on the faucet in the sink, and jump-started the pilot light on the stove. He dumped in a box of penne and popped open a jar of Ragù. Birdie thought of Ian, and how he used to cook for her when she needed not just nutrition but nourishment. She should have called him when she knew it was over after Elliot's mom's funeral. She should have told him something rather than telling him nothing. He'd taken care of her, and she'd been selfish and squandered that, and when she met Kai, she'd convinced herself that she didn't need taking care of, which was an easy excuse for knowing that she was compromising herself. But everyone needed taking care of from time to time, and Ian had already understood that when Birdie still had so much left to learn. Carter had taught her about kindness and generosity in his own way, but theirs was never a grand love story. So yes, she realized as Elliot dumped cold sauce on the pasta, she should have dialed up Ian and filled the silence, even if what she'd had to say was difficult and wouldn't have been what he wanted to hear.

Elliot slid a bowl over the table, and she grunted a thank-you, but neither of them spoke, each of them waiting for the other to admit his or her wrongdoing. Birdie knew she still had some growing to do, but not now, not with Elliot.

At bedtime, which was essentially after dinner because there was nothing else to keep her occupied, Birdie slipped into the tiny bathroom and peeled off her clothes, excruciatingly aware that she was forcibly trying to stop herself from thinking of Elliot and how, if she weren't furious with him, she wouldn't have minded if he peeled off her clothes.

She met her eyes in the mirror. *NO. NONONONONONO.*

She was mad at him, *she was mad at him.* She studied her reflection, the hint of fine lines that she'd have to have blasted off, the purple circles under her eyes that there wasn't much to do about now, and tried to remind herself why they had started fighting in the first place. The issue was, she suspected, that these days she was too frequently engaged in too many squabbles, even if they were worthy squabbles, righteous squabbles. Sebastian and the studio and the press and Nelson Pratt and her sister, and Kai if he ever thought to reach out to her, but maybe that was a one-sided battle, since he never did think of reaching out to her.

And now Elliot.

It hadn't always been this way, the squabbling. In Barton, it was just with Andie. They were constantly at each other's throats over sisterly things, stupid things: who stole what from whose closet, whose turn it was to drive the car on Fridays (rarely Birdie since she didn't have much of a life unless she was doing a school play), why someone's eyeliner was missing when she'd just bought it brand-new at the mall. Their parents—Susana and her dad—almost always took Andie's side because she was a relatively obedient teenager who lived up to the household expectations, and Birdie was in near constant peril of academic probation, which made her grouchy and moody and misunderstood around the house. And also, she suspected, lacking the type of intelligence her parents valued. Which only furthered the sisterly complications.

In the early years of her career, she didn't have the confidence or the power to go looking for trouble. As her star rose, she supposed that her assertiveness did too. She didn't make petty demands, and plenty of actors did. But she did expect respect and parity, and now, despite her fame, despite her box office guarantee, none of it mattered because it was so much easier, even in this decade, to point fingers at a hysterical woman instead of asking the man to take accountability.

In the bathroom, she spun the rickety RV faucet, splashed her face with questionable water, and sighed. She thought again of Elliot taking off all her clothes, slowly, piece by piece, button by button, and a charge flew through her like she'd been plugged into a socket, like they could work through their issues by making out on that flimsy mattress on the bottom bunk. She lingered in the cramped bathroom until her pulse slowed, but when she emerged, flushed and looking anywhere but at him, he was down to his shorts. Which certainly did nothing to quell her racing heart, her racing mind.

"Sorry," he said. "I run hot at night."

She remembered. How sweaty he'd gotten when they holed up together because she'd just bought the apartment and the central air wasn't yet installed. How slick his skin had been against hers, how she'd liked it because she took it as a compliment, as if she were setting him on fire.

This morning, at 6:53, she grabbed a black hoodie off the table and threw it over her head. She'd thought it was hers, but it smelled like Elliot, it felt like Elliot, and though she knew both feet were firmly planted on the Winnebago floor, it felt like the world was spinning again for a moment. When she collected herself, she slipped outside. It was just daybreak, and the air was chilly and clear.

She punched in Imani's number. It rang once and went to voicemail. Probably still asleep, which was just as well because Birdie needed coffee before talking her publicist down from another emergency. She didn't know exactly what that emergency was, but she assumed her publicist hadn't called her five times in the early hours of the morning to discuss the Nordstrom half-yearly sale. Birdie clomped back up the steps to the RV, making no effort to be quiet for Elliot, still asleep in the top bunk. If she was awake, he was awake, she resolved as she slammed a cabinet door in search of instant coffee. Like many things of late, Birdie didn't consider the outcome of her actions, which was why when

Elliot moaned from the top bunk to please keep it down, she wondered why on earth she'd woken him in the first place.

"Birdie," he groaned. "Shhhhhhhhhhhh."

She opened another door just to close it loudly again.

"*Birdie*," he grumbled again. She saw him roll over in the top bunk and fling an arm off the side. Then he stilled, like he had fallen back asleep again. Which was so audacious. So rich. So exactly like Elliot. She was infuriated all over again. In her business, you felt first, thought later. You leaned *into* every emotion, not away from it. So she was leaning in, so far in, she nearly tipped over.

She marched back to the bunk beds and planted herself right in front of Elliot's (annoyingly beautiful) resting face. He really was asleep. In less than a fraction of a second, he was asleep while she nearly died from lack of coffee.

She jabbed his shoulder. He let out a little whimper.

She jabbed his shoulder again. He growled.

She jabbed it one more time, and his eyes flew open, just a few inches from hers.

"What?"

"We have a problem," she said because it was the first thing that came to mind. "We have a very serious problem."

Elliot blinked twice, then a third time, and his gaze moved to her lips.

Then before she even knew what she was doing—she always did act first and think second—she leaned in, grabbed his face in her palms, and kissed him.

25

ELLIOT

ALL ELLIOT KNEW was that Birdie had woken him up and suddenly she was kissing him, and he didn't know what happened between last night and now, but Jesus Christ, he wasn't about to stop and ask. Then his brain caught up with his desire, and he pulled back and stared at her.

Birdie returned his gaze unblinking. He could feel his pulse in his neck, his breath turning jagged. Then, either she lurched back toward him or he lurched back toward her, the gap between them flattened into nothing. His lips were on hers, his hands in her hair like he wanted to swallow her. He did. He hoisted Birdie up to the top bunk, and then she was straddling him, and his brain was white noise and fuzzy electricity and heady desire that he didn't think he'd felt in, well, seven years.

Elliot sat up to meet her, as if he couldn't tolerate even a slip of air between their bodies, then he pulled her down on top of him, his hands making their way under her hoodie. He wanted to take his time but simply could not. His fingers danced along the flesh of her waist, then over her rib cage, and, oh god, her skin felt perfect, like a goddamn miracle, and then he went to unclasp her bra but discovered she wasn't wearing one, and that made him absolutely frantic, just completely crazy, something rising in him like he'd been hungry for Birdie for seven long years and now he was more ravenous than he'd realized.

Birdie let out a little moan as he swung the hoodie over her head and threw it to the floor, then she repositioned herself right on his extremely obvious hard-on. *Hard-on* wasn't even the right word for it, he thought. He felt like he was armed with a fucking torpedo. Had he ever wanted something more, someone more? She eased back, then up, over him, and both of their breaths hitched, and then she was atop him, skin to skin, his tongue exploring her mouth, his hands exploring her breasts. Her hips were still moving in a perfect rhythm, like they were made for each other, like she couldn't stop herself any more than he could.

"Fuck, Birdie," he managed. "Jesus, fuck." He knew that he had questions for her, that they should talk about this, but he couldn't remember what his questions were, and he certainly didn't want to talk about *anything* right now.

He flipped her onto her back, and his lips made their way down her neck, then toward her nipple, which he couldn't help himself: He grazed his teeth over it, okay? He fucking nibbled her nipple because she was absolutely goddamn delicious, and that's when Birdie startled, jolting an inch or two away from him.

She blinked quickly, then again, as if she had disappeared into one of her fugue states of make-believe and had now snapped out of it. And Elliot saw it clearly, unavoidably: that he had to put a stop to this before they got in even deeper.

"Oh no," he said, and rolled beside her, flopping one arm over his face and resting the other on his crotch because maybe that would help disguise just how badly he wanted her. "Oh no," he said again, then repeated it a third time.

Birdie pushed herself up to her elbows and turned toward him, her bafflement giving way to stoniness. "*Oh no?*" she hissed.

"No, Bird, that's not what I—"

She waved a hand as if she wasn't interested in his explanation, covered her breasts, and slid down to the floor. She scooped up the hoodie and threw it over her head so quickly, all he could see was the beautiful curvature of her spine, and then no skin at all.

"I am such an idiot," she said. "I cannot believe—" she started and stopped, then shook her head, flexed her jaw, and strode toward the front of the RV.

"Birdie, please, let's—" Elliot scrambled upright, wrapping the blanket around his waist, and hopped down. It felt like seven years ago all over again. When he had so much to say but said none of it, and he wasn't even sure what to believe about whatever it was that she said. "Birdie," he called again. Her back was to him in the driver's seat. She had jammed the key into the ignition and was flipping it over and over, as if maybe, suddenly overnight, the RV had repaired itself.

"It's fine," she said. "Please, do not make this worse."

"No, it's not fine," he said. "We should—"

He didn't get to say exactly what they should do because someone pounded on the RV's front door and they both startled and jumped.

"Shit!" she whispered.

"Shit," he replied, glancing down at his state of half nakedness.

"Could we have honestly been followed?" she asked. "Dammit! You like this, me in your hoodie? Dammit, Elliot!"

"The press, I know." He grimaced, like Birdie could always circle it back to her publicity hit.

"Mona," she snapped. "I'm talking about Mona."

And that's when he remembered his own quandary of being found in a state of sexed-up hair and a still relatively visible erection. Mona, yes, but also Francesca. If he were photographed looking like *this*, and she put together any sort of logical conclusion, he'd have crossed so many lines with her that he doubted he'd ever be able to find a job in the industry, much less with her, again.

The door clattered one more time.

"Birdie?" a woman shouted. "Birdie? Please tell me this is the right RV, and I'm not beating down the door of some retirees who are enjoying a road trip?"

Elliot looked at Birdie. Birdie looked at Elliot.

Imani, Elliot thought. He'd forgotten that he'd texted her late last night because he doubted they could find a mechanic first thing, and he assumed that she was the one who could fix this. He hadn't expected her to show up in person. He definitely hadn't expected her to show up in person first thing before he could tell Birdie that he'd reached out to her team rather than discuss it with her first. He dodged Birdie's stare as he walked past her and down the camper's steps. He suspected that if a look could wilt a man, he'd be in a puddle on the ground, helpless, immobile, like an amoeba. That's what Birdie Maxwell could do to him: turn him into an invertebrate.

He hoisted up the blanket around his waist for good measure, then flung open the door.

If he thought he was calling in the cavalry, well, in what would turn out to be a series of foreseeable errors over the past day, Elliot O'Brien had gotten it totally wrong.

26

BIRDIE

CANNOT BELIEVE YOU called them," Birdie seethed, while Imani and Sydney, her agent, parked at the laminated dinette as if they were setting up a war room. "Do you think that I need babysitters?"

Birdie was in no mood to be chewed out by Imani, who had turned up with Sydney, as if it took the two of them to wrangle her into submission. As it was, she was spiraling about her idiotic make-out with Elliot, and the last thing she needed was her two parental figures giving her a dressing-down about all the ways she had made things worse for herself. She already knew she had made things worse for herself.

She hadn't *meant* to kiss him, obviously, when she marched back inside the RV, but somehow she simply *had* ended up kissing him, and further, it had been *exceptional*, and now she was just setting herself up to be emotionally annihilated again, and *good god*, how many times could a girl make an utter fool of herself? She wanted to strangle Elliot but also she wanted to strangle herself, but since that wasn't possible, she focused on him.

"No! I don't think you need 'babysitters,'" he whispered back. "I thought they would send a tow truck, not personally make a rescue appearance."

"I told them I was in San Francisco, you dickwad," she said.

"And I told them we needed some help," he replied. "You're welcome."

"I didn't thank you," she snapped, too loudly, and Imani looked up from frantically typing something into her phone. "I am not *helpless*; you didn't have to go around me and bring in my *handlers*. I do not want to be *handled*."

Birdie had been working with Imani since she was twenty-five and landed that movie with Kai. At the time, Imani was a magnetic junior publicist who had been a star debater at Spelman and applied all the ruthless wisdom that she used in debate tournaments to her client roster. She was known for both her exceptional brain and her killer shoe collection (indeed, this morning, she had paired her athleisure tracksuit with a pair of lug-soled combat boots as if she were lacing up for battle), and there was almost no jam that Imani couldn't finesse, no reporter she couldn't woo. She was diplomatic when diplomacy was called for, she was cunning when cunning was called for, and she was irate when fury was called for, which Birdie had only heard about but never witnessed. Now she suspected that she was about to get a first-row view.

"I don't need a lecture," Birdie said to Imani, whose stare was darting between her and Elliot, while Sydney clucked her tongue from her perch at the table. "I didn't need you two to show up and hold my hand. I'm doing this on my own."

"How's that working out for you?" Imani asked.

"Perfectly fine except that my genius best friend is also a moron who clearly hasn't had this hunk of junk serviced in a decade."

Elliot bristled like he took umbrage at calling the camper a hunk of junk, which she thought was actually a pretty generous description.

"Do you have something to say?" Birdie turned toward him.

He opened his mouth, then closed it.

"I thought so," she said, like they were having an actual conversation.

"So you haven't checked your phone this morning," Sydney piped in. Sydney was a hardheaded divorced mother of two teens, so needless to say, she'd seen some shit on her watch. She was feared in the industry for her negotiating tactics, but fabulous to her clients as long as they remained on her good side. She treated herself to a day spa one Friday of every month, and though she was a natural brunette, she'd been blond for as long as Birdie had known her, and Birdie had never seen so much as a centimeter of a root. Sydney was that meticulous.

"I've checked my phone this morning," Birdie said. "I actually called you, Imani, but you didn't pick up." She held up her screen like this was proof. "Then I lost service again. I can't be blamed for the lack of Wi-Fi in the middle of a godforsaken rest stop."

"I don't think this is even technically a rest stop," Elliot interrupted, but all three women glared at him, so he hoisted the blanket up higher and shuffled toward the back to get dressed.

"We must have been in a dead pocket, driving up here," Imani said. "And if you are so on top of things, then I assume you've seen the article."

"You'll have to be more specific," Birdie said. There were probably seven hundred articles zooming around the web about her right now.

Sydney yanked her head toward Elliot.

"His article."

"His article?" Birdie's stomach flipped. "What article?"

When had Elliot filed his article? She hadn't even known he'd finished it. He certainly hadn't run it by her, hadn't shared even the smallest hint of the details about what Carter said, what Carter felt. Had he waited for her to pass out last night, slipped out to the parking lot, skulked around until he found a signal, and blasted it to the *Times*, then slipped back into bed, and then proceeded to *make out* with her this morning?

She was going to kill him. Really. With her bare hands.

"I just texted it to you."

Birdie's phone buzzed.

The headline read: **PART 2: AMERICA'S SWEETHEART DOUBLE-FAULTS**

Birdie huffed air out of her nose like she was about to blow her top. She glanced toward the back of the Winnebago, but Elliot had ducked into the bathroom, which was probably for the best in case she spontaneously combusted from rage.

"Keep reading," Imani said.

"I'm going to go back there and murder him." She didn't realize she had said this aloud, but Sydney clucked her tongue again, indicating either deep approval or deep disapproval, and Birdie didn't have the slightest clue which.

"I'm not sure that murder will help your public image," Imani said. "But if you do, make sure it's not with a tennis racket."

"Imani!" Birdie barked.

"It would be a pity," Sydney said, sliding her reading glasses up her head. "To off a man that beautiful, but don't worry, Bird, I'll happily help you bury the body."

Birdie could taste blood in the water.

She hoped that it wasn't hers.

Part 2: AMERICA'S SWEETHEART DOUBLE-FAULTS

By Elliot O'Brien

Our quest to find Birdie Robinson's anonymous suitor has brought us to the glittering landscape of Los Angeles. Deep in Silver Lake, through winding, unmarked roads, we land at a picturesque bungalow with a freshly painted deep navy door and a picture-perfect man behind it.

Meet Carter LeRoux, retired professional tennis player whose best showing at a tournament was the quarter finals at the US Open in 2011, and now tennis pro to the stars. Which included Ms. Robinson at one point in their recent past. LeRoux, who has an easy demeanor and an infectious laugh, greeted me with a joyous baritone, a rescue dog straight out of ASPCA magazine, and skin that looked like it had a pricey antioxidant regimen.

Ms. Robinson was feeling shy, having been so derided in our first attempt at reconciliation with Chef Ian Sands, and opted to linger behind. I assured her that if it were good news, I'd immediately text her and unite the happy couple. Unfortunately, it was not good news. In fact, so far, Ms. Robinson is now love-thirty, and the question she now faces is: How many points will she play while continuing to swing and miss, to take an ace right to the far corner, to double-fault at match point? (Forgive the tennis puns, I couldn't help myself.)

Mr. LeRoux, as he explained to me, is currently engaged. His happy home is filled with photos of his stunning fiancée, the life they've built together, and one photogenic, extremely well-trained rescue dog, Lucy. If I weren't a nomadic reporter who so rarely stayed in one place, I'd have asked if I could have adopted Lucy out from under them. Or have the couple adopt *me*.

Though Ms. Robinson and I are operating under the theory that the letter is several years old, Mr. LeRoux assured me, and I believed him, that he is not the sort of man who trips down his past with regrets. He rarely thinks of our favorite actress, he said, though he clarified and said he is certainly a fan of some of her movies, though he couldn't name many when pressed. He finally managed to cite *Love Bomb*—not exactly a deep dive into her résumé. It seems that while Ms. Robinson lingered on the notion that Mr. LeRoux could be her potential happily-ever-after, Mr. LeRoux hasn't lingered on her much at all.

Which led me to the question I asked myself while leaving his bungalow. What if no one in her past actually wants to reconcile? What if we go on this quest and her ex-suitor has changed his mind (not outside the realm of possibility, given Ms. Robinson's recent press about both her temper and her behavior), or what if we simply come up empty? Will Birdie Robinson, who always gets her happily-ever-after on-screen, simply forge on alone?

⇒ 27 ⇐

ELLIOT

ELLIOT EMERGED FROM the camper bathroom, where he'd splashed water on his face and brushed his teeth and pulled on a pair of sweats and the button-down Birdie had worn yesterday, to a significantly chillier vibe than when he'd gone in. And things hadn't been particularly warm to start with. The make-out session had been a massive miscalculation, not just because his feelings for Birdie were blurring together in some sort of mosh pit of love and lust and protectiveness and regret and irritation and professional responsibility. All Birdie had to do was tell Imani or Sydney, and all Imani and Sydney had to do was tell Francesca, whom they surely knew, as members of these circles tended to, and that would be that. He'd promised his editor that he could keep it aboveboard, and it had been three days and all had gone to hell.

Birdie Maxwell made Elliot do all sorts of reckless things.

"Why are all of you staring at me?" he asked from the rear of the camper. He glanced down to ensure that he didn't still have a hard-on. Thankfully, no.

"The article," Birdie screeched.

"What article?" Elliot asked, then took a few steps toward her. Until he got a better look at her face, which was curled up into an unnerving blend of rage and beauty, like she was some sort of ethereal goddess of fury, and he stopped cold.

"*Your article,*" she shouted, and took her own three steps toward him. "Carter is engaged? Carter couldn't even name one of my movies? Carter has a fucking rescue dog named Lucy?"

"That . . . that . . ." Elliot sputtered.

"You could have *at least* told me that Carter was engaged before I *had to read it* with the rest of the world. Did you not have enough time yesterday? Did you not have any opportunities? Were the four hours in this godforsaken rattling box on wheels not enough? The night spent sleeping under each other—"

Imani gasped and Sydney popped her eyebrows, so Birdie aborted the tirade for a brief interlude.

"No, I meant in the bunk beds," she said to them, and they both visibly relaxed, like Elliot was goddamn sexual napalm, but then maybe his reputation preceded him with them too. *It's all consensual fun and games until you're thought of as a gigolo,* he thought.

"Birdie," he said.

"Your TV voice, O'Brien. Do. Not. Placate. Me. With. Your. TV. Voice."

"Bird," Elliot said, trying to recalibrate. "I didn't know the piece published. It was a draft. It wasn't meant to—" He shook his head. He knew this sounded flimsy. Ridiculous. Excuses that even a middle school teacher wouldn't accept. But that didn't make his story any less true. "Yesterday, when the engine was . . . going, and you pulled off the road, I guess I thought we might die?"

Imani snorted, and Sydney shushed her, even as Birdie crossed her arms and narrowed her eyes.

"And, so I uploaded the draft," Elliot rambled. "It was a draft, I promise. I swear. I swear on . . . whatever is most valuable to you." He watched Birdie try to think of the most valuable thing that she kept close to her heart, and when she didn't offer it, he continued. "Francesca and I have a system. I have no idea why she ran with it."

He winced, genuinely pained that his petty words were flying around the internet. He'd been childish and catty when he was pounding the story into his laptop. He was sick with jealousy over Carter's amiable, easygoing affection for Birdie, and he was annoyed with her for . . . he couldn't even remember why they were squabbling yesterday, but, well, the conflation of those two things meant that he wrote a draft just for himself. He did that sometimes: wrote the vomit version to get it out of his system. Those iterations were never meant for an audience other than of one. And now Francesca had put it live on the site? He had figured that Francesca would be pissed he blew his deadline last night; he didn't think she'd go ahead and publish the piece without him signing off. Which, of course, he couldn't do, because cell service went out as quickly as it came last night, here, on the side of the road in the middle of fucking nowhere. He was used to this sort of hiccup in remote locations, sparse, run-down cites. He and Francesca had a language: *DRAFT* meant he was just trying to salvage what he could before the signal blew up, and he'd return to it as soon as it was safe to do so.

"The article, the way you made it sound like I am destined to be alone forever—" Birdie was already in the middle of a thought when she started in on him again. Elliot watched her chest rise, like she was gearing up to detonate. "Which, it should be noted, is completely fine. Who says I need a *guy*? Who says I need true love? Maybe *true love* is just a misguided fairy tale that we see in the movies."

"I didn't, I don't—" Elliot tried to recalibrate. "I wasn't trying to—" He understood that this was not the moment to point out that she was the very one selling the fairy tale and selling it well.

"You promised me that you would have my back," she said.

"It wasn't meant to get published," he said again. "I promise on . . ." He tried to drill down to something that only she would understand, some shared sense of intimacy that meant something to them both. "I promise on . . . our prom date."

Birdie blanched at the reference, like either she never thought of that night or she was surprised that he still did. Her glare had gone unreadable, the woman who Elliot was always so sure he could read. Before she could say another word, Imani's phone clattered loudly on the RV table. All four of them jumped.

"Oh," Imani said, hopping up and running down the front steps, like nothing about this fight was permanent. "Mechanic is here." Sydney clapped her hands together, as if she, too, was done with this, trailing Birdie's publicist out the door.

"Thank god someone here can perform cleanup," Birdie said, then turned to follow her team.

"Birdie—" Elliot started. "Come on. We can't get through this if we're fighting."

She froze with her back still to him, then spun quickly and marched right up to the tip of his nose. Under any other circumstances, Elliot would clasp both of her cheeks in his palms and kiss her until she couldn't breathe.

"There is nothing to get through anymore, Elliot," she spat. "We're not doing any of *this* anymore. Call your editor, tell her I'm out. I don't need to invite more scrutiny, and I certainly didn't expect that scrutiny to come from the one person I'm supposed to have trusted."

Then she stormed out of the camper and slammed the rickety door behind her.

It figured, Elliot thought, that the first woman to ever really leave him would be the only one he ever wanted to beg to stay.

28

BIRDIE

BIRDIE WAS DONE. Done with Elliot. Done with driving this ridiculous landboat. Done with this whole notion of being sunny and compliant because somehow demanding respect both on set and occasionally off it now mandated that a woman seek the company of a man to rehabilitate her reputation. She never should have trusted Elliot O'Brien—*a reporter!*—to take care with her story, to protect her vulnerability. Such a thing only worked out in her movies, and there was a reason that her rom-coms were fiction. *Fiction*, she huffed to herself while the mechanic rattled around in the engine and whistled that they were lucky that the entire thing didn't catch fire and explode.

The RV, it turned out, was rusting from the inside out and also needed a new belt of some sort, and of course, Mona had neglected to change the oil in god knew how long. Imani offered to drive her back to LA while the mechanic fiddled around under the hood, but Birdie found that she just wanted to go home. She didn't have any rational explanation for this—she'd spent a decade pretending that Barton was irrelevant in her story—but the thought of Los Angeles and its ghosts was too haunting, and the thought of New York and her empty apartment was too pathetic. She wanted to see Mona, and she wouldn't have even minded the company of Andie, a notion that caught her off guard.

"So you'll be okay driving home with him?" Imani had nudged her head toward the RV.

"I think the better question is if he'll be okay driving home with *me*," she replied. Elliot had disappeared inside to call his editor, and though Birdie was itching for another fight, she heard him on the phone, sounding chastised and embarrassed, and she decided to wait it out, not out of kindness, but so that he'd feel pain not all in one blow but bit by bit for the rest of the day. She was angry at herself for kissing him. She was angry with him for kissing her back. She was angry that she couldn't kiss him forever, actually, but she couldn't, she shouldn't, she mustn't.

An hour later, she was sitting in the back of the RV, unwilling to even meet him midway at the dinette, make small talk, listen to the radio the way they used to in carpool or had on the way down to LA. *Sweet dreams are made of cheese.* She felt the curl of her smile but recalibrated. She wouldn't make this easy for him; she wouldn't just roll over and forgive him, which she figured he expected her to do because he was used to women going easy on him.

No. *No.* If Elliot had something to say, if Elliot had something to *do* (to her), kissing her—even if she started it, she knew she started it, okay?!—after publicly humiliating her, not to mention walking out of her apartment all those years ago, was not the proper order of things. *You don't just get to kiss a girl and have her swoon, have her world spin differently on its axis*, she thought. Even if that's exactly what would have unfolded in one of her movies. In fact, he *had* just kissed a girl, and she *had* just swooned, but only for a minute, and Birdie was wise enough, strong enough, to pull herself out before she spiraled. She stared toward the front windshield, at Elliot's back, and knew how easy it would be to spiral for Elliot O'Brien.

She'd been spiraling since she was twelve. Now, at nearly thirty-five, she wanted to think that she knew better, that she was wiser. She worried, however, that neither of those things was particularly true.

29

ELLIOT

ELLIOT HAD ALWAYS considered himself to be excellent at reading his subjects, and yet now he had absolutely no idea what to do next with Birdie. It had been hours since she'd spoken to him, and even as he curved the RV into his parents' old driveway, Birdie was as stony, as impassive, as she had been when she first read today's story.

Mona was waiting for them outside the house, and she was a markedly easier read. Elliot knew immediately that she was furious with him. Not because of twintuition. Because of the look on her face. Lines pointing downward, a glare that stretched from her forehead to her chin. Birdie glanced out the window and saw it too.

"Christ," she said, like Mona was angry with her too.

"It's me, not you," Elliot replied.

Birdie stared at him like she was waiting for him to say something more. But Elliot had already apologized. He'd reached Francesca back in the parking lot, as promised to Birdie. He was mortified that he'd even written such a thing—that Birdie Robinson needed a man like she needed oxygen. He knew that he had humiliated himself even more than he had humiliated her, even if the internet piled on her, the easy mark.

"It wasn't a draft, O'Brien. Why would I have run with a piece marked 'draft'?" Francesca had asked, like she needed her already-on-thin-ice hotshot reporter second-guessing her. "This isn't my first rodeo. If you think I'd just publish something because it's been graced with your byline, you should lasso in your ego, although if I gave you enough rope, I think we both know what would happen."

She was speaking in metaphors, but yes, he understood this to mean that he'd hang himself on his own hubris. Like he'd done with the payoffs, like he'd done with his sourcing.

"Fact-checking verified the piece," she said. "It wasn't Carter. And he is engaged."

Elliot wondered how fact-checking could ever verify how love soared and faltered, but he wasn't in a position to argue.

"Okay, but I still would prefer a shot to rewrite it, edit it," Elliot said. "Birdie is pretty upset."

"Since when do you give a shit about if you're hurting a subject's feelings?" Francesca barked out a laugh. "Are you *asking* to get fired?"

"No," Elliot parroted. "I am certainly not asking to get fired."

"Great," she replied. "Then we agree. The story stands. Now, goodbye."

Hours later, with the RV parked in his childhood driveway, he started toward Mona with her grimace and her curled fists and, he knew, her oncoming extremely wordy dressing-down. He stopped for a beat, glancing toward Birdie's house, which was now blessedly free of TV vans, and he imagined Andie chasing them off with a baseball bat. Then he heard Birdie scream from inside the camper, and even though they weren't speaking, he flew up the steps and flung the door open like he was goddamn Superman. But she pushed past him and raced toward Mona.

"Shit," she cried, her face pale, her eyes wild. "*Shit—*"

"What?" Mona asked. "Are you okay? What can I do? Tell me."

Birdie was staring at her phone, mouth agape, chest visibly rising and falling. Then she held up her screen toward his twin.

"What?" Mona asked, beside her in an instant. "What are we looking at?"

Birdie lowered the phone in front of her.

"A letter," she whispered. "I got a second one."

30

BIRDIE

"THIS IS RIDICULOUS," Mona said once they were back inside.

"I'm completely aware," Birdie whined, sliding out a chair at Mona's kitchen table and sinking into it, as if her legs couldn't hold her for another second. She honestly wasn't sure if they could hold her for another second. "But don't kick a girl when she's down."

"Not you, Bird. I understand why you'd get dozens of love letters. I meant the copycat. I meant that the copycat is bullshit. At least the first guy had a little gumption, some nerve."

Birdie flopped her head down to the table and moaned.

"Fame is intoxicating," Elliot offered, as if this could be the only explanation. Actually, it probably *was* the only explanation. Friends and lovers and coworkers and even fans forgive all sorts of things when you're famous. Until they have a reason not to. "Also, it could just be the first guy, doubling down," Elliot added. "Like a trail of bread crumbs trying to lead you back to him."

Birdie dropped her hands and stared at Elliot. She didn't know why she hadn't taken her first instinct more seriously—that it could have been Elliot all along. He'd denied it, sure, but like that meant anything. Words were words were words. She, of all people, recited words all the time that meant nothing, *were* nothing, other than fictional little entities that flitted from her mouth and then dissolved. So it would be so clever of Elliot, Birdie thought, to pitch this article, to disguise his true intentions, to pull back the curtain at the final hour and reveal himself like it was a triumph.

She narrowed her eyes, suspicious. He certainly seemed game this morning. Had certainly returned her (absolutely moronic) kiss with as much gusto, if not more. She replayed the scene while Mona and Elliot bickered between themselves, and she wondered if a human could spontaneously combust from unrequited lust. If she could just blow to a million pieces, right here in the kitchen where she used to ask Elliot for help in geometry because she probably could have figured out how to use the protractor, but it was much more interesting when he leaned over her shoulder and explained it.

"My hunch is that it's a new guy," Mona said. "Why send a letter to your house initially, if he could have just emailed? Why follow up a second time when you're out here already looking for him? Actually, why bother with any of it and not come clean?" She drummed her hands on the counter, then waited, as if the two of them had any answers.

"It's the romantic gesture," Elliot said in his irritating TV voice. Birdie was starting to suspect that he slipped into it unconsciously whenever he thought he should be the authority in the room but really was just overcompensating. "Maybe this guy mistook who you were in movies with who you are in real life and thought you wanted, *needed*, the gesture."

Sounds like you know what you're talking about, Birdie thought.

"So someone has to *mistake* me to fall in love with me? Extremely flattering, thank you."

Elliot blew out his breath. "That's not what I—"

Mona interrupted. "Okay, okay, whatever you two are sniping about, drop it." Birdie bit the inside of her cheek, and Elliot turned pink. "Yeah, I'm not oblivious to this extremely bad juju circulating between you two right now," Mona added, like a teacher chastising her students. "Also, if this *is* a plot right out of the movies, then I think we need to discuss the elephant in the room."

Birdie felt the blood drain from her face. After all she'd been through the past few weeks, she didn't have it in her to fight with Mona. Now she wondered if she could spontaneously combust by choice. That would be so much easier than cleaning up the mess of Mona knowing about Elliot, about their night together. The omissions they'd embraced, the lies they'd told.

For a long time, really since she was twenty-five and her fame outpaced even her wildest ambitions, Birdie had thought that she knew everything, which was a blessed relief compared to her first eighteen years. She'd believed Sydney when she said that Birdie was sitting atop a mountain. She'd believed Imani when she said that Birdie was untouchable. She'd blossomed from the theater loser at Barton to someone the whole world fell in love with, and so she thought, she supposed, that she was invincible.

But that form of adoration was much flimsier, much more delicate, than she realized. Climbing the mountain took so much effort; falling off it required only a simple mistake. A slip of your foot, and you tumbled all the way down. So if Mona knew about her long-simmering feelings for Elliot, if she had discovered that she and Elliot had actually spent the night together in her apartment at twenty-seven when she was on a break from Kai, and that they'd explored every last inch of each other's bodies until they were sweaty and exhausted and a little delirious, well, then, it wouldn't be much of a surprise. Her foot had slipped, her ankle had turned, and she tumbled over the side of the crest.

The doorbell clanged unexpectedly, and Birdie, already on high alert, jumped out of her chair like a panicky house cat. This reminded her of Imani, and Imani reminded her of the apology video, and the apology video reminded her of Sebastian. And Sebastian, needless to say, reminded her of Kai. The very last thing she could handle right now was a come-to-Jesus moment with her best friend when she was already unraveling at the seams. Birdie well knew that Mona wasn't a child any longer, but the three of them had understood the math both implicitly and explicitly, as expressed by Mona at prom: Birdie and Mona. Elliot and Mona. The lines were never meant to intersect.

Birdie had assumed Elliot would remember the Cheetos. It had been a gimme, an easy lay-up. She'd gotten them intentionally at the rest stop as a test. If he remembered how they once raided the vending machine at the school cafeteria, how she had been there late for a rehearsal of *Little Shop of Horrors*, how he had been there late because he was getting in an extra workout after swim practice. They were starving and delirious. Elliot suggested they break into the cafeteria, and Birdie, trying on the role of rebel much like she tried on the role of Audrey from *Little Shop*, jumped at the chance. Really, it was just to spend time with Elliot.

The cafeteria had been padlocked. Birdie remembered even now how Elliot howled and she dissolved into a fit of tears at that.

"Do. They. Think," Elliot had sputtered between gasps, "that people"—*breath*—"would choose"—*breath*—"to eat here"—*breath*—"voluntarily?"

It was true. The school lunches were abysmal. Birdie had to

squat down to stop from peeing in her pants, she was laughing so hard. They could have gotten into his Accord, gone to a drive-through by the strip mall on the way home, but they were in deep now, and the fun was in the adventure of it.

"To the vending machines!" Elliot had said, a finger in the air like he was suggesting they storm the castle. His hair was still wet from his swim practice or his workout, and Birdie thought he looked like he was fresh out of the shower. She would have liked to have seen him fresh out of the shower.

"To expired Cheetos!" Birdie had cheered, and they scrambled down the dimly lit hall to the machines outside the gym. She didn't know what she was thinking would happen. That he would glance over at her and something electric would pass between them, like it had that week in carpool when Mona was out with mono, and he'd lay her down on the weight benches and do all sorts of torrid things to her with his mouth, with his hands? Even then, she had an aptitude for romantic comedy, for wish fulfillment.

Neither one of them had any cash for the vending machine, but Elliot was undeterred. He hit the buttons in random order, over and over again, claiming he had heard that sometimes you could short-circuit the wiring and swamp the motherboard. These sounded like words he was just saying to appear knowledgeable and not actually a real thing, but Birdie didn't want to say anything to break the magic spell. There weren't many boys she knew who accepted her at face value, who made her feel perfect even when she was well aware, thanks to her parents, of her shortcomings. When the buttons didn't work, he butted it with his hip several times until Birdie started giggling again and he said, "What?"

And she said, "You look like you could have auditioned for the musical. You have some pretty good hip movement going, some really nice thrusting." And she immediately felt her face glow red, her ears burn. She probably had hives all over her chest. The forthrightness, the audacity. But she decided that she was going to play the part, the ingenue, the girl who could roll up her sleeves and get 'er done. Also, she thought Elliot was looking at her with, well, she wasn't sure, she wasn't in any way an expert on men, but he looked . . . delighted. Entertained. Happy. This new role, she could finesse.

"Step aside," she said, fluttering her hand to usher him away. He held his arms up like *Whoa, okay, let's see what you got, Birdie Maxwell*, and she stopped and assessed the machine, like it was a problem she needed to solve. She took five steps back.

"Birdie," Elliot said.

"I got this," she said. She didn't. But she was operating from a place of relative lunacy being in such proximity to Elliot, like he was a drug and she'd injected him into her bloodstream.

She took in a deep breath and then closed those five steps between her and the machine, hurling her body against the front window with a thud and bouncing off it onto the floor. Elliot's eyes went wide, and he was beside her in an instant, crouching down and meeting her where she was.

"You okay?" he asked. "Jesus, you are actually bonkers."

Birdie's shoulder was throbbing, but she was well into the part now, the role of a lifetime, wooing Elliot O'Brien. He was so, so close, and she could have tilted toward him and kissed him. If she were a different person, if she were in a film. Instead, she looked past him, and there, on the ground, were at least half the items from the vending machine.

"Look." She nudged her chin.

He spun around, folded next to her.

"Jackpot!" he cried. "Oh my god, Birdie Maxwell, I think I love you!" Birdie froze, stunned, taking it too literally, of course, while he crawled toward the loot and held up three bags of Cheetos triumphantly, with flushed cheeks and this goofy side-grin on his face. So she told herself to play along. To play it cool. Just hearing Elliot say it aloud, even if he only meant it because of the Cheetos, was enough for her that night. Birdie opened her palm, and he threw her a bag. Then Elliot slipped to his butt and leaned against the machine, and they ate all of it, the whole bounty, together.

Birdie was sure that she would love Elliot O'Brien forever.

And now he hadn't even remembered. Hadn't remembered those stupid stale Cheetos. How he'd loved her for them. Which meant that Birdie's suspicion that he had written the letter was only lukewarm, not at all grounded in fact. *Fact*. That was Elliot's territory anyway.

The doorbell rang again, and Mona lurched toward the foyer. Birdie seized her chance.

"It was you," she whispered at Elliot across the table. "It was *you* all along, wasn't it." She hissed this like it wouldn't in reality please her. It would under any other circumstances but these. Possibly under these too but she'd need time to gather herself. "This is all part of some weird journalistic mind-fuck or gotcha to, like, write the gossip story of the century."

"*What?*"

"I don't know what you're getting out of this, but there must be something." She breathed like she had ingested gasoline and lit a match. She wanted to burn him. She wanted him to burn him alive. And then if he begged her to rescue him, well, she'd consider it. "You easily could have sent that email when you got off the RV. When I was distracted. When I was talking to Mona."

"*What?*" Elliot looked apoplectic. "*What are you even talking about?*" But his face was the color of a beet, and his skin looked clammy, like he was unprepared for an interrogation and hadn't yet thought of an excuse.

Aha, Birdie thought. *The student has become the master. Truth, fiction, facts, what did it matter?*

"Confess," she said, pulling out a chair and taking a seat. "I have nowhere to be until you do." She'd wait all day—hell, all week—until he finally did.

31

ELLIOT

ELLIOT HAD NEVER once had a panic attack in the field. Not when he was being shelled in Iraq, not when a senator cornered him at a urinal in the Capitol and threatened bodily harm, not when his single-engine plane dipped too low, too fast in Senegal. But sitting at his childhood kitchen table, with Birdie throwing accusations like that senator nearly threw punches, Elliot thought that his chest might actually combust. Right there. In his parents' mundane kitchen, which hadn't been updated since the early 2000s. He supposed that death really could catch you off guard.

Elliot tried to stammer out a denial. But he also knew that he resembled a boiled lobster, which likely meant that Birdie only suspected him more. He opened his mouth. Closed it. Opened it again. He tried to catch his breath while thinking of something witty to say. It wasn't totally outside the realm of possibility, he could see, that he could have sent one. Both. If they'd actually had an *adult* conversation about whether or not the electricity that pulsed through him at a hotly charged clip still pulsed through *her* at a hotly charged clip, well then, maybe they could get down to being honest. But they hadn't, they weren't, and they were both to blame for that. Elliot had a literal job to do. Keep it aboveboard. Be fucking platonic. That's what Francesca had stipulated without knowing what she was asking for but asking for it all the same.

He tried not to think about this morning when she reached for him, which meant that was just about all he could think about—her with bed-head hair and lips that were full and pink. And her smell. His blood throbbed. He didn't know if he could even come close to describing her smell other than to say that she smelled like Birdie Maxwell, like her skin emitted a pheromone designed just for him. He wanted to bury himself in the crook of her neck, right between her shoulder and the arch toward her ear, and live there forever.

He heard Mona at the front door, her voice low, and exhaled to possibly slow his pulse. He had limited time to refute Birdie's accusation, and he had to do it crisply, sharply, with no room for doubt.

"Why would I send you a love letter?" he finally whispered back. "Why would I possibly concoct such a thing? You know that I only deal in facts, not fantasy."

Birdie pursed her lips, prepping a reply, but then there were footsteps approaching in the hallway, and then Andie burst into the kitchen. Flushed and fists on her hips like she was aiming for a brawl.

"You realize I have better things to do than be your private escort down the block, right? The photographers are gone. You're welcome, by the way."

"Hey, Andie," Elliot said, lifting a hand. She was a welcome distraction, he realized. A diversion that gave him time to think up an alibi.

"I didn't text you," Birdie said. "I didn't ask for an escort. I'm capable of walking down the block by myself, my god, Andie."

"I did," Mona replied. Then, to Andie: "Birdie got another letter."

Andie looked from Birdie to Mona to Elliot and back to Birdie again. "You have got to be kidding me."

Mona ignored Andie's irritation. "That time in LA when you lived with her. I thought we could use some perspective," she said. "We need all hands on deck to connect the dots."

Andie raised her eyebrows, and so, too, did Elliot. Despite being an intrepid reporter, he'd forgotten about that, and he thought he'd remembered everything when it came to Birdie.

He half listened to the three of them bicker, Birdie's hands flying around as she argued, the tips of her fingers still orange, and he suddenly remembered something else he'd forgotten: that evening in high school, when she was rehearsing for that show, *Little Shop of Horrors*. That night, he hadn't needed to do a workout after swim practice but he knew she'd need a ride after rehearsal. He loitered by the auditorium, and when she emerged, she had that vibrant heady glow that she always had when she was in her element. He had a girlfriend then, AnnaMarie Baker, whom he mostly genuinely liked, and Birdie was off-limits anyway. But still. She walked out of the auditorium, and she didn't see him at first, so he had time—seconds that felt like they stretched for eternity—to simply watch her, to indulge in that fantasy he found himself playing in his mind at night when he couldn't sleep and stared at the ceiling instead. *What if Birdie had been mine instead of Mona's?*

Finally, she glanced in his direction and gave him that crooked smile that he could get high off of.

"Need a ride?" he asked, trying to keep it casual.

"Yeah, but I'm so hungry that I might actually chew your arm off."

Elliot honestly wouldn't have minded, nearly offered it up as a snack. But he proposed they try the cafeteria, and when that was locked, they ransacked the vending machines. God, they were desperate for the Doritos. He remembered now how she threw herself against the machine with a commitment that honestly daunted him, and then she raised her arms in triumph when the contents spilled forth, like a broken slot machine in Vegas. They sat on the floor and made a dinner out of stolen junk food, and he watched her lick the tips of her fingers after inhaling those Doritos and thought that she was perfect. That he didn't have to be anyone else for her: not the star swimmer, not the intrepid editor of the paper, not the straight-A honors student. Just him. Just her.

Doritos. Something clanged in Elliot. Maybe that's what she'd meant in the RV earlier. Maybe she'd gotten mixed up or maybe he was now mixed up and it had been Cheetos. He eyed her and wondered which one of them had it wrong, and if it really mattered anyway. But this is what Birdie Maxwell did to him, made him debate ridiculous things like which processed snack food they'd looted that night from the Barton High vending machine.

"Look," he heard Andie say as he tuned back in. "Will someone just read me this second letter? Wasn't that the point of calling me here? I know this is a huge shocker, but I actually have better places to be than solving my sister's PR crisis."

"I didn't ask you—" Birdie started.

Andie held up a rigid hand as if to say, *Do you ever shut the hell up?*, and surprisingly, Birdie did. She passed Andie her phone and grumbled, like she was doing her little sister a favor.

"From lovesick@gmail.com," Andie read aloud and rolled her eyes. "'Dear Birdie.'"

It seems that you are by now well versed in the art of anonymous love letters. So I thought I'd roll the dice, play my hand, see if the signs lead us back together. I've always wondered if I gave up at exactly the wrong moment or if you did. But either way, I've also always thought that we each deserved better—not from someone else, but from each other, and if we'd been a bit better, maybe it could have lasted forever. So I thought I'd put that out into the world and see if we maybe, possibly, could have a chance for a sequel.

Xx

Andie handed the phone back to Birdie and looked toward Mona. "I mean, this is all so intriguing, but again, I'm here why?"

"I wanted your insights on LA. You're the one who spent real time with her since she left," Mona said. "Though I have to say, I'm really not a fan of a bandwagoner. So unoriginal, right? But still, we need to consider him."

"I'm not *considering* any of them," Birdie said. "I'm doing this because the world hates me. Actually, I'm not doing it at all anymore. I quit."

"So now you quit?" Andie asked. "Just because it got tough?"

Birdie flared her nostrils and looked like if they had been alone, she would have escalated this into a wrestling match in the front yard.

Andie rolled her eyes. "Anyway, I only worked for her for about a year."

Elliot furrowed his brow. "When was this?"

Andie shrugged. Looked at Birdie. "After she moved to LA the second time. That ridiculously large house that wasn't necessary."

"I sold it," Birdie snapped.

"Whatever," her sister replied. "It was about six years ago."

"And who were you with then?" Mona asked Birdie. "I lost track."

"Nice." Birdie sulked. "Very feminist."

"I meant I can't remember. Not that there were so many."

Andie glared at Birdie. Birdie glared at Andie. Elliot didn't know what he was missing.

"Simon," Andie said. "I remember that Simon was around all the time."

"Well, Simon is next on our list anyway," Elliot said. "The day after tomorrow. We're going to Vegas."

"I'm not going anywhere," Birdie said.

"Simon was always pretty great," Andie interjected. "I never really understood it. That whole thing. Why he put up with it."

"*I'm literally sitting right here,*" Birdie whined.

"But, per your own words, you're not going anywhere," Andie said, looking like she was starting to enjoy this. "So you're just going to have to grin and bear it."

Birdie pushed back her chair and stomped to the front door, as if she'd do exactly what she didn't want to do just to prove Andie wrong.

"So what am I telling Francesca about the rest of the series?" Elliot called after her. He rose from the table and trailed her. "Are you in or are you out? Because either way, I have to finish this."

"It seems to me that you didn't need me in LA. With Carter," she said, pivoting toward him.

"I *did* need you," he replied. Then, before he could help it, he said again, "I still do."

They locked eyes for a beat too long, like it was only the two of them in the room, and Elliot's insides bottomed out. He hoped Mona didn't detect anything. He hoped Birdie didn't either. That longing, that pang, that want.

"I would just like to reiterate that I'm still rooting for the first guy." Mona tutted behind him. "Seems like the second one is capitalizing on a trend. Gross. The worst. Actually, he disgusts me."

"So a man who is interested only because he knows I'm taken." Birdie said. "There's a trope for that in movies. Usually pops up just at the end of act two."

"So we're at the end of act two?" Elliot asked.

"That implies that my life is literally a rom-com, Elliot. I think the past few weeks have clearly disproven that."

"Well, you never know until the closing credits," he said. When she didn't reply, and Andie opened the front door, he called out, "See you here on Thursday morning? I'm going to find Simon with or without you."

The door slammed by way of answer. Elliot hadn't managed to stop hoping for a different ending with Birdie. If their history was any indication, his heart would probably hang on the line until the screen went black.

32

BIRDIE

BIRDIE AND ANDIE did not speak on the short walk home. Dusk was falling, and a few houses had chimneys smoking; one that still needed to take down its Christmas lights three months later. It was beautiful, she thought, even if she hadn't expected to find much beauty in Barton. But that, she was starting to realize, was her own issue. Not *all* of her issues, but some of them. The sense of not belonging in her brainy household, the sense of invisibility that went along with it, the sense that her little sister was always outshining her, which shouldn't have been the natural order of things. Still, she was almost thirty-five now, and heaving around a chip on her shoulder—even if that chip had forced her to be independent, self-reliant, hardworking, stubborn, all qualities that launched her into superstardom—wasn't doing her much good anymore.

She and Andie had never really discussed that year when Andie had lived with her in Los Angeles. Just like, she realized, how she and Elliot had never discussed the night in her apartment in Tribeca. Once could be excused. Twice meant it was perhaps a pattern. Three times—with Ian; four times—with Kai; and actually, maybe her avoidance was pathological. For the better part of a decade, she'd been coddled by Imani and Sydney, said yes to by a thousand people who knew they had no other option but to say yes. No one ever bothered pushing back. No one ever offered lukewarm approval like her parents did, like Andie did, and now the pushback had become a very public tsunami, and Birdie was out here pretending she could do the same old things and not drown. She couldn't. She was halfway to the bottom of the ocean.

At the time that Andie moved in with her, six years ago, Birdie had skyrocketed to A-list and needed someone around her she could trust. It was about a year and change after Elliot, right in the middle of Simon, which meant it was also right when Kai, now engaged to his high school sweetheart, popped back into her life.

Andie, who was already tepid about working as an assistant and taking orders from Birdie (but who was saving up for her master's degree, and Birdie paid her generously), did not approve. The first time Kai showed up outside the gate of her new Brentwood home, Birdie had been at some event—she couldn't remember which now—with Simon. Simon was an easy date to industry events. He was used to fancy people from his job managing high-end hotels, so he didn't mind breaking away on red carpets for her solo photos, he didn't mind that she was gone for weeks at a time on location, didn't mind that she was becoming neurotic about her place in the industry even while gaining more power with each film. He didn't know anything about Kai (of course), but by then the two of them, Birdie and Kai, had their secrecy down to CIA clearance. No one knew other than those who did. And those who did kept their mouths shut. Also, Birdie had kept everything completely platonic since Kai's team had announced his engagement two years back. She thought this was important: that she was on the correct side of morality, even when Kai tried to tug her across that line by texting and calling and emailing, all of which Birdie returned irregularly, as if this gave her cover.

The night when Kai rang her security bell over and over until Andie finally relented and buzzed him in was the first time he'd made a mistake in years, publicly calling attention to himself on the street outside her house. And so it was also then that the rumors about their history very quietly began to take root on the internet, even though Birdie had stopped sleeping with him, tried to stop even thinking of him.

He was drunk because Kai was often drunk, and Andie, as unimpressed by meeting the world's biggest action star as she was by being a blood relative to the world's biggest rom-com star, put him in the guest room, where he fell asleep half-dressed, and called Birdie and demanded she head home. Birdie remembered, even now, that she'd made an excuse to Simon at the event, that Andie had sprained her ankle and needed help. What adult needed help with a sprained ankle? But Simon kissed her and stayed behind because rubbing elbows with VIPs was important for his own job, and for once, Birdie was relieved to be with someone who bought into the celebrity of it all. She rushed back to find Kai snoring facedown atop the duvet with one shoe dangling off his foot, and Andie standing there with crossed arms. Their own mom had left their dad for someone new, and Andie was understandably puritanical about infidelity. But Birdie hadn't seen Kai in ages, she told Andie, and that was true. She'd been faithful to Simon, just like in a few years when this pattern repeated itself with Carter—Kai hurling himself against her front door because by then he had her gate code—and she was faithful to Carter too. It was just that Kai always took up emotional space, lurking in Birdie's cerebral background, a sickness for which she had no cure.

Still, that night she roused him and kicked him out before Simon got back.

Now, with the sun setting in Barton, she and Andie stopped in front of their childhood home. Andie had always been a better person than Birdie, that much was clear. The next morning, she told Birdie to cut Kai out of her life entirely. That he was a cancerous tumor, that she owed it to Simon. But Birdie couldn't, couldn't commit to such a thing, even if she wasn't the one chasing Kai, even if she had abandoned him completely once his team arranged the fake engagement to Haley. Eventually, months later, it became obvious to both of them—Andie and Birdie—that their arrangement was untenable: Andie's judgment, Birdie's obstinance or paralysis when the phone rang at midnight or Andie was cleaning out Birdie's inbox and saw Kai's emails (which Birdie did not return but left there all the same). So she fired Andie or Andie quit. It didn't really matter which—they screamed at each other as Andie threw her clothes into a duffel and revved up the 4Runner, and the damage had been done to their sisterhood, which wasn't even all that seamless in the first place.

What made it all the more punishing for Birdie was that she knew by then that she didn't even really love Kai. Not in the way that she had loved Elliot. Kai had his pick of any woman on the planet. The actual planet. But Elliot had rebuffed her when it mattered, when it was just the two of them with so much naked history between them. So maybe Kai was what she deserved, whom she deserved: a man who was half-present, dubiously faux-engaged, and who once said to her, "You're, like, ninety percent what I'm looking for." Birdie hated herself for trying to convince him that he could live without the ten percent rather than convince herself that she was already everything that someone else might want. But who did want her one hundred percent? Not the person she actually hoped it would be in the first place: Elliot. So she kept Kai's pleas close to her heart because at least that was something. At least it wasn't nothing.

The sun had nearly tucked behind the horizon on their street in Barton when Birdie finally decided to forge a peace with her little sister. "I wasn't that bad of a boss," she said, toeing a crack in the sidewalk because it kept her eyes occupied.

"You were a dictator," Andie replied. "You were grouchy and demanding and very rarely thankful or appreciative. I know it was a job, but, like, we were sisters, Birdie."

"Are sisters."

"But you treated me like an employee. And then there was . . . that asshole. I mean, honestly, Bird, fuck him."

"But you *were* an employ—" Birdie started, then caught herself picking an entirely different fight. She stopped, inhaled. "So then this whole thing, Sebastian Carol, the studio shutting us down, the apology video—it must have delighted you."

"You think that I get off on my sister being publicly shamed?"

"I think you thought I should be shamed for a long time coming."

Andie blew out her breath, which sounded acutely like her patience was being extremely tried.

"Birdie, this is your whole problem. You always think everything is about *you*. I have spent approximately zero minutes thinking about your video meltdown, your professional liabilities." Andie stared at her until Birdie had no choice but to meet her gaze. "I have a life outside my famous sister. I have a girlfriend, I'm prepping my dissertation, I'm packing up our entire childhood because our parents are in Spain. I have . . . like, other shit going on. If you ever came home, ever called, you'd know that."

"I can't wait to hear all about your dissertation," Birdie said, and Andie rolled her eyes because they both knew that wasn't true. "Okay, but I *do* know you have a girlfriend. Heather," Birdie said. "I met her. I like her."

"Heather and I broke up nine months ago," Andie said. "Her name is Dre."

"Oh," Birdie said, her eyes right back to that crack in the sidewalk. "Okay, well, maybe I could meet Dre. I am sure I'll like her too."

"Maybe." Andie shrugged and started toward the door, like they were so far gone it didn't matter one way or the other. Maybe it didn't.

But maybe it still could.

"Hey," Birdie said to her sister, who hesitated for a flicker, but then opened the front door and slammed it behind her. It struck her suddenly that there was nothing stopping her from making sincere amends. Other than her pride. Really, other than herself. That it was that simple. Like an equation that Andie had probably worked out long before Birdie did because Andie really always was one step ahead of her in math.

She probably owed a lot of people apologies. Not a filmed apology like Imani and Sydney had insisted on. Birdie knew she sounded insincere and was grimacing like she was battling a bad case of food poisoning. That the lighting was too perfect, that her makeup was immaculate when it should have been running down her face, that her stylist had given her blowout too much pep, her clothes too much starch. What people needed was a real, heartfelt, down-on-her-knees, from-the-bottom-of-her-soul apology.

She stood outside her childhood home as the light faded and

the temperature dipped. The lights from the neighboring houses twinkled. The smoke poured out of chimneys. If she inhaled deeply enough, she thought maybe she could smell mulled cider on a stove somewhere or maybe that was just her imagination, the embellishment that she was always adding to a perfectly fine reality.

She stared up at the first stars in the cloudless, chilly sky. She knew what the script would dictate she do. She knew how her character would be rewarded. She just didn't know if it was too late in the act for the audience to believe that she could change.

BLIND ITEM:

We have an early Valentine's teaser! Want to know whose heart might burst at the seams? Well, the star who is on everyone's brain these days: BiRo. One Miss Birdie Robinson. A different little birdy sent us a blind item that we thought was a perfect love potion for our subscribers.

We hear that Ms. Robinson's anonymous paramour is a high roller who likes the penthouse life amid the showgirls. Will theirs be a happily ever after? A roll of the dice.

⇒ 33 ⇐

ELLIOT

ELLIOT WOKE UP the next morning with an itch to write and with Birdie on his brain. Francesca had blessedly gone quiet for the morning—a quick text about her kid's violent stomach bug, which was obviously not a positive, but Elliot took his wins where he could get them these days with her. He tossed his phone to the foot of his bed and rolled to his back, staring at the ceiling. He had to figure out how to convince Birdie to trek to Vegas and sit down with Simon and see where it could lead.

His future, not to be too dramatic, depended on it.

He was beginning to suspect, however, that he needed to take a clearer-eyed look at how he defined his future. He'd gotten greedy with his shortcuts. He'd gotten in so deep that he couldn't assess when he was blurring the lines and when he was walking right over them. Maybe Francesca had been right to put boundaries around his work. Maybe Mona had been right to put boundaries around Birdie. Maybe he was too arrogant for his own good and too reckless to be reliable. Maybe he slept with women all the time because it was easier than being alone. Maybe being alone reminded him of the one pure thing that he'd had and how that was gone too. Maybe the brilliant Elliot O'Brien was actually a fool: he was working so hard on a series of articles that ran counter to exactly what he wanted. Birdie. Birdie was what he wanted. Who he wanted.

Elliot pushed up to his elbows, smelling waffles and coffee wafting from downstairs. He should come clean with Mona. Tell her the truth about that night in New York all those years ago. How was he expected to write the rest of this series if he couldn't be honest about his part in it? But he thought of how angry she'd be and couldn't bear one more calamity. He flopped back on the bed.

Tomorrow. He'd tell her tomorrow.

Then, as if Mona had read his mind, the door to his boyhood room burst open.

"Come on," Mona sang, "I made your favorite breakfast."

She bounced onto his bed and jumped on top of him like she used to when they were kids. It was one of the singularly odd things about being orphaned, even as an adult in your midthirties. How specific and granular your memories were of a time when your parents were still alive, and how you could carry on in all the same ways, but without them, everything shifts just five or ten degrees, so nothing is the same at all.

"Get off of me," Elliot said with a huff, just like he always did when they were kids too.

"Okay, but hurry up or else I'm going to eat all the waffles." Mona really always did level with you.

He pushed himself up to seated, then swung his feet to the floor and was surprised at how delightful he found this: his sister's wide-open enthusiasm for the everyday mundanity of life. Sometimes, he resented that she'd claimed Birdie as her own, that even as he so profoundly loved her, Mona got there first. But other times, like now, he saw it with utter clarity: that he and Mona were all the other had.

He wiped the sleep from his eyes and found a T-shirt in his drawer that read *Barton Varsity Swimming* and tugged it over his head. He thought again of Birdie, how he lingered at school for her after that rehearsal with the Cheetos or Doritos or whatever, how he'd been wearing his full varsity garb like that would impress her. How he thought that maybe it had, but what did it matter?

He wound his way downstairs and found Mona halfway through a Belgian waffle.

"It's been like thirty seconds," he said, then reached for the other half.

"Sit," she replied. "I have another one coming."

He sat, surprised at how grateful he was to be taken care of, even for something as simple as a homemade breakfast. Mona was so often looking out for him, he realized now. And he mostly repaid her by nagging her about Caltech, by quietly—and sometimes less quietly—judging her choices.

"Do you think Birdie is really done with me?" he asked. "I mean, with the articles?"

She hovered by the waffle iron, pouring the batter in, watching it sizzle before she closed it.

"I think," she said, "that if you want Birdie to trust you, you need to give her a reason to. So my advice to you is to give her a reason to."

Elliot sighed, squeezed his eyes closed, and pressed his fingers to his lids like he was staving off a headache. "So *you* think she doesn't trust me?"

"I think I'm the wrong person to ask," Mona said. "There are only two people who can answer that. And one of them is you."

34

BIRDIE

BIRDIE HAD UNEARTHED a mountain of pillows and sheets last night from a box that Andie had earmarked for Goodwill, and she was piled under the entirety of the bedding when her phone started vibrating again on her nightstand. She'd already muted nearly all her notifications: Twitter and Instagram and text and email. She knew what America thought of her; she didn't need the play-by-play. But she'd forgotten to set the ringtone to silent, so here it was, haunting her. Had been for the better part of the morning and afternoon.

She heard the door to her room open, then her sister's thundering footsteps.

"Oh my god," Andie said, flinging the sheets off Birdie, as if Birdie's hideaway aggrieved her personally. "Get. Up."

"Hey!" Birdie snapped, flopping onto her back. "I wasn't bothering you. I thought that would make you happy."

Andie grabbed the phone and held it directly in Birdie's eyeline. "Elliot. Elliot O'Brien has called you nine times in the past three hours." She dropped it onto Birdie's belly. "So do you want to tell me what's going on or are we still pretending that you can handle this all on your own?"

"I thought you were totally disinterested in my business," Birdie said.

"I am. But even I can see that when a world-famous movie star is hiding in a pillow fort, it's a pretty pitiful cry for help. But a cry for help all the same." She paused. "Also, I found this cashmere sweater in your duffel bag, and I'm keeping it, so I came up to say . . . thank you. And I suppose in return, I can be a little generous with your problems. But that could wear off in about ten minutes, so I suggest you hurry."

Birdie groaned and flung an arm over her eyes, like she couldn't bear to tell Andie the truth if she could see her. She felt something soft smack her in the face, then opened her eyes to see Andie hovering above, armed with a pillow.

"You do not get to resort to violence!" Birdie cried just as Andie pummeled her one more time.

"It's ironic," Andie said, "that the girl who has everything still behaves as if she has nothing, still mopes up here feeling sorry for herself."

"I don't have everything," Birdie said. "I am very bad at math, for example."

Andie clenched her jaw like she was about two seconds away from losing every last ounce of her patience. "Why is Elliot calling you so desperately? When you just saw him yesterday."

Birdie moaned and forced herself upright, leaning back against the headboard.

"It's complicated," she said.

"No shit," Andie answered.

Birdie looked up at her sister, who seemed like she knew more than Birdie had expected.

"What does that mean?"

"It means that anyone with eyes and even an extremely limited emotional IQ knew that you were in love with him since puberty."

"What? That's not true. That's not accurate at *all*."

Andie pinched up her face. "Come on, Birdie. You can be more convincing than that. You're a better actress than *that*."

"Whatever you think you know—"

Andie waved a hand, stopping her. "I know that when we lived together in LA, I saw you make a series of truly trash choices. I saw you choose a bad man over a pretty good one. And I suspect that you had already long ago chosen an even better one."

"Elliot," Birdie muttered.

"Elliot." Andie nodded, plopping on the bed, unspooling next to her.

They lay in silence for a long beat. Birdie rolled on her side toward her sister and noticed that the aquamarine hue in the sweater Andie had swiped from her really brought out the gold in her irises, made her blond hair even more golden. Birdie should have shared more often, more generously with her—it would have cost her nothing.

She hesitated, deliberating.

"Elliot and I slept together. About seven years ago," she said finally.

Andie's eyes grew to globes, and she clamped both hands over her mouth, like she was trying not to scream.

"I know," Birdie said, and allowed herself to grin. That in a normal world, if she were a normal person, she could share such a delicious juicy detail with her sister and revel in it.

"And?" Andie asked. She turned onto her own side, so they were parentheses now. "And then?"

"It was . . . it wasn't realistic. It could never happen."

"Why?" Andie asked.

"It was Elliot's decision," Birdie said, her shoulder rising, then falling. "I can't blame him."

"You can blame him however you fucking want to!" Andie said, and Birdie jolted back, like she honestly couldn't believe her sister was taking her side. Or maybe she couldn't believe that after the past few weeks she'd had, anyone who wasn't on her payroll was taking her side. "He doesn't just get to sleep with you after all those years, then decide that it was a mistake. He is such a manwhore," she added.

"I don't think that we can say *manwhore* anymore," Birdie said.

"Fine. Whatever. Start at the beginning. Spill everything."

Birdie sighed and blew out her breath, steeling her nerve, steeling her guts. She hadn't told anyone about any of this. Not back then, not since. It was embarrassing, humiliating, made her feel exactly like she was back in high school, itchy and ready to flee.

Then, in what she considered a real display of growth, she met her sister's eyes and decided that maybe she should say it anyway.

35

ELLIOT

ELLIOT HADN'T HEARD back from Birdie by the time he and Mona were settling in for the night. Mona was entertaining vegetarianism for reasons he didn't ask about because she was cooking, and it wasn't often that he had a home-cooked meal. This made him think of Ian, which made him think of Birdie, which was actually hilarious because he never stopped thinking of Birdie. She was the only thing his brain was processing, like a storm siren blaring *Birdie Birdie Birdie* until he evacuated.

He'd checked his phone four times at the dinner table before Mona finally chided him.

"She told you that she didn't want to do this anymore. You called her, she didn't answer. You have to let it go. You don't always get what you want, which, I know, is sort of new for you."

"But I'm heading to Vegas tomorrow. And it would be much better for the story if she joined."

"It's always about the story with you," she said, and forked at her tofu, looking a little sad. Elliot wasn't sure if it was the tofu or the situation with Birdie or just, like, the situation in general.

"Anyway, aren't journalists supposed to be able to adapt, react in real time? Just react in real time."

"She's honestly the most infuriating person I've ever met," he answered, which did not address her question at all. He pushed his own tofu around, then settled on a green bean with crispy onions, a dish their mom used to make, which made him wistful.

Mona raised her eyebrows. "Hmm." She chewed slowly, like she was exaggerating her point, but it could have been her cooking.

"What's that supposed to mean?" Elliot set his fork down.

Mona moved her plate away. "She only gets under your skin because you let her."

"And what's *that* supposed to mean?" Elliot said more loudly than he'd intended. He'd been meticulous over the decades, keeping his feelings about Birdie from Mona.

"Don't you find it odd," she asked, "that you've been with, um, your fair share of women—is that a respectful way to say it?—and I don't think I've ever seen you get worked up, tied in knots, over anyone like you do with Birdie. It's been, what? Three days? And you want to strangle her."

"Exactly. She's infuriating."

Mona rose and took her plate with her, and it clattered in the sink. Elliot, who considered himself to be nearly always prepared for his job, was not prepared for this. Did Mona know about their night together? Did Mona know about the extent of his feelings? He felt like the room was tilting, like everything was coming undone beneath him. She returned to the table with a slice of apple pie from the grocery store and a tub of vanilla ice cream, which she slid over to his place mat.

"I'm only irritated with her," Elliot said carefully, "because she and I agreed to do this together. I take my work seriously. Even if she doesn't."

Mona nodded, then picked off a piece of the piecrust and savored it.

"Everyone knows how seriously you take your work, Elliot. Try a different answer."

"Oh, I see, so because you *don't* take work seriously—" he started.

She waved her hand in a flash. "Do. Not. Demean. Me. With. Your. Brand. Of. Bullshit."

"I'm not—"

Mona's eyes flared, and he stuttered, then stopped.

"I happen to love running the bar, Elliot. I happen to love taking out the RV with my friends, looking for alien life. I happen to love living here, even though you think I should have aimed higher. You aimed higher, and so what? What has that gotten you?" She paused. "No, seriously, El, what do you have in your life besides work?"

Elliot slunk lower in his seat, pushed the ice cream tub a few inches away from him. He didn't want to fight with Mona, and it wasn't like she was wrong. He offered up a small nod, an acknowledgment that he'd stepped in it.

"I'm trying," he said, but he wasn't really. He'd filled his life up with ambition and work and meaningless sex because everyone needed a contact high every now and then. He used to have things he loved—the cut of the water when he was flying in a fifty free, the camaraderie of a newsroom when everyone got slaphappy, the way that he'd land in a foreign country for an assignment and the air was electric, not just because of the career opportunities but because he'd spend downtime exploring bazaars or football matches or hole-in-the-wall local cafés. Now he worked for the work, for the accolades. The exploration—in just about every aspect of his life other than breaking a headline—had dimmed. Maybe, he realized, he was tired. Maybe, he considered, he was lonely. He thought of Birdie in carpool, of Birdie in the RV, getting all the lyrics wrong, singing loudly anyway. Maybe—his heart lurched—it was time to do something about it.

His twin sighed, pulled back a chair, sat back down right beside him. She rested a palm on his arm.

"Remember when we first moved here? And we met her out front?"

Elliot had absolutely no idea where she was going with this. "Of course."

"And then how we started school, and you were immediately beloved because, well, you're you. And Birdie and I just . . . I mean, we're not you."

Elliot swallowed. If he and Mona were really going to discuss this, get into it, maybe it would go better than he thought. Maybe he really could tell her about their night together, and that he'd tried to do the right thing—walked away—when Mona called him the next morning, but that it wasn't the right thing at all.

"Anyway," Mona continued. "For a long time, she and I were all each other had. I mean, yeah, some of her theater friends or whatever, but let's be honest, they weren't great company since they tended to break into song with no notice, and that was tiresome from the get-go. Like, hello, our lives are not actually *Glee*."

Elliot smiled. *Sweet dreams are made of cheese.*

"But we're grown-ups now. You know that, right? You know that we can be friends with one another, and it's not like I have dibs on Birdie. Maybe I thought that when we were, like, thirteen. Or," she said more quietly, "at prom. But that's because you

had this whole goddamn town on your side. I just had Birdie."
She paused, as if to make sure that he heard her. "You can call her
up now and chew her out for being a narcissist, or you can call
her up and tell her that you're sorry you guys are fighting. You
don't have to worry about me having my feelings hurt because I'm
the third wheel on this. You're allowed to be friends without me."

Friends.

Okay.

"I've called her nine times today," he said.

"Well, you know Birdie, she never met a dramatic arc that she
didn't want to make at least one scene longer."

He did know Birdie, and he thought her love of the dramatic
arc might just be the cure for the thing that ailed him. Maybe he
needed more fantasy in his life, maybe he needed to get swept up
in the electricity of her wild imagination. But of course, then
there was Francesca.

"I'm going to Vegas tomorrow," he said, "with or without
Birdie."

Mona bounced her head. "The dogged reporter until the bit-
ter end."

"Would you want to come?" he asked, startling himself but in
only a good way. "I mean, I'd like it if you came."

Mona's face cracked open into a smile, her eyes dancing with
surprise. "Absolutely. I'll have someone cover the bar."

"The O'Brien twins take a road trip." Elliot grinned.

"Vegas, baby," Mona said. "You know I've always liked to
gamble."

36

BIRDIE

BIRDIE WOKE THE morning after her confession to Andie feeling like she'd consumed all the cheap vodka in the Barton vicinity. She *had* consumed all the cheap vodka (the cheapest) in the Barton vicinity. Andie was still asleep and snoring beside her with red plastic cups and an emptied bottle on her floor. They'd made a 7-Eleven run last night after dark because their parents had drained their liquor cabinet before they left for Spain. The 7-Eleven was the only place nearby that was open past 10 p.m., and since they were merely looking for something—anything—with alcohol, it worked out just fine. Birdie had worn a baseball hat nearly down to the top of her nose and tugged Andie's neon hoodie over her head, but even then, the cashier had raised his eyebrows and said, "Whoa, Birdie Robinson. Rough out there for you these days."

And Andie had snapped, "Oh shut up, Matthew, and mind your own business," which surprised Birdie perhaps more than it surprised Matthew, and she lost herself to a fit of giggles that she couldn't control until they were halfway home.

Once she was properly boozy, Birdie had finally told Andie the whole story about Elliot. Which was also a story about Kai.

The night of the premiere, when she ran into Elliot for the first time in years, she had been obsessing over Kai. She knew he was terrible for her; she knew that whenever she thought of him, her stomach cratered out and her anxiety spiked. They'd been entangled for two long years, off and on, in fits and starts, with Kai returning to her on unpredictable whims, as if his entire purpose was to keep her off-balance. It had started on set, as Andie had already pieced together when Birdie was relaying all of this. He was a superstar by then, seven years older, famous beyond famous. Birdie was the hot new ingenue, having landed the lead opposite him after one of the casting directors saw something in that Oregon lighthouse indie film and decided she should be a bona fide movie star. Kai knocked on her trailer door the first day with a bouquet of flowers the size of a St. Bernard, and Birdie was smitten. That he made the effort, that he noticed her.

Within two weeks, they were spending all their free hours in his trailer (his was much nicer than hers), and one day, he leaned over and kissed her, and Birdie's brain short-circuited, like his kiss was so potent that it scrambled her mind. He stood up and locked the door to his trailer, and then he proceeded to take off her clothes, followed by all of his. The whole time, Birdie was thinking, *I cannot believe that Kai Carol wants to sleep with me, Birdie Maxwell, from Barton, California.*

Even though she'd already been with Ian, and Ian was objectively wonderful. But he wasn't worldly like Kai. He wasn't beloved like Kai. He wasn't magnetic and powerful, which Birdie knew weren't reasons to fall in love with someone, but that he chose her? Well, she'd be a liar to say that it didn't matter. It did. Kai Carol could choose anyone on the planet, literally, and he chose her.

Once the movie wrapped, they kept going quietly, stealthily, like the secrecy was half the fun—Birdie flying into wherever he was whenever they both had a free weekend. Until it was announced that Kai was engaged. Birdie learned about it from a gossip site in a retweet on Twitter. She cried and called him up and screamed at him, and he assured her it was just for show. That audiences wanted him to be the sort of man who married his high school sweetheart, not an up-and-coming starlet or else sure, babe, of course he would have been thrilled to go public with her instead. But Birdie was the one he loved, she was the one he needed. She was the one he dreamt about.

The night she ran into Elliot at the premiere seven years back, Kai had called her to wish her good luck. She hadn't heard from him in four months, since the engagement. That night, he called to say that he was working out a plan to end it, that he couldn't go on another day without her.

"Wait for me, baby. Give me a little time. Then it will be you and me. I want us to get married. I want *us* to have babies."

Birdie demurred. She'd been clear with him that as long as he was with Haley, contracted or not, he was off-limits. She had her own memories of her mom leaving them, and even when Kai tugged at all of her seams, she tried to be stalwart, she tried to hold steady. But she heard the promise in his voice and wanted to believe him. She was too embarrassed by the moral squishiness of it to share with Mona, and she didn't have many other friends.

And then she ran into Elliot (literally). In a tuxedo. At the bar.

The only boy she had ever loved in a pure, perfect, uncomplicated way, the only boy who had made her feel like she wasn't settling if she was only Birdie Maxwell. Maybe Ian had made her feel that too, but then Ian wasn't Elliot, and that, Birdie supposed now, was never his fault.

It had been electric from their first hello. Everything else became background noise at the party other than Elliot, here, in front of her, all grown up. He wiped his drink off her dress, then leaned in to kiss her cheek, and her whole body nearly detonated. The only thing she cared about was getting him home, letting him do whatever he wanted to her, letting her do whatever she wanted to him. They replenished their gin and tonics until she was buzzed enough to let him follow her to the bathroom, where he pushed her up against the wall as if they both understood that they were combustible. He lingered an inch away from her, breathing, just breathing, until a noise rose in his throat as if to say, *Are we doing this? I think we are doing this*, and she nodded, because mostly, she wanted to just devour him whole. And then he closed the inch between them, and Birdie thought her heart might give out.

"Do you want to see my new apartment?" she'd asked, pointedly, clearly, when she found the will to pull back from his lips.

"Yes," he replied simply, hungrily. "Yes."

They could barely make it to her waiting town car before they tore into each other. His hands were all over her body, leaving imprints on every last inch of her skin. Hers worked their way under his shirt, over his face, through his hair, onto his belt buckle.

"So we are definitely doing this?" Birdie managed. After a decade of wanting, she needed to be sure it was real, he was real.

"Yes," he said again, "we definitely are."

Birdie thought she might be having an out-of-body experience, but not like when she was with Kai, when her disbelief was because of the fantasy of him. Rather, this time, it was because of the reality of Elliot. *Elliot!* Whom she had loved and dreamed of and wanted since she was old enough to want such things.

"Wait," he managed in the back seat, sounding very much like he did not want to wait. "Not in the car. I don't want this to happen in a car."

It was all she could do not to straddle him and pull him inside her.

They held it together until her apartment building, where Birdie frantically pushed the elevator button while Elliot nibbled on her shoulder, and then once they stepped inside, his hands snaked up her thighs, under her dress, and pushed her underwear aside, his fingers diving into her. And she was ready for it. He buried his face in her neck, and she whimpered at how good he smelled, how good he felt. Like he belonged there. When the elevator doors opened again, he pulled his fingers out from inside of her, and she nearly begged him to keep going. She fumbled with her keys until the latch blessedly unlocked, and they stumbled inside, then he kicked the door closed with his foot, never missing a beat, and pressed her against the front foyer wall, flipping her so her back faced him and he could unzip her dress, tooth by tooth.

The dress dropped to the floor, and she turned to face him, braless, exposed, in nothing but her black thong and her heels.

Elliot took a step back to stare at her, his eyes roaming all over, everywhere, like she was fucking edible. He looked animalistic, wild, and Birdie loved every moment of it. His hands found their way to her hips again, and he stepped closer, half an inch away.

"I've wanted to do this to you forever," he said, his voice low, hoarse.

Birdie swallowed. She didn't think she'd ever needed something so desperately, not even with Kai. She was on fire. Everywhere.

Elliot sunk to his knees, his fingers winding their way over the elastic of her underwear. He gazed up at her. She nodded. He started with his lips on the inside of her thighs. Slowly. Gently. Driving her wild. She spread her legs open an inch, then another. He accepted the invitation and slipped a finger inside her and, when she gasped, slipped in another.

"Jesus, Birdie, I—" He lost his breath then, and it was just as well because she wasn't capable of talking. He pulled her thong lower, then down to her ankles, and she kicked it aside, and then his tongue was inside her with exactly the right amount of pressure, and he worked his fingers again, and she cried out for him because she didn't want him to stop.

He glanced toward her and grinned.

"Tell me what you want me to do to you. Because I know what I've been imagining. Forever. But I want what you want. So tell me, Bird."

"Everything," she managed. "I want you to do everything."

He nodded and then his mouth was back, his tongue probing, and Birdie wanted to make it last. But she was slipping away, her body on fire, her breathing ragged. He sensed it and refused to relent, sucking and pressuring and intuiting exactly the right spots to make her absolutely crazy. She was sweating and her breath was hitching, and her palms were flattened against the wall as if they were holding her up. They were. She couldn't even feel her legs anymore. Finally, when she thought she was going to pass out from how fucking good he felt, he pulled back and said, "More?"

And she whispered, "Please."

And he worked his fingers and his thumb to exactly the spot that even Kai had never found. And then she was cresting and tipping over over over, nearly leaving her body, wondering if she would ever stop. When she did, finally, the room was spinning, and he rose to his feet, and she led him to her bedroom, and they did it all again, only this time, it wasn't just his fingers that were inside her. He kept his eyes on her the whole time, like he couldn't believe it, like if he looked away even for a second, none of it would be real. For Birdie, nothing had felt more real, nothing had felt better.

They kept at it all night. Every time Birdie thought she had to come up for air, Elliot pulled her under again, as if he'd been starving for her body for a decade, and now he needed every second, every inch of her.

"My god," Andie said from the floor of Birdie's childhood bedroom. "My. God."

"I know." Birdie nodded. "Trust me. I know."

"So explain to me why you're sitting here with me, and not over there with him? Because if you don't, I may. And I've been a lesbian since birth." Andie refilled her vodka and swallowed it in three gulps, then clutched her chest. "Oh god, does that burn." They were both going to regret this in the morning.

"Because then he left," Birdie said. "Just like he does with every other woman. I wasn't any different than anyone else."

"Explain," Andie said. "Let me be the judge."

Birdie wasn't particularly interested in reliving the humiliation, but her brain was buzzy and her tongue a little numb, so she didn't stop herself. Maybe she'd feel better, to have Andie share in her embarrassment, tell her what she could have done differently all those years ago.

The next morning, she decided to call in sick for work. She and Elliot hadn't discussed what any of this meant, other than that they couldn't tell Mona just yet, but she didn't want him to leave. She knew that much. Maybe, she told herself in the months afterward, she was wrapped up in the fantasy, the way that one of her characters would have been: daydreaming about how the two of them could last forever. Even though she'd been certain that being with Elliot was grounding, true, the realest thing about her now gargantuan make-believe life. But regardless, when she woke, Elliot wasn't there. His pillow was still indented, his side of the bed still rumpled and smelling vaguely of his shampoo, and yet Birdie was all alone. Her chest got tight, and nausea crested in her throat. She buried herself under the sheets in a cocoon to get a grip. It didn't help.

After so many years, she'd finally gotten what she wanted, and then it hadn't been real at all. He'd panicked, she assumed, and fled.

She found her phone on the nightstand. Nothing from Elliot. She triple-checked her email, her spam, her texts. Definitely nothing from Elliot. But Kai. Kai must have heard that she left with someone the night of the premiere because he was all over her phone. Twelve texts. Two emails when she didn't return the texts. Three missed calls.

She replied to his last text.

> **BIRDIE**
> **Hey. Sorry. Been busy.**

He replied immediately, like he was clutching his phone in his palm, staring at it until it buzzed.

> **KAI**
> **I need to see you. In NYC. Coming now.**

And she knew that Kai wasn't what she wanted. Wasn't *who* she wanted. But she wasn't in any emotional state to deal with her heartbreak alone.

She pushed herself to standing, then stumbled to the bathroom to brush her teeth. She typed back: **OK.**

She was applying mascara when she heard her front door open, then close.

"Hello?" she called, surprised that Kai had made it there so quickly or that her doorman had buzzed him up without asking, but then she wasn't thinking clearly. She wandered to the living room and found Elliot standing there with a bag of bagels.

"Hey," he said, holding them aloft. "Bagels."

"Oh," she replied, trying to steady her voice. "I thought you left." Her brain felt staticky, her tongue thick. She started to say more but then couldn't figure out what it was that she wanted to articulate.

"Look," he said, staring down at her feet. Her stomach coiled. He sighed. Set down the bag on her dining table, ran his fingers over his face, his two-day-old stubble. "I think, this has been—" He stopped, stuttered, then stopped again, seemingly no more sure of what he wanted to convey than she was. Like in the bright light of the morning, he'd reconsidered everything. Birdie hadn't. Birdie would have flown to the moon and the stars for him, she thought, but then she realized that she'd invited Kai over so easily, so quickly. Maybe she didn't know what she wanted any more than Elliot did. But it was irrelevant. Because he kept talking.

"I just—" he tried again. "Mona called me," he said finally. "Birdie, I don't want—"

"It's okay," she said, not because it was in any way okay but because she didn't want him to see how much he was about to wreck her. She didn't want to hear his excuses. Didn't even know if they were true. Maybe he just wanted to get her out of his system, an itch that needed to be scratched. He wouldn't be the first guy who had just wanted to fuck someone famous.

Her panic was rising like a tide—she needed to pull it together before Kai turned up. Not even because she cared if she offended him, but because she'd be absolutely humiliated if Elliot knew that she'd agreed to fill his side of the bed before it grew cold. She didn't even *want* to fill his side of the bed; she was certainly *not* going to sleep with Kai regardless of what sort of grand gesture he pulled off this time. She wasn't sure how this had all happened—Elliot and bagels and Mona and her action star who seemed to call only when she was on the cusp of forgetting him. Maybe she really did go into a fugue state, a place of make-believe, when everything got hard.

"No," Elliot replied as her brain spiraled. "It's not okay. Not really. None of this is okay. Nothing about it is okay."

Birdie didn't know if he was saying that he regretted their night or he just regretted the clarity with which he now saw the situation, but she resolved that she didn't want to find out, didn't want to hear just how deep his regret ran. To learn that she was now disposable, it was just unbearable, too much.

"It *is* okay. It's totally fine." She nodded. "We're consenting adults. It's not a big deal. You should go. I think your jacket is bunched up in the foyer." She really was a spectacular actress.

"*Birdie*," he said. "Please, let me explain. Can we talk about this—"

The phone on her wall buzzed—her doorman. Her brain buzzed along with it.

"That's work," she managed, though it nearly broke her. "I actually need to start my day. We can pretend this never happened."

"Birdie, that's not—" Elliot started, but she had brushed past him, scooping up his tuxedo jacket in one hand, swinging her door open with the other, as if she were ushering him out. She was, although she didn't understand why. But the doorman was still ringing, and Kai was downstairs waiting. Birdie didn't want

Kai the way she wanted—had always wanted—Elliot, and she didn't necessarily even want a man, but god, if she had one, she wanted someone who was going to lay it all on the line for her. Elliot was already backpedaling away from the line.

"Right." Elliot nodded and shoved his hands in his pockets. He stopped right in front of her in the doorframe, met her eyes, and it was all Birdie could do not to crater. "I'm sorry about all of this. I'm sorry to walk away from you."

And Birdie wanted to scream, *Then, don't, goddammit, do not!* but, well, Elliot O'Brien had always been out of her league and maybe she'd forgotten that.

He got into the elevator, and that was the last time Birdie saw Elliot until seven years later in Monads.

"So you never even heard him out?" Andie said last night. They were both drunk on the vodka by then, and Birdie's stomach was beginning to curdle.

"I didn't need to hear him explicitly reject me even more than he had." Birdie shoved her face into a pillow on her bed, then thought better of it and curled around it, like that might ease her digestion.

"Birdie, you are such a fucking moron." Andie sighed. "This is like the cliché in one of your movies where the guy is trying to pour his heart out and the girl is too stupid to listen."

"No," Birdie said. "He was always going to choose Mona. If that was even a legitimate excuse, not just a reason to bolt. But, like, for my own ego, let's pretend that it was real . . . How can I blame him for that?"

"Elliot isn't a liar, so stop it with that," Andie said. "He's a lot of things, and definitely a bit of a slut—"

"We also can't say *slut* anymore," Birdie said. "We're entirely sex-positive."

"Fine, whatever. He is known to appreciate the female form. But still not a liar, and I kind of can't believe that you've spent seven years telling yourself that he is. You really are the queen of make-believe," Andie said, and Birdie lifted her head and punched her in the arm. "Ow!" Andie yelped. "And also, Mona is a big girl. You should give her some credit. Or maybe the both of you should."

It hadn't occurred to Birdie that Mona and her sister could be friends now, though of course it made sense: both living in Barton, both with shared history.

"I don't think she'd want either of you sacrificing on her account. You guys aren't kids anymore," Andie added.

Birdie sat up and inexplicably guzzled more vodka. She thought she might puke but couldn't stop herself. "It's not like he didn't have the chance over the past seven years to tell me that I'd misunderstood, that I'd read the situation wrong," she said. She thought of the kiss, of his hands on her breasts in the RV.

"Don't forget, I met Kai." Andie sniffed. "That one time in LA when he passed out in your guest room. I'd pick Elliot any day of the week. I'd pick Simon any day of the week over him. Fuckin' movie star, more like a gigantic asshole."

Simon. Shit, Elliot was leaving for Vegas in the morning to interview him. In her confession to Andie, Birdie had forgotten all about the present mess of her life, not just the past mess of it.

"Simon was a good guy," Birdie echoed, her words getting slurry.

"Yes, but I think it's obvious that Elliot wrote the letter," Andie said.

"No, I asked." Her eyelids were feeling heavy now. "Besides, it's okay, it was all for the best."

Once Elliot was in the elevator the morning after, Birdie dialed back down to her doorman, told him he could send Kai up.

Three minutes later, there he was. Kai Carol in the foyer of her new apartment. He ran his palms over her shoulders then down her arms, where he clutched her hands and made her promises all over again. He couldn't stay, he said, as he kissed her neck, and Birdie squeezed her eyes shut and tried not to think of how Elliot had turned her to molten lava when he did the same. But he had to see her, he said. He saw pictures of her at the premiere, he said. He thought about all sorts of untoward things he wanted to do to her, he said. He was coming undone, he said, at the thought of her moving on without him. He was leaving Haley imminently, calling the "engagement" off, he said. *We don't even live together. It's all an act, I promise.*

He had a flight to catch to Rome for some junket. Birdie couldn't remember for what now. But he asked her to wait for him, and Birdie, having already been rejected by the one man she realized she wanted but couldn't have, found it was easier to simply nod yes. She would wait for him. She didn't have any reason not to.

Andie was silent on the bed beside her for a long time, and Birdie thought that maybe her sister had fallen asleep. She liked that notion: that the two of them had reached a sort of peace, a comfort where they could share a bed like they were kids again. Then Andie said, "How did no one ever know this about you two?"

"About Elliot and me?" Birdie shrugged. "That wasn't difficult. We were the only two who ever knew about it. We kept our mouths shut. I didn't want to upset Mona when it was obvious that he'd already chosen her. What was the point?"

"No, about you and Kai Fucking Dickwad. You two combined could literally, like, provide solar power to Earth from your wattage."

"Oh," Birdie said. There had been rumors, of course, especially after he showed up at her Brentwood house when Andie was there. Some posturing on Reddit and various fan forums. But his team had denied everything and sent him to rehab as a distraction. He probably needed rehab all the same. A year or so later, he made one final effort—buzzing Birdie's gate again. This time, Carter answered. That time, Birdie rebuffed him completely, but Carter wasn't in it for half measures, and Birdie couldn't promise him that she wasn't complicated, that her situation wasn't complicated.

"He wrote it," Andie said. "He definitely wrote it. He wants to fix what happened that morning, make it right."

"Now you think *Kai* wrote it? Not Elliot?" Birdie's insides lurched at the possibility. Kai was her kryptonite, even all these years later, and she didn't have the fortitude to embroil herself all over again. He'd ended the years-long engagement, faked or otherwise, finally, but he'd never reached out to Birdie afterward. Not even when his brother publicly eviscerated her, not even when she could have used his defense. Or maybe he *had* reached out by sending her an anonymous letter, and maybe it had taken her years to find it because she never went home.

"No, idiot. Elliot," Andie said. "Or at least, he wrote one of them. Maybe both of them?"

"He's called nine times today," Birdie said. "I never picked up."

"If he calls again," Andie said.

"If he calls again," Birdie said, finishing her sentence, "then I will."

They passed out. Elliot never called.

≈ 37 ≈

ELLIOT

ELLIOT GAVE BIRDIE the benefit of the doubt and waited for her in Mona's driveway until 10 a.m. It was a long drive to Vegas, and he'd booked a room at Simon's hotel, which meant with a stop for gas and assuming the RV didn't blow, they'd get there right around check-in time. He didn't want to wait any longer.

Birdie had been clear—she was out. Just like she'd been clear that night when they'd finally been together. He'd thought they could discuss it the next morning; thought he could tell her what Mona had said, that he had every intention of making this stick, making it last. Birdie was unlike any other woman he'd been with, cared about. She was an inexplicable mix of quixotic and dramatic and hilarious and self-conscious and completely liberated. She was droll and pithy and funny, both unintentionally and also because she could deliver a line perfectly, and he couldn't explain it—their draw toward each other—she felt like his missing half, for no tangible reason other than that they clicked. The ephemeral, inexplicable magic of falling in love.

But there was Mona, on the phone when he went out for bagels while Birdie was still sleeping. She'd just called as a check-in, surprised that she hadn't heard from him in several days. She hadn't meant anything by it, the call. Didn't have an ulterior motive. In fact, she didn't say anything about Birdie because she, of course, didn't even know that Elliot had spent the night exploring every millimeter of Birdie's skin, committing every noise, every nuance, every nook of her body to memory. That night, they'd drifted off for a few minutes but he woke around 2 a.m. and just rolled to his side and stared, and she must have sensed it because she fluttered awake; she said, "You're still here," and her electric smile illuminated every angle on her face, and he said, "I'd stay forever if I could." And she said, "Well, I wouldn't be against that," and then he reached for her, his hands on her lower back, then her hips, then anywhere else he could make her crazy with.

But the next morning, Mona was in his ear, and Elliot remembered her boundary, one of the few things his sister had ever asked of him. Women were not a rare commodity for Elliot, even if Birdie was. How difficult was it—how deeply had he betrayed his sister—to covet the one woman he shouldn't have? Mona was the only family he had left now, and so he paid for the bagels and talked himself into leaving Birdie behind, although he didn't know if he had the guts, the fortitude, to do it. It turned out, he didn't have to—she never gave him the chance to figure out how he could stay. He'd always thought that if they'd decided together, united, they could have figured out a way. It *had* to be the two of them if they were going to face Mona, and when Birdie didn't even try, Elliot told himself that he'd gotten it all wrong. Birdie could have had anyone by then. Why did he imagine that it would be him?

Today in the driveway, Birdie wasn't going to show. And Elliot

intrinsically knew it. Still, that didn't mean it didn't pierce him—
that Birdie could untangle herself from him again so easily—and
the cut ran deep, slicing right through.

"All right," Mona said, her eyes pointed down the street toward the Maxwell house. "Enough. I know I get on you about
work, but you do have a job to do. So let's do it."

"I thought you told me to care *less* about my job."

"I did," Mona said. "But I don't want to have to hire you as a
busboy at Monads if you blow this."

"Why would I have to get a job as a busboy at Monads?" Elliot felt his face burn. Just how much did his sister know about
his life that he wasn't aware of?

Mona squinted up toward the overcast sky. "El, Francesca and
I are friends, you know that, right? Remember you brought me to
that thing . . ."

Elliot had forgotten. He'd been dateless for a media awards
dinner last year, so Mona drove up (in the camper) to attend. She
and Francesca had gotten on like a house on fire.

"We're friends online." Mona sighed. "She DMed me this
week. Told me you might need some backup. Implied that you
would need some backup." His twin paused. "You know that I'm
here as backup, yes? That you don't have to always be the one
leading the way."

Elliot blinked and tried to gather himself. This entire week
when he'd been trying to project strength, Mona knew of his
weakness. And she was just waiting for him to let her help.

"I should have told you," he managed.

"You should have trusted me," she replied.

"I do," he said.

"Sometimes," she answered, "when it's convenient for you."

"It's a relief that you know," he said, and he meant it, "that everything depends on this story for me. That I have to get it exactly right."

Mona started toward the camper. "Not everything depends on it, El. Some things do, sure, but not everything."

The drive to Vegas from Barton was interminably boring. Straight highway, deserted land. The RV still smelled a bit like Birdie, of her expensive Parisian perfume, and Elliot found it hard to get his head on straight in the plume. He'd already outlined the article—the work he was going to have to put in to make all the parts line up just right, so he couldn't distract himself with the buzz of work in his brain. He'd called Francesca from his driveway after he and Mona cleared the air, after the considerable stress bubble in his chest deflated, and promised her an article by a midnight deadline in time for tomorrow morning's news cycle.

They pulled onto the Vegas Strip by midafternoon. Mona was driving because she was better in traffic in a vehicle the size of a small home, and she veered the Winnebago into the giant circular driveway of Simon's hotel. A towering eruption of a fountain spurted gallons of water behind them, and a mob of tourists and valets stood at the ready at the front door. Mona opened the door, grabbed her overnight bag, and handed the keys to a perplexed attendant who was eyeing the camper like it was a mountain he couldn't scale.

"I know where every ding is on this thing. Take good care of her," she said, then marched toward the lobby.

Elliot trailed behind her, the whoosh of the automatic doors welcoming him and blowing back his mop of hair. He saw Mona disappearing into the casino, which was just as well: he had work to do and needed to find Simon. He approached the front desk, which had a cascade of crystals adorning the entire wall behind it in typical understated Vegas style.

"Welcome to the Boulevard," a receptionist said. "Checking in?"

"Yes," Elliot said. "Mr. Halstead is holding a room for me—two beds. Under *O'Brien*."

She clacked the keyboard of her computer, but before she landed on his reservation, Elliot heard his name being called from across the lobby. He turned to find Simon Halstead walking his way with his arms wide open. He took four steps toward him, and they clapped each other's backs like old friends. Which they were.

Elliot had met Simon six or so years ago when he was on assignment in London. This was after the night with Birdie but before Simon had gotten involved with her. Elliot was in the UK for a long stint, so the paper put him up at a hotel in Kensington where Simon happened to be the manager. They weren't too far off in age, and Elliot would decompress at the bar when he wasn't holed up writing or near Parliament reporting. Most nights, when he was solo, Simon would join him for a pint before turning the shift over to the evening staff.

Elliot hadn't seen Simon since he'd moved back to the States after the gig in London. But they'd stayed in touch over email, partially, he supposed, because of Birdie. Mona had been the one to tell Elliot that Birdie was in London for a shoot and getting hounded by the press daily. Throngs of photographers chasing her cars, hordes of them outside Claridge's, where she was staying. Elliot had purposefully placed a moratorium on all things related to Birdie Maxwell since he walked out of her apartment a year earlier, as if even a hint of her in his life would send him snowballing, running back to her like at the end of one of her rom-coms, but he couldn't say this to Mona.

Did he know anywhere she could go? Mona had asked. *You know London as well as anyone. A friend she could stay with, an apartment to crash at?*

As a matter of fact, he said, he did. He emailed Simon, who assured him that she would be well taken care of at his quiet boutique of a hotel. No one would think to look for her there. Mona told Birdie, and Birdie checked in, and six months later, Elliot heard that she and Simon were a thing. He knew he couldn't be possessive over someone who was never his, but his jealousy planted roots all the same.

Today, Simon flagged over a bellman and had him whisk Elliot's bags up to his room.

"Let's get a drink," Simon said. "Before we get into the rest of it, let's get a pint."

Elliot laughed. "You know I'm on a deadline, right?"

"You were always on a deadline," Simon replied, which wasn't incorrect.

He and Simon moved through the Boulevard's lobby, past a towering glass art installation of two vibrant red colliding hearts, and with the clang from the casino in the distance competing with a pitter-patter from a waterfall by the elevators.

"You sure about this?" Simon said.

"Not particularly," Elliot said. His plan was a high-wire act, and there were a million ways he could stumble, career to the ground, crash and burn. "But half of my job comes from trusting my instincts, and I think this is the hand I need to play."

"It's Las Vegas," Simon concurred. "That's the only way to go. As long as you know when to walk away before you lose everything."

38

BIRDIE

BIRDIE WAS ANCHORED to her childhood kitchen floor, her back pressed against the refrigerator, downing Andie's homemade hangover cure of tomato juice and vinegar and maple syrup, when Mona's text came in.

MONA

vegas baby

She swallowed the rest of Andie's concoction, the syrup sliding out the bottom of the glass and down her throat, which nearly made her gag, the 7-Eleven vodka still a slushy bomb in her gut. Andie, who was even more hungover than Birdie, had run to the store for hangover cure ingredients, then returned to bed an hour ago, though it was two o'clock in the afternoon.

BIRDIE

ur in vegas?

Mona texted back an emoji of a moneybag, which Birdie took to mean yes.

So Elliot had left without her, which immediately infuriated her. That he hadn't stuck around, that he was so damn good at his job that he didn't need her involved in the first place. Exactly what he did seven years ago. Left when he should have stayed.

She'd assumed that he'd call again this morning, and then she'd cave, at least having made him work for it. Birdie did truly want to get to the bottom of the letter, letters, for the sake of her career. She doubled back over that notion. Why did this have to all be in service of her career? Maybe it would be nice, she thought, to have a steady companion, to have someone other than her team to cheer for her successes, to offer an outstretched hand when she faltered. She reached for her phone in the kangaroo pocket of Andie's neon hoodie and tried to think of a single person she could call now, someone who wasn't on her payroll, someone who wasn't Mona because she couldn't call Mona about everything that was brewing inside her.

She dipped her head back against the refrigerator, closed her eyes, and tried to breathe.

Why was she thirty-four and alone? And she didn't mean single. She never really valued marriage, was lukewarm on having kids, and wasn't interested in a relationship simply for a warm body in the bed beside her. But she had a sister she barely spoke to, parents who packed up the house without her knowing, and a best friend in Barton whom she hadn't visited in four years. She had casual friends in the industry and liked her personal trainer and facialist well enough, but they weren't on a texting level, and certainly not mental-breakdown-crises texting level.

Jesus Christ, she thought, the notion hitting her like a tsunami. *I have an army of people around me but I'm so goddamn lonely.*

She swiped her phone open before she could talk herself out of it. Found Ian's old Yahoo email in her address book. She was surprised to still have it, honestly, and had no idea if it would reach him, if he would read it even if it did. But it felt like the right place to start.

Dear Ian,

I know you don't want to hear from me, but I thought it was important that I try. Risking your well-deserved anger. I wanted to tell you that I was sorry. For moving to Los Angeles and ghosting you. For being careless with your heart when you deserved the opposite. I was shitty and selfish, and you were nothing but wonderful and kind. And I shouldn't have blindsided you at the restaurant. I'm sorry about that too.

I don't expect a reply, and you have the right to hate me forever. But I wanted to apologize anyway, because it's the right thing to do, and also, because I truly do regret how dismissive I was with your heart.

Yours truly,
Birdie Maxwell

Her hands were shaking by the time she was done. She read it once while holding her breath, then hit send before she could second-guess it. Maybe if she could say the brave thing to Ian, she thought, she could also say brave things to Elliot.

Her stomach lurched, and she rose from the floor too quickly. She saw stars behind her eyes, and the kitchen floor tilted. She steadied herself, guzzled a glass of water, and marched up the steps into her sister's room.

She couldn't do this alone. Well, she could. But she no longer wanted to.

"Andie." She shook her sister's shoulders.

"Go away," Andie moaned and dove under a pillow.

"No, come on, wake up."

Birdie grabbed the pillow and swatted Andie like they were ten again.

"Stop. So sick. No vodka again forever. I think 7-Elevens may be out permanently too."

At the mention of vodka, Birdie felt bile rise in her esophagus. She sat on the side of Andie's bed, then flopped beside her and stretched out.

"I need your help," she said.

"Fuck off," Andie groaned.

"I need you to drive me to Vegas," Birdie said.

"Drop dead," Andie replied.

"It's for Elliot," Birdie said.

There was a long pause, and Birdie wondered if Andie had fallen back asleep. Or perhaps had died. They'd gotten drunk enough last night that anything was feasible.

Then: "For Elliot?"

"Partially for Elliot," Birdie conceded.

Andie popped open her eyes, pushed to her elbows, and stared at her older sister. Then a wide grin spread across her grayish face.

"All right," she said. "Let's go."

39

ELLIOT

ELLIOT WAS MEETING Simon for dinner at 7 p.m., then he'd do the interview, then he'd pound out the story and fire it off to Francesca.

He checked his phone every ten minutes for something from Birdie. He didn't know what he was expecting. She'd always been ridiculously headstrong, and he was a fool to think that she'd call and apologize, say that she was on her way, say that she couldn't live without him. Or maybe that's what he needed to say to *her*, he thought as he showered, then thought it again as he shaved, then thought it a third time as he pulled on a suit because the restaurant at the Boulevard had a jacket-and-tie requirement even though Simon had said since he was his guest, not to worry.

Simon was waiting for him at the bar. The hostess, lithe and beautiful, nodded and said, "Oh, Mr. Halstead, your table is ready." She was exactly the type who would normally turn Elliot's head, but now he didn't even consider it, didn't have to repress the *urge* to consider it. He could still taste Birdie on his lips from two days earlier, from that kiss in the RV. He could close his eyes and the image of her nearly in his lap, top off, no bra, was imprinted on the back of his lids. *God, she was edible.* A charge ran through him. Maybe the two of them were so electric because it was so long in coming, maybe it was because it was off-limits, a reality check he got when Mona called while he was at the bagel store. Maybe it was just that when you wait for someone, something, for so long, it's going to be either the best thing you've ever had in your life or an utter disaster.

He supposed that Birdie was actually both.

At their table in the back of the restaurant, Simon waved over a waiter and ordered a bottle of Malbec, and Elliot set his phone down between them. He thought of Carter, and how he'd told him that Birdie was always holding out for someone else. He hated how much he still hoped that it was him, even though she wasn't here, even though she'd made it clear that she was done.

"Okay if I tape this?" he asked Simon.

"Sure, no problem," Simon said, like a man who had nothing to hide. He didn't, of course. Elliot already knew that, but it was important for the integrity of the story to be certain, to get him on record. Readers would pillage the comments section with questions about plot holes and conspiracy theories if he hadn't. Also, Elliot wanted to, needed to, prove to Francesca that he could still play within the rules. He'd given her three names. He'd interview all three. He could be the pro she relied on again.

He pressed record.

"So you met Birdie Robinson when? How?"

"Well, I first met Birdie Robinson at the cinema," Simon said. "Like most of us did. *Crazy Foolish Heart* convinced me of my virulent heterosexuality. If it had been socially acceptable to put up posters of an American movie star in my adult bedroom at twenty-five, I would have."

"*Crazy Foolish Heart* being her breakout romantic comedy, nearly a decade ago. With Kai Carol."

Simon nodded. "Then, of course, I met her in real life three, three and a half years later, when you emailed and said she needed somewhere to stay. That she needed help."

"First impressions?" Elliot asked. None of this was a necessary ingredient for the article, but he was curious to hear a different perspective, if Birdie was as vexing, as confounding, to Simon as she had been to him.

"Well, initially, you have to get past the fact that you already feel like you know everything about her," Simon said. "The dichotomy of celebrity is that you are at once completely familiar with someone, and yet you are acutely aware that you know very little in actuality. Then you have to parse out, for yourself, if you are only intoxicated with the fame or if the other stuff, the stuff underneath that veneer, is appealing."

Now Elliot nodded. He'd known Birdie since before. Before fame, before wealth, before personal chefs and premieres in Tokyo and covers of magazines. And for him, none of that mattered. For him, she was simply the girl he'd fallen in love with at twelve, and for whom his heart still carried a blazing bright torch.

"How long were you together?" Elliot asked.

"A year or so. Though I was in London part of the time, back and forth, before jumping back to the States more permanently. So a year, but that timeline may have been fuzzy. And to be fair, there were difficult moments, with the time zones, the distance, the long-haul flights." Simon appeared to have no malice, which Elliot admired.

"Could you have made it work?" Elliot probed. "Even with all of that?"

Simon took a moment to consider it. "How can you know if anything could have worked?" he said finally. "With different circumstances, with different obstacles, with different personalities. The thing about Birdie is that she is quite clear in who she is."

"And who is that?" Elliot was genuinely desperate to know.

"An enigma." Simon smiled. "What I discovered about Birdie Robinson is that she may be unknowable. And if you can accept that, live with that, then she's your perfect match. And if you can't, then there's really nothing else to be done."

Elliot furrowed his brow and made a mental note to revisit this part of the conversation when he played it back while drafting the piece. He didn't think Simon had her quite right. He was certain that Birdie was entirely knowable; he'd known her once back in Barton, and for snippets of their time together as adults, in her apartment that weekend; when her guard was down in the RV and she so mangled the lyrics of the Eurythmics, he knew her again. Maybe the enigma of Birdie wasn't that she was unsolvable, it was that you had to know both the equation and the solution at the same time. What made Birdie tick and how to keep her ticking. He thought that he did.

"So I should ask you," Elliot said, "did you write her a love letter? Either years ago or just a few days back?"

Simon paused as the sommelier crossed the room with their bottle of Malbec, then uncorked it and poured a taste that merited Simon's approval. Both of their glasses were filled, and Simon raised a glass.

"To Birdie Robinson," he said.

"To Birdie Robinson," Elliot concurred, though he'd rather have toasted Birdie Maxwell.

Simon savored his sip, then set his glass down thoughtfully.

"When I think of Birdie, of the time I spent with her," he said, "I sometimes wonder why I was never struck by that lightning bolt, if I missed something—"

"What was there to miss?"

"That's the thing," Simon said. "I don't think there was. That incalculable magnetic pull is either there or it isn't."

Elliot wondered if Simon knew how close to the bone he was cutting. How his magnetic pull had been so strong it was nearly fatal with Birdie.

"But?" Elliot asked.

"But it wasn't for me, for us. So no, I did not send her an unrequited, anonymous love letter. But you already knew that."

Elliot nodded. He just needed Simon on record so no one could doubt that he'd covered his bases, interviewed the men Birdie cited, double-checked his facts.

"I did already know that," he agreed.

"So how do we see this through?"

Elliot reached for his glass and eased back in his chair.

"First, we drink this wine, because I sure could use it," he said. "And then, armed with a little bravery, we finally come face-to-face with the truth."

40

BIRDIE

BIRDIE STARED OUT the dust-specked passenger window of Andie's ten-year-old 4Runner as the lights of Las Vegas broke through the darkened sky. She wasn't quite sure what her plan was, what she needed to say to Elliot, what she needed to say to Mona. She didn't know how this got her any closer to finding the anonymous letter writer unless her instincts that it had been Elliot all along proved correct.

Andie cursed at another bug that splattered on the windshield, then sprayed the glass with fluid and turned on the wipers. For a moment, everything in front of them went blurry, then clear again. *Wouldn't it be nice if it were just that easy*, Birdie thought. *Blurry, then clear again.*

She'd called Imani about an hour ago and told her what she was doing, and Imani fell silent, weighing all the ways that the situation could go wrong. Finally, she said, "I assume you know the stakes of this?"

"I do," Birdie said.

"Well then, I'm going to give you my blessing. Be honest,

be . . . yourself, Bird. I think this could pay more dividends than any sort of spin I worked my ass off for."

"That's what I needed to hear," Birdie said. Though that was more of a platitude, something nice you say to wrap up a conversation. She didn't actually know what she needed to hear because she hadn't been this terrified in a long, long time. Maybe since she first moved to New York. Or maybe when she first went to Kai's trailer and let him seduce her. Or maybe when Elliot walked out of her apartment and she wondered if she should chase him but did not. One of those things was among the best decisions of her life. Two of them were among the worst. All three were leaps of faith.

Birdie hadn't been to Vegas in years. She'd had invites to conventions, to restaurant openings, to front-row seats at pop-star residencies, and it wasn't that she wasn't tempted, but Vegas elicited nothing but bad memories. The last time she had been to Vegas was with Kai. Well, not with him. They'd hadn't arrived together since they were technically *not* together, and they were in the habit of dodging the press to keep the rumors at bay. It was a few months after Carter had kicked him off her property, and so also a few months since she and Carter had split.

Kai was not a particularly good poker player but, like many rich men with bulging egos, he had an outsized impression of his talents, so enjoyed a weekend or two every month at the casinos, losing money that he didn't bother counting, ogling women whose names he didn't bother learning. He always booked a suite on the top floor of the Wynn, like he enjoyed making it easy for fans and paparazzi to track him down. He waved to the cameras when he saw them; he routinely stopped for autographs when asked. Photos were even better. Sometimes he kissed chubby babies, and sometimes his publicist planted stories, like he'd performed the Heimlich on a patron at the breakfast buffet (Kai drank only protein drinks for breakfast, so *as if* he would be at a breakfast buffet, Birdie had thought at the time). Whatever served the narrative was what Kai Carol served the public. A fake fiancée, a fake breakup, it didn't matter.

He had texted her back then and begged her to come. Said he had big news that he couldn't wait to share with her. Birdie hated herself for how much she wanted to hear that. That maybe finally he had chosen her, called off the ruse with Haley. That maybe, six years after she met him on set at twenty-five, they finally could go somewhere in public together, hands entwined, heads high.

He'd booked her a room at the Venetian so no one would link them, and said he'd have his assistant leave her his key at the Venetian's front desk. By then, Birdie could barely go anywhere without being recognized, so he reserved a tinted-window SUV that could meet her at the parking garage and drive her down the Strip to the Wynn. Birdie had a wig that she had kept from one of her sets that she wore whenever she just needed to blend in— mousy-brown hair, medium-cut bob (her character had been a third-grade teacher who fell in love with a widowed dad who happened to be a secret billionaire; it opened to the biggest weekend in romantic comedy history to date)—so she wore that too.

On her way to meet him, tucked inside this monstrously sized vehicle, under a pile of fake hair, she caught a glimpse of her reflection and thought: *What has happened to you that you equate all of this with happiness?*

Kai was waiting for her in his room, and despite the PR stint in rehab a few years back, he'd been drinking, though only to the point of being ludicrously charming. Birdie loved how he tasted with liquor on his tongue, and he swept her up in his arms, literally, and swung her around.

He set her down and kissed her again, and Birdie remembered, even now staring out at the oncoming lights of the Vegas Strip with Andie driving beside her, that it didn't feel like she thought it would, how it used to. She leaned in to him again, pressing herself so close that there wasn't even a sliver of light between their bodies. She went through the motions—sighing and little gasps of breath and smiling when their lips came apart—but it felt like another role she was playing, and if someone had called *cut*, she wouldn't have had any problem turning it all off. Kai tugged her shirt over her head, and her wig went lopsided, and he laughed and straightened it, as if maybe this was all pretend for him, too, as if he liked her better when she was an amalgamation of whoever he wanted her to be.

And for some reason, there with her slightly crooked wig and down to her bra, Birdie thought of Elliot. And how he was one of the few people in her life, or had been anyway, who hadn't asked her to change. How he embraced her imperfections, how he met her exactly where she was, even if he'd walked away. It had been almost four years by then since their weekend together, and Birdie was shocked that he was the one she thought of now.

"What's your news?" Birdie had said to Kai. She didn't want to think of Elliot and tried to squash him from her mind.

His face wrinkled in confusion and then opened into surprise, like he'd forgotten why he arranged this. Birdie thought, *Please pick me please pick me please pick me please leave her please leave her please leave her please love me.* Even if this all felt flat now. She was in too deep, sunk costs, and it was easier to keep going.

And he said, "Oh right! I'm signed on to do Marvel. Highest payday in history when you add in back end." He looked absolutely fucking delighted.

Birdie took a step away from him, folding her arms around herself like a straitjacket.

"You called me here, urgently, after years of being apart, not even speaking, to tell me that you *signed on to Marvel*?"

He looked only slightly less delighted when he said, "Well . . . yeah? Jesus, Birdie, I thought you'd be happy for me."

"You thought I'd be happy for you?"

He reached for her hand, which would have meant uncovering her half-exposed breast in her demi-bra, so she did not reach back.

"Well, yeah," he said, then moved toward the bar to pour himself another drink. "You know that Haley doesn't get it, she's not in the industry. I thought you would."

"*You thought I'd get it?*" Birdie couldn't decide if she was angrier at the audacity of mentioning his real/fake fiancée to her or at the audacity of this entire thing.

He put his palms on his hips like he was an elementary school principal. "The point is: you were the only person I wanted to share this with. So I thought you'd be happy. I thought we could celebrate."

Birdie felt like such a fucking idiot. She swiped her shirt off the floor and frantically tugged it over her head. The wig was entirely crooked now, but who cared? What was the difference? Acid rose in her throat, and if she'd bothered to eat that day (she had not), she would have vomited all over his stupid fucking suite. She wished she'd eaten that day just so she could do so.

"Birdie," Kai said, once her hand was on the door. "Come on, babe. Don't be like that. We have a good thing here. You and me."

But they didn't. Kai had a good thing. Birdie had nothing but years of waiting for him to decide she was worth it.

"Okay," he said to her back as she swung open the door and steeled herself to walk away from Kai Carol forever. "But I think you're gonna regret this."

She heard him shaking a martini shaker like he was James goddamn Bond. She adjusted her wig and slammed the door behind her. The SUV was still idling in the garage. She managed to wait until she made it back to the Venetian to absolutely come undone. Of all the things that Birdie Maxwell hated, of all the things she'd been running from since she was eighteen, it was being a fool.

Now, three years later, Andie had her head out the window, screaming at a guy in a sedan on the Strip who refused to let her over. The Boulevard was the next turn-in, and Birdie honestly would have found it poetic if they'd missed it and had to circle back. Circle back to Simon. Circle back to Elliot. Taking the long way around. That was a metaphor she could appreciate.

But then the sedan driver rolled his eyes and waved Andie in, and then, in no time at all, they were at the valet.

"You ready for this?" Andie asked before a kid hustled over to open the door, take her keys.

"No," Birdie said.

"Awesome," Andie replied. "That's what makes it even better. For once in her life, the actress goes in totally cold."

41

ELLIOT

LLIOT HAD NEVER much liked gambling. Losing money for sport wasn't something he could afford on a journalist's salary, and so much of it was left up to chance that he probably wouldn't have enjoyed it even if he'd had the dough to lose. Simon was winding his way through the casino floor with Elliot close behind. There were bright lights and too many cigarettes and bings and bops and clangs from the slots. It was disorienting, Elliot thought. Enough to make you lose yourself.

The high rollers' tables were tucked in the back, behind a velvet rope, with security granting entry. A burly guy in a tight-fitting suit nodded at Simon, then pinched the latch on a rope and allowed them through.

Kai Carol was unmissable.

He had an entourage behind him and a beautiful woman on each side, like he couldn't make up his mind. Which, given everything Elliot knew about Kai Carol, sounded exactly right. He was in an expensive-looking navy tapered suit, and Elliot was relieved that he'd thought to wear his too. It wasn't that he cared if he was dressed appropriately, but he wanted Kai to know that they were sparring partners. That even with all the fame, all his disgusting wealth and private jets and entry to just about anywhere in the world, Elliot was on his level. *Out of professionalism*, Elliot told himself. Not because of Birdie. Though it was mostly because of Birdie.

Kai was staring at his hand and looking displeased. Elliot thought that for an actor, he sure as shit couldn't bluff. But he was absurdly handsome, with perfectly supple, perfectly moisturized skin, a haircut that probably cost as much as Elliot's rent, and a jawline plastic surgeons would covet. Did covet. He had a heavy Rolex on his wrist, and his shirt was unbuttoned just enough to look casual but sharp. *This guy*, Elliot thought, *knows how to play a part*.

Kai shook his head and placed his cards down on the table.

"Dammit," he said. "I'm out."

One of the women leaned closer and whispered something in his ear, and he swiveled toward her, delighted. He pushed back his chair and stood, as if she'd proposed that they go up to his suite and undress. She probably had. Kai Carol, Elliot could see, had that way about him. Sheer magnetism.

"Mr. Carol," Simon called as they neared the table. He held out his hand, and Kai, upon noticing Simon, did the same. They were old acquaintances, the professional sort anyway. Though Kai was renowned for his suite at the Wynn, he'd become a regular at the Boulevard's tables.

Simon hadn't been all that surprised when Elliot called a few days back. He'd heard the rumors about Kai and Birdie over the years, even if nothing had ever been confirmed, the press had never run with it beyond some early speculation. Besides, Simon had told Elliot over the phone, he'd never blamed Kai for why he and Birdie hadn't worked out. If Birdie couldn't shake Kai from her system, that said more about Birdie or perhaps about her compatibility with Simon than it did about anything else. Regardless, he confirmed, yes, Kai was in Vegas these days during his downtime.

Elliot pondered this for a while after they hung up. If he'd ever reach a place of such placidity about her. It was all so adult, so subdued. But then Elliot's feelings for Birdie had never been subdued, and that, he thought, was the point.

"Ah, Mr. Halstead," Kai said while vigorously shaking Simon's hand. "I've lost enough money to call it a night. Or at least take a breather and check in with my accountant." He grinned, and his immaculate white teeth were matched only by his immaculately cratered dimples. *It should be a crime*, Elliot thought, *to be born so good-looking.*

"We always appreciate your patronage," Simon said. And he appeared to mean it. "I wanted to take a moment to introduce you to my old friend Elliot O'Brien," Simon said.

Kai's smile faltered for only a flicker of a second, microscopic if you weren't looking for it. But Elliot was. And it brought him immense satisfaction to know that Kai recognized his name. That Kai was following the story. Then Kai bounced back to his outsized, magnanimous persona.

"Mr. O'Brien, a pleasure," Kai said, extending his hand and gripping Elliot's with a professional firmness. "Here for some poker?"

"Sadly, I am terrible at the game," Elliot replied. "I'm completely unable to bluff."

Kai raised an eyebrow. A single eyebrow. Elliot assumed he'd honed this for the camera, but still, it was an art.

"Ah, well, I'm on my way out," Kai said. "I can only lose so much money at once before I need some fresh air. Nothing is breaking my way tonight, it seems."

"Do you mind," Elliot said, slipping so easily into his reporter voice that Birdie would surely call him on it if she were here, "if I asked you a few questions before you do?"

Kai grinned like he was used to people asking all sorts of questions. Whether or not he wanted to answer them was an entirely different story. But then he'd gotten good at dodging sticklers, Elliot knew.

"Sure, why not." Kai shrugged. "But first, how about a drink?" He looked at Simon, who flagged over a server, who then rushed off to the bar. "If we're going to get into this," Kai said, "it's probably best to first have a drink so we all know exactly where we stand."

42

BIRDIE

BIRDIE WAS RECOGNIZED in the lobby of the Boulevard, of course. Most people kept their distance, but she could feel the long stares, the slightly turned heads, as if people didn't want to gape but couldn't help themselves.

Andie checked them in while Birdie signed a few autographs and snapped a few selfies and forgot, for a moment, that she was technically publicly reviled. Then an older woman smacked her lips together and said, "To think I always thought that you were the nice girl from next door, picking fights with Sebastian Carol, calling that nice young man at the bar a"—she lowered her voice to a whisper—"*fuckwad*. I would like a refund."

And Birdie surprised herself by biting her urge to correct the narrative, telling the woman just how much she had gotten wrong—that both of those men deserved it. Instead, she reached into her wallet and pressed two twenties into the woman's palm, saying, "Here you go. A refund. Consider us even."

And then a couple of twentysomethings started clapping and whooping at her gumption, and Birdie thought, *Maybe this isn't about pleasing the public, maybe this is about pleasing myself,* and something took flight in her, the weight lighter on her shoulders, the pressure in her chest a little bit less heavy. She'd been America's Sweetheart for so long that it hadn't occurred to her that she might not even want to play that part any longer. She offered a shy wave to the cheering twentysomethings, and they offered proud fist pumps in return, and then Andie was back, having checked them in.

"I need to get to the casino," Birdie said. "Mona told me that Elliot is with Simon. I should probably go talk to them both."

"I'll drop the bags in the room," Andie replied. It was a relief, Birdie thought, to have an ally, not one on her payroll like Imani or Sydney, but an honest-to-god partner who had no ulterior motive. "You can do this, Bird. It's gonna be okay."

Birdie nearly threw herself around her sister and wept.

Birdie followed the sound of the slot machines and soon found herself on the casino floor. She walked up and down the aisles looking for Elliot, her pulse accelerating with each passing moment. She'd had a full six-hour drive to figure out what to say to him when he confessed that he'd written the letter or letters, but she still wasn't quite sure how to speak her truth. She was getting there, but vulnerability was much more accessible when it was scripted, when she was emotionally availing herself on camera. What did Carter used to say? That she was too busy living out someone else's story. Well, duh. That was all so much easier than this.

A few casino patrons did double takes, but mostly they were much more invested in the machines or tables in front of them, so Birdie was able to wander relatively unselfconsciously. Her posture sunk just slightly, and she shoved her hands into the pockets of the joggers she'd borrowed from Andie, but she liked it here, in the world of normals. She'd always been striving for validation with her career, since she'd been eighteen and fleeing Barton, so she'd never much paused to ask herself why she couldn't just be content with what was. What she had. Who she had. When Kai picked *her* of all people to fall in love with, if she'd considered that she was deserving of more than his half promises, maybe the rest of her personal life could have been more fulfilling, could have been entirely different.

She stopped in the middle of the blackjack tables and tried to get her bearings. Mona had texted that Elliot and Simon had a dinner reservation, then would be at the casino, but neither of them was anywhere to be found. Something bubbled up from years back, early in their relationship, when Kai was set to spend a weekend lost in the haze of Vegas.

"They wine you and dine you at the high rollers' tables, Birdie," he'd said. "It's like they're made for our type." *Our type.* It had both revolted and titillated Birdie at the time. Now it just revolted. He'd wanted her to join him for the trip but she'd had a photo shoot in LA the next day for a cover. It was one of the few times she'd turned any of Kai's requests down.

She tapped the arm of a waitress passing by.

"The high rollers?" she asked.

The waitress offered a smile. She'd recognized Birdie, Birdie could tell right away. *Please don't say something please don't say something please don't say something*, Birdie thought. She just wanted to be anonymous for one more moment, out here searching for a boy like any other heartsick girl in the world.

The waitress nudged her chin toward the corner. "That way."

"Thank you," Birdie said and reached for her wallet to tip her.

"No, stop." The waitress waved her away. "It's just my job. And besides, I think he may be waiting for you." She smiled again, wider. "You deserve a happy ending, Ms. Robinson. Like your movies. I knew you were just telling that dick off, the director— he's been here with his brother, likes to grab onto things that aren't his, like my ass. A lot of us appreciated what you did, even if no one says that online." She nodded at Birdie, and then pushed her way through the crowd to deliver her drinks.

Odd, Birdie thought. That the waitress would know that Elliot was here, waiting for her. But maybe coincidences weren't just found in the final pages of her scripts. Maybe, for once, some of that romantic good fortune was going to shine on Birdie Maxwell too.

43

ELLIOT

ELLIOT AND SIMON and Kai had retreated to the bar tucked away behind the high rollers' tables so that Elliot could record the interview without all the competing noise. He needed to be sure that he got Kai Carol on the record crisply and cleanly, so that Francesca could pull the exact quotes and leave no room for doubt with readers. And no doubt with her: his job would be secure, his ass no longer on the line.

"So, you and I have a friend in common," Elliot said to Kai. They'd each ordered bourbon, like they were trying to outmacho each other. Elliot had never liked bourbon, but he wasn't about to wilt in front of Kai Carol, world's biggest movie star.

Kai's eyes crinkled in something like delight. He knew why Elliot was here.

"Ms. Robinson," he said.

"You've followed the articles?" If Elliot were wired differently, he'd have been flattered.

"Of course."

"And . . . we can acknowledge that you and Birdie were . . . involved off and on for several years?"

Kai pursed his lips, inhaled, then smiled. "Well, I guess the cat's out of the bag," he said. "Bravo to you for being the first reporter to nail us down. Before, it was all just smoke and mirrors."

Elliot didn't like the way he said *us* like they were still a living, breathing entity, like they were still connected.

"So you know what I'm here to ask you about, then," Elliot pressed on.

"Before you do ask, what did she say about me?" Kai said.

"Birdie?"

"I assume she sent you here? You're here on her behalf?" Kai's smile faltered. "I do owe her a call, after the thing with my brother."

It would have pleased Elliot greatly to tell Kai Carol that Birdie hadn't said a goddamned thing about him.

"No, not from Birdie. I did a deep dive on Reddit." Elliot shrugged. "You were caught once on camera outside her gate. Someone had the photo, even if it never made its way into the press."

"Ah," Kai said. "Reddit. I admit that is one of the far-flung corners of the internet where my team strictly prohibits me from going."

"You need a team to prohibit you from googling yourself?"

Kai found this hilarious. He dipped his head back and howled his famous howl. Elliot wanted to fucking hate him, and part of him did. But he was so magnetic, such a goddamn movie star, that even he, Pulitzer Prize–nominated reporter, had a hard time staying completely objective. It wasn't difficult to understand why Birdie got trapped in his orbit, even when it was self-destructive. Kai Carol's gravitational pull was impossible to withstand.

Before Elliot could ask a follow-up, he saw Mona rushing toward the security guard outside the velvet rope. The security guard shook his head and held out a hand, spurning her, so Mona bounced on her toes and waved frantically toward Elliot, then Simon, who locked eyes with the guard and waved her in.

"She's here," Mona said, out of breath.

"Where are you coming from? Why are you panting?"

"I was on a roll at the Encore," she said, "when she texted me."

"Who is *she*?" Kai asked, and Mona froze for a beat in recognition.

"Birdie," she replied once she composed herself. "Birdie is here."

"Birdie is in *Vegas*?" Elliot barked.

"Birdie is in *Vegas*?" Kai said with unbridled enthusiasm. He rubbed his hands together like he could not *wait* to see her, and Elliot reversed course and decided that he didn't like him. He didn't like him at all.

"Birdie is at the Boulevard," Mona heaved. "This is what I'm trying to tell you."

"Birdie is at the Boulevard?" Simon parroted. He looked concerned and said, "Excuse me. I need to get back to work." And quick-stepped toward the security guard and whispered something in his ear. The guard picked up his walkie and spoke into it as he hustled off.

"How did she . . ." Elliot started.

"I texted her," Mona finished.

"You texted her?" Elliot repeated.

"I didn't think it was right, knowing that a couple of dudes were going to sit around and debate her future."

Elliot had only vaguely filled Mona in on his plans, hadn't shared all the details about Kai, so he didn't know how she'd ascertained how it was going to play out. Still, he supposed she had a point. The way she was looking at him—he was unnerved. How much more did Mona know than he'd realized? For a long time, as kids, they'd told each other everything, and sometimes they hadn't even needed to articulate their thoughts aloud. They'd shared a womb, they'd spent their early years inseparable. Maybe she'd been more in tune with his feelings for Birdie than he'd given her credit for.

"I haven't seen Birdie in ages, since we were last in Vegas, actually," Kai said, like this was the final scene of a script written just for him. "This is wonderful!"

Then Elliot remembered why he was there. Not for Birdie but for the *article*. For the *job*. For his *career*. Just like he always was. He raised his phone to capture Kai's response to the question he'd come to ask.

"So." He cleared his throat. "Since you know why I came, I'm just going to ask you outright."

Kai nodded. Elliot felt his pulse accelerate, like he needed to know the answer and simultaneously didn't want to.

"Did you send Birdie an anonymous love letter? Hoping to win her back?"

There was a commotion behind Elliot—a din of voices, a huddle of whispers—but he was locked into Kai and refused to break eye contact. But Kai's gaze floated over Elliot's shoulder and grew wide. Then he leaned closer to Elliot's phone so that his voice was loud and clear.

"Yes," he said. "I did. I sent Birdie Robinson a love letter. A mea culpa of sorts, because I really screwed that whole thing up, and with some distance, I've realized that it was the biggest mistake of my life. Letting Birdie Robinson go was the most catastrophic, disastrous error of my life. Quote me. Print it. Blast that to the satellites. I messed everything up with Birdie, and I've changed, and now I'll do anything to win her back."

Elliot heard a gasp from just a few feet away and recognized the sound. He could have identified her anywhere; he could have picked her voice, her breath, out of a crowd. He turned to find Birdie standing with Simon, both hands clenched over her mouth, like she hadn't seen this coming. Like Kai was perhaps the one she'd been out there chasing all along. Not him. Kai.

Not me, he thought. *Him.*

≈ **44** ≈

BIRDIE

BIRDIE DIDN'T KNOW why she hadn't pieced it together. Kai and Las Vegas. Elliot and Las Vegas. Obviously, she knew in the back of her brain that Kai could be here, but she'd assumed Elliot had come only for Simon—she'd never even mentioned Kai and figured her omission was enough to keep Kai out of this. But now her mind was moving in slow motion, through mud, through quicksand, and she was sinking and sinking and sinking.

Kai's arms were wrapped around her in an embrace so tight it was nearly claustrophobic, then he pulled back and clasped her cheeks in his hands, his breath minty like he was expecting her.

"Birdie," he said. "You came for me."

Her heart was pounding in her chest; her blood was pooling in her ears. She'd waited for Kai to pick her, choose her, for so many years. She'd almost never had the strength to turn him down, to walk away back then, even when he was ruinous for her. Even when he dangled her along with empty promises of breaking his engagement and emptier words that never proved true.

Now, just like back then, she couldn't assess if she had wanted this ending or should run from it.

She untangled herself from him.

"You sent the letter?" she asked.

He was a decent actor, but she thought she'd be able to tell if he was lying. Not that she understood why he would lie. Kai could have just about any woman he encountered. And for so many years, she'd wanted it to be her. How to reconcile that something in her gut, small but throbbing, told her that she had an honest-to-god *real* choice this time, that she could choose differently?

He nodded. "I did."

"You knew she lived in Barton?" Mona asked, her eyes narrow. Birdie had forgotten she was there. Her arms were crossed, and she had a sour look, a sour vibe about her, like anything that Kai would say would be wrong. "You *mailed* her a letter in Barton?"

Kai froze for a fraction of a beat, and Birdie doubted that anyone else saw it, but then, she wasn't just anyone. She'd memorized the lines in his face, the glimmers of expression, the subtleties in a drop of an eyebrow, a twitch of his lips. Sometimes, when he was sleeping, she'd wake and just stare at him, like all she'd wanted to do was breathe him in and will him to choose her like she would have chosen him.

"Yes," Kai said.

"Yes?" Elliot echoed.

"Yes." Kai's hands were back on Birdie's cheeks. "Birdie, I owe you a multitude of apologies. I was awful, and you were wonderful, and you didn't deserve any of it. I've changed. I've realized the error of my ways."

"When did you mail this letter?" Mona asked, suddenly an intrepid detective.

"Does it matter?" Kai said.

"Am I to seriously believe," Mona asked, "that you two were actually, I mean, I knew you did a movie together but—"

Birdie turned toward her best friend and nodded. "I stopped it when he got engaged," she said. "But he promised me that wasn't real, promised me I was the only thing that was." She'd never told Mona because she'd never told anyone, and though there had been those unconfirmed rumors from time to time, as she'd said to Andie just last night, exceptionally adept PR maneuvers had managed to squelch most of them before they planted roots.

Andie. Where was Andie? Birdie took a small step back from Kai. She would like her sister here, the only one she'd told about Kai. The only one she'd told about Elliot.

"Wait," Mona said, like she was doing the math in her head. "Why didn't I, how didn't I . . . ?"

She faltered, then winced and composed herself. She shot Birdie a look that said: *You could have told me*, and Birdie knew immediately she was right. But she'd gotten used to keeping Kai a secret in those years. It occurred to her that maybe she kept him a secret not because she had to, rather because she was so mortified at what she'd gotten into. Running when he called. Accepting his attention in half doses. Buying into his flimsy promises, his dubious claims about calling off the allegedly fake engagement. Birdie was so busy seeking his approval that she lost sight of the wisdom of the people who really mattered.

Kai pulled Birdie into a hug again, and on instinct, despite her revelation from just a moment earlier, her arms found the broad part of his back. It felt nice, nicer than she'd expected, and though she told herself this didn't have to be a slippery slope, she could push off of him and walk away, she also suspected this was a convenient lie to salvage her pride.

Birdie eyed Elliot from the embrace, waiting for him to intervene. *Intervene*, she found herself hoping. *Tell me he has it wrong. Tell me it was you.* But Elliot was looking pale and a little sweaty, as if even though he'd gotten the answer he'd expected for his article, it turned out it wasn't the one he wanted.

"Come back to my suite," Kai whispered in Birdie's ear. "Please. Just to talk. I have some things I need to say."

Birdie didn't particularly want to go back to his suite but thought maybe he'd apologize. For dragging her through so much over the years. For making her wait over and over. For not rising to her defense when his brother swung his ax and felled her. She didn't realize how much she wanted to hear his apology, how maybe an apology could mean closure or at least a new beginning.

"Elliot?" she asked, all the same. One last chance, just for safekeeping.

Elliot kept his eyes on her, then lifted a shoulder.

"I guess we solved it," he said.

It should have been a triumph. Instead, it felt like a defeat.

45

ELLIOT

FOR ONCE IN his life, Elliot had absolutely no idea what to write, how to file this story.

He flopped back in the chair in his room, sighed, redoubled his efforts. He almost never had writer's block. Thought that writer's block was just something that lazy reporters cited to get out of doing the work. He'd figured he'd mapped it all out—come to Vegas, confront Kai, write a triumphant piece that would secure his future at the *Times*. The issue was, he'd only just realized, that if he secured his future at the *Times*, he'd throw away any shot of a future with Birdie.

He should have found a way to tell Mona how much Birdie meant to him. He should have found a way to just tell Birdie once and for all how much she meant to him. He could have said that she turned him to stardust, that he wanted to spend every second of every day with her, that he couldn't believe he was such a complete fucking moron seven years ago, walking away or letting her push him out. Maybe they'd both put up boundaries the next morning because that was muscle memory for them. But maybe muscle memory causes the rest of your heart to atrophy. Elliot didn't want to atrophy anymore.

"You realize," Mona said from one of the queen beds when Elliot sighed so loudly that he couldn't be ignored, "that this doesn't all add up, right?"

Elliot turned to stare at her. It was as if she were reading his mind. Twins. Still.

"What do you mean by that?" He had a pit in his stomach that was lurching toward illness.

"Kai didn't answer me back there when I asked him. About mailing the letter," Mona explained. "Like did he really know that Birdie lived in Barton? Because I was under the impression that basically no one had any idea, other than the people who knew her from back then, and I guess, like, Simon, who knew because you were friends with him first." She paused. "Although to be fair, I didn't even know they were screwing. Maybe I don't know what I'm saying."

"Oh." Elliot deflated even further. Mona's theory was not nearly as promising as he'd hoped. "Well, he obviously knew she was from Barton. He just didn't answer you because he was distracted." How could he not be distracted by Birdie?

Mona raised her eyebrows and pushed off the bed. "Okay, well, you can't say that I didn't try to help you. But I guess you really can only lead a horse to water." She retreated to the bathroom. From behind the door, she called, "But I'm not hiring you at Monads."

Elliot reached for his phone. He could at least try to fight for Birdie, even if he suspected that he didn't stand a chance against a man whose face was on half the billboards on Sunset Boulevard. He typed in her number and stiffened while it rang. Four rings later, and he was rolled to voicemail. He jabbed his screen and hung up. He was willing to do a lot of things for Birdie Maxwell, but leaving her a desperate message while she was getting reacquainted with Kai felt like a low even he couldn't stomach.

Elliot cracked his knuckles and rolled his neck around three times. *Fine.* He'd write the story that would save his job. It might not be particularly helpful to Birdie—writing about a years-long off-and-on romance when Kai may or may not have been engaged, piled on top of her fallout with his brother. The public would probably say she was aggrieved, desperate, that maybe her fight with Sebastian was just a way to get Kai's attention all over again. Or maybe the opposite would be true: maybe the article would be tremendously helpful, and she and Kai would be the newest media darlings, and Birdie would be forgiven for all things.

Either way, if he filed the story, he'd lose the girl.

But work was work was work. Work was the one thing he could rely on. So he did.

Thirty minutes later, he'd written the draft. It wasn't perfect, but it was down on the page at least, and Francesca would be thrilled. He squeezed his eyes shut. *Don't send it don't send it don't send it.*

But when given the choice, personal or professional, Elliot O'Brien was always a pro.

46

BIRDIE

KAI KISSED BIRDIE as soon as the latch on her door clicked shut. And really kissed her. A muscle-melting, brain-dizzying type of kiss that Birdie had always been a sucker for. This time, she did indeed feel her blood pulse, and small zings of electricity coursed through her from limb to limb, but mostly she thought of Elliot. How when they'd kissed in the camper just a few days back, it had been more than palpable sparks and jolts of lust. It had been an animalistic, set-your-body-on-fire, impossible-to-stop type of connection. She *had* stopped it, though barely. And now she could hardly remember why. The *why*, she reminded herself, was that he'd already walked out on her once, but god-dammit, she of all people read enough scripts to know that some-times you needed two bites of the apple, two shots at the bullseye, two swings of the bat, before you hit it out of the park. If she really wanted to start fresh, not just with Elliot, but with *herself*, maybe she needed to forgive him for the ways he had hurt her and forgive herself for the ways she had inflicted her own damage.

By the time she wrapped her brain around all this, Kai had whisked off her shirt, like they were falling back into bed so easily all these years later.

"Wait," she said, putting her hands on Kai's chest and pushing him back a few inches.

"Baby," he murmured, "I don't know if I can." He pressed his hips against hers, and part of her wanted to cave, to let him do whatever he wanted because that's how it had always been between them. She was easy for him, in just about every way.

But then something dawned on her: the question Mona had asked downstairs on the casino floor.

"Kai," she said, her arms folding across her breasts as if he didn't have a right to them anymore. "How could you have known where I lived? How did you know to find me in Barton, not Medford? California, not Oregon?"

Birdie specifically remembered that she'd never corrected the record about her childhood hometown with him. Kai spent his early years globe-trotting with his famous dad and model mother, and she was worried he'd judge her, for barely graduating high school, for growing up in a split-level midsized home that could probably use some renovations in a town that definitely needed a makeover. And then months, years, went by, and once she was in over her head with him, it felt too late to be honest, and she felt too foolish about what a stupid thing it was to lie about in the first place. She never wanted to give him even a sliver of a chance to find fault with her—which, she supposed now, she couldn't blame Kai for. That was on her. She was so busy concocting a version of herself that he'd love that she forgot that one day he might find out the truth after all.

"I—" Kai started, then dropped his hands from her shoulders and to his sides. "Fine, very well."

"Fine, very well, what?" Birdie asked. The hairs on the back of her neck stood up. This all felt too familiar. The dread, the ominousness, the way she was waiting to be disappointed.

"The second one," Kai said. "I was the one who sent you the second one."

"You were the one who sent me the *email*?" Birdie wasn't sure if she felt rage or relief. "Not the letter?"

Kai nodded and glanced to the floor. When he met her eyes again, his were damp and set to spill. "I just . . . I just couldn't bear the thought that you were out there without me, Birdie. I had Galen set up a dummy email. But *I'm* the one who wrote it. Not him. Me."

Galen, Kai's assistant. Kai required his assistant's help to woo back the woman he allegedly loved.

"So you sent me the email because you didn't want me to be with someone else? Or you sent me the email because you wanted me to be with *you*?"

He offered her an apologetic grin. "Is there a difference? What does it matter? I'm here. You're here. Let's see where this goes. I've been missing you like crazy, baby."

But there was a difference, and it *did* matter. Not wanting her to be with anyone else was not enough; it was more of a half-hearted gesture that was spurred from coveting her, not from loving her completely.

"I need—" she started.

"What do you need?" he murmured, and stepped closer, pressing his lips to her collarbone, though she was still clutching her chest and the whole thing was clumsy and awkward. Birdie didn't think she'd live to see the day when Kai Carol was awkward at anything.

"Wait, Kai." She pulled away, thinking of Kai's brother and

the mess he'd mired her in. "If you had this epiphany, why didn't you say something about Sebastian to the press? You could have spoken up, defended me. You could have *helped* me."

His face fell. "Bird, you know that's complicated for me."

"Complicated *for you*? I risked everything to stand up to him on set, and I probably *lost* everything by standing up to him, and it's complicated *for you*?" Birdie suddenly thought she was going to be sick.

"He's my family, Birdie," Kai offered, and honestly, Birdie was ashamed to realize that years ago, that would have been explanation enough for her, that she was Kai's second choice, but hey, it made sense when he explained it that way. But she'd tangled with Sebastian because she'd earned the right to be powerful, and she'd tried to revive her career with this stupid letter because she was tired of giving her power to everyone else: to him, to the studio, to her handlers, to the public. And it had been a dumb idea, to pitch herself as a girl out here in search of a boy, just like in one of her movies, but at least it had been *hers*. At least when she fell on her face, she could own that fall.

"I need some air," she managed, like her throat might close or like her stomach might lurch through her throat before it did so. "You can stay. Or you can go. But I need some air."

It occurred to her that Andie might return to the room and find Kai Carol there and possibly Mace him, but she couldn't concern herself with Kai's well-being any longer. She reached for her shirt, throwing it over her head, then she fumbled for the door. Out in the hallway, she took deep, gasping breaths like maybe this whole thing was suffocating her.

She thought she heard Kai on the phone behind the door and stilled herself. Probably calling his own team or Galen because he still needed people to help him out of a jam. Birdie thought of

Andie and of Mona and of Elliot: she needed people, too, but in a different way than she'd thought she needed them when she fled New York four days ago for her wellness retreat and ended up in Barton.

She jabbed the elevator button down. She wasn't sure where she was headed or how her next scene would be written, but for the first time in a very long time, she knew that she didn't want to, absolutely couldn't, leave it up to anyone else.

47

ELLIOT

THE ELEVATOR WAS taking forever, and Elliot's stomach was in a full-on revolt, a cramp building in his side. He wished he could blame it on low blood sugar or abject hunger because he'd barely been able to eat at dinner with Simon, but he knew, because it was his actual gut, that it was much more about the story he'd just filed about Birdie. What was wrong with him? Why had he written something so counter to his own personal interests? Why wasn't he fighting for Birdie, even if it meant going up against an admittedly magnetic movie star? Elliot had never been daunted by a thing in his life, and yet here he was, wilting.

He poked the elevator button again, then again, then stepped back to watch the numbers tick down. His fingers dug into his abdomen, trying to press the cramp away, like he used to when he got winded after a freestyle sprint in a meet. Just as his muscle blessedly relaxed, the elevator doors whooshed open.

His brain took a few seconds to catch up to what was in front of him. Who was in front of him. Like seeing Birdie alone in the elevator was a mirage. He thought he'd be better prepared to face her. He'd had decades, literally two decades, to figure it out. To say, *It's been me all along. Don't you want it to be us too?*

He stepped into the elevator. She looked up at him, seemingly as surprised to see him there as he was to see her.

"Elliot," she said, her voice intentionally steady, like it was taking every ounce of energy she had to keep it so.

"Why aren't you with Kai?" he asked. "Is everything okay?"

She shook her head, then stopped herself. "I don't—" She lifted one shoulder and let it flop down. "I don't really know anymore."

The doors lurched closed, and he took a step closer, but something about her face implored him to give her some space, so instead, he turned and stood in front of her even though it was awkward, with his back to her, when what he really wanted was to sweep her up in his arms, wrap her legs around his waist, and pin her against the wall.

"I need you to be honest with me," Birdie said quietly. Maybe it was easier that way. Not facing each other. Not facing the truth or the consequences. "Did you send me the letter?"

Elliot went hot all over.

"Kai just told you that he did," he said. "Why are you still asking me?" He considered lying, telling her what she wanted to hear, but then, he wasn't certain what she wanted to hear.

Birdie stepped next to him, then slammed her finger on the elevator's emergency button, and the descent came to a halt with a lurch.

"What are you—" Elliot started.

"It's time that we did this, that we really had it out," Birdie said.

"By holding up an elevator?"

"I don't have the luxury of privacy," she said. "Of anonymity. This is as good a place as any."

"Okay, but—"

"Stop." She waved a hand in front of his face. "*Stop.* I don't want to argue about whether or not someone else is waiting for the elevator, and how I'm a selfish person for doing this here, now."

"Okay," Elliot said.

"Okay," Birdie answered, though it was more of a huff.

They stared at each other. Elliot clenched his jaw. Birdie chewed her lip.

"Did you send me the letter?" Birdie asked again.

"What happened with Kai?" Elliot responded.

"That is not an answer, Elliot," she snapped.

Elliot leaned against the side of the elevator wall, then pushed the bottoms of his palms against his eyes.

"Bird," he said. "This is all really a mess. I . . ." He paused. Then: "Do you want me to have written you the letter?"

"I asked you the question first!"

"I am just trying to do my job, Birdie," he said.

"I am not your job!" she shouted.

"Then why am I even here?" he shouted back. "You don't seem to want me personally and now you don't seem to want me professionally. What can I do to satisfy you?"

"You're the one who said you had to walk away from *me* that night."

"And you're the one who didn't even wait for an explanation. You literally pushed me out the door. If that doesn't say *regret*, I don't know what does."

The seconds ticked past, and he frowned at Birdie and Birdie frowned at him. And Elliot, who always had the answers and when he didn't have the answers found inventive ways to come up with them, could not understand how they kept getting stuck here, how he kept getting it so wrong with the one person with whom he wanted to get it right.

48

BIRDIE

BIRDIE WAS STANDING in front of Elliot, willing herself not to cry, feeling like a broken compass. Her feelings pointed everywhere, pointed nowhere, and offered absolutely no sense of bearings, no sense of direction or where she wanted to go next. This was why she relied on Imani and Sydney. They told her what to do, and she, in turn, then knew how to feel about it. But that wouldn't do anymore, it wasn't *enough* anymore, so from here on out, it was going to get harder, but maybe, also, that meant it was going to get better.

"Kai sent the email," she said finally. "But he didn't send the letter."

She saw something unlock in Elliot, his chest heaving up and down, like it was being freed from a weight he hadn't realized he was carrying.

"You're certain?" he asked. Something like worry passed over his face, but then he composed himself. Elliot the pro reporter back at it.

Birdie bounced her head, and her voice cracked. "Mona was

right, the question she asked. Kai never knew where I grew up. He couldn't have mailed a letter to the house—he didn't know that house existed."

As she said it aloud, Birdie realized how preposterous this was: that for as long as she'd been pining over Kai, he'd never even known where she'd come from, who she was at her roots. That had been her fault, the lies that became foundational in her narrative, but finally she had a chance to correct them.

"So I'm going to ask you for a final time," she said. Her hands were shaking, then the rest of her trembled too. "Did you send me the letter, the actual letter, the one I found in a box in my room?"

Elliot stepped closer. Birdie's breath picked up speed. She didn't dare move.

He reached for her chin and tipped it up toward his. She wanted to sink her face against the security of his palm, let him hold her there forever.

"Birdie," he said gently. "I did not write that letter. And I guess what you have to decide is if you're telling me that you wish I had."

Then he dropped his hand and released the emergency button. They were going down again. No closer to answers than when they started.

49

ELLIOT

THE BOULEVARD BAR was packed, and the wait for the food was interminable. Elliot's brain was still racing at a dangerous speed; his pulse was still keeping time along with it. Birdie had veered toward the hotel's exit as soon as the elevator hit the ground floor, and he watched heads swivel in her direction as she skittered out into the cool Vegas night.

Sitting at the bar replaying the elevator encounter—her vulnerability, the closeness of her breath to his—he knew with sudden clarity that tonight's article to Francesca, all about Kai, unraveling the truth of their relationship, was a mistake. He'd thought he could be impartial when it came to Birdie, but he'd overcorrected, been too removed, too distant, too rule abiding to save his job, even if it cost him the girl. But the girl, he knew with lightning-bolt certainty, was the only thing worth fighting for. He didn't know why it hadn't occurred to him until now that he didn't have to file any damn piece that he didn't want to.

The air caught in his throat at the revelation. That for once, for the first time, he could choose differently, he could prioritize something more foundational, more important. He'd spent his whole life chasing the get at any cost, and now the cost would be Birdie. It was too high a price to pay.

His fingers were trembling when he pulled his phone from his pocket. He needed to get to Francesca in time.

Her voicemail bleated in his ear.

"It's me," he said, "please don't run the article. It's not ready. You can't. I said some things I want to take back. Please, just . . ." He ran his hands over his face. "I know I'm pleading here, and I know I don't deserve a grace period, but give me a day. Please."

He hung up and stared at his screen as if he could will her to ping him back. Then he caught Simon's eye from across the room and nudged his head up as a hello. He tipped the rest of his martini down his throat, closed his eyes, and sighed, waiting for it to take effect.

"Nursing a bruised ego?" Simon said once he made his way over to him. He passed Elliot a second martini. He really was an excellent host.

"Something like that," Elliot said. He checked his phone again. *Fuck.*

"I'm not sure that anyone can solve her, Elliot. If it's any consolation," Simon said, mistaking Elliot's distress for Birdie drama when he was mostly just furious, just sickeningly upset, at himself. "But you knew her before all of this pomp and circumstance," Simon said. "So if anyone could be the one to solve the equation of Birdie Robinson . . ."

"Or Kai could. Kai will."

"Kai Carol is a fucking buffoon." Simon snorted. "Do you know how much money he loses in my casino?"

Elliot's text buzzed, and his heart detonated. But it was only Mona.

MONA

> Ok for me to borrow your laptop? My phone
> doesn't have good service up here.

Elliot didn't reply—Mona would do whatever she wanted anyway, and he clicked over to his texts to Francesca, but there was nothing. *Fuck fuck fuck.*

"Hey, did you hear me?" Simon said, pulling Elliot's focus. "You're down here nursing your second martini thinking that Kai Carol has you beat, and what I'm saying to you is that Birdie needs someone who was her equal long before she knew what back-end revenue was or flew to Dubai for twenty-four hours to shoot a perfume commercial for a million bucks."

"I just wanted to solve this for her, you know?" Elliot said.

"For her?" Simon posed, then shook his head. "Or for you? Very different questions, very different answers. And respectfully, I think Birdie is well capable on her own."

Elliot sighed and drained his second drink.

"Mate," Simon said, resting his hand on Elliot's shoulder. Elliot waited for his old friend to offer something insightful, for him to tell him he hadn't blown it, that he still had his shot. But instead, Simon, so good at getting his guests what they needed, not necessarily what they thought they wanted, simply let his hand linger, then slid the stool back beside Elliot and sat. Simon couldn't fix this for Elliot, and Simon already knew that.

No one else could fix it, solve it, resolve it, predict it, heal it. Who was going to do any of it in the end, if not him?

50

BIRDIE

BIRDIE WAS OUT in the middle of the crowds on the Strip. The temperature had dropped and the wind was kicking up, the late-winter air smelling like snow. Under the night sky and with the flashing lights and cacophony and street performers, she blended in with all the tourists, and it was a relief to just be Birdie Maxwell from Barton, California. She zipped up the collar on Andie's Costco coat, which she'd borrowed, like maybe she could get lost in it. Like maybe it could swallow her up and take her troubles along with it.

She obviously hadn't expected to see Kai, much less have him plead for another chance. In her former life, just a few weeks earlier, nothing would have brought her more joy than a Kai Carol mea culpa. But now she couldn't help but wonder if his mea culpa actually changed anything for her. If, even with all their history, she wasn't always going to put on a front for him, shade her story or herself with all sorts of small untruths. That's what she'd grown excellent at both on-screen and off, and maybe, she thought, it was time to leave that strictly for the camera. Maybe it was time to revisit Birdie Maxwell.

Birdie Maxwell was not Birdie Robinson.

Birdie Maxwell liked sitting shotgun in Elliot's Honda on the way to school, singing nineties music and frequently getting the lyrics wrong.

Birdie Maxwell liked school musicals that she took too seriously when half the sets were haphazardly painted and sometimes tipped over in the middle of the second act.

Birdie Maxwell liked vending-machine Cheetos inhaled on a cool linoleum floor and passed back and forth, like a secret, with Elliot until the tips of their fingers were bright orange and sticky.

Birdie was half a mile down the Strip now, away from the hotel. She could keep walking, stay out most of the night. Or she could pivot and return to face the complications that were waiting back at the Boulevard. In a script, Birdie thought, maybe Elliot or Kai would come running after her, shout into the wind until she heard him, then kiss her in front of the fountain at the Bellagio as music soared in the background.

But that was a Birdie Robinson feature.

She spun around without second-guessing herself. She'd thrown herself into this whole endeavor because she'd wanted to regain control of her own narrative, and then, as soon as it got difficult with Ian, she'd retreated like she only got one shot to change her trajectory. When had she become someone who took no for an answer, who took a punch to the chin and refused to get back up? Elliot had assured her that she could carry on, push through, persevere, but she'd been so humiliated after Ian that, she supposed, it was easier to pretend that she didn't have agency anymore, that her story had already been written.

Birdie stopped, her heart beating so hard that she could hear her own pulse in her neck. She tilted her head toward the sky, and it was then that she noticed it was snowing. In Las Vegas. She fluttered her eyes against the flakes and tried to just breathe. Snow in the desert. She opened them and stared down the Strip, at how everyone was now gazing upward, as if no one else could believe it either, like it was some sort of miracle.

Birdie felt her face crack into a grin and blinked back a surprise of tears. In Vegas, anything was possible; anything could happen.

Then she started moving, double-timing it back to the hotel. If she wanted her own sort of happy ending, she really was going to have to write it herself. And for the first time—or maybe the second—since everything cratered around her, Birdie truly believed that she could.

51

ELLIOT

ELLIOT MADE IT back to the room after three and a half martinis. The half had been a mistake. He fumbled with the key card, dropped it, picked it up, but then Mona swung the door open.

"Goddammit, you're a mess."

"At long last, I'm as messy as my twin sister," he said, his tongue feeling swollen, thick.

"What's that supposed to mean?" she said, color rising to her cheeks, her fists curled like she was ready to come out swinging.

"Nothing." He sighed. "It means nothing." All Elliot wanted to do was make contact with his pillow.

"I cannot believe you," Mona said. "Are we really doing this again?"

"No," he said, face-planting on the bed. "We are not doing it again."

"I'm going to tell you for the last time, Elliot. I know you think I blew it, that I should be working for NASA or at the very least some biotech firm in Palo Alto. But I am *happy*. I like Monads, and I like our old house, and it's pretty fucking ironic that you think I'm the one who is stuck."

Elliot felt his shoulders curl closer to his ears. He knew she was just warming up.

"Just because I don't live this high-wire life doesn't make it any less fulfilling. And I think—" Mona took a deep breath. "I think you should, like, figure out why you are so tied to the validation from your career. When, I mean, look, Elliot, we're not getting any younger. We'll almost be as old as Mom and Dad were soon . . ." Her words drifted, but she didn't need to say anything else. They both knew that whatever he was chasing had something to do with his parents and mortality and leaving a mark on the world, but goddammit, the chase was exhausting, and he was beginning to realize he was sprinting down a dead-end street. Sprinting for the sake of it, not because it made any sense. "Also," Mona said. "I think you should talk to Francesca. Ask for a vacation, take some time to just be a human, not a reporter. I think she'd agree, and you could start fresh."

Elliot groaned into the bedsheets. She was right. His brilliant twin sister had figured out how to live her life all on her own terms while he was busy judging her. He shifted and rolled on his back and found her glaring at him from across the room.

"I'm sorry, you're right," he said. "And I'd be happy to talk to Francesca if she doesn't fire me after tonight."

"She's not going to fire you," Mona said.

He checked his phone one more time, but there was nothing from his editor, and his eyelids were tugging him toward sleep.

"She is," he said. "But it's just as well. I shouldn't have accepted this assignment in the first place. I should have done everything differently. If I could go back in time, I'd start over. I'd rewrite it all."

52

BIRDIE

IRDIE RACED INTO the lobby and scoured the bar for Elliot. She had things to say to him. They had things to say to each other. She felt the stares and the long gazes from the patrons, and she decided to let them look. Birdie Maxwell hadn't turned her life upside down to become Birdie Robinson to hide away from the attention. She smiled and waved, and when three people asked for a photo, she cheerfully said, "Of course!"

She could do this on her own terms. She really could. She'd never been one to cower at the first sniff of rejection, and she wasn't sure why—or how—she'd become the sort of person who did so now. Birdie Maxwell was tired of hiding. Tired of listening to everyone else. Tired of the carefully curated persona. Who ever said that America needed her to be their sweetheart? Who ever said that audiences couldn't differentiate between a woman they'd like to know exactly as she was and the roles that she played?

She thanked the last picture taker, then felt someone tug on her elbow and turned, and there was Simon.

"We didn't get a proper hello," he said, all British charm and sparkle, and Birdie gratefully welcomed his embrace.

"I'm on an apology streak," she said when they disentangled. "Do I owe you one too?"

He laughed. "No, you and I were always fine with each other. Before, during, since."

Birdie nodded, relieved that after so many things she'd gotten wrong, she hadn't gotten this wrong too.

"Elliot went upstairs, though," Simon said. "A few drinks to the wind. A story to fix, he said."

"*My* story," Birdie said. Acid burned up her throat. "And I don't think *he* can fix it."

"Well, you might want to give it a beat," Simon offered. "Let him sober up, stop feeling sorry for himself."

"What does Elliot O'Brien have to feel sorry for himself over?" Birdie retorted.

Simon laughed again. "I think a lot of people could say the same of you."

Birdie raised her eyebrows. She'd forgotten how normal Simon was, how adjusted he was to the pomp and circumstance of celebrity so that he was utterly unfazed by its lunacy. The Birdie Maxwell in her adored him for it. She pulled him into a hug again.

"It's great to see you, Simon," she said. "And that's fine, about Elliot. I have my own plan anyway, so I'll give him the night. Nothing I have to say can't wait. It's been twenty years. What's one night more?"

Simon's face broke into a smile. "Birdie Robinson has her own plan. Perfection."

"Birdie Maxwell does," Birdie smiled back. "Birdie Robinson is just grateful to be here." She paused. "Speaking of which—I need a favor."

53

ELLIOT

ELLIOT WOKE TO blinding morning light pouring through the drapes. His mouth felt like sandpaper and tasted even worse, like the olives from his martinis last night, but if the olives had curdled on his tongue. He creaked his head up an inch. Mona's bed was empty.

He patted down the bed, in search of his phone. He thought he might vomit, but he couldn't be sure if it was his hangover or if he was about to see the article he'd written about Birdie and Kai. His palm landed on his device, and he pulled it in front of his face, prepared for the worst.

Oddly, he had only a few notifications. None from Francesca. None from the *Times* app. He felt his forehead furrow, suddenly significantly more awake. He logged on to the app and searched for Birdie's name. Nothing since his last story. He didn't know if he should rejoice that Francesca had pulled his story or assume that she'd had enough when she did pull his story and was now ghosting him. *Shit.* He exhaled and was thumbing over to his email when he heard the key beep in the door, and then his twin burst in.

"Morning, sunshine," she said, and held up a paper bag with grease oozing through. "I brought doughnuts for breakfast. Well, brunch, since it's almost noon."

"Noon?" Elliot shot straight up. "*Noon?*" He hadn't even noticed the time on his phone.

."You were sleeping." Mona flopped a shoulder. "I figured you needed it."

Now Elliot was frantic. His fingers flew over his screen and landed on his texts. Nothing from Francesca. *What was going on?* He wasn't sure if he'd been fired or was simply being ignored, but either way, Elliot reverted right back to pro reporter and doubled down.

> ELLIOT
>
> **F—you'll get your story by end of day. Thank you for the grace period.**

He hit send before he could retract his thank-you because they were not really a relationship of thank-yous, but he wanted to show her appreciation all the same.

"We're going to Clay Dodara at 3 p.m."

"Clay Dodara? The magician? I thought . . . I thought we would head back home." Elliot didn't want to drag Mona's oddball interests—magic was right up there with extraterrestrials—because that would only kick them right back into a fight, but he had less than zero interest in sitting through some magician's matinee show for a packed house of tourists. She might as well have proposed that they divert their drive to Area 51.

"Birdie got us tickets," Mona said casually, like she was testing the waters. "I didn't want to say no. Besides, he's been sold out for six months. Nelson said he's incredible."

There was so much to unpack in that sentence that Elliot didn't even know where to begin. *Birdie* got them tickets? *Nelson* said he's incredible?

"I wanted to get a jump on it, head home," he grumbled.

"Well, I'm going to Clay Dodara. I guess you can drive back without me."

Mona knew damn well that Elliot didn't want to spend three hundred miles by himself in the RV. She was always able to press his pressure points and get him to bend to her will. Well, not always. But most often. Sometimes she had to play the long game.

"Fine," Elliot replied. "*Fine.*"

"Fine," Mona said, a grin spreading across her face. She threw him the bag of doughnuts. Elliot reached up to grab them on instinct. *Instinct*, he thought. When it came to Birdie, he needed to start trusting his own.

54

BIRDIE

BIRDIE WAS CALMER than she expected to be. She and Andie, who was beside herself with excitement about the house seats to see Clay Dodara, walked to the Bellagio early, the sidewalks pooling with puddles from the snow that had come and gone and already melted. Simon had left their tickets at the front desk, so Birdie pinged Mona and told her to meet them there. She wanted to get a move on.

Clay Dodara was the hottest ticket on the Strip. Birdie wasn't particularly interested in magic, wasn't interested at all, in fact. But he'd done a TV special that had blown the minds of even the toughest of critics, so Birdie had grudgingly tuned in a few months ago in her trailer, and what she liked most about him—or, she should say, what she needed most from him—was that he always invited an audience member up onstage to participate. And Birdie needed to participate.

She intentionally had muted Imani's and Sydney's texts this morning, of which there were many—checking in, saying hi, trying to be casual but also likely frantically waiting for updates. But this was something she could do on her own. This was something she was *going* to do on her own. They could read about it when everyone else did. And if it backfired, if it didn't go exactly as planned? Well, then Birdie had started over before, and there was almost nothing in life that stayed permanent if you didn't want it to.

Birdie and Andie loitered in the Bellagio lobby, Birdie trying to be inconspicuous, trying to calm her nerves. She chewed on her thumbnail and shifted her weight from one foot to the other until finally Andie said, "What is wrong with you? Is this about Kai? Please tell me this isn't about Kai."

Andie had returned to the room last night to find Kai red-eyed and sniffling on a love seat in the suite's living room. It took her twenty minutes to cajole him to leave. Birdie suspected he'd talked himself into crying just so someone would catch him doing so.

"It's not about Kai," Birdie said, just as she saw Mona and Elliot stroll into the lobby, Mona looking giddy, Elliot looking like he'd ingested E. coli–laced beef. Birdie understood because she, too, felt like she had ingested E. coli–laced beef. But the show had to go on.

"Hey," Birdie said to Elliot.

"Hey," he said back but did not meet her eyes.

They found their seats and waited for the lights to dim, and soon, Clay Dodara, in a tux, with extremely gelled hair and very white teeth, was in front of them. Just a few minutes in, Andie and Mona, sitting between Birdie and Elliot, were pie-eyed, giggling, astounded at Clay's sleights of hand, at his ability to make a horse disappear. (Yes, he really had a horse onstage. This was Vegas.) About an hour into the act, the house lights came up for the big finale, and Clay ambled to center stage, directly in front of them. Birdie's breath quickened. When she'd envisioned this last night, it had seemed brilliant, foolproof.

"I'd like to request some audience participation," Clay was saying. "A volunteer?" The crowd began to cheer, and hands flew into the air. Clay's eyes settled on the seats directly in front of him. "Wait, ladies and gentlemen, please wait for a moment," he said. "I believe I see—yes, I definitely do—is that Birdie Robinson in row three?"

The cheers turned to squeals, and Birdie felt every stare from the entire two-thousand-person venue on the back of her neck. *Shit shit shit shit.* What had she been thinking, asking Simon to phone Clay to pull her onstage? She raised a hand meekly to acknowledge the crowd.

"Birdie Robinson! I can't have you in my audience and not demand that you come onstage. Get your ass up here," Clay called. The auditorium absolutely lost it, and if Birdie had felt like enjoying herself, she would have floated on the high of this adulation for days. Alas, she was too consumed with regretting her plan to enjoy it.

"Birdie," Andie whispered into her ear, "I think you're supposed to go up there."

Birdie nodded and pushed herself up with the armrests on her seat, her legs so wobbly she wasn't certain she'd hold steady. In any other circumstance, she'd remind herself that she was an *actor*, a total *pro*, and she'd stitch herself into a mask, a costume, and carry on as if this were all an act. But it wasn't. She had to do this as Birdie Maxwell, and it was absolutely fucking terrifying.

She made her way down her row, and then up the stairs, to where Clay was beaming. He gave her a quick hug, then bowed, as if she were royalty. She'd only met Clay once in passing, and she knew that he loved nothing more than a celebrity collaboration, which inevitably drew views to his YouTube channel, so she wasn't particularly surprised at his enthusiasm. She was doing him as much of a favor as he was doing her.

"Birdie Robinson," he said, holding one of her hands and raising their linked arms in the air, like they'd just won Olympic gold, "it is an honor."

The crowd went completely nuts. Just bananas. As if they'd forgotten that Birdie was no longer their sweetheart, as if she'd been forgiven for everything. It would have been easy, Birdie realized, to simply get swept up in Clay's act, to set aside her plan and let Clay encourage a redemptive arc that she would ride like a wave. But it had dawned on her last night that she didn't want anyone else to be responsible for her own happiness: not Imani, not Sydney, not Ian, not Carter, not her parents, not Andie, not Kai, and not Elliot either.

So she steadied her breath, reminded herself that she was more self-reliant than she'd gotten used to, and then she reached for Clay's mic.

55

ELLIOT

ELLIOT WAS DUBIOUS, even grouchy, about wasting his time at some ridiculous magic show in a packed house full of tourists when he could have been writing. But now Birdie was onstage, and he found he could barely breathe. There was a moment, initially, when Birdie looked like she couldn't breathe either, and Elliot wanted to run up there and wrap himself around her, like what she needed was protection. But then he saw what he knew almost no one else in the theater did: she stitched herself together and grew taller, bolder, stronger, all with a nearly undetectable shift in her posture. Elliot detected it, though, because he was made to read Birdie Maxwell like a well-worn book. Every page, every sentence, every line. He'd been reading it since he was twelve.

"Thank you so much for inviting me up here, Clay!" she said, her voice dancing, her tone animated. "What an absolute surprise. I hope you don't intend to saw me in half. My agents would be quite unhappy if I were sliced in two today."

"Your agents may be, but maybe not that ex of yours, the chef?" Clay retorted. The crowd roared.

Elliot saw the tiniest of flinches behind Birdie's eyes, but she played along, the good sport. She had to know that just about every phone in the auditorium was trained on her, that fingers were flying over their keypads to update every social media app possible. Which reminded him.

Francesca was going to kill him if he didn't scoop this first.

He tugged his phone from his jacket pocket.

"What is she doing up there?" Mona hissed in his ear. "Is this why we came here?"

"Shh," Andie said. "It will be okay. Give her some credit. Also, Elliot, put your fucking phone away. You don't have to be a reporter at all times on all things."

"Do you know what's going on?" Mona snapped. "I don't like this one bit."

"Maybe it's not up for you to like," Elliot said, surprising himself, that he'd choose Birdie's side over his twin's. He set his phone back in his pocket. Andie was right: he could be a reporter when all of this, whatever it was, was over.

Mona scowled. Elliot scowled back. They all turned their attention back to the stage.

"Yes, well, about that ex," Birdie was saying. "Well, about everything. If you don't mind, Clay, can I steal your spotlight for a second?"

"I'm pretty sure it's already been stolen," Clay replied, "with or without asking my permission."

The audience's applause was thunderous, and Birdie, Elliot was relieved to see, broke into a genuine grin that reminded him of high school, of her belting out those songs. He wondered if it was possible to die from an exploding heart, and if so, if that was going to be his fate.

The lights dimmed, and a spotlight went on. Clay faded to the back of the stage, and then it was just Birdie, beautiful Birdie, all by herself. The auditorium hushed to a near-dead silence.

"So," she said. "Well, gee. I thought I'd be better prepared to say something now."

Someone in the mezzanine shouted, "Birdie, you can dump me anytime!" And that seemed to electrify the audience all over again, which in turn electrified Birdie.

"Whew, okay, well, thank you, kind sir," she said, and Elliot could sense her relaxing, so he unclenched his own jaw, his own shoulders, which he was holding up to his ears. "So . . . I guess some of you are aware of what's been . . . happening in my life these days," she said. Her voice was still a little wobbly, and Elliot found himself squinting, as if he could telepathically will her some confidence. Birdie carried on. "So, um, while I have your attention, I wanted to say something to you guys, the public, the people who have made my career." She inhaled, smiled, and continued. "I owe you all a real apology. Not the canned, filmed thing that you saw a few weeks ago. But from me. Just . . . me. I screwed up on set. I thought I was doing the right thing by speaking out against our director, um, you guys know Sebastian Carol, but I turned something private into something public—um, I guess like what I'm doing right now—and that cost a lot of people their jobs. My fight with Sebastian was not the right one to have, and for that, I'm sorry."

Someone a few rows behind Elliot shouted, "Fuck the patriarchy, Birdie!" and Elliot was pretty sure he saw Birdie blink back a swell of tears.

"Anyway," she said. "Obviously, since then, I've been in sort of, um . . . a personal spiral."

"Jesus," Mona muttered beside Elliot. "What is she doing?"

"Her own thing," Andie said. "She is doing *her own thing*. It's amazing."

Birdie kept talking. "And, um, in this personal spiral, I guess, you now know that I am also a bit of a mess when it comes to my love life. I'm not the girl you've come to know at the movies—sunshiney, easy, or really all that interested in getting married actually. And . . . well, I don't want to drag anyone else into this public morass of my messiness. So, since I'm already canceled, I want to say that my hunt for my anonymous ex is over."

The crowd stirred and everyone started talking at once. Then the booing began at the back of the house. Elliot spun around. How could anyone *boo* her? How could *everyone* boo her? He jumped to his feet, then felt Mona's hand on his arm, pulling him back down.

"No, no, it's okay," Birdie said. "I know you want the happily-ever-after. I get it. I do. I've spent ten years acting out that happily-ever-after, and it's hard to let go of." The booing droned on, and Elliot, who had never been violent, never had the urge to hit a person in his life, wanted to excoriate every single ticket holder. One by one. Let him at them. He'd clock them all right in the nose even if he broke all his knuckles.

"You can't quit now!" some woman shrieked.

"How can you do this to us?" someone else cried. "We need to find Mr. Anonymous!"

Birdie shifted from one foot to the other.

"What I'm trying to say," she managed, pulling the mic too close, feedback blaring throughout the theater, "is that it doesn't matter who wrote it. We can have a happy ending without it."

"The hell we can!" another woman yelled.

Birdie glanced around, her eyes searching. Whichever way

she'd imagined this would go, Elliot didn't think she'd imagined this. She was trying to write her own ending, her triumphant independent ending, and the audience, who had grown so used to her fairy-tale happily-ever-afters, wasn't biting.

Clay stepped forward from the shadows, ready to steer the ship back to his show.

"Okay, okay," he said. "Come on, friends, let's go easy on her."

The booing started up again, but Clay held his fingers to his lips and, incredibly, the entire venue stilled.

And that was precisely when the back doors to the theater clanged open and Kai Carol strode in. He did have immaculate timing, Elliot thought. He always knew exactly when to ride in on his horse, a white knight, ready to save the damsel in distress.

56

BIRDIE

BIRDIE DIDN'T KNOW what she was expecting in this grand plan, but having Kai bound onstage was definitely not on her agenda. As soon as the crowd realized what was happening, they were back on their feet. The booing turned to screams, and even Clay Dodara looked a little gobsmacked, like never in his wildest magical ideas could he have dreamed of something that would garner this much press. His eyeballs had dollar signs on them; Birdie could practically hear him counting up the rising tally of his YouTube subscribers.

Kai landed in front of her and held up his arms, his fists curled into balls, like he'd just won a marathon.

"What are you doing here—" Birdie started. She thought she'd been clear last night, but now he was in front of her, now he was in front of *two thousand* people, and Birdie felt off-balance, uncertain. She looked out toward the house seats, to find Andie, Mona, Elliot, but the stage lights were bright, and she could make out only shadows.

"Birdie," Kai said. He placed his palms on her cheeks, like he always did. Why was he always assuming he had the right to her focus, her body, her gaze? "I wasn't honest last night."

Birdie's stomach dropped.

"I wrote you both letters. It was me."

"You what?" Birdie yelped.

"I got nervous last night—when you asked. I didn't want to show my hand, play all my cards, but—" He dropped his head now, a perfect leading-man touch. He glanced back up at her with lonely, welling eyes. "It was me, babe. I don't want to live without you."

He turned toward the audience.

"Also," he said, "I want to make something clear, not that she has asked me to say this. But my brother, Sebastian, well, I love him. But he can be an arrogant asshole, and I don't want anyone blaming Birdie for what happened on *Love Grenade*. I've reached out to the studio, told them I'll step in for my brother if they'd like me to, and it looks like the movie is going to get back on track."

He turned back toward Birdie like this was the greatest gift he could imagine, him saving her movie, him saving her broken heart. Then he was down on one knee. And Birdie wasn't sure if she was going to pass out or puke.

He reached into his blazer pocket.

No no no no no no.

"I saw you here—with the livestream, I mean, and I just knew I had to make it right, Birdie. I knew I couldn't live another day without you," he said.

And then there was a little black box in his palm, and then there was an enormous diamond inside the little black box, and then the audience reached a decibel that Birdie thought would shatter the space-time continuum. Birdie had no idea when Kai would have found the time to buy a ring with a small glacier on it, but she envisioned him running into some fancy jeweler in the ground-floor level of the Wynn, pointing to a ring—it didn't matter which one as long as you could shoot it from a wide-angle lens—and billing it to his room.

"Holy shit," Clay managed into the mic. "Holy fucking shit."

Birdie's eyes floated over to him, like maybe he could save her, but he looked frothy, giddy, and so her gaze shifted back to Kai, who was making gestures to the audience to be quiet.

"Guys, guys," he said. "Shh, we need to hear Ms. Robinson's answer. We *have* to hear Birdie's answer."

Birdie blinked quickly and tried to speak, but her tongue felt anesthetized; her brain was complete static. She'd wanted Kai for so long, and yet now she no longer wanted him at all. *At all.* And if she could evolve so much as to spurn Kai goddamn Carol, she clearly could evolve in other ways too. Like being completely fine if she stayed single forever. Like being more than okay if she had to *pivot* to an indie horror film because at least that might feel authentic.

"Ms. Robinson?" Clay prompted.

"Ms. Robinson?" Kai echoed sweetly.

And then Birdie heard a voice from the audience, and everyone turned, and it wasn't who she expected, because she expected Elliot. But Elliot could never save her, because that was the stuff of movies.

So she watched in complete disbelief as her best friend, Mona, shouted, "It's Birdie *Maxwell*, you fucking fuckball," and then pushed through her row and landed onstage. "And you didn't write that first letter. I know because I did."

57

ELLIOT

ELLIOT THOUGHT HE was having a stroke. Or an aneurysm. Or a psychotic break. Something. Anything to explain why his twin sister was onstage dressing down Kai Carol by explaining that there was no way he could have sent that anonymous letter because she was the one who had.

He heard Andie mutter, "What the actual hell?" under her breath, so he figured he wasn't, in fact, having some sort of brain malfunction, and he grabbed her arm and said, "What is even happening?" and she simply turned to him with saucer eyes and shook her head.

Mona had swiped Clay's microphone and was demanding that Kai get to his feet.

"And put that stupid black box away," she snapped. "You're not proposing to my best friend. You're not showing up here and lying after all those other years of trapping her under false circumstances. Yes, I did a deep dive last night. Not again."

The rumble in the audience began low and picked up speed, like they were all just realizing that their two favorite movie stars had real, not just internet-rumored, history. And they were lucky enough to be witnessing it, here, now, all for the price of admission to a Clay Dodara show.

"I didn't mean—" Kai started, tilting toward the microphone, as if the public record was what mattered here. He faded and stared at Birdie, and Elliot muttered to himself, "Don't do it, Birdie, don't do it. Do not give that man another inch."

"Kai," Birdie said, and squeezed her eyes closed.

"Please," Kai pleaded, and Elliot realized that this might be the first time in Kai Carol's whole life when he had to fight for something, when something actually had stakes. *What an absolute prick.* Then he felt his phone vibrating in his pocket and pulled it out.

Francesca.

Of course she wanted the story, of course she wanted the scoop. Of course she knew he would be there, involved in some way. She just didn't know how much, how deeply his involvement ran. It ran so deep that he couldn't separate Birdie's pain from his, her shock from his shock. Goddammit he wanted to help her, but he also intuited that the best way to help her was to stand right here, unmoving, and let her hold her own. His thumb hovered over his screen, and then he shoved his phone back into his pocket. For once, the scoop could wait, and Elliot found this absolutely liberating.

"I don't understand," Birdie said, turning to Mona, as if Kai was already irrelevant. Elliot's heart soared. Literally, actually soared. Well, figuratively actually soared, but he suspected if a heart could really soar, his would be suspended in midair right now. "Mona, you're not in love with me."

Mona stared at her shoes and shifted her posture. "No, no, I mean, I love you, Bird. But . . . well, I wrote it for Elliot."

That soaring heart careened straight down to the ground and splattered. Elliot nearly jumped over the two rows in front of him out of sheer astonishment.

"You wrote it . . . for Elliot?" Birdie squeaked.

The theater had fallen so quiet that if a heart *could* soar, you would hear its little wings flapping.

Mona sighed, cleared her throat, looked out to the two thousand ticket holders who were getting way more than they had paid for.

"I made Elliot promise. Years ago. At prom. You remember, right?"

Birdie nodded. Elliot swallowed.

"And, I mean, you don't know this, Bird, but seven years ago, when you guys were together—"

"Wait," Birdie interrupted. "How do you know about that? Who told you?" Elliot saw her squint in his direction. He hadn't said a word, he'd promised he wouldn't tell Mona, and he hadn't.

"No one told me, Birdie. That's the whole point. That Elliot went to the premiere that I knew you were at too and went dark for the night, and then neither of you mentioned that you'd even run into each other, and then you never even mentioned each other again to me *at all* other than weird, stilted one-off questions and answers? I know I just run a dive bar, but it wasn't difficult to piece together."

Elliot felt the blood drain from his face, and though the spotlight made Birdie glow—she was impossibly beautiful even in the middle of a disaster—she looked peaked herself.

"And I wanted to ask you about it," Mona said. "I wanted you to know that you could tell me anything! I didn't have a right to claim you simply because you were my best friend, and because

Elliot got all the good things when we were growing up. What I said back then, at prom, was stupid and selfish, and I love you two more than anything, anyone else, on the planet." Mona inhaled, then kept going. "Anyway, I called Elliot after the premiere, and I asked him how he was doing, what he was up to, and . . . he didn't say a word. Dead silence about it. And I realized what a disaster I had made of everything. That the two people I wanted the most happiness for couldn't even share it with me."

Elliot's jaw had nearly come unhinged. *Mona called him that morning when he was at the bagel store as a setup so he could tell her, so she could give him room to tell her if something happened, and she would have been happy for him, for them, and instead, he didn't trust her to do so, so he went back to Birdie's and walked away or they both pushed each other away, more likely, and then he and Birdie spent the past seven years losing time.*

"So anyway." Mona sighed. "You were supposed to come home a few years ago, for something, maybe Christmas, I can't remember. And, I mean, I feel like a proper idiot now, but I typed that note up and dropped it in the mail, thinking you'd find it and realize that it could only be from Elliot, and my screwup wouldn't have set you guys too far off track."

"But I didn't come home," Birdie whispered.

"But you didn't come home. Not for years, not until now," Mona said, her voice breaking. "And, Birdie, I am so, so sorry. I'd forgotten about it, and then when you brought the letter to Monads last week, I thought that you'd figure it out. And then when you didn't, I thought that if you two spent time together in the RV, *then* you'd figure it out. I didn't mean for it to spiral." Mona turned toward the audience. "Elliot, I'm sorry, too. I commandeered your laptop last night and got Francesca's email—I wrote her and told her I'd make this right for you. Explained myself. She agreed to give you a minute to find out the truth. So you have. And I'm sorry."

Then Mona swiveled back to Birdie, who stared at his twin sister for a long beat. Elliot was paralyzed, unsure of what to do, if he had any part in this, if he should bound up onstage and tell Birdie that he'd loved her since the day they met when she had skinned knees and lopsided braids and that weathered copy of *The Lord of the Rings*. Or if he didn't have the right to tell her any of this anymore, now that it was so late in their saga. He was shaking, his body so amped-up on adrenaline and stress and dopamine and serotonin.

Then the applause started in the back of the theater, like a low rumble of thunder. And someone shouted, "Girl, what are you waiting for? Where is Elliot? Go get your Elliot!!" And then the rest of the venue joined in. Explosive, booming clapping and howling and cheering.

And Elliot wanted to run to her, fly right up those stairs, elbowing past Kai Carol and sweeping Birdie up into an embrace that he didn't think he'd ever let go of. But this had to be Birdie's story, he told himself. This had to be the ending that she wanted to write, not him. So he held his breath, and he tried to abate his trembling, though it was futile and a losing battle in all respects.

Then, just when Elliot began to feel foolish for holding out hope, Birdie broke her gaze from Mona and turned toward the adoring crowd. She turned right toward him and smiled.

58

BIRDIE

ELLIOT. *ELLIOT.*

That was the single word running through Birdie's mind. She had to get to Elliot. She forgot that she was onstage in front of two thousand people. She forgot that every one of those two thousand people had their cameras trained right on her. She forgot that Kai Carol was standing just a few feet away from her with an elephant-sized diamond ring still in the palm of his hand.

She spun out toward the auditorium.

Elliot.

Birdie bit her bottom lip, then allowed herself to give in to this moment, this ridiculous turn of events that had cost them both so much time together but maybe was exactly how it should have been written.

She took one long, cleansing breath and realized that the crowd was absolutely losing their minds, screaming at a decibel reserved for rock royalty. Then her face split open into a smile that was so wide, it would have hurt under different circumstances. But now it felt hard-won, and it felt glorious. Birdie felt *glorious.* Through the glare of the lights, she managed to find Elliot's eyes, and he found hers, and she nodded, so he nodded, and then she watched him bound—literally leap like an actual superhero—over the first two rows of seats, and then he was taking the steps two by two, and then he was in front of her.

"Birdie," he said, and she couldn't really hear him over the shrieking, but she didn't think she needed to.

"Elliot," she said, and she knew he couldn't hear her either, but no one cared.

"I can't believe you did this," he said. "It's brilliant. *You* are brilliant."

"Well," she said, "this wasn't exactly how I planned it."

"Close enough," Elliot replied.

"Close enough," she agreed, because it was.

"I have so much I need to say to you," Elliot said.

"But maybe not now," Birdie replied. "In front of two thousand people?"

Elliot turned to look out to the theater, like he only just realized they had an audience.

"Oh my god," he said.

"Welcome to my world." She smiled.

"Can I stay for the rest of my life?" he semi-shouted so he could be heard above the ruckus.

"Yes," she shouted back. "As long as you know you're about to be thought of as my plus one."

"I couldn't dream of a better title in my life."

The noise of the crowd was earsplitting, and because words were pointless, they stared at each other for a long beat.

Then: "I would really like to kiss you now," Elliot mouthed.

"I would really like you to kiss me now," Birdie mouthed back.

And he took a long glance at her, like he couldn't believe this was actually happening, and Birdie wanted to tattoo his adoration onto her insides, hold it close to her chest forever. And then he tipped forward, and the roar from the audience was deafening, but all Birdie could hear was her breath, and his breath, and the rush of blood that made its way to her ears as his lips met hers, and hers met his. Birdie sunk into his chest and kissed Elliot like she'd never kissed anyone before, and to be fair, she'd had a lot of practice. Screen kisses, air-kisses, faked kisses, and yes, some real kisses too. But it felt different this time, with her first love, with, she suspected, her last love too. She felt the urgency of his mouth, his tongue, his hunger, and she lost herself in the headiness of how he smelled, how he tasted, how he felt against her.

After some time, long enough that every part of her was tingling, and she mostly wanted to hustle offstage and take Elliot back to her room, he pulled back.

"You wrote the perfect ending, you know," he said.

"You're the writer here," she replied. "Not me."

He shook his head. "This one was all you. I'm too dark and twisted to write something like this."

Birdie laughed, out of both disbelief and utter joy. The thing was, she thought, maybe she had been too.

"I'm going to kiss you again," Birdie said. "Just so I'm certain this sticks."

"It's sticking," Elliot said, already tilting forward. "Like glue."

59

ELLIOT

SIMON HAD A car waiting for them at the back entrance of the Bellagio. The driver hopped out, opened the door for them both, then gave them their privacy, as if Simon had instructed him to do so, which he probably had.

Elliot and Birdie sat pressed together in the enormous back seat of the Escalade, like any inch between them was too much. He turned toward her and was surprised to find that he was choking up, blinking back tears.

"Bird," he said, his voice hitching.

"Aw, don't do that," she replied. "Then I'm going to cry too."

He nodded, took a deep breath, tried to steady himself. He couldn't remember the last time he cried, and the feeling was both discombobulating and comforting, like nothing made sense but at the same time everything did.

"Can you believe Mona?" Birdie smiled. "I guess she really is a genius."

"I'm sorry about seven years ago," he said, not because he didn't agree with her about Mona but because he'd never been more desperate to say what he needed to. "I shouldn't have left. I never, ever should have walked away from you." He wanted to tell her everything, to make sure she knew that she was more valuable to him than anything else he'd ever thought was precious in his life.

"And I shouldn't have kicked you out before I heard what you had to say," she said, moving her thumb over his cheek, where a tear had streaked down before he could stop it.

"I've spent a long time telling myself that I would have let you talk me into staying," Elliot said. "But now I know that you shouldn't have had to talk me into anything. Birdie Maxwell doesn't have to negotiate to be loved."

"I think I thought that I did. At least for a while. Maybe we both got it wrong back then."

"If I could do it over, I would have told you that I loved you, that nothing, not even Mona, could make me leave."

He watched Birdie's eyes flare wider, then the brightest of grins illuminated her face.

"Did you just tell me that you love me?"

Elliot hadn't even realized that he had, but once he replayed what he'd said, he was perfectly content, perfectly sure of it. "Yes," he said, mirroring her grin. "I definitely did. I definitely do."

Birdie laughed, dipping her head back and letting the joy overtake her. Elliot thought she had never looked more exactly like herself, never looked more beautiful. He thought of that girl on her porch reading *The Lord of the Rings*, of singing ABBA or Queen with the words all wrong. God, he was going to love her forever.

"I don't think even the best screenwriters in the industry could have crafted this," she said just before Elliot covered her mouth with his because he couldn't not kiss her for another second. They didn't stop, not when her phone buzzed and buzzed and buzzed, and not when his rang over and over again, and he was certain it was Francesca, who he hoped would forgive him, but none of it mattered. Nothing mattered but her, him, them.

Birdie pulled back for the briefest of hiccups and said, "Me too, by the way, me too."

Elliot furrowed his brow. He couldn't even remember what they'd been talking about, like kissing her short-circuited his brain. "Me too what?"

"Me too, I definitely did. Definitely do," she said, but she could read on his face that he was still lost. "Love you. I love you, Elliot O'Brien. And I want you to stay forever."

Elliot wondered if he had ever been this happy. He hadn't been, he knew. "I will."

"Then it's settled. You'll stay forever."

"Where the hell is our driver?" Elliot yelped, tipping toward her and kissing her neck. "I need to get you back to the hotel room."

Birdie laughed again, and he thought he could listen to that laugh for the rest of his life and never grow weary of the sound.

Birdie opened the passenger door and shouted, "We're ready!" And though he knew it was to the driver, Elliot thought it was for the both of them too.

Two decades. Seven years.

Finally.

They'd never been more ready.

He couldn't wait.

⇒ EPILOGUE ⇐

Dear Readers,

*I've convinced Elliot and his editor to let me take the wheel,
dictate this update in the column that retains his byline. I
wanted to write my own ending, even as much as I trust
Elliot, even as much as I love Elliot, I thought I should be in
charge of my own story. So, I'd like to reintroduce myself.
I'm Birdie Maxwell from Barton, California. And I apologize
for not introducing myself properly before. That's my bag-
gage, not yours. It's been three weeks since Mona told us
the truth, and Elliot and I then told each other the truth,
and I see your tweets, I read your Instagram comments.
Don't be mad that I've gone silent, taken my life behind the
curtain, away from the audience who made my career. I
know I owe you all a debt of many things. I don't take any
of that for granted. But Elliot and I needed some time to
build something just for ourselves, to settle into twenty
years of an ending we didn't see coming.*

After we returned to California from Vegas, we decided to get away, see how it felt to be alone together after everything that had swirled around us. We took a week to just be, and for an actress who bounces from one story to the next, and a reporter who does the same, the time away, to just live inside our own bodies, to just breathe inside our own minds, was a revelation. We talked about what we could have done differently, what we'd like to do moving forward, how keeping secrets was dangerous, how protecting our loved ones—and ourselves—doesn't have to come at the expense of personal happiness. Does that all sound too vague, too much like a greeting card? Well, I'd like to think that I'm still entitled to a small bit of privacy, but if it helps, I'll tell you that you've never been kissed until Elliot O'Brien makes your knees go weak. Elliot is taken (sorry), but I hope you all find someone out there who makes you go weak in the knees, however they do so.

We're heading to San Francisco later this week to clean out Elliot's apartment and to stop into Ian Sands's Chez Nous for some of his delicious mussels. It seems that an honest apology can mend even the most heartless of breakups, and Ian generously accepted mine. We all do stupid things when we are young. Some of us do stupid things even when we are older. The grace of living is that it's never too late for contrition, and it's never too generous to accept that contrition when you can. Speaking of which, no one is mad at Mona. And if you're ever in the middle of California and need watered-down beer, please head to Monads and say hello. I hope to spend more time in Barton from now on, so maybe you'll even see me in the back room at the dart board, crushing Nelson Pratt and collecting some wadded-up cash from him when I do. (Emotional growth doesn't happen overnight, okay?)

After San Francisco, we'll stop in Los Angeles for a few months, since I'm now set to direct Love Grenade. The entire crew has been rehired, and I've already asked them to forgive me for the many mistakes I'll make along the way and also in retrospect. Elliot reminds me over and over again, when I doubt myself, that sometimes quieting the critics in our own minds is just as important as quieting the critics on the outside, so I'm trying. From there, we're not sure what's next. But we've agreed that we'd like to start over somewhere, a place that feels wide-open and also like home, and I can't speak for Elliot, but I'll go anywhere with him, even in a rickety RV, and just the possibility of the road rising to meet us is enough for me now.

Is this too much like an ending to one of my movies? All smooth sailing? Neither one of us is naive enough to believe that there won't be more obstacles. There always are. Even after the credits roll. Especially after the credits roll. But I've learned it's so much easier to hurdle over those obstacles when you have a partner to hold you steady as you leap, to offer a hand to catch you in midair.

So, dear readers, whatever you're waiting on, whomever you may love who doesn't know it, get on with it. Say the hard stuff, do the difficult things. I can't promise that saying the hard stuff and doing the difficult things will always reward you. But the cost of not being brave, of not being honest, is so much higher than the risk of failure. Fail. You'll get back up. Fail again. You'll get back up a second time. Then one of these days, you won't mind getting knocked down, or even if you do, you'll bounce up faster, more agile, ready for whatever comes next. It took public humiliation and a magician and an errant proposal for me to realize all this. I hope, for you, it takes a little less.

Love shows up in our lives in so many different ways. My advice, not that you asked, is to keep your eyes open to its many forms. Great loves can be found in sisters who drive six hours with punishing hangovers because you asked them to; in best friends who hope only for your own happiness; in editors and crews who forgive your professional stumbles; in publicists who come to your rescue when an ancient RV breaks down in the middle of nowhere.

I'll leave you with this: picture-perfect happily-ever-afters might just be what you find in the final five minutes of my movies. But don't mistake that sort of make-believe for the gritty, honest goodness of reality and all the ugly beauty that comes with both heartbreak and new discoveries. You are smarter than you know and more formidable than you realize, and however love finds you, when it's the good stuff, the very best kind, hold on.

Birdie Maxwell Robinson

ACKNOWLEDGMENTS

SOME BOOKS COME easier than others, and as thrilled and proud as I am of the pages you just read, *Take Two, Birdie Maxwell* did not come easily for me. I burned down my first four drafts, deleting them nearly entirely, and I don't think that *grateful* even begins to describe my debt of gratitude for my editor, Kerry Donovan, for her patience, insight, and guidance, as well as for my agent of almost two decades, Elisabeth Weed, who provided much the same. These brilliant women read draft after (terrible) draft and trusted me to transform those garbage pages into something that sparkled. I will always be immensely thankful to them for holding my hand along the bumpy journey.

The team at Berkley is genuinely the very best in the business, and I feel so, so lucky to have them in my corner. Craig Burke, Claire Zion, Christine Ball, Tara O'Connor, Dache' Rogers, Jessica Mangicaro, Hillary Tacuri, Mary Baker, and so many more: every single person at Berkley champions their authors, and it's a complete joy to collaborate with them all. Laura Dave, always one of my first early readers, read an absolutely trash draft of the book and was kind enough to offer smart, incisive notes. Berni Barta and Michelle Weiner at CAA are the best kind of women to have in your corner, as are all the women at The Book Group, including DJ Kim and Brettne Bloom, superstars each. A few others who offered wise counsel and encouragement: Julie Clark, Andrea Peskind Katz, and Rochelle Weinstein.

My family remains my best support team, even ten books in. Adam, Campbell, Amelia, my parents, my brother and sister-in-law, and a special shout-out to my other sister-in-law, Molly, who is like my personal Instagram publicist.

Many moons ago, I actually received an anonymous love letter in the mail one summer while I was home from college. I never tried to find who sent it (I remember finding it more alarming than romantic, so please, let's not all start putting pen to paper and mailing off our wildest desires to the ones who got away), but I suppose I owe that letter writer my thanks. Without him (or her), Birdie Maxwell may never have found her own happily-ever-after. Silver linings are found in every storm.

Keep reading for a preview of

THE REWIND

by Allison Winn Scotch
Available now!

The Night Before

FRANKIE HARRIMAN TOOK a long last look in the mirror on the back of the bathroom door of her decently appointed hotel room. The lighting was, as expected, quite grim, but even without the shadowing and the unflattering overtone of yellow, she startled herself. She fidgeted with the hem of her oversize wool sweater, tried tucking it into the waist of her Levi's, then decided that made her look like she was trying too hard, so untucked it, but she still wasn't happy. She turned to the side and gave herself a final once-over. It would have to do. The rehearsal dinner invite had called for *College Chic!* and this was all she had: her old J. Crew fisherman sweater that she'd dug out of a box in the back of her closet in her Los Feliz apartment and her vintage Levi's, which she now bought at a used-clothing store on Fairfax, but she may just as well have been wearing the ones from 1989, the year they graduated. The last time she'd set foot on campus at Middleton University.

She had been as surprised as anyone that she willingly ac-cepted her freshman-year roommate's request to be a bridesmaid (how do you really turn that sort of thing down?). Months later, she checked off "Yes! Party Like It's 1999," rather than "Y2Nay," on the invitation, and after sealing the envelope and dropping it in the mailbox on the corner outside her office, it wouldn't be a lie to say that she regretted it and immediately thought of a mil-lion and one excuses as to how she could bail last minute. She always had excuses at the ready, and to be honest, half of them weren't even lies: her artists inevitably got themselves into trouble or she was headed out on tour or there was some sort of unfore-seeable crisis to manage.

But here she was despite all of that. At April and Connor's wedding. At Middleton after a decade. With a magenta taffeta bridesmaid's dress with an oversize bow on one shoulder hang-ing in the closet next to the hotel robe. There were so many places she would rather be—anywhere, really—but she knew she owed it to April to show up and stand beside her when she vowed herself to Connor for life.

She'd tried to convince herself otherwise. She'd poured her-self a whiskey a few months back, the day before she had to go to a wedding shop in Beverly Hills to pick up her bridesmaid's dress, and dialed Laila Simpson, the college friend she was still tightest with, and ran through why her presence wasn't really necessary. She'd stayed in closer touch with Laila than April in the years since they graduated; whenever Laila was in LA, they toasted each other and got drunk at whichever hotel bar Laila's pharma-ceutical company was putting her up at. That afternoon, Laila went quiet on the other end of the line for a beat, then said, "You know, Frankie, you have this big, incredible life, and I'm never here to tell you how to live it, but April gave you a shoulder to

lean on when you needed it, and it's probably time that you recip-
rocated." Frankie knew she was referring to the night they graduated from college, when the two of them—Laila and April—had
hailed her a cab and hugged her goodbye and called her the next
morning to make sure she was okay, but she hadn't thought about
all of that in so long. It was easier not to think about any of that.
Because that's how Frankie marched forward. By never looking
back.

Frankie wanted to protest, to say, *But there are bigger reasons,
more terrifying reasons for me not to come.* But that wasn't true.
There was just one.

Ezra Jones.

Tonight at the hotel, Frankie tousled her blond hair one last
time in front of the mirror and swiped on bright red lipstick. She
checked her teeth and ran her fingers under her armpits because
she couldn't remember if she'd put on deodorant. She knew she
was more frazzled than usual (as a former child piano prodigy,
Frankie Harriman had been trained like a show dog to overcome
any nerves), so she stared at her reflection until her pulse slowed,
and she told herself that Ezra Jones was just a small sliver of her
past, a hiccup, a forgotten glimpse. She didn't have to speak to him,
she didn't even know if he'd be here at April and Connor's wedding, and she certainly didn't ask. Frankie often advised her musical artists on how to avoid drawing unnecessary attention to their
weaknesses, and she thus knew that asking was doing just that.

Her phone beeped on the nightstand, and she turned away
from the mirror and flipped it open.

"You ready?" Laila asked. "I'm almost there. I'll be in the lobby
in five."

Laila was crashing with a girl Frankie didn't remember who
was two years behind them in college but who had returned to

get her master's in something related to literature. (Laila had told Frankie, but she hadn't been paying close attention.) Laila had stayed in touch with this woman all these years because she was better at those things than Frankie.

Frankie pushed her shoulders back and reached for her coat, then her purse. She stuffed her CD player into her jacket's oversize pocket and flipped her yellow Sony headphones atop her hair. She had Night Vixen's early cut of their new album but never gave them feedback until she'd listened to it at least twenty times. She kept hearing new things, new nuances with each spin, but then that's what made her the best at what she did.

Frankie held her head high as she swung the door open and strode down the hall toward the elevator. She heard the door latch behind her and told herself that she was Frankie Harriman, music manager to the stars, and she was capable of anything. She'd eradicated Ezra Jones from her life once before. How hard could it be to do for one weekend more?

EZRA JONES POPPED open the black velvet box one last time. The ring, naturally, was still there. He didn't know why he worried it wouldn't be. But nevertheless, it was reassuring to see it secured away in its place, sparkling and magnificent, a single two-carat solitaire. He thought of his mother and how much he wished she were here so he could call her and share the news. She was always happy for him, whatever his choices.

A knock on the door startled him, and he closed the box with a start and tucked it into the inside pocket of his coat, which was slung around the mahogany wood chair in front of a matching desk. Ezra had sprung for a suite, which felt a little foolish now— he didn't want his old college friends to think he was being flashy about his bank account—but it was too late to do anything about it. Besides, he wanted tomorrow night, New Year's Eve, to be special. Mimi was coming, and it felt like exactly the right time, the right moment to make a new start, even if this was the place where plenty of things had come to an end.

"Hello?" he called from behind the door, then unlatched the safety lock.

"Dude!" He opened the door to find Gregory Mason standing there with open arms, double fisting two large bottles of booze. Gregory, whose brown hair was shaggy and who still looked about twenty-two despite a half-hearted attempt at a mustache, bear-hugged him like they hadn't seen each other in years, which wasn't quite true. Gregory had moved to Portland three summers ago, but they'd stayed close. They'd planned a trip to Prague last summer that Ezra bailed on last minute—instead, he went to Nantucket with Mimi for her work retreat—and Ezra was relieved that Gregory didn't seem to hold a grudge.

Gregory entered like Ezra's suite was his own, plunked the alcohol onto the mahogany desk, and flopped on the bed, rolling onto his back to unwrap his scarf and unzip his bright red puffer jacket. "Drink, my friend, you must drink. It's the only way to see this through." He rolled back over, then pushed up to his elbows and eyed Ezra.

"I'm fine," Ezra said. "I'm totally fine. I'm better than fine."

Gregory gave him a long up-and-down stare, as if his gaze were a lie detector, then he hopped to his feet and grabbed one of the bottles and took a swig. "You know that she's here, right?" Gregory didn't need to elaborate: *she* was Frankie. Ezra didn't bother to ask how he knew such things because Gregory always knew such things.

"Mimi's coming," Ezra offered. "So I'm honestly fine. She's

flying from Kansas City to Chicago tonight, Hartford in the morning—I have a car bringing her." He grabbed his bright blue iBook from the desk. "I was just about to check on her flight."

"Mimi." Gregory sniffed.

"I'm sorry again," Ezra said.

Gregory shrugged like he knew there was no use in holding it against him. "I'm just saying that Prague is significantly more awesome than Nantucket."

"I know." Ezra nodded. Because he did. "It was just . . . it turned into a thing." He didn't mean to sigh but did anyway. How could he explain that Mimi was upset that everyone else was bringing a plus-one to the retreat while her plus-one was in Prague with his college buddy, and so, rather than disappoint her, he canceled his own plans.

Gregory moved on and refocused. "Your shirt is buttoned wrong," he said, and Ezra glanced down at his plaid flannel (*College Chic!*). Gregory's always-animated face slowed for a beat, and Ezra knew he was worried. He was one of just a handful of Ezra's friends, well, really his only friend, plus Frankie, who knew how deeply his anxiety used to run straight through him.

"This doesn't mean I'm not fine," Ezra said, unbuttoning, then rebuttoning, but Gregory held the bottle between them until Ezra finally sighed and reached for it and drank. It burned all the way down, deep into his gut, and he shuddered.

"Special Portland blend." Gregory smiled. "I know a guy." He paused. "We used to know each other intimately but fortunately now are still on speaking terms. Because, you know, the booze."

Ezra took this to mean that Gregory was still happily single, as he had nearly always been since he'd come out their senior year. Ezra never understood his rotating lineup of men, how it didn't unnerve him not to have a steady partner, how Gregory seemed to delight in the chase. For Ezra, the chase was the most arduous, exhausting part. Give him the evenings in pajamas and Blockbuster rentals, give him morning breath and bed head, give him the assured companionship over dinner, the shared *New York Times* crossword, the intimacy of being on a first-name basis with her parents.

"Have another," Gregory said. "I suspect you'll need it."

Ezra tipped the bottle back and drank again, and this time, it burned a little less, felt a little better. "I don't even have to see her," he said. "I mean, I guess I have to see her, but I don't have to *see* her. It's been ten years. Who said I have to care?"

Gregory cupped his shoulder and said, "My man," and shook his head, like he was in on a secret that Ezra didn't yet understand, and then he grabbed his scarf and his red puffer and also the two bottles of booze and said, "Let's hit it. We have an hour at the hotel bar before we head to Burton."

Ezra didn't want to make a big scene about the ring in front of Gregory, who, he knew, would make it into an even bigger thing because Gregory was all about delighting in the dramatic. Until Ezra got on bended knee and slipped his grandmother's ring on Mimi's finger, he just wanted this for himself. He'd planned to put the ring in the hotel room safe, but that would draw attention to it, so instead, he reached for his coat where it was stuffed in the inside pocket and said, "Okay, just promise me one thing."

And Gregory turned, with the door ajar, and said, "Anything."

"Just don't let me . . . I mean . . . Look, I don't want to turn this into a *drama*. You know, with Frankie."

"I got you," Gregory said. "I'll be the buffer."

Ezra didn't really know what exactly that meant. He envisioned Gregory rushing over to form a human wall between

Frankie and him if ever they were in the same vicinity. But Gregory said it with such confidence, with such enthusiasm that he decided to trust him; he seemed to be an expert in making peace with exes, and when peace couldn't be found, at exorcising their ghosts. Ezra had never exorcised a ghost in his life.

ALLISON WINN SCOTCH is the *New York Times* bestselling author of nine novels, including *The Rewind, Cleo McDougal Regrets Nothing, In Twenty Years,* and *Time of My Life.* She lives in Los Angeles with her family and their two rescue dogs, Hugo and Mr. Peanut.

Ready to find
your next great read?

Let us help.

Visit prh.com/nextread